POKER GAME

POKER GAME

by
Fletcher Knebel

Doubleday & Company, Inc.
Garden City, New York
1983

Library of Congress Cataloging in Publication Data

Knebel, Fletcher.
  Poker game.

  I. Title.
PS3561.N4P6 1983   813'.54
ISBN: 0-385-18429-8
Library of Congress Catalog Card Number 82-45613

For Audrey, Hollis, Lauren and Scott

1

The night it all began, he lost a wad on successive hands, suckered by miscalculation and his own aggressive style of play.

The damp thick night lay sluggish on skin and spirit. The university had emptied, the last of the dogwood blooms had blown away like yellowed scraps of paper and gypsy moth caterpillars had begun munching the leafy canopy over Nassau Street.

Doug dropped the second of the two hands after Gary, high on the board, checked on the final round of seven-card stud and Doug bet the $10 limit. Gary promptly raised $10, got a call from Doug and swept the pot with an ace-high flush.

It hurt. Doug thought his straight had clinched the contest. But it wasn't so much his erring judgment or combative impulses that troubled him, or even the fact that Gary gulled him into betting a losing hand. It was rather that flicker of disappointment, shading into disinterest, when Gary glanced at his hole cards, a look that hinted at a worthless hand.

"I walked into that one," said Doug Perry, with a sigh. Beneath his genial exterior, he was a keen competitor who disliked losing, especially to Gary Jameson. Head-to-head combat with Gary invariably sharpened his battle senses.

"Blind hog picks up an acorn now and then." Gary, a city boy and specialist in codes and ciphers, relished rustic aphorisms.

Zap! Mentally projecting a flash image, Doug Perry saw Gary stripped naked as an eel: pale, skinny legs, shriveled penis in a graying nest, a lump of a belly, hairs strewn like withered weeds on a concave chest. Thus fortified by his rival's shrunken image, Doug could deal with Gary from a superior plane. An old ploy, used since boyhood, but it rarely failed him.

But his secret weapon could not control Doug's memory which now called up the scene of another swampy night under this same kitchen drop lamp on Pretty Brook Road. Then Gary feigned similar dissatisfaction and lured Doug into raising what proved to be Gary's easy winner, tens full against his own straight, wasn't it?

Jesus, what an oddball memory. As sharp for trivia sometimes as his computers.

Gary more than once had seemed to transgress one of the Sunday-night poker game's unwritten rules, the one against peripheral deception—that moody shake of the head when inspecting a gold-plated hand, that fingering motion as if about to fold unbeatable cards, that long sigh of resignation when pulling three kings on the draw. Okay at the Elks Lodge perhaps, but not in THE game.

They had frowned on both visual and verbal deception ever since the game began forty years ago with players drawn from the Institute for Advanced Study, Princeton University's faculty, the Nassau Club and the Palmer Square commercial crowd. A historic game, some claimed, even though the action couldn't match those $500 Wednesday-night pots at the Italian-American Sportsmen's Club.

The Sunday-night game had a pedigree, they said, in keeping with the graceful ivied New Jersey town with its appetite for narcissism. A haven of old trees and older money, Princeton was peopled by scholars, pollsters, psychologists, writers, artists, computer nobles, rich frayed Tigers tottering back to the collegiate lair, marketing soothsayers, retired politicians and diplomats as well as the financial platoons that trooped off daily to New York and Philadelphia. Dubbed the "golden ghetto," Princeton was F. Scott Fitzgerald's "green Phoenix" rising out of drab Jersey flatlands.

The history of the Sunday-night game and Princeton entwined like lovers. At one period the players often gathered in a book-walled den of the stone-and-frame house on elite Library Place that once belonged to Woodrow Wilson during his university days. John von Neumann, the math wizard from Hungary who designed some of the first computers, had played in the game's early years, they said, and even Albert Einstein showed up one night in his cyclone hair and ragged sweater to kibbitz. More recently George Ball, Under Secretary of State in Kennedy and Johnson years, had taken an occasional hand as had authors John McPhee, Peter (*Jaws*) Benchley and Carl Schorske, the historian who won both a Pulitzer Prize and a five-year McArthur Foundation "genius" grant in the same year.

Players boasted that they took part in the world's only endowed poker game. The Sunday-night sessions owned $5,000, bequeathed by a whimsical academic, once holder of the Andrew

Fleming West Chair in Classics at Princeton. His will stipulated that the interest be used "to provide a $1.00 ante for each hand of poker so long as the money shall last in each calendar year." Thanks to high interest rates, players in some years enjoyed several months of subsidized gambling.

Marshall Ingersoll, a player until recently, had often vowed to augment the endowment via his own will, and this night Stan, the host, channeled the talk toward the departed Ingersoll and his infamous $83 debt.

"Hey, Jay, did you get a check from Marshall yet?" Stan, the game's cigar smoker, was busy with his chores as banker. He shoved new stacks of gold, blue, red and white chips to loser Doug Perry who paid over another $50.

"You kidding? Zilch." The overhead light glinted on Jay's russet beard. Jay McNaughton played unorthodox poker based on a theory of random action spun by a graduate student at the University's Woodrow Wilson School where McNaughton headed Latin-American studies.

"Have you written him about it?" Gary Jameson fingered his waved, sprayed hair. The cryptographer had recently begun a new sub-rosa affair, so rumor had it, and transferred his barbering from a shop on Witherspoon to more expensive styling at the Princetonian on Nassau Street. "He could have forgotten."

"I called once before he left town. That's enough. I'm not in the collection business." Jay walked over to the kitchen counter and took another beer from the cooler. Sausages, rye bread, pickles, pretzels and potato chips surrounded the cooler like a besieging army. Empty beer cans stood about and an odor of stale beer merged with the muggy air.

"It's been five months, right?" asked Milt. "He's a real bastard to fink out on eighty-three bucks. Christ, he's making good money."

"Yep. Big bucks." Doug Perry, like the others, classed Marshall's offense as cardinal—welshing on a debt of honor. Also Doug felt personally victimized because he had introduced Ingersoll to the game. Ingersoll had been the top systems programmer at Princeton Dataflo, the company Doug headed, until he had left five months ago to take an executive post with a computer concern in California's Silicon Valley.

"Face it, tiger," said Ira. "The guy's a prick. I never liked him."

"My mistake," said Doug. "When he asked to play, I should have finessed it."

"Trouble is, Doug, you can't say no to anybody." Hugh shook his head though his tone was affectionate.

"It's not Doug's fault," said Jay McNaughton. "I'm the pigeon who took Marshall's check."

"If it were me," said Larry Warfield, "I'd threaten to go out there and bugger him in the front office of . . . What's the name of that outfit, Doug?"

"Bytex Labs."

"Hey, you guys," protested Buck, "let's play poker."

"Yeah," said Al. "Deal!"

Larry Warfield, trust officer of the town's leading bank, dealt a hand of seven-card stud, "Common card at the end if too many stay." A late flurry of betting yielded a $130 pot to the winner, Jay McNaughton. Stan returned to his favorite topic as soon as the cards were tossed in.

"There's no reason Jay should stand the loss," he said. "Why don't we all ante up eight or nine bucks?"

"Good idea, tiger." Ira stripped a ten from his winner's roll.

"No," countered Jay, "this is my problem . . . Besides, you know, I won a fair amount from Ingersoll. He had a habit of clenching his jaw whenever he had a good hand, so he was easier to read."

"You noticed that too?" asked Ira. "I thought I was the only one who spotted it."

They all looked at one another a trifle sheepishly, then burst out laughing.

"Hell, we all knew it," said Larry Warfield when they quieted, "but true to our rigorous code of frank and open communication, nobody said a word."

"Wrong, Larry," said Jay in his professorial way. "The unwritten rules say 'thou shalt not deceive by word or gesture.' They don't forbid astute observation of the clues dropped by others."

"Marshall didn't exactly clench his jaw," said Stan. "It was more of a little bulge right here." He pointed to a jaw muscle.

"Yeah, kind of a tremor," said Doug. "And never when he bluffed. Only when he had good cards. I was sure nobody else knew."

"Play poker," demanded Buck.

"Deal," said Al.

They played for another half hour, closing on the stroke of midnight with the ritual hand of show-down. Then they lingered, drinking beer in the humid night, prolonging the warm ribbing spirit that had prevailed throughout the game. Stan lit his third cigar. Hugh saluted Buck's birthday in song. "Only man in America," said Milt, "who manages to go off-key on 'Happy Birthday.'" Larry Warfield told another camel joke. Jay McNaughton, an officer of Amnesty International, said an uncle in Indiana had tried to buy stock in the organization, thinking it was a multi-national weapons manufacturer. Ira topped his own Jewish mother story of the previous week. But they could not shake loose from Ingersoll's fiscal perfidy. Nothing like it had happened in their time.

Hugh, the game's oldest player and unofficial custodian of its lore, reckoned that actually one would have to go back twenty-five years to the celebrated case of Barney Pilgrim to find a rival for Ingersoll's delinquency.

"Barney Pilgrim?" asked Doug. "Wasn't he the guy who jumped off Palmer Stadium?"

"Right. I'm the only one left who played in the game with Barney." With his white hair and pink, unlined face, Hugh had the look of an overage cherub. "He gave somebody his check for fifty dollars—a lot of money back then—and the check bounced. A few nights later under a full moon, the night before the Yale game, he jumped off the top wall at Palmer Stadium. The borough police carted him away in a sack."

"Yeah, but he'd gone off his rocker," protested Stan. "It wasn't a fifty-buck bad check in this game that did it."

"True." Hugh nodded. "The bad check was just another symptom. Barney had always been scrupulous about money. I'm just saying that Marshall is our first case of a bad debt in a quarter of a century." He dwelled lovingly on the last phrase, rooting the game in the loam of antiquity.

Riding home with the windows of his BMW down and the damp night air washing over him like warm suds, Douglas Perry reflected on Marshall Ingersoll's violation of their sanctuary. For poker devotees like himself, the Sunday-night game offered a familiar refuge in an unruly, random, terrorized, perplexing world. In the game one knew all the rules, always inviolable, never complicated. One felt safe, among one's own kind, comfortable, master of one's fate save for the whims of Lady Luck with whom

all were smitten and who smiled now on this favorite, now on
that, without regard to intelligence, craft, means or social class.
And within the immutable rules, one could vent the classic urges
of a turbulent competitive society: bluff, deception, merciless attack, swift retreat, bombast, threat, squeezing out rivals, boast,
feint, sporadic bursts of recklessness.

Doug Perry played the game of poker as he played the game of
business, hard and straight within the rules, yet always with a
touch of compassion. He hated to crowd any man against the wall,
except in those games for high stakes that he occasionally played.
In the big-money games with strangers, he applied maximum pressure, gave no quarter and sometimes ran risky bluffs for hundreds
of dollars that set his blood racing. For the rest he was an amiable
but firm executive whose personal life vacillated between intem-
perance and disorder. He waded through chaotic weekends, then
welcomed Sunday-night poker as a bracing warm-up for the major
game on Monday. He liked the friendly gambling sessions not
only for the competitive skirmishing, but for the kind of rough
tenderness that infused male animals at play.

If rivals at cards, the players were also friends—some of them
close—and they gathered once a week as much to enjoy the com-
panionship as to test one another's mettle. Once Larry Warfield
suggested the inclusion of women, but they hooted him down, vot-
ing derisively to preserve their all-male sanctuary.

By refusing to honor his debt, Ingersoll had torn the delicate
fabric tenting that refuge. The game went on, attractive and con-
soling to the participants, only so long as all abided by the conventions of palship. He who flouted them became a pariah. Even
should Marshall now reimburse Jay ten times over, he could never
play in the game again.

Two cars waited to turn left at the traffic light at Elm Road as
Doug hummed along Stockton on the drive to the white-brick
home on Hun Road.

"Doug!" Someone called from a waiting car. Doug did not recognize the voice, but tooted his horn in acknowledgment.

At once, as the sound fell away in the muggy air, his thoughts
veered from poker to work. His called name echoed in his skull, a
summons to arms. Doug. Douglas. Big Doug to business rivals.
Sweet man to some of the women, including Pru McNaughton,
whom he'd taken to bed. Douglas Roper Perry. The names rolled
away, familiar, exhortatory, property of that bodily compound of

flaw and grace, vice and virtue, that held this steering wheel. He knew his faults. A stubborn, if often betrayed, faith in salvation through a rapture of the senses, a failing for good whiskey, happy hours and lively women, impulses toward the outrageous, a tendency to confuse monogamy with tedium, impatience with the staid, the ordinary, the conforming. On the plus side, he knew the value of the ethical code passed down from his preacher father, and he rated himself as generous, reliable and lucky.

If in playing the game of life hard and fast and in his often overindulgent leisure hours, he had lost a wife and daughter, he at least did not blame them. Nor did he unduly miss Joan, that sweet-tempered, comfortable woman with a yen for the stability he could never provide. As for nine-year-old Judith, he missed her ferociously at times and always looked forward to his trips to Short Hills where his daughter lived with mother and grandparents.

As he drove past Drumthwacket, the governor's mansion, he slapped the wheel as if to banish self-scrutiny. He returned instead to the poker game. A bit absurd really, even as a warm-up for the main game on Mondays, and no doubt to be listed among his character defects. Seven or eight men huddled about a table, studying numbers and symbols on small, rectangular pieces of pasteboard with the fervor of ancient diviners seeking to foretell the next caprice of the gods. The ebb and flow of those colored chips representing money, itself a baffling token of past work and chicanery, faith and exploitation, trust and grinding toil. The game offered players an excellent excuse to escape personal responsibility. If a man lost, he blamed it on the cards. If outwitted, rotten luck. If he stayed too long on poor hands or tried too many bluffs, what a run of miserable cards!

And the posturing. Eight males bragging, boasting, preening and faking, the cult of machismo in miniature, each man playing out a part as predictable and as stylized as Chinese opera. Every player concealed himself behind his mask or shield—Larry Warfield behind his raucous jokes, Jay McNaughton behind Latin-American politics, Gary Jameson behind his bromides, Hugh behind his history. Delusion gripped them all. Plodding Stan fancied himself a future governor and cool, calculating gambler. Ira believed himself an irresistible lover and the intellectual superior of anyone in the game. And what remained when the role ended? With the exception of the eccentric classicist who endowed the

game, players vanished leaving but a fragment of their inner selves
to the common memory. When they died, only shards remained: a
name, a skill, an exploit, a mannerism, an act of desperation like
the unknown Barney Pilgrim's death leap from Palmer Stadium.

As he drove past the Hun School where a few lights still shone
in the prep school's faculty quarters, Doug heard the high shrill
chant of cicadas. In the pulsing drone, he thought he could distin-
guish the call of a single male, pumping his resonating organs with
the same monotony as Gary Jameson and his poker clichés . . .
"Eighter from Decatur" . . . "Little duck" . . . "Nothing wild
except the players" . . . "Winners tell jokes, losers cry, 'Deal!'"

He turned into Hun Road toward the old house of white-
painted brick, its low profile framed by the tangled woods of
Stony Brook. It looked as rooted, as solid and permanent, as it
had for the last twenty years. Yet it gave him no particular comfort. It was more than two years ago that Judith had driven off
with her mother and he was alone here now. But, truthfully, he
was a restless man, and home had always been but an interlude.

As he stood in the driveway, a dark sedan pulled up across the
road at the foot of the long esplanade, bordered by majestic oaks,
that swept to the Hun School far up the grassy slope. Someone
stepped out. A car door slammed.

"Mr. Perry?" Less a question than a courteous statement.

Doug faced the street. A man walked toward him, his shape
framed in the feeble light of a clouded moon. Unusual at this
hour, nearly one o'clock. Neighboring houses showed only garage
lights that now burned all night in the wake of an epidemic of bur-
glaries.

"Yes." Doug met the stranger at the end of the lawn.

The man wore a suit and striped tie. His belly protruded like a
pregnant woman's. "Marshall Ingersoll said I'd find you home
about this time." He breathed heavily as if from strenuous exer-
tion.

"Marshall Ingersoll!"

"Yes." The stranger blinked. "Why, has something happened to
him?"

"Not that I know of. It's just that some of us were discussing
him a few minutes ago."

"At the poker game?"

"Well . . ." Doug felt stirrings of alarm. The man looked
harmless enough, beefy and stolid with a neutral, almost vapid, ex-

pression. But it was well after midnight in a residential area where few people were still awake. A dog barked. Probably the McCleerys' Irish setter.

"Look, I know this is an extraordinary way to meet you. I should have called for an appointment, but we face a time factor here." The man doled out his reassurances in a slow reasonable tone. He was obviously accustomed to disarming strangers. A detective? Social worker? Maybe a priest?

"I see." Doug studied him again. "Perhaps if you'd give me your name and some clue as to why you want to talk to me, we might continue this inside."

"No. Out here is fine. I'll only take a minute." His quick, raspy breathing seemed to stress his references to speed. "My name is Kramer—Otis Kramer—and like you I'm in the data-processing business." He put out his hand.

Doug met a moist palm. "So what's this all about, Mr. Kramer?"

"Otis, please." He mopped his forehead with a handkerchief. The night pressed down. Thunder growled on the muddy horizon like distant artillery fire. "I'll make this fast. I used to be with Bunker Ramo, also Hewlett-Packard. Now I've got my own consulting shop, and on this job I'm under contract to Washington."

"Washington?"

"Sorry, the deal's classified, but I'm sure you can guess . . . To come to the point. Tomorrow morning you're going to be offered an immense amount of money for your new chip—the Katwar 23, right? Washington wants you to agree to the sale in principle, but to string out negotiations for a couple of weeks, reporting everything to Washington. I'm your contact."

"Whoa. Just a minute, man." How the hell did he know about the Katwar 23? Of course rumors circulated in the industry, but this flabby, short-winded stranger had the exact name. . . . *Zap. At once a disrobed Kramer flashed into view. Enormous feet, swollen thighs, a huge white belly with patches of hair like drifting seaweed, fleshy breasts and—an X-ray bonus—lungs clogged with nicotine.*

Doug felt much better. "You're going too fast, Mr. Kramer."

"I apologize for showing up in the middle of the night." Actually, returned to his clothes, Kramer looked blandly officious, quite unapologetic. "But I had to act fast. The offer will be made tomorrow morning at your Princeton Dataflo office."

Doug decided to end it. "Look, Kramer, I have no idea who you are, who you represent or what this is all about." The thunder rumbled somewhere over Trenton. "If you want to talk business, call my office in the morning and make an appointment through my secretary."

Kramer smiled, first crack in his mask of plastic neutrality. "Sorry, but I'm driving back to Washington tonight."

Driving through the night to Washington, almost a four-hour run? Not like the high-priced computer consultants Doug knew. They flew charter out of Trenton on short hauls, rode first class to the Coast, invariably took the Concorde to Paris.

"In that case, I'll say good night. I have a full day tomorrow." Doug edged away. Turning his back on this man didn't seem like a good idea right then.

"Please, Mr. Perry." Kramer advanced a step.

"No, that's it." Doug raised his palms. "Time to break this off."

Kramer shook his head in disbelief. "You're making a big mistake, Mr. Perry. You'll realize that before noon tomorrow. Just remember what I said. Don't sign anything. Here." He held out a card. "Call me after the offer, please. A matter of national security."

Doug watched as Kramer walked back to his car with heavy swaying tread. The dark sedan, an American compact of some kind, moved off at once, turned into Russell Road and disappeared in a lament of tires. Doug could not catch the license number.

He read the card in the tiled kitchen beside the long planked table. Reflections danced on burnished copper pots that hung like tribal trophies near the stove.

Otis M. Kramer
Data Processing Consultant
1951 Pennsylvania Avenue N.W.
Washington, D.C. 20004

Other data included his office and home telephone numbers, a computer network address and another for cables: OTKAM. Doug shoved the card in a pants pocket.

He undressed upstairs and climbed into bed. Entwined dolphins carved on a mahogany headboard were a reminder of the passions once shared here with Joan. "Did you win?" she would mumble when he slid in beside her on those Sunday nights years ago.

Later, after Dataflo's early run of profits, she no longer inquired about money and Doug himself cared chiefly as a measure of his skill as a player.

Of what concern poker skills to Doug Perry, that haphazard amalgam of hedonist, driving executive and lover of freaky exploits? He once bought a half dozen baby bonnets and tied them late at night on the heads of the trite pop sculptures that wealthy Seward Johnson had placed around Princeton. Another time he answered a column of kinky ads in a flesh magazine's personals section in the name of Ira Bickstein, the fellow poker player who preened on his amorous skills. Bickstein, a top mathematician at the Institute for Advanced Study, was deluged by letters from sexual virtuosos of varying age, race, sex and nation. One night Doug brought a live piglet to the poker game and awarded it to the first man to win both ends of a high-low game.

Well, he did like to gamble, and winning was the only gauge of ability. Several times a year a hankering for the big no-limit games hit him like a fever. In Las Vegas, Miami, Los Angeles, New York and London, he had played in games where one could win or lose thousands of dollars in a night. Once in London he bet $1,900 on a single card. In a hand of five-card stud, he bluffed out a player holding two pairs with his own broken straight.

Occasionally he did skip the friendly Sunday-night game, catching a movie, watching the tube or making a dinner party. Several nights he fetched Prudence here to help fill the empty spaces while her husband Jay McNaughton continued his faithful attendance at the poker game.

Doug held that the love game, like poker and business, had its own rules. Honor had limitless facets. While he would never bug out on a gambling debt like Ingersoll, he would take Ingersoll's woman without a qualm if the flame burned hot enough. In any reasonable code of conduct, he considered himself straight and reliable. Yet his failings bothered him. Why did he frequently drink too much? How about his affinity for the bizarre and nutty? Did his ceaseless busyness shield him from a panic of loneliness?

Certainly not on the outside. There Doug Perry, a pounding tennis player, fast-run skier and accomplished businessman, had it made until the recent downturn in company profits. Princeton Dataflo was struggling now, true, but he was a fighter and he had vowed to pull the company out of the red. And who was this exterior Perry, the man who would turn his company around? Well, a preacher's kid, Methodist turned agnostic, independent voter, computer president, member of the Nassau Club, New York's University Club and San Francisco's Bohemian Club, also an insider at the annual summer frolic of America's men of power at the Bohemian Grove.

Thoughts swam lazily as the curtain of sleep lowered. Seriously now, how come *Playboy* and *Penthouse* did not fan his erotic fancies, but the lingerie and female jeans ads in the Sunday *New York Times Magazine* did? And how come . . .

The thunder receded, a muttering over Pennsylvania. Tomorrow when a mystery caller might or might not offer a bundle for the Katwar 23 belonged to that fickle temptress, the future. His mind flushed a last set of conflicting images like a covey of startled birds. Doug Perry fell asleep as usual on a train of ambiguity.

2

Insiders at Princeton Dataflo counted on their new, still secret chip to seize leadership in the surging computer industry's latest and most sophisticated race. Having achieved phenomenal miniaturization of the machines that had converted the Western world into a vast sea of invisible information held on microscopic scraps of silicon, computer executives now feverishly sought some means of protecting this fact-and-number glut from the pack of thieves, swindlers, data crackers, spies and numbersmiths who preyed on electronic files.

The great data banks held their knowledge bullion behind the flimsiest of shields. Computer crooks falsified the paperless records of commercial and savings institutions. In some banks clever programmers had snipped odd sums from thousands of accounts, diverted them to a single fictitious name and then withdrawn the loot. In Britain a mail-order-house programmer stole $85,000 by a similar method. In the United States thousands, even millions, of dollars were transferred illegally from one account to another via simple electronic instructions from programmers bent on fraud. One West Coast bank transferred $2,000,000 to the New York account of a firm's branch office. By the time the bank discovered the eastern branch did not exist, the money already had been withdrawn. In one metropolitan bank a teller manipulated accounts from his computer terminal and embezzled millions over the years while keeping the bank's books in precarious balance. Bank officers generally shied from prosecution of embezzlers for fear resulting publicity might entice still more employees to match wits with the computer. Experts estimated that 90 percent of computer thefts went unreported.

The new electronic methods of storing information enabled canny swindlers to plunder corporate treasuries with surprising ease. One computer security consultant estimated that "electronic thievery" cost American companies $3,000,000,000 a year. In New England clever operators stole the password directory of a computer time-sharing company, thus gaining access to data in some 8,000 corporate computers. In New Jersey, a computer technician manipulated an oil company's electronic records, permitting a gang to divert $20,000,000 worth of fuel over a span of years. In California an engineering student, breaking simple electronic codes, compelled a utility company's computer to order deliveries of $1,000,000 worth of goods to unguarded platforms during night hours. He collected and resold the booty.

For sheer volume of computer fraud, the great Equity Funding Corp. scandal of 1973 topped the list. Conspiring officers managed to create almost $200,000,000 in bogus company assets by loading the computer with fake insurance policies "sold" to more than 60,000 nonexistent people, all properly listed in the machine by name and number. These policies on ghostly souls were sold in turn to other companies under the industry's reinsurance practices. The scheme and the company's bloated stock finally collapsed when a former employee took his suspicions to authorities.

In addition to bank fraud and corporate larceny, the infant computer years had given electronic license to the rape of individual privacy, the snatching of trade secrets, compromise of national security, diversion of payrolls and the theft of inventions. While similar crimes marred the old pen-and-paper days as well, the dazzling speed of computers permitted the new data burglars to accomplish in a few minutes what once took weeks or months. The more powerful the computer, the more vulnerable to piracy became its electronic hoard. Computer crime even built its own vocabulary with such samples as *piggybacking,* meaning to hook a terminal onto a private computer network to intercept, modify or change data, or *masquerading,* meaning the use of authorized passwords by people who stole or misappropriated them.

All this had come with a rush that startled the businessmen, educators and bureaucrats who relied on the electronic repositories as they had once depended upon millions of tons of flimsy papers filed away in metal cabinets. Doug Perry often compared his computer world to a precocious boy of four who suddenly starts smoking cigars, running factories, making millions, wooing voluptuous women and buying race horses while at the same time paying tribute to a brand-new electronic Mafia.

Another Princeton Dataflo executive put the state of the art in more traditional, if pedestrian, terms. "As the huge computer industry moves toward maturity," said Dataflo's vice-president Lindbloom on a TV panel show, "if it is to grow, it must confront and solve its gravest problem—data security."

Doug Perry knew that his company's new wonder chip, the Katwar 23, met that privacy challenge head on, and it was the Katwar on which he and other executives counted to put their company back in the black. This morning the device was very much on his mind as he wheeled his well-traveled BMW past the lush green lawns and wooded stands of Forrestal Center, a thriving parklike spread on U.S. Route 1 where the wealthy landlord, Princeton University, rented to corporations on fifty-year leases.

It wasn't, however, a chip named Katwar but his own reputation for bizarre exploits that produced the day's first problem at Dataflo. Doug's secretary accompanied him into the No. 1 office with its frosty-lime-fabric wall covering, its visual display terminal, a large Arnold Roth caricature of Doug missing a ball at the net despite a tennis racquet the size of a billboard and on another wall a spectacular Tom George abstract.

"Busy already, Mr. Perry." Edith Yeager, a decorous, mothering secretary with luminous sheep's eyes, looked stricken. "People have been calling. One of them's still on hold."

"What's up?" Doug's juices quickened. He liked the days that started off on a quirky, unexpected note.

"Oh, something about a leaflet, Mr. Perry." Edith's doting eyes hinted that she knew more than she admitted.

"A leaflet?" Sounded trifling for a rugged morning challenge. "Who's on hold?"

"Mr. Gary Jameson."

"Can't shake that man. Okay, I'll take it."

His poker rival, the only player able to hook Doug's ego, was calling from his den at the Institute for Defense Analyses where he worked as a cryptographer or "cryppy" as the codes-and-ciphers trade had it.

"Doug, what do you know about this flyer?" Jameson's opener was not overly friendly.

"Nothing." Alarms failed to sound. Actually, at the moment, Doug's thoughts had veered once more to silicon chips and a mysterious stranger who was supposed to offer him a fortune that morning. "What flyer, Gary?"

"The orange one that's all over town, especially out here."

"I haven't the least idea what you're talking about."

"I'm talking about the leaflet that urges us to move our shop to Forrestal Center." Suspicions fluttered.

"Never heard of it." Doug's gaze strayed to the video terminal. Had any electronic mail been left for him over the weekend?

"Isn't the phrase 'Department of Offense' your favorite name for the Pentagon?"

"Favorite, no. I did use it in a joke I told at the game a week ago."

"Why 'Offense,' Doug?" The line grew chilly.

"Because it was necessary to the joke, cryppy." Doug's equanimity began to fray. "Say, what the hell is this?"

"You want me to read through this propaganda for you?"

"What propaganda, for Christ's sake? You're talking in riddles, man."

"Should I read the leaflet to you?" Gary enunciated as if speaking to a small child.

"Of course. What else? Obviously it's ruined your morning."

"Okay, it's in big, black type on orange paper."

"Tiger, tiger."

"This isn't funny, Doug."

Edith popped her head into the doorway. "I have one here, Mr. Perry. It might be easier if you read it yourself."

"Wait a minute, Gary." Doug took the orange sheet. "My secretary just handed me the incendiary document. Hold on."

IDA, GO WHERE YOU BELONG!

To: Institute for Defense Analyses
      (Special attention Gary Jameson and
      other cipher freaks.)

Instead of spoiling a lovely residential neighborhood
with your ugly building, your juvenile codes and ciphers
and your hush-hush work for the Department of

Offense, move your electronic military factory to Forrestal Center.

That's where IDA belongs.

Why?

Because Forrestal Center is named for James V. Forrestal, the first Secretary of Offense, who freaked out on the job and plunged to his death from a sixteenth story window of the Bethesda Naval Hospital. Trapped in paranoia, Forrestal (Princeton, 1911–15) believed that Communist persecutors were hounding him through Pentagon corridors.

While the authors of this leaflet hold no brief for the glacial Soviet Union, it is obvious that United States foreign policy, obsessed like Forrestal with fear of Communism, has led the nation into one extravagant military blunder after another until we now face bankruptcy.

As a mercenary of the Pentagon, the Institute for Defense Analyses should make its home in the industrial park named for a man who helped mold the military policy that has drained the U.S. of thousands of young lives and hundreds of billions of dollars and changed the world's image of America from Thomas Jefferson to Dr. Strangelove.

IDA: Move to Forrestal Center. You belong there.

Signed:
Princeton Committee for Sanity in Foreign Affairs.

"All right, I've read it," said Doug. "Quite a blast at you people."

"Do you agree with it?" Jameson's tone had turned frigid.

"No. It makes a point, but the plot's too simplistic. Why?"

"I'm asking you straight out, Doug. Did you have anything to do with writing, printing or distributing this?"

"Of course not. What the hell do you take me for, Gary? When I pull a stunt, I put my name on it. I don't go anonymous—ever."

"Then I apologize, Doug." He sounded sincere if somewhat disappointed. "There were some clues, frankly, pointing your way, the 'Offense' bit, my name singled out from the group here, you know, and also you're out at Forrestal."

"Sounds like juvenile campus stuff to me. Weren't undergraduates picketing you last month again?"

"True enough. I'm sorry, Doug. They've got us churned up here this morning."

Doug visualized Gary Jameson's office at IDA, a solemn brown-brick building on a wooded unmarked site on Thanet Road where the American flag flew. Out of gratitude for the cipher-cracking contracts the Institute received from the National Security Agency in Washington? Were the clever cryptanalysts now trying to divine the source of the leaflet? Were roars of outrage echoing down soundproofed halls, upsetting pale and plastic-badged scholars at their craft of plucking the covers off foreign secret writing? Would encrypted protests fly to Washington over computer networks? The Institute, a high-priced nest for mathematicians, code breakers and computer specialists, operated in a clandestine mist, ruptured only by sporadic demonstrations by Princeton University students.

"Our security has turned the flyer over to the FBI," said Jameson.

Ah yes, Washington had been alerted. These sprouts of dissent would soon become weeds of subversion in the electronic log of the Bureau.

"Then you'll know the perpetrators soon enough, Gary. Don't let it upset you, man."

"It bugs me that only my name appeared on the sheet, not even the director's."

"That's the breaks. See you next Sunday night at Hugh's."

A light blinked at the base of Doug's phone. He picked up the instrument.

"A man from Mexico City who says it's urgent, Mr. Perry."

The voice on the line spoke measured English with a Latin accent. "Thank you, Mr. Perry. My name is Carlos Rey Quinto from Mexico. While it is an imposition to make this request on such short notice, I would like to see you today about the purchase of one of your chips." He pronounced it "cheeps." His voice had a heavy, brooding quality. "The interests I represent are willing to pay considerably above market price."

"Just which chip are you interested in, Mr. . . ."

"Rey. A new one. It has not reached the market yet."

"I'm wondering how . . ."

"I've heard it called the Cat Word Twenty-three," Rey cut in. "That may be a distortion. Your computer gossip gets garbled sometimes crossing the border."

"Where are you calling from?"

"The Nassau Inn. I stayed here last night."

"Okay. I'll see you for lunch at the Scanticon Hotel here in the center. Meet me in the lobby at 12:45 if that's convenient. I'm tall, sandy hair and I'll be wearing a plain blue sport shirt, no tie."

So last night's fleshy stranger with the raspy breathing knew more than Doug gave him credit for. He fished in his wallet, drew out the card. Yes, Otis Kramer in D.C. "Edith, ask Susan and Tony to come in. Put an urgent tag on it."

A few minutes later Doug Perry looked across his desk at Susan Lindbloom and Tony Canzano, vice-presidents who had helped steer Princeton Dataflo into the profitable years. The three had been friends since college days in Boston where Doug studied engineering at M.I.T. and Tony and Susan majored in mathematics at Boston University. Then Susan Lindbloom, the steady judicious Swede, had spent ten years at IBM while Doug worked at RCA and Tony Canzano earned rapid promotions at Burroughs before they regrouped to found Princeton Dataflo.

Although Doug, the forceful entrepreneur, held the top job and the final word, the three friends operated as near equals. All major decisions had been unanimous. Lindbloom took the deliberate cautious role, Canzano liked breezy innovations, while Doug Perry played it as he did the Sunday-night poker game, steadily aggressive with sudden venturesome flings that often paid off, occasionally flopped and always ran on the rim of risk. They trusted one another completely, but seldom let another's game plan pass without challenge.

Casual dress had become the company style set by the three executives. Like Doug, Tony wore open-neck sports shirts in summer and turtleneck sweaters in winter. Susan wore simple cotton dresses, sometimes a slit skirt with blouse and figured vest. Tony had once fired a less than whirlwind salesman partly because he insisted on wearing tie and jacket around headquarters.

"Excuse the short notice," said Doug, "but it seems that before we take Katwar to market, we have a couple of mystery guests to cope with." He sketched the post-midnight meeting with Otis

Kramer and the phone call from the Mexican. "Anybody heard of either of them?"

Susan shook her head.

"Never heard of Kramer," said Tony, "but Woody Kauffman at K-Squared Systems was talking the other day about Carlos Rey or Charlie King as he called him. Seems this Rey, a weird character as Woody tells it, has become one of the big dp brokers on the international scene. Clients all over the map."

"I assumed Washington would get word of the Katwar," said Susan, "but I'm a little surprised they know about it in Mexico City."

"Well, the trade press has picked up rumors," said Doug. "On Friday, *Computerworld* called Edith about a reported new chip."

"We're getting famous." Tony Canzano grinned, superlative dental caps flashing against his dark skin. He had broken three front teeth in college during a touch football game along the Charles River.

"Nothing particular to decide here," said Doug. "Mainly I wanted to keep you both informed."

" 'No man who is correctly informed,' to quote Macaulay, 'ever takes a dim view of things,' " said Canzano. His first love was baseball, his second English and Irish literature.

"I wonder how much the Mexican will offer?" asked Lindbloom.

"It'll have to be good." Doug frowned at the Arnold Roth caricature of his poor net play. Actually he thought he covered the front court better than most. "If we get the expected bids from IBM, Control Data and Wang, I figure we should net a couple of million a year for some time—and man can we use it."

"I suppose Kramer was hinting that the CIA has taken an interest in our chip." Canzano, a toucher, laid a hand on Susan's arm. "Maybe this Rey is fronting for somebody in the Communist bloc."

"Better proceed with caution, Doug," Susan added.

"Don't worry. I'll let him do the talking."

"I hope he can come up with a respectable offer. We're getting close to the bone." Susan handled the company's finances.

"How close?" asked Tony.

"Three more months on our reserves. Then we'll have to call our bankers."

They discussed the tight fiscal situation and once more mentioned their hopes for the Katwar. Then Doug stood up. "Okay, Susan, how about getting Eric in Washington to run us a good check on Otis Kramer? And Tony, do you have the time today to dig into Carlos Rey's background?"

"Sure. I'll give it all the time it needs."

"Try Chico Aller at Barclays for a starter. He handles the bank's line to big Latin money. I guess that's all. . . . Oh, I almost forgot the leaflet." His account of Gary Jameson's querulous call evoked laughter.

"You're not the type for anonymous pamphleteering, Doug," said Susan.

"I saw one of those flyers on Nassau Street this morning," said Tony. "Hell, I never did know what they do at IDA. . . . And I almost forgot too. We landed three top-of-the-class engineering kids." Canzano handled the company's personnel including hirings and firings. "Two of them phoned me at home last night."

"Where are they from?" asked Doug.

"One from your old school, one from Caltech and the other, a black guy, from Carnegie."

"How much did we have to pay?" Susan turned a shoulder as if to avert the blow.

"Thirty-one K," said Tony. "I had to go two grand over budget. These kids are worth it."

"I just hope we find the money to pay them," said Susan.

"Ah, we'll have good news with the Katwar. . . . And talking of good news, the Phillies made it three in a row over Chicago yesterday." Tony jerked a thumb over his shoulder. "That's it for the Cubs."

"Baseball!" scoffed Susan.

Doug made several calls, tapped out on his word processor two letters that Edith would polish into shape, then set off for his luncheon at Scanticon, a hotel conference center.

He walked along winding College Road, a thoroughfare for such companies as RCA, Prudential and IBM that looped through grasslands and cool stands of hardwood, a forest-park setting favored by corporate America in its flight from the decaying tax hungry cities. Here dwelt natural beauty, serenity and elegance with not a needy family nor mugger within miles. Here life wore a bouquet of affluence and ease. Here at Forrestal Center business could be done in the modulated, unruffled tones of a network anchor man reciting faraway global horrors on the evening news.

Here were no frenetic sirens, no squalid tin shacks or teeming slums, no bag ladies bivouacked in rags, no emaciated children or ulcerous beggars. Here business might live like the beautiful people, clean, isolated, content, forever wrapped in pleasantly profitable thoughts of that mighty engine, the consumer.

Brisk winds from Canada had blown off last night's junglelike miasma and fashioned one of those rare diamond days, bright, flawless, gleaming, charged with promise and marred only by the muffled but unrelenting groan of traffic along U.S. 1 and the haze of exhaust fumes hanging over the highway like a sullen shroud.

Compared with the fresh June day outside, the man Doug met in the Scanticon lobby was a tub of despair. Short, saddled with flesh, dark-haired, his black eyes peering through thick misted lenses, Señor Rey gave off melancholy undulations. They had no trouble spotting each other, and as they exchanged greetings Doug decided he had never before met such a transparently unhappy man. The Mexican seemed soaked in grief, his toxic spill contaminating the brick-and-copper lobby like leaking chemical wastes. Wary in the manner of strangers about to square off over money, they walked to the Courtyard Restaurant and took seats looking out on the cobbled entrance area.

Carlos Rey followed Doug's lead in choosing a cold watercress soup and shrimp salad, but evinced scant interest in food. He squinted behind the dull lenses, squirmed in his chair, failed to glance at the shapely waitress and smoked two cigarettes, strong Gauloises Caporal, from a small blue pack.

"You're a broker in hardware, is that right?" Doug wondered at the source of the man's profound malaise.

"Yes, yes, Mr. Perry." Rey coughed as he inhaled. "My clients are scattered through the Americas and Europe, a few in Asia and Africa. All in data processing. Most of my customers want hardware, but I make some software deals too."

"How about the Soviets? You have any customers in the Warsaw Pact countries?"

"Absolutely not." Rey looked, if possible, more pained. "None of that, none of that. I got burned once on a Czech deal. Never again."

"Do you know an Otis Kramer in Washington?"

"Kramer? No."

"How about an Ellwood Kauffman here in Princeton?"

"Ellwood? No." He appeared to search his memory. "Oh, wait.

I think . . . a big man, stout, they call him Woody? K-Squared Systems?"

"That's right." Doug studied his man.

"Yes, I did meet him at the National Computer Conference last month. I'd forgotten he lived here. I'll have to call him." The prospect failed to cheer Rey. In fact, nothing seemed to lighten the dolorous cloud in which he brooded.

After more sparring, Doug steered the talk directly to microcircuits. "Where did you hear about our new chip, Mr. Rey?"

The Latin raised his palms, spraying ashes over his soup. "I'm not at liberty to disclose my source. You understand? So many tangled interests, one hesitates, one hesitates . . ."

Doug smiled. "Let me try another angle. What's your understanding of our chip's capabilities?"

"They say your Cat Word Twenty-three is the best chip for security ever made." He shaped a small space with thumb and forefinger. "Only so big, right?" Rey went on to describe the configurations and talents of the micro masterpiece with reasonable accuracy. "It protects the data like no other, so I've heard."

As Doug pursued his questioning, the shrimp salads arrived in the hands of the fetching waitress with the olive skin and sculpted bosom. Doug's eyes lingered on her. Rey paid her no attention whatever. They talked some more, approaching in ever smaller circles the target of their meeting.

"And you want to buy our new piece of hardware?"

"An exclusive franchise for three years. My client is willing to pay above market price. Handsomely above, I'd say."

"And your client is who exactly?" Doug tried to fix Rey's eyes with his, but the Mexican's gaze veered away.

"That must remain confidential, you understand?"

"We never sell to unknown parties. If they're overseas, there's the little matter of export licenses, for one thing."

"With this client there is absolutely no problem. That I can assure you." Rey lit another cigarette, inhaled gloomily, glancing at Doug through the veil of smoke. "I might add, just between us, that the customer is anxious to make a considerable personal gift to the individual who provides the key to the sale."

Doug frowned. "Careful, Rey. Up here people would call that a bribe offer." At least this would make juicy retelling for Susan and Tony.

"Oh no, no, no." Rey melted in a pool of protest. "You misunderstand, Mr. Perry. I was speaking of the broker, in this case myself."

"You get a commission, don't you?"

"Yes, but if this particular deal works out, I'll get a handsome additional gift. In American terms, a bonus."

Doug did not believe him. Rey had spelled under-the-table payment to Perry in capital letters. The man was not only despairing, he was slippery. Yes, Susan, he would proceed with caution. "You realize, of course, that this chip isn't much good to a computer manufacturer without the circuit diagrams, chip layouts, software and technical help?"

"Yes. The customer would need your technicians for a month or so. Is that about right?" Rey's voice was dipped in melancholy.

What made the man so disconsolate? Blighted sex life, sour liver, guilt over bribe attempts, twisted childhood, *Weltschmerz?* "A minimum of a month, yes."

"My client would need exclusive use of the, er, Cat Word, for three years before you sold it elsewhere."

"And if we met that condition, what would your people offer for the package?"

"Assuming the circuits function to specifications and that everything worked out as promised?"

"Naturally."

"And that this chip, as rumored, offers so many cipher keys—a billion billion, they say—that it would take a machine hundreds of years to break a message?"

Rey's question, reflecting the approximate potential of the Katwar, capped Doug's wary probing. There was no doubt now that somewhere, somehow, the dolorous Mexican had picked up information about the chip that only insiders were thought to possess. The Katwar was indeed, if not a miracle as publicists were accustomed to hail each computer advance, at least a shining wonder of the new miniature electronic technology. In size and function, Katwar would have stunned such a computer pioneer as John von Neumann. A flake of specially treated silicon no larger than a clover leaf, the chip held a maze of microscopic circuitry permitting the automatic encryption of all data flowing through a computer.

The Katwar 23 offered an astronomical number of secret cipher keys for commercial and military users. Mathematicians estimated that it would take a cryptanalytic computer, working nonstop at the speed of light, centuries upon centuries to crack Katwar's se-cret writing. This magic sliver of silicon resembled a tiny coffin. So minuscule was Katwar's wiring that regular light could not be used to etch the grooved circuitry. Instead, electron beam lithography, a new technology, fashioned the circuits in a basement room so antiseptic that the technicians wore masks, and giant filters con-tinually scrubbed the air.

PDF officers felt confident that they had won the industry-wide race to perfect an encryption chip that could withstand assault from the professional cryptanalysts as well as from the canniest electronic thieves. "Now the banking system and the Pentagon can breathe easier," Doug told Susan and Tony, "while we breathe money—for a change."

Carlos Rey waited, an abstraction in pain behind his smoke screen. Doug, a nonsmoker, found the pungent odor of the Gau-loises difficult to tolerate.

"You're on the right track, Mr. Rey." He waved the smoke away. "Our Katwar 23 encodes in such an ingenious way that it would take the world's fastest code-breaking machine many life-times to crack security."

"Just as I heard." Rey's smile had the pale flame of the bed-ridden.

"And where did you hear it?"

"I can't, I can't . . . so many conflicting loyalties."

"So, your people would offer how much?" Money, with its flinty edges, would at last hack through the psychic smog.

"Assuming all goes as promised?"

"Of course."

"In that case"—Rey coughed, swiveled his thick lenses toward Doug—"nine million dollars."

Doug kept his poker face. Nine million! No need to gain the upper hand by zapping the Mexican into lumpy nudity. After ex-penses that would mean a windfall of almost $8,000,000 or the equivalent of PDF's net in its best four years—unhappily now but a memory. Doug made swift calculations. In the computer world's competitive maelstrom, no inventor could hope to keep exclusive possession of a new piece of hardware for more than a year or two. By the time a company finished a legal battle against patent infringement, the computer industry's swirling progress had swept the contested item into the sludge of history. Clearly this bid, if bona fide, would yield Dataflo more profits than would the open market.

"Nine million." The repetition issued from a cave of gloom. "In gold if you wish, Mr. Perry."

"Gold might be very nice, Mr. Rey." As they settled into after-lunch coffee, Doug found himself pitying the Mexican. No one should have to shoot life's rapids while burdened with such desolation. He had an urge to jettison all dealing and devote himself to healing Carlos Rey.

"Excuse me for a moment." He bowed slightly to the broker, pushed back his chair and walked from the room. He felt compassion for the man. Had he been responsible only to himself, Doug would have put business aside and spent the afternoon trying to help the conflicted Mexican, perhaps urging him into therapy. Lending a helping hand came naturally to him. He was, after all, a preacher's son. Still, he did have his obligations to Susan and Tony and the rest of straitened Dataflo, and he realized that much as he would prefer otherwise he must bargain with Rey without regard to any psychic infirmity. He paced the lobby beneath huge copper chandeliers for some minutes before returning.

"Sorry," he said, when he seated himself again.

"Ah, those intestinal bugs." The assumption came naturally to a life-long resident of Mexico City. "I would advise the new tablet called . . ."

Doug waved the suggestion aside. "Thanks, *amigo,* but this is more complicated—a thing perhaps of the spirit. You understand?"

As a Latin, Rey either understood or pretended he did, forbearing renewal of crass commercial talk. He waited, draped in distress, until the American reopened the subject of money. Several minutes elapsed before Doug's talent for hard, sharp bargaining returned in full.

"Two things, Mr. Rey. First, I know my executive committee"—he looked appropriately solemn in honor of that body's instant creation—"will want more than $9,000,000 for exclusive use of the Katwar. We can easily get ten or eleven, perhaps more, supplying it to our regular customers who'll get pissed if we give your people an exclusive." He bluffed with his Sunday-night face.

"Second, it's futile for me to go back to the shop this afternoon without the name of your client. We'd be wasting each other's time."

"May I assume you'll weigh my client's offer in good faith, in good faith?"

"Of course." Doug bore in. "But we must have the name. Absolutely essential. You must know that."

"May I have your word the name will be held in confidence if the deal falls through?"

"You have my word." He was beginning to regard the Mexican's misery as an affront. By what right did Rey poison his surroundings? "Let's get on with it."

Rey leaned across the table. "The name is Ossian, Ltd." He lowered his voice as though for the bereaved. "Nassau, the Bahamas. It's a young company, but heavily capitalized with American, German and Swiss money. They're specializing in computer supplies in Third World countries. Here's some data on their credit rating."

Glancing at a sheet stuffed with numbers, Doug noted that Ossian, Ltd., had a $20 million line of credit with one New York bank and major reserves in another.

"They're cash heavy." Rey said it with an awe Doug could appreciate. They were both, after all, acolytes in the cathedral of money.

They soon wound up their business. Doug would carry the offer back to the newly born executive committee while Rey went to New York on other brokerage missions. They walked through the lobby, autumnal in its coppery hues, and Doug waited until a cab arrived.

"Well, good-bye for now." Doug put out his hand. "Give my regards to Otis Kramer."

Rey's dark eyes flashed in surprise, a rent in the Mexican's pall of melancholy.

"Kramer?" Rey feigned ignorance, but did not quite, Doug thought, bring it off.

"Oh, I forgot. You don't know the man." But surely Rey did. Doug was confident of that now. Buoyed by the discovery, even though blind to its meaning, he walked into the pouring sunshine, leaving Carlos Rey, that agent of unimpeachable despair, standing in the shadows.

3

On this sparkling June day, Kate Warfield, twenty-three-year-old daughter of Larry Warfield of the Sunday-night poker game and the Second National Bank's trust department, sat hunched before a computer terminal in her upstairs room of the Warfield home on Lake Drive. A long picture window overlooked Lake Carnegie where Princeton crews skimmed their narrow shells through spring mists or skaters scoured the ice on cold winter days. Large color computer chip layouts, posters of rock bands and Swiss railways surmounted a wilderness of clothes, books, records, tennis gear and computer journals, through which Kate had hacked a pathway to the outer world. Actually, she had long since vowed to stamp out vestiges of teenage clutter, but old habits died slowly.

She tapped the ENTER key of her ivory-colored terminal with a touch of feathers. A small green square sprang to the screen, shivering as if in anticipation of action to come.

VM/370 ONLINE

Kate logged in: L. She typed her account number: 174093

LOGON AT 13:11:38 EDT MONDAY 06/21/82

She tapped her invisible password: KATWAR

CMS/SP VER 1, PLC 14 – 82.172

Kate thus gained access to time-sharing on Princeton University's computer, a maze of wires, microscopic paths on silicon wafers and magnetic disks that electronic engineers admired as a majesty of simple logic. In essence, this IBM 3081, like all other computers, dealt with but two digits, 0 and 1, that were formed by either high or low voltage levels on minute metal trails acid-etched into the silicon. The machine operated via lightning-swift electrical impulses which everyone took for granted and which no one, from Ben Franklin to modern Nobel Laureates, completely understood.

Although Kate had entered the University's computer, she might as easily have tapped into machines belonging to the Educational Testing Service, Rutgers University, Princeton Dataflo or a half dozen other facilities. In fact, any data processor in central Jersey would have been proud to have the woman on-line, for Kate Warfield currently starred as the hottest gossip item in the Princeton area's computer community.

Thus far only officers and top employees of Princeton Dataflo knew of Kate's precise contribution to the chip that would soon make electronic and cryptographic history with her name attached. While a compact team of engineers had developed the chip and its auxiliary circuitry, the trio knew that Kate's genius for seeing whole, new patterns on the screen of her mind had enabled the team to score its triumphant breakthrough.

Kate occasionally recalled the night last winter when rich, vibrant colors saturated her mind and offered like a gift of jewels the solution to the puzzle of the coding algorithm. After months of elusive, drifting fragments, the stuff of forgotten dreams or fevered hallucinations, now suddenly appeared this solid pattern, this other reality that could be handled, measured and duplicated. It had dimensions, texture. It did not fade away like aged voices, but stayed front and center on the living stage of her mind.

Kate could remember the exact place and moment when the surge of inspiration overwhelmed her. She had been working with the engineering team for months, had gone to bed late on the night of January 10. From her snug cocoon beneath an electric blanket, she could look through the window on frozen Lake Carnegie, fringed by skeletal trees that creaked and snapped in the moaning wind. Moonlight shimmered on the ice like sequins.

She was tired to the bone, and when she closed her eyes she felt unstrung by fatigue. Her eyelids fluttered, her neck ached and she knew that sleep would be long in coming. She forced her mind away from work, far from that tiresome chip. Instead, she saw herself dancing at a new spot in Trenton the previous Saturday night. She could see the pale, frantic kid with burning eyes as he flailed his drums and cymbal. She could hear the beat, feel her body bend to the rhythm. Then in a flash, without leave and against her will, her thoughts shot back to the basement computer room of Princeton Dataflo.

And there it was, the coding algorithm, or the precise procedure to solve the problem that had baffled them for so long. It burst on the theater of her mind in brilliant color, showering greens, purples, blues and reds in those deep liquid tones peculiar to computer graphics. She saw the algorithm, first in a series of design steps that would lead to the chip, as a great pattern that was as plainly and as minutely visible as parts of the human body in the big anatomical chart she had studied in prep school. She lay quite still, fearful that the slightest movement might dissipate the enchanted spell. For the image, pulsing in vivid colors, was a thing of enchantment. Kate had done enough exploring, both in mathematics and computers, to know that this was a rare moment, one untarnished by doubt. She knew with the certainty of long-proved equations that this throbbing pattern held the answer to the team's long search.

She did not lay immobile for long. Discovery charged her, sent tremors racing from head to toe. She threw off the covers, slid out of bed and pulled on the clothes she had draped over the armchair just a few minutes earlier—jeans, sweater, wool socks. Her parents were asleep. Downstairs she put on her winter boots, noted the time, 1:38, and decided it would be reckless to ride her motorcycle over icy roads. Larry Warfield always left keys to the family Chevy Malibu hanging in the kitchen. She drove the car out to Forrestal Center and hurried into the Dataflo lobby.

The night security guard looked up from his copy of *The National Enquirer*. His uniform bulged at the waist and his long, brooding face had the claylike pallor of people who see little sunlight. "What's up, Miss Warfield. You just left here."

"Brain storm, Duddy." She signed his entry-departure sheet, then fished her security badge, complete with photo, from her leather tote bag and pinned it to her gray sweater.

Duddy Atkins locked several desk drawers with the elaborate deliberation of a man who doesn't have enough to do, stood up with a busy jangling of keys and led Kate downstairs and along a brightly lighted corridor to a door that bore admonitory crimson lettering: COMPUTER RESEARCH. AUTHORIZED PERSONNEL ONLY.

Atkins waited while Kate unlocked the door with her numbered key. "Don't work all night now," he cautioned as he plodded off.

But she did. She sat for hours before Susie, the computer on which the team tested its endless theories aimed at producing an invulnerable encryption chip. She flashed graphics on the screen, fed the machine long strings of numbers, equations, measurements. She hit the coffee maker three times while rebuking herself for risking caffeine jitters. A sense of satisfaction, of completion, slowly spread, at last suffused her whole body. Each step checked out. Nothing went awry. Oh, sure, there were the usual bugs, a gap here and there, but nothing that could not be handled later when they moved into the design phases. The algorithm worked. The picture that had seized her mind while she snuggled in bed and thought of dancing had proved out.

It was almost an anti-climax when Jerry Dunn, the systems analyst and boss of the engineering team, arrived at eight o'clock. A neat, meticulous technician who worshipped punctuality and order as his mother had adored saints, Dunn had an unruly thatch of red hair that gave strangers a false clue to his character. Led by the ungovernable hair to expect a comfortably disoriented man, people found instead this human timetable, all straight lines and angles.

"I've got it!" Kate bounced off her operator's chair and struck a statuette of triumph, right leg thrust aggressively forward, arms raised, hands fluttering.

"Show me." Dunn ran his fingers through his tangle of hair.

His crest reminded her of bursting sunrise. "Okay, it's like this, Jerry love." She kicked the roller chair back in place, sat down before the screen. She tapped the keyboard, triggering first a set of numbers, then a series of geometric designs and patterns in flowing color.

Minutes passed. "Show me more," said Dunn quietly.

Additional patterns unrolled on the screen. Save for the breathing of the two specialists, the only sound in the acoustically designed room was that of Kate tapping the keyboard. Time slipped by unmeasured.

"Hey," said Dunn at last, "I think you may have it. . . . Yeah. Elegant, Kate. I thought the solution was a couple of months away. Of course, we have a long way to go, but right off it looks good."

Other members of the team, engineers and cryptologists, began arriving, Bill, Steve, Florence, Gavin, Art. All heard bits and pieces of the discovery story and Kate told of leaping out of bed so often that she caught herself sounding like a recording. Freddie Pond, a cryptographer and the team's clown, named her "Queen of Codes," crowned her with a reel of magnetic tape and predicted she'd take Duddy Atkins as her royal consort.

The day turned into a long merry liquid smoky celebration.

Doug Perry arrived at nine-thirty followed in a few minutes by vice-presidents Susan Lindbloom and Tony Canzano. Marshall Ingersoll came in from his day off. By late morning they were drinking champagne, and at noon Freddie Pond went home and returned with his stash of marijuana, a *sin semilla* brand heavy with resin. The grass coaxed them into mellow dancing to the music of Chick Corea on Steve's portable stereo. Sedate Susan Lindbloom kissed Jerry Dunn and everyone kissed Kate. Doug led her in an undulating hula.

A month later, after the algorithm had been checked and rechecked and the first sketches of circuit diagrams had been made, Doug, Susan and Tony summoned Kate to Doug's splashy head office. They dubbed the new chip-to-be the Katwar 23 to commemorate her name and age and offered her 5 percent of the chip's earnings if Kate would remain with the company another five years. She accepted and walked out the door—a millionaire on the hoof. Later, methodical Stanley Fowler, the Stan of the Sunday-night poker game and a partner in Princeton's leading law firm, drew up a formal contract for her.

Princeton Dataflo officers, seizing the Katwar like a life preserver, slapped a top-secret label on Kate's breakthrough and muzzled members of the production team. But the new world of computer networks was a leaky one for secrets and soon rumors began to circulate.

Gary Jameson called on Doug, reminded him of the agreement reached with the National Security Agency by a committee of private and academic cryptographers. Papers on new research should be submitted first to the NSA, according to the voluntary pact. Doug took up the matter with Tony, Susan and Kate. Tony favored turning over the Katwar designs to the government's code-and-cipher agency, but Doug finally ruled that they'd sell the chip on the open market or to a mainframe manufacturer. Either way, NSA could buy the security chip like anyone else in the American computer community. Doug mentioned this decision casually to Gary at the next Sunday-night game.

By summer word of Kate's brilliant work was spreading widely through the volatile world of data processing.

If the computer universe of the '80s belonged to the young, Kate Reilly Warfield was the youngest and brightest sun in the galaxy of invention.

A slim prodigy with a crooked smile and a mass of curly hair the color of melted midnight, Kate had a fierce unflagging current of energy. She was not beautiful. Picked apart, she had hollow cheeks, sharp eyes, long, thin legs, narrow hips and a chest that no one would ever call bosomy. She kept in almost constant motion, crackling with wiry vitality, striking quick, little disco poses that illustrated her speech like animated cartoons, teasing her hair, tapping her feet and glancing this way and that as if fearful of missing something of critical importance.

A puzzle addict in childhood, Kate became a computer bug as a preppy at Princeton Day School where she scored a perfect 800 on math in the College Board SATs. She also collected arcane movie trivia, played on the girls' ice hockey team and gulped enormous exotic blends at Thomas Sweet's Ice Cream hangout on Nassau Street. For a time her parents feared she might develop into a single-minded grubby mathematics grind. But as a junior at Princeton Day, Kate budded into the familiar complexities of adolescence. She became a rock fan, designed some of her own clothes, ignored the rubble in her room, fell in and out of love, experimented with a half-dozen shades of lipstick and took to dancing until the small hours at parties.

Although the math and computer star protested that she had "the same number of brain cells, fourteen billion, as everyone else," her classmates credited her with triple the normal cargo. Yet few peers dismissed her as an oddball, and no one called her a nerd. People responded to her quirky vitality, bursts of energy as heady as those of her Kawasaki motorcycle and as inexplicable as the electricity that surged through the binary gates of her computers.

Bewitched by her perfect College Board math score and tales of her computing exploits, college admissions officers wooed her on behalf of such hallowed halls as Harvard, Penn, Chicago, Caltech and, of course, Princeton. "That girl is a cinch to endow a chair at her alma mater before she's forty," said one.

But Kate chose Rutgers, the state university, for its computer-science department, headed by Saul Amarel, a family friend who had taught her adventuresome computer games like Star Trek long before her first lipstick. She was graduated with honors and now neared her Ph.D. in computer science, approaching the halfway mark on completion of her doctoral thesis: "The Design of Search Algorithms and the Possibility of Obtaining Polynomial Bounds on Their Complexity." Meanwhile she had spent weekends and many nights at Princeton Dataflo with the symbols, circuit diagrams and chip layouts that eventually became the Katwar 23.

But work and the doctoral thesis were far from her mind this first day of summer on the banks of Lake Carnegie where breezes whispered through the weeping cherry trees and fleecy clouds overhead sailed toward the Jersey shore. Kate was absorbed in devising a birthday present for her father.

Accessing the computer where streaming electrons performed feats to rival the life and death of far galaxies, she set about making Larry Warfield an invincible poker player. Building on a computerized study of poker by Nicholas V. Findler, a computer scientist at the State University of Buffalo, Kate had delved into the mathematics of the game for some time. If her program proved successful, and if her father heeded the advisory printout on the odds for a vast variety of situations, he would become the Sunday-night game's leading player, assuming his normal grasp of the psychological and character aspects did not weaken.

She typed a command to summon her poker program from the computer's infallible memory, studied the opening lines as she twirled a strand of her frizzed black hair around a finger.

Someone rapped at the door.

"Damn." She hated to be disturbed when seated before the altar of her terminal. Did Catholics tolerate interruptions when taking Communion at the rail? How about Moslems prostrate toward Mecca?

"Who's there?" Her voice grated with irritation.

"Prudence McNaughton, dear. Your mother said you might let me look at that famous computer of yours."

"Just a sec." She'd forgotten. Peggy Warfield was entertaining a dozen members of the Monday Book Club at luncheon.

Prudence McNaughton, wife of Jay McNaughton of the Sunday-night poker game and the University's Woodrow Wilson School, was what Kate regarded as stuffy class as opposed to what her father called classy stuff: old WASP money from Boston, Mt. Holyoke College, Present Day and Pretty Brook clubs in Princeton, imposing home on Independence Drive, always chaired a committee at the annual hospital fête, played smashing, aggressive tennis and rode her ancient creaking bicycle all over town.

"Come on in, Mrs. McNaughton." But Kate opened the door only halfway. "I was just checking out a program."

"I'd love seeing how you work it." Pru McNaughton edged into the room where stereo amplifiers shared the book shelves with computer journals, records, cassettes, textbooks, detective thriller paperbacks, a pair of skis and a framed color picture of Kate as an ice hockey player back in prep school. Sunlight poured through the open window and a breeze curled up from the lake.

Kate, seldom a partner to malice, didn't trust this woman. What was this sweet defenseless look doing on the face of such an utterly confident, and probably predatory, female? She thought of calling up her private weapon for dealing with irritating characters, but decided she didn't need it today.

"Do you mind, Kate?"

She minded fiercely and was about to unsheath a verbal stiletto when she halted herself. Now why be nasty to this woman who was guilty of nothing more offensive than curiosity? Prudence had no way of knowing that Kate hated interruptions. After all, it was her mother's fault for encouraging Prudence to come up there. Time to move out to her own place. Long overdue, in fact.

"What would you like to see?" She forced herself to be pleasant.

"Oh, anything that you've worked out and that I could see on your screen, I guess." Standing beside Kate, Prudence McNaughton pointed to the terminal.

"How about something on your Monday Book Club?" Kate looked up with a smile. "I worked up some probabilities on the members last month."

"You did? That would be fascinating, Kate."

"Some of it is, well, clinical." Should she actually run the book club file?

"I don't mind."

Kate dismissed her poker program and typed a message summoning the book club data from the dustless storage bins of the University's $4,200,000 machine. Wavering green letters fled across the video terminal.

MONDAY BOOK CLUB. 17 MEMBERS.
Kate stroked a number: 1041
MENOPAUSE PROBABILITIES
Current: 3. Next Five Years: 7. Next Ten: 14.

"Would you like to see more, Mrs. McNaughton?" Kate gathered her brows in a proper technician's squint. "I have lots of data."

"Good heavens." Prudence McNaughton's look of helplessness evaporated. She glanced sharply at Kate. "Why yes, I would."

1044
DEATH PROBABILITIES
Current: 0. Next Five Years: 2. Next Ten: 4.

Kate looked up. "There's more stuff in the club's profile." She evinced professional unconcern.

"Perhaps you could show me a few more." Pru McNaughton now eyed the screen as she might a neighborhood busybody.

1047
ADULTERY PROBABILITIES
Current: 3. Next Five Years: 6. Next Ten: 9.

Prudence coughed behind her hand. Who were those two other errant wives? But, of course, the computer couldn't know her secret. Not a soul knew that. Or did they? She began to dislike this silent box blabbing its statistical gossip.

1048
POVERTY PROBABILITIES
Current: 0. Next Five Years: 1. Next Ten: 2.
1049
CANCER PROBABILITIES
Current: 2. Next Five Years: 5. Next Ten: 7.
1050
MAJOR DENTURES
Current: 5. Next Five Years: 8. Next Ten: 11.

"Thanks, Kate." Prudence McNaughton had had enough. "Your machine certainly dredges up the dreary side of things."

Kate stood up. "Just the facts of life as the members get older." She shaped a disco pose, arms angled, pelvis sunken, choreographing the onslaught of age.

Prudence McNaughton picked her way down the stairs, bearing enough gossip to divert the Monday Book Club for weeks from its earnest pursuit of the inner Nabokov, Updike, Borges, Lessing, Roth, Didion, Cheever and Grass. But, honestly, could the computer—or Kate—know about the affair with Doug? Just what was a probability, anyway?

Kate settled back with a sigh of relief. With college out for the summer and the Katwar 23 packaged and ready, she could concentrate on the program designed to make her dad the town's top poker winner. She ordered the computer's memory to swallow the book club once more and regurgitate the card-game study.

Let's see now. After a sample opening deal of five-card stud, Larry Warfield had a nine of hearts up and a ten of clubs in the hole. Two players showed face cards and a third an ace. What should Larry do? Triggered by Kate, electricity shot through miles of wiring in the mainframe computer, glancing here, detouring there, shying, racing, searching, snatching at odds as the machine sped toward possible solutions. The process engrossed the computer as thoroughly as did that other problem for a Woodrow Wilson professor several thousandths of a second ago: If the Soviet Union fired twenty hydrogen-headed missiles at the United States, what were the odds of Minneapolis-St. Paul surviving? New York? Los Angeles? Sioux Falls? Now, a sliver of time later, should Larry Warfield call, raise or fold?

It was in the cool of the evening, as the summer breeze died and the lake mirrored tawny shafts of fading sunlight, that Peggy Warfield broached the subject of her daughter's computer inquiries into the destiny of Monday Book Club members.

A warm hearty woman, built like a tank, Peggy Warfield bristled with a militant brand of her daughter's energy. Mrs. Warfield was fascinated by successful people and social standings, and she went armed with celebrated names which she dropped as purposefully as a combat vehicle planting land mines.

She faced her daughter on the screened porch across a glass-topped coffee table. "I think you owe me an explanation, young lady, for whatever it was you showed Pru McNaughton this noon." Having a genius in the house did not deter her from the grave responsibilities of motherhood.

"Oh, Mother." Kate let her facial printout register uncharacteristic boredom. "Must you use that old cliché, 'young lady'? It's always a tip-off that you're off on one of your lecture trips."

" 'Young lady' is a perfectly acceptable phrase. I heard George Kennan use it just the other day."

"George Kennan?" Kate flamed the name with incredulity. She rated her mother's practice of buttressing shaky parental admoni-

tions with quotations from notable Princeton residents as quite unfair.

"Don't detour from the subject, Kate." Mrs. Warfield was stern but contained. She had taken this whole business of Kate's "gift" to a psychotherapist last year. Leaving aside math and computers, she asked, shouldn't she treat Kate as she would any other postgraduate-age daughter? Absolutely, agreed the therapist, thereby earning her $65 an hour and a reputation, quickly spread by Peggy, for sagacity.

"All right. I'll lay it out straight." Kate went into a dance pose, shoulder lowered, one arm extended. "You know that I detest people who come into my room, especially when I'm working. So I decided to shake her up."

"And just how did you do that, dear? Prudence wasn't totally coherent, I must say."

Kate ran over the book-club data, from menopause to major dental disasters. "You can have hard copy on it if you're all that interested."

"Kate, I'll thank you not to take that patronizing tone with me." Peggy, whose vitality, like her daughter's, usually sought wider spaces for its expression, heaved from her chair and began to stride about the porch. "I can't understand why you have to pick our book club for your research when you have the whole world open to those machines of yours."

"Mother, must you stomp around like that?"

"I'm not stomping." The porch nevertheless shuddered.

"It sounds like stomping to me." Actually Kate thought these gymnastic outbreaks were as funny as the flings at discipline. She enjoyed sparring with her mother. Not nearly as stimulating as concocting a dp program, but diverting as far as family-type entertainment went.

"Kate, you know I'm not overly concerned about what the women in the book club think." Peggy adjusted the upholstery on her splendid bosom, a feature which her daughter had failed, distressingly, to inherit. A matter of Larry's family genes, no doubt. "What does concern me is you. There are enough tales circulating, trying to make you out some kind of freak. With your skills, dear, we have to be especially careful. I don't want you known as a kook."

"Who says I'm kooky?"

"There were some unpleasant references to you at that authors' do last week at Prospect House."

"Is that the same party where you talked to Joyce Carol Oates?"

"That's the one." Peggy preened. How sweet of Kate to recall her rewarding moment beside a resident literary star.

"Do you think I'm freaky, Mother?"

"Indeed not. You're a very normal young woman with a special gift. Let's keep it that way."

"Then don't let people barge into my room."

"I admit that was a mistake."

Both women knew they had negotiated an unspoken compromise. Kate would keep her unconventional research to herself while Peggy would protect her daughter's privacy.

The ringing of the telephone interrupted their kiss of reconciliation, a slight brushing of lips on cheeks. Kate answered, listened briefly, then said, "I'll come right out."

She turned to her mother. "I have to go out to Dataflo. We've been had. Somebody's planted a Trojan horse."

"A what?"

"Computer talk." She snatched up her leather tote bag and headed for the porch door.

"But dinner, Kate. The lamb's almost done."

"I'll eat it cold later." The door slammed behind her. "Sorry, Mother."

Kate stowed her bag in a compartment of the Kawasaki, settled her helmet on her head like a space warrior, gunned the motorcycle and roared off toward Harrison Street.

4

They stood looking sadly at Susie, a faithless servant guilty of betraying the pinched company that had given the machine a secure air-conditioned fireproof home.

Susan Lindbloom, for whom the computer was named, Doug Perry, Tony Canzano and the red-haired systems analyst, Jerry

Dunn, gazed at the metal box as they might at an old trusted retainer apprehended in the act of making off with the family silver.
As always Susie, or "the beast," as computer toilers often called
their charge, rested mute while her busy interior silently gulped
millions of facts that would be regurgitated in familiar patterns
deemed essential to the survival of Western civilization. A swift
efficient worker, Susie was a mainframe computer of sturdy talents.

Linked to a national computer network, she had run off a number of routine chores in near-record time. Her triumph, for which
she would rate footnotes in computer and cryptographic histories,
was her service as the electronic drafting board for incredibly
complex designs for a coding chip. In time these designs matured
into that scrap of silicon, that powerhouse of encryption, the ulti-
mate in computer security tools, the Katwar 23. And it was this
service in producing Katwar that now bred such dismay in the
PDF executives gathered near the computer's sleek flanks.

A gong sounded like a fire alarm, notice that someone sought
admission to Susie's security-steeped hideaway. Jerry Dunn
opened the metal door and in kited Kate Warfield like a fitful
breeze, black hair piled in a mound, eyes darting about and her
canted smile sloping toward the plastic security badge, complete
with photo, above her heart.

"What's up, gang?" Kate struck one of her postures that came
and went so swiftly that most people were aware only of a blur of
movement.

Doug Perry recognized her "ready for action" stance, left heel
raised, pelvis tilted and right fingers pointed skyward. He had
known the girl and woman for years, had always noted how she
managed to inject the inanimate circuitry of computers with a
vague but unmistakable sexual coloration, a kind of erotic dye
that coursed through the machines as steadily as the electricity
that powered them.

"Someone has gotten into Susie," said Doug, "and may have
stolen our prescription for Katwar."

"How do we know?"

"Jerry discovered some secret instructions." Susan Lindbloom
nodded toward the systems analyst. "Here, look." She handed
Kate a slip of paper. The proof of villainy looked at first glance
like a quite ordinary computer printout.

% ps al

TTY	F	S	UID	PID	PRI	ADDR	SZ	WCHAN	COMMAND
1:	1	W	7	10	10	2506	9	121444	–
2:	1	W	0	11	10	2423	7	121504	– 2
3:	1	W	0	12	10	1371	7	121544	– 2
4:	1	W	0	13	10	1454	7	121604	– 2
5:	1	W	0	14	10	2712	7	121704	– 2
6:	1	W	0	15	10	2255	7	121644	– 0
7:	1	W	0	16	10	2340	7	122004	– 2
8:	1	W	7	17	40	1537	9	65416	–
8:	1	W	0	61	40	2656	9	65444	–
8:	1	R	0	62	115	3006	17		ps al
101:	1	W	0	7	10	1257	7	121404	– 7

"Not very impressive, is it?" Dunn shrugged. "It looks just like a normal listing of what's going on inside the beast, right? But, as it turns out, too normal."

"Oh, yeah. You were testing how the system would behave without Arpanet." Kate pointed to the copy. "But that last line is a network terminal. It shouldn't be there when the Arpanet is turned off."

"You've got it." Dunn nodded several times. "It's just luck we caught it. Turns out that someone was starting up his own version of GETTY for the Arpanet line. Acted just like ours most of the time, but when the unknown user typed his magic user name, it gave him access to everything in our system. Didn't even log in a job, so we never saw a thing."

"Trojan horse, huh?"

"Yep. No mistake about it." Dunn paid homage to the artistry of the interloper. "Classic case. Beautiful animal, Kate. Even after we saw the extra process, it took us six hours to figure out how the damn thing got started in the first place."

"Let me get this straight," said Tony Canzano. "Can we tell from the last line of the list what terminal on Arpanet got our stuff?"

"No way," said Dunn. "This animal left no traces."

In the ancient Trojan horse legend, Greek soldiers hid inside a huge, wooden horse which the befuddled residents of Troy, a city near the Aegean coast of what is now Turkey, permitted to be wheeled inside their city. The Greek legions, who had laid siege to Troy for years, boarded their ships and pretended to sail away. Under cover of night the hiding Greek soldiers slipped out of the wooden horse and opened the gates of the city. Warriors from the returning Greek fleet swarmed in, sacked the city, slaughtered the Trojan men and made off with the women.

The implications of the Trojan horse planted inside Princeton Dataflo's computer were immediately apparent to those gathered about the machine. Susie was hooked into Arpanet, a nationwide network of computers originated by the Advanced Research Projects Agency of the Defense Department. People left electronic mail for one another while computers traded data with computers on this web that embraced more than three hundred of America's largest and swiftest data-processing machines as well as several computers abroad.

As he stood with his staff and stared at Susie, Doug felt his anger rising. Dataflo's first strike into the big money—money that would stave off the threat of insolvency—jeopardized by an unknown thief! He felt as he had once at the poker table when he drew a rare four-of-a-kind only to have his four eights topped by an opponent's four tens. Just when the Katwar promised to reshape Dataflo into a highly profitable company, robbery shattered the promise. Had his luck run out?

Of course, they had no evidence that anyone actually had stolen the designs of the Katwar chip, but the tool for robbery—a file of numbers ordering the machine to disgorge all its contents on command to an anonymous fact-snatcher—rested inside the machine itself. And the person who planted that subversive instruction could extract Katwar secrets via any of hundreds of terminals linked to Arpanet, summoning data through interface processors that connected each computer to the network, then over lines stretching from coast to coast. At this moment someone several thousand miles away might be building a duplicate Katwar with just enough subtle change to mask the chip's origins. How to find the culprit? Even more difficult, if and when found, how to prove he stole the designs? Electronic thieves left no fingerprints. Doug's deepening rage fed on frustration.

Pressures of the long day already had frayed his nerves. First the brush with Gary Jameson over the IDA flyer, then the session with Carlos Rey, that tub of gloom, followed by more calls from around the country as sharp traders picked up rumors of Katwar. Other PDF business had taken Susan Lindbloom to Philadelphia for the afternoon, so the triumvirate could not meet on Rey's bid until evening.

Doug, Tony and Susan had just settled into their session over sandwiches at Doug's desk when Jerry Dunn called with the ominous word about possible rifling of their company's secrets. Carlos Rey was forgotten as they hurried downstairs. Now, standing beside the machine with Jerry Dunn and Kate Warfield, the angry Dataflo officers faced the paramount question: Who had violated Susie?

"If I find the guy, I'll throttle him with my bare hands." Tony was furious. He'd been without a raise now for two years.

"Not if I get him first." So had Susan.

"Could be a prank, of course," said Jerry Dunn, "somebody leaving a trademark just to prove he could get away with it."

Doug glanced at Kate.

"Don't accuse me." Kate threw up her hands. "I knocked off that kid stuff years ago after I sneaked into Educational Testing's IBM 3031." She savored her old feat. "Pretty neat, though. They never caught me."

"So that's how you scored your perfect 800 in math?" Tony teased.

"You kidding? The only thing I tapped into was the ETS salary list. In case you want to know, I can tell you what anybody out there makes."

"How about others on the Katwar team?" asked Doug. "Any of them likely to do it as a joke?"

Kate pondered. "Only one, I guess. Freddie Pond, the youngest of the cryppies. Freddie likes to spook people."

"I thought of that. I called Freddie at home." Jerry Dunn apparently would tick off suspects as methodically as he checked the work of the Katwar team. "He swears he didn't do it."

Tony Canzano touched Doug's arm. "Say, this isn't one of your stunts, is it, Doug?"

"Not guilty. I don't play around when big money's involved."

"Who do you suspect, Jerry?" asked Tony.

"Hold it." Doug raised a hand. "Let's do this systematically. First, let's find out who had access to this room. Agreed?" Susan and Tony nodded.

"Okay, let's go over the names." Doug pointed to Dunn. "You make a list, starting with the five of us here now."

In a few minutes they had listed twenty-three people, chiefly engineers and cryptologists who worked with Kate on the new chip but also including four employees who had signed the registration book at the door. Anyone not entitled to a numbered key and special security badge had to sign in and out of Susie's presence. The four registrants, all from other Dataflo departments, were quickly dismissed as suspects. They either lacked the necessary expertise, the time to tinker, or both.

"Now I want a signed statement from each person here," said Doug. "May sound untrusting, but I want this done properly." The five people wrote briefly and then Doug glanced through the papers. "I have never touched the beast in my life!" Susan Lindbloom. "Not me, guys," wrote Kate. "Why would I snitch my own chip?"

"Okay," said Doug, "we all seem to be clean. No surprise. Now let's go over the other names on Jerry's list and take our time about it."

An hour later they had narrowed their prime suspicions to three people, two young electrical engineers who worked with Kate on the encryption algorithm and Marshall Ingersoll, the systems programmer who had left the company five months before to become an officer of Bytex Laboratories. A producer of computer components, Bytex Labs was located in so-called Silicon Valley between Palo Alto and San José, California.

"As for Ingersoll," said Doug, "you ought to know that he left town owing an $83 poker debt to one of the players in our Sunday-night game."

"Is that supposed to be incriminating?" asked Tony.

"It's a fact to consider." In Doug's mind a man who would welsh on a friendly gambling debt was capable of limitless iniquities.

"Hardly seems world shaking," said Susan.

"True," Doug conceded. "Not to be compared to the big reason why Ingersoll is more than an ordinary suspect."

Tony nodded. "You mean the super-user?"

"Right. Only three people had super-user passwords to this machine." Doug laid a hand on one of the computer's terminals. "Jerry Dunn, Marshall Ingersoll and myself."

In the world of data processing, a super-user password enables its holder to gain access to any and all material in a machine. In mainframe computers the super-user password would be to the individual passwords as the master key is to the room keys in a large hotel if the master key also enabled its holder to slip through walls and ceilings.

"So if he had the super-user, why bother to plant a Trojan horse command?" Susan paid only routine attention to the company's technical matters.

"In case we changed the super-user password after he left," said Tony promptly.

"Did we?"

Jerry Dunn nodded. "Just Doug and I have the new one."

After a span of silence, Kate said, "I remember Ingersoll was here that January morning when we celebrated with champagne and grass. Is Bytex on the ARPA network?"

"Oh yeah." Doug nodded. "Been on a couple of years. Marshall kidded about it his last day here, saying he'd be in constant touch via electronic mail."

"Has he?"

"Haven't heard a word from the guy by any means."

"Here's the latest ARPA list." Jerry Dunn stepped over to a printout hanging on the wall. "Bytex Labs is one of a dozen hosts in the Bay area."

"So what's our next move?" asked Susan.

"We let Jerry and Kate go for the night," said Doug, "while we continue this up in my office."

Kate swept up her tote bag. At the door she struck one of her quick poses. "Don't worry too much, you guys. If anybody stole our Katwar, it'll take them a year to figure out how to produce it."

Doug shook his head. "Eight or nine months is more like it. And suppose they've already started?"

Three hours later the Dataflo triumvirate had about exhausted possible lines of inquiry as well as themselves. Personnel printouts covered Doug's desk, coffee mugs held cold dregs, Tony yawned and Doug paced about near the Tom George painting, a churning sea of color.

"I'll agree, Doug, that evidence points toward Marshall Ingersoll," said Susan, "but we ought to interview the other people on our list with plenty of care."

"Right." Absorbed in thought, Doug continued to pace.

"What about Jerry Dunn?" asked Tony. "He's had more opportunity to fiddle with Susie than anyone else."

"No." Susan was emphatic. "I know something about Jerry. He's a man of conscience. He sold some property on Witherspoon to a friend of mine. Jerry gave his word and he refused to change it, even though he could have made another five or six thousand when prices zoomed up before the settlement. No, Jerry is scrupulously honest."

"Besides," said Doug, "why would he ever expose the plant if he'd done it? Also, he has daily access to everything Susie does anyway." His anger had subsided, but now helplessness fed it anew. Had the Katwar indeed been stolen, invisibly siphoned over hundreds of miles of wire to appear briefly on some distant video screen and then have its image erased forever? If so, how could he ever prove it? Such a crime was like a safecracking with no fingerprints, a kidnapping with no victim, a murder without a corpse. The frustration was galling.

"Look, here's the best we can do right now," he said. "Tomorrow I'll fly out to the Coast and start nosing around the Valley, see what I can dig up on Marshall and Bytex Labs. I'll stay out there and then make the Bohemian Grove encampment. A few days around my own camp, Micro Mall, is worth a dozen computer conventions, believe me.

"Tony, you and Susan quiz everyone on Jerry's list. Also, Susan is handling the check on Otis Kramer and Tony is covering Carlos Rey. A couple of weird characters, those two, and I've got a hunch they're tied together some way. . . . Sound okay?"

"What about Rey's bid for the Katwar?" Tony stood up and stretched.

"That'll hold for a while. If they're ready to go nine million, maybe we're underestimating our little nugget."

"All right," said Susan. "And Doug, have some fun out there. You deserve it."

"Yeah, fun mixed with some lucky business maybe now and then at the Grove. . . . But fun's hard when you dream of red ink."

"Cheer up." Susan held up a V sign. "Robbed or not, we'll be first with Katwar."

Doug remained at his desk for a few minutes after his two vice-presidents left. He read a Merrill, Lynch report on Bytex Labs and phoned Tilly, the company's travel specialist, to book him economy class on United's nonstop flight the next day from Newark to San Francisco.

As he turned to leave, the phone rang.

"Hey, Doug." It was Kate Warfield. "I've been thinking. I know Pam Ingersoll, Marshall's daughter, and also her mother, Marjorie. Why don't I go out to Sunnyvale and do some snooping? Damn if I want my chip stolen by some glitch chief who never put in a minute's work on it."

"Can you leave tomorrow?"

"Sure, I could go right now."

"Call Tilly and get her to put you on United's flight to San Francisco. I'm already on it. We'll ride out together."

"Which class?"

"Used to be first. Now when you travel for Dataflo, you go economy all the way, baby."

"I'm no baby, babe."

"Okay, Kate. See you tomorrow."

He sighed as he hung up. The boss and the prodigy, a goodenough team. But he had no great hopes. They were looking for an invisible needle in an electronic haystack.

5

They rolled south from San Francisco's International Airport on the expressway through Silicon Valley where flowering fruit orchards had fallen to the armies of the new micro civilization. Here hundreds of smokeless, landscaped factories, some decorated as gaily as nursery schools, produced minuscule semiconductors and other artifacts of computerdom's Lilliputian era. Here lay the golden land of High Tech where engineers and entrepreneurs lived out the American dream while unskilled production workers settled for waning dreams.

"Hey, Doug." Kate shouted into the whipping wind. He had ordered their rental car, a Fiat sports convertible, and let her take the wheel. "I like you."

"I'm glad. Not every boss can claim as much from the hired help."

"Hired help!" She feigned outrage. "I'm a consultant, thank you." She knifed the Fiat between two lanes, passing flying strings of cars. "I wasn't talking about relations at the shop. I mean I like you personally."

"And I like you, Kate." It was an understatement. In the hours on the plane, far more time than he had ever spent with this computer *Wunderkind,* he had found her fetching, very feminine with a sassy brand of humor. And beneath lay a vein of vulnerability that evoked protective urges.

"My dad warned me about you. He said you'd probably make a pass."

"Oh." He found this direction vaguely troubling.

"But then he always thinks every man will proposition me."

"Worried father, huh?" Doug's voice warred with the drum of traffic. He had learned more about Larry Warfield, the ribald officer of the Second National Bank, in a few hours with his daughter than he had in a decade around the poker table. "Well, he can rest easy. This is a business trip."

"Just business?" The wind whipped her hair into streaming geometries.

"All business."

"How dreary."

He was not surprised. The air around Kate snapped with sex. She struck her suggestive poses, she flirted and her tumble of energy had a vital, earthy core. On the plane ride from Newark she had sprinkled the conversation with remarks her mother would have called indecorous.

Still he had not expected such a broad hint. A new element had been added to the easy boss-prodigy rapport. The wind brought a glow to her thin cheeks and a pixie smile flickered. She awaited his response with an air of mischief. No question that she stirred him and no question, he told himself, that he would do nothing about it.

"Did that remark mean what it sounded like?"

"Who knows." Her voice said no, her sloping grin said yes.

"Look, Kate, we're out here on business. That's one thing. Second, we're in the same company, and office affairs spell trouble. Third, I'm older than your father. You're twenty-three."

"Wrong." She shot a look of triumph. "I'm twenty-four—or will be next Thursday."

"Age is only part of it. Your parents are both friends. They wouldn't like it, and I don't propose to get in some sticky emotional tangle with the Warfield family."

"You make it sound so heavy. Do you think I'm a kluge?"

"Come off it. If you weren't so foxy, we wouldn't be talking like this."

"Okay, boss." She whipped past a van driven by a bearded man who waved a beer can at her.

She switched to talk of California, a state she was visiting for the first time. The air was warm, fresh. The late afternoon sun swelled, tomato red, as it sank behind the western hills flanking the Pacific.

On the fringe of San José they put in at a ranch-style motel called the Chanticleer, napped in their rooms and dined in the motel's Gay Nineties restaurant in a booth of polished oak. Above them a stained-glass globe drooped strings of colored beads. Over drinks Kate told of running the Monday Book Club probability profile for Prudence McNaughton.

"I thought at first I might have to splat her with my secret weapon, but she was so easy to handle, I didn't need it."

"Secret weapon?"

"Oh, I have this patented system to hex people who give me trouble. What I do is imagine them stark naked and then put them . . ."

"What!" Doug couldn't believe it. "You do what?"

Kate did a quick imitation of undressing. "I picture them in the raw. You can't imagine what a leveler that is. Take a phony bitch like Pru McNaughton who pretends to be so sweet and fragile. If I ever had to undress her, I'll bet that naked she'd turn out tough and knobby, and if I X-rayed her heart, it would be cold as winter."

Pru tough, knobby, cold? Not the Pru who just last week yielded like soft springtime murmurs. No, Pru's flaw was that head stuff, forever testing herself and others.

"Kate, you're incredible." Doug shook his head. "I thought I was the only person who did that. Do you know that I've been mentally undressing people ever since I was a kid?"

"You too!" Her shriek made heads turn. A waiter stopped short to look at her. "Do you just do it with certain people when you feel you have to cut them down to size?"

"Right. I did it again Sunday night at the poker game to a guy who manages to push my buttons."

"Doug, you of all people." She gloated over their mutual sorcery. "And I always thought you were so poised, confident, you know, really had your shit together. I started doing it about the sixth grade when I had a terrible inferiority complex with all those pretty girls and smooth boys."

"Me too." He beamed. "About that time in grade school and for the same reason. Now I can't stop. It's an automatic crutch."

"The john too?"

"The john?"

"Oh, I always stick them on the john after I strip 'em. No way then can they upstage me."

"Great idea." He joined her laughter. "Never thought of that, but I might do it from now on. Thanks."

"Imagine! Doug Perry another closet stripper." She broke up again. Nearby diners turned, wondering what this noisy couple found so amusing.

"You know I did it once to the Vice-President." Kate shot off a new wave of laughter. "Remember that time he received the prize winners of the post-grad computer contest in Washington. Well, I felt awkward when we entered his office, so I just stripped the dude, sat him on a back-yard two-seater and gave him a Sears catalogue. Made my day."

"Who would have thought that Kate, the girl genius, felt inferior to anyone?"

"Or Douglas Perry, the big computer tycoon?"

"You're terrific, woman."

She became suddenly shy despite her crooked smile. "Doug, you know I never told anyone before about my stripping trick."

"You're the first person I've told, Kate." Their private theaters of the absurd had created a bond.

Coasting easily now, they talked about Otis Kramer and Carlos Rey, about the home office and Katwar, then about themselves. Doug told her of his clash with Gary Jameson over the leaflet attacking the Institute for Defense Analyses.

"He had the right tribe, but the wrong Indian." Kate, sipping at a Margarita eyed him over the glass.

"I don't get you."

"Since we're into confidences, I'll trust you with a big one." She offered her broken smile. "I helped write that blurb. The idea originated with a joint anti-war committee, Princeton and Rutgers students and postgrads that I belong to."

"I didn't know you were political."

"I wasn't until this year. Then I began to realize how dangerous that gang in Washington is. They're on a course that could blow up the world. . . . What did you think of our throwaway?"

Doug reflected as he toyed with his scotch. "Frankly, I thought the reasoning was lame. To link IDA's work with whatever mental illness Forrestal had is pretty farfetched."

"No it isn't." Kate shook her head. "Washington's foreign policy today is a mirror of Forrestal's paranoia. And IDA's contracts gave us a good handle to show local people how the system works."

"Local angle on doomsday?"

"Sure, why not." She bridled at his sarcasm. "People go numb. They have to be jabbed awake, and it's always better to hit them with something close to home."

"Even if I agreed with you, the anonymous angle would put me off. If I want to blast somebody, I believe I ought to sign my name."

"I wanted all of us to sign." She reached out to touch his hand. "But I got voted down. You know why? Because Jameson's niece, Mary Ann, is on the committee. That's why he got named especially. She hates the whole idea of IDA."

"That I never would have guessed."

"That's strictly between us, Doug."

"Of course. But your secret won't keep. The F.B.I. probably has half the committee names by now."

"I couldn't care less. It's time to speak out. Do you blame us, Doug?"

"No. At your age I wanted to change the world." Memories rained. A Socialist Party rally where he spoke. The patrician woman in green who welcomed him to a brief affair because he worked in the second Adlai Stevenson campaign. The hot summer he quit work to march at Selma.

"But it's not a question of age at all." She was indignant and embattled now. "If we don't defuse this horrible game of nuclear chicken between us and the Russians, we'll all be dead, you characters who are forty-nine just like us twenties."

"Forty-seven, please."

"Whatever. I mean it, Doug. I'm giving this fight all I can. You know, my mother's a do-gooder along with her celebrity chasing. She's on all the disaster and disease lists—gives fifty dollars to stop acid rain, diabetes, starvation in Somalia, the Moral Majority, you name it. Me, I'm sticking to one issue, saving the world from the nukes, but I'm going to give it lots of muscle."

They chatted along about themselves and their aims, work, music, more politics, the other sex, health, peeves . . . life's ambiguities, the great unknowables, the crazy meat on which men fed and for which they prayed, raped and killed . . . blood-red sunsets, the erosion of hope, ambition and desire, the tinsel of charity and the cancer of illusion.

"I haven't swapped confidences like this since Charlie." Again that touch of shyness.

"Charlie?"

"My first big love years ago. Charlie was okay, but my math scores bugged him. He felt inferior. Silly, right?"

"Oh, but I understand. If a man hasn't made it in some way, pushed his own skills to the utmost, then he rarely has the self-confidence to handle a brainy woman."

Kate raised her glass. "Not like you can cope with me, right?"

"Right." This woman honed his senses. She was a female John von Neumann mixed with more than a dash of Jane Fonda. He admired her passions, was intrigued by her flirtatious style and her extraordinary vitality, this unique daughter of Larry Warfield. Kate warmed him.

"You're still married, aren't you, Doug?"

Her question broke into his thoughts. "Yes. Joan's been talking about a divorce. Frankly, I haven't made a move one way or the other. My mind's been elsewhere."

"You've been living alone some time, right?"

He nodded. "Two years. Joan left soon after we came back from a trip to Central America. Jay McNaughton's specialty is San Luis, you know, and he gave us introductions to his friends there. Actually, it was San Luis that put the final scene to the Perry soap opera."

"How so?"

"Jay's friends are mostly poor Indians out in the boonies. Remote mountain villages. Plantation towns. Joan was uncomfortable there. She saw only the dirt, the poverty, the backwardness. Judy and I loved the Indians and their colorful life-style and clothes. They're kind gentle people. In fact, Judy still writes to one Indian woman, Silvia Ticpan, a nurse in a town called Montes."

"I'd love to travel in that Indian mountain country," she said.

Kate made him feel good. Yet he envied her too. He sensed that in some deep intuitive way, she knew more about life and how to live it than he did at twice her age.

"I think you have a secret I'd like to share."

"A secret?" She thought reflexively of codes and computers. He was Doug Perry and she was not, after all, telepathic. "About what?"

"About life and people and what's worth fighting for, that kind of thing."

"Oh, I doubt it. I think you're way ahead of me there." She lowered her eyes. "I like you, Doug. A lot."

"Same here, Kate."

A new awareness settled down like a third person between them, welcome yet strange in custom and portent. Conscious of the growing bond, they began to treat each other with care and restraint. Doug saw not just a brilliant prodigy of the computer age, but a complex woman with much to learn and even more to teach. He knew he would pay attention.

As they dined, then lingered over Irish coffee, they turned to business, searching for the best way to track down whoever might have filched the design of Katwar. Kate would look up her friend, Pam Ingersoll, and perhaps the mother, Marjorie. Doug would call on friends in the computer industry, including a college classmate he had phoned from the airport. If Bytex Labs planned to produce a new security chip, word might have seeped around the Valley. Doug would not confront Ingersoll himself until he knew a great deal more than he did now.

Later Kate drove the Fiat into San José in search, she said, "of music, a singles bar or whatever's the scene around here." Doug, too tired for bar cruising, opted for bed. He caught a half-hour of TV, watched hypnotically as a florid evangelist in a pleated fawn-colored shirt and giant black bow tie pledged that the Kingdom of Jesus would transfigure any viewer who sent in twenty-five dollars to keep this spiritual peach melba on the air. Doug had just switched off the light and settled into his pillow when the phone rang.

"Hey, Doug." Pounding music shook the line. "Lots of action here. I had to undress one fast operator before he did it to me. Better change your mind and come on out."

"Another night. Have one on me. I'm going to sleep."

It took him less than five minutes.

A chauffeur-driven Mercedes-Benz delivered Doug Perry to the portico of Eniplex, Inc., one of Silicon Valley's top chip manufacturers. Hatched by a band of engineers, fugitives from Honeywell and Digital Equipment, Eniplex in less than a decade had vaulted from a standing start into that *Burke's Peerage* of corporate America, the *Fortune 500*.

Sprawled on the outskirts of Sunnyvale, the compound resembled a cross between a tennis ranch and a resort hotel. Rustic redwood buildings, none more than two stories high, rambled across a flowering meadow. Covered walkways linked the structures and angled like strands of a cobweb to such unbusinesslike appendages as tennis courts, pond with resident ducks and geese, volley-ball court, barbecue pits, paddle-ball cages and an outdoor cafe where at this morning hour a few employees socialized beneath striped beach umbrellas.

Doug knew that somewhere in this luxury spread, screened behind redwood walls, workers labored to produce vast quantities of semiconductor chips. They treated slices of silicon with a mixture of gases, including the dangerous phosphine and arsine, printed patterns by photolithography, bathed the wafers repeatedly in acid to etch the circuits, cut them into small pieces, then attached the tiny chips to lead frames by microscopic gold wires. In a final operation, the chips were embedded in plastic packages about the size of jelly beans which, in turn, were mounted on small boards, thirty-six to a board, ready to serve as the brains or memory of a computer capable of shepherding millions of bank transactions a day or tracking a satellite as it spun around the earth.

Solemnized by a visitor's badge above his heart, Doug was escorted to the office of his friend, M.I.T. classmate and fellow camper at Micro Mall, the retreat of computer executives at the Bohemian Grove north of San Francisco.

"Doug!" James Taliaferro surged across the sunlit room from a desk holding two video display terminals that looked like hooded friars. "Haven't seen you since last summer. You look great, guy."

Sunlight poured through an enormous picture window overlooking the parkland recreation area. Wide green lawns framed a distant swimming pool. Taliaferro, a tanned clump of a man, moved like a bar fighter.

"Thanks, Jim. So do you." Doug felt the pride of success in Taliaferro's grip as they shook hands. A battler, the Eniplex boss lived to win. "I appreciated your sending the car for me."

"It's yours as long as you're around." He swept his arm toward the window. "How do you like our spread?"

"We're in parkland too back in Princeton, but nothing like this. You Coast people have it made."

"The age of Aquarius on a chip. If it weren't for sky-high housing costs, traffic jams, acid fumes at work and chemicals leaking into the water table, our production people would call it paradise. As it is, they grumble like hell."

Taliaferro moved to a corner brightened by emerald cushions on wicker furniture. Motioning Doug to a chair, he sat down like a ball that might bounce back up. They brushed off personal news as they might lint from a sleeve, then plunged into trade talk.

"The grapevine says you have a new security chip that'll burn up the market." Taliaferro lit a cigarette after Doug declined. "I envy you, but we're sticking to what we know best, the memory boards."

"We hear we may have some competition from the Valley, Jim."

"Which outfit?" Taliaferro exhaled a shaft of smoke.

"Not sure." Doug hesitated. He wanted to move more slowly, feel out his old friend first. Who knew the interlocking interests in this maze of new factories where semiconductors sometimes grew beside hot tubs and Jacuzzis? They sparred for several minutes.

"Come on, Doug," said Taliaferro at last. "What's the matter? You don't trust me?" Impatiently he flicked ashes from his cigarette. "You didn't fly out here this far in advance of the Grove just to shoot the breeze."

"Okay, okay. I do need help and also you ought to know what's up for your own protection. What we say has to stay in this room."

Taliaferro grinned. "No Watergate bugs in here. You have my word. Shoot."

"First, what's the reputation of Bytex Labs?"

"Okay, as far as I know. I'm acquainted with Mal Purvis, the top man. He was to be Paul Ellenbogan's guest up at the Mall, but Purvis will be out of the country, so Paul's bringing up Marshall Ingersoll instead. Your old employee was made executive v.p. at Bytex last week."

The news took Doug by surprise. "Fast climb. Ingersoll's only been out here five months. . . . Is Purvis a friend of yours?"

Taliaferro squinted through the smoke of the dying cigarette. "No, just an acquaintance. Frankly, I'm not sure I'd like to do business with the man. Can't tell you why either. Just something kind of . . . he's an operator, on the devious side. I guess that's it. Why?"

Doug sketched the Trojan horse story. "So naturally we have suspicions about Ingersoll. I saw a lot of him at our Sunday-night poker game. It's not just the debt. A whole mishmash of hunches leads me to wonder about him, just as you do about his boss. And I can't explain why." Nuances, fragments of gestures, a glimpse in an unguarded moment, a sudden impression, scraps of speech drifting in memory. Nothing indictable.

"Why the hell did you design a new chip on a computer that's hooked into Arpanet? Must be a thousand people using terminals on that network."

"We're on the network because we need data from a lot of hosts: NASA, Rand, Stanford, Lincoln Labs, you name it. But Christ, nobody on the network can take from us unless we send it." Doug resented Taliaferro's implication of poor judgment. "To steal from us, you have to plant a secret command in our machine and that means an inside job. You know all that, Jim."

"Easy enough to check your operating system, see if anybody hid a command in there." Taliaferro squashed out his cigarette.

"Oh no, it isn't. It's practically impossible to check. We found our Trojan horse plant by pure accident."

"I can't believe that." Taliaferro frowned. "Of course, I'm out of touch with the technical side now, but that seems . . ."

"How many computers do you have here at Eniplex?" Doug cut in.

"Three DEC BAX and a lot of micros."

"Ask your top technical man how long it would take him to check his beasts for hidden commands."

"Okay." Taliaferro walked to his desk and punched buttons on his phone. "Steve, I'd like you to settle a little argument for us." He relayed Doug's question. "No, no, I mean the basic commands." He sat on the edge of his desk as he listened.

Taliaferro shook his head in apology when he returned. "You're right, Doug. Our dp manager says it would just be a matter of luck to find a plant."

"That's the way it goes. Hell, Jim, we're all wide open at the skull. Any savvy programmer with a yen for larceny can suck our brains out. Until, of course, all your stuff is enciphered via our Katwar."

"I see what you mean." Taliaferro, self-interest aroused, leaned forward to his wicker chair. "So, what can I do to help you?"

"What I need most is some inside word on upcoming products from these companies." He named the computer enterprises in the Valley that had nodes on ARPA. "Of course, I'm looking especially at Bytex."

"Hmm." Taliaferro gazed out the long picture window. Two women were sunning themselves by the pool. "Paul Ellenbogan at Logiware is your man. He's the Valley's No. 1 specialist on cryptology. If something's going on with an encryption chip at Bytex Labs, Paul should know about it. Also, since you know him from the Mall, confidential talk should come easier."

"Yeah, I get along fine with Paul at the Grove. But if Ingersoll's to be his guest, won't that cramp his style with me?"

"No, no. He puts his Mall friendships first. Paul's solid."

Through his secretary, Taliaferro made arrangements for Doug to meet Ellenbogan at six-thirty at the Bold Knight in Sunnyvale. "Paul's anxious to get the word on your Catbird chip."

"Katwar. The Katwar 23."

"Katwar, right. Let's go have lunch."

They selected melon, eggplant Parmesan and iced tea from the elaborate menu at the outdoor Eniplex restaurant where both employees and officers dined. The two executives sat at a redwood table beneath a beach umbrella spangled in black and yellow. A warm summer breeze skipped down the Valley.

"Beautiful layout, Jim. You struck it rich."

Whenever they met, at least once a year at the Bohemian Grove, they measured each other's financial progress like small boys counting marbles or baseball cards. Hell, thought Doug, they might as well match income tax returns.

"We were doing fine until this quarter. Now, just between us, we're flat or maybe a bit behind last year." It had been years since Jim had admitted slippage of any kind. "But you ought to make a mint with your Katwar. Am I right?"

"We sure hope so." Doug moved his canvas chair to get out of the sun. "Jim, I'll level with you. We're in trouble. We've been running a deficit for more than a year. We need the Katwar to

haul us back in the black." And that, he thought, was putting it
mildly.

"I hate to hear that." But Taliaferro looked less than grief-
stricken.

"But even in good times, our shop is nothing like this." Doug
waved at the pastoral scene.

"Maybe we shouldn't have gone the playground route. Some
outfits skip the sugar and take their work straight. Like Allen
Michaels over at Convergent Technology who calls his place 'the
Marine Corps of the computer industry.'"

"If you can make it in pleasant surroundings, why go the Spar-
tan way?"

"You ought to know the answer to that, Doug. You spell it
J-A-P-A-N." Taliaferro beat time to the letters with a spoon. "We
may all have to do a Marine Corps act or watch the Valley turn
into Poverty Pit. Those Japanese chip makers are grabbing the
market fast. Why they bothered to steal tech secrets from IBM is
beyond me. They were outselling us on their own. They could ruin
us."

"If it's not the Nips, it's the Krauts," said Doug. "We were better off when they were shooting at us."

Paul Ellenbogan, whom Doug had known for several years as a
fellow camper, was a crisp businessman who wore a figured blue
tie and spoke as if he'd been weaned on an encyclopedia. He had
knife-sharp views on everything from the weather to the neutron
bomb. Although their dinner at the Bold Knight went pleasantly
enough, enlivened by an exchange of Bohemian Grove anecdotes,
Ellenbogan could offer little of value about computer cipher work
in the Valley. He "guessed" that Bytex Labs was "into encryption" because he'd heard that Bytex had ties to the National Security Agency in Washington. He noted that when Data Encryption
Standard, the computer code in general use commercially, was
adopted some years earlier, the National Security Agency, which
spent lavishly in the computer field, used its enormous influence to
weaken the key. Some experts even believed that NSA managed to
place a secret part in the chip, enabling the code-breaking agency
to eavesdrop at will on American corporate computers in the interests of protecting the nation. Of course, that was all history
now, he said.

Since Logiware was easing out of ciphers and codes, Ellenbogan preferred to shower Doug with tales of his company's newest venture. Logiware, it developed, had patented a new video game called Folkblast, featuring 8,192 ways to kill a human being —scalding water, arrows, guillotine, drowning, stones, gunfire, missiles, axes, burning at the stake, hanging—and 8,192 historical characters of varying levels of wickedness. For each villain Logiware engineers had devised a perfect death, suitable to his personality, niche in history and satanic dossier. The player's goal was to select a fit mode of liquidation, using a dozen or so clues. Lurid graphics converted Folkblast's screen into a gory execution chamber.

"As you can see," said Ellenbogan, "this gives players more than 67,000,000 combinations, so the game promises great market durability. Our psychologists say it's sure-fire—we all have murder in our hearts, no?—a judgment validated by a market test we did in Oklahoma. People went wild for it, married couples especially. We're launching the game this fall with 300,000 machines at $695 a copy."

"Have you tried it yourself?"

"Sure. I scored next-to-perfect on Attila the Hun. The clues involved horses, so I had him dragged by the heels behind a horse at full gallop." He wet his lips as he relived the dispatch of the barbarian despot. "Actually, you were supposed to chop off his hands first and then have him dragged by a galloping horse."

He had another near miss on Torquemada. The game's designers decreed that the ideal death for the Spanish Inquisitor General called for two red-hot bars which the executioner slowly pressed through the eyeballs and brain. (The player got bonus points if he had one glowing shaft held by a Jew and another by a Moor.) Ellenbogan, somewhat less imaginatively, merely skewered the fifteenth-century Dominican monk on a heated poker.

"But a mass market?" asked Doug. "Sounds like the players have to know too much history."

"That's all supplied in the clues. Both pupils and teachers love the game." The pedagogical prospects put fire in Ellenbogan's eyes. "We tested one near a high school in Tulsa. The principal said the kids learned more history from a month of Folkblast than they did in a semester of class. We found the same thing in bars. Drunks will play Folkblast all night." He smiled benevolently. "They learn while they kill."

This lucrative alliance of education and murder, however

merited by the victim's crimes, left Doug less elated than it did Ellenbogan. He made his good-byes soon after learning that Logiware, anticipating a sales bonanza, was already experimenting with such refinements as Girlblast, Mateblast, Doctorblast, Bossblast and for the export trade, Jewblast and Arabblast.

Kate, itching to give her report on the day's sleuthing, awaited him in the Chanticleer's Gay Nineties bar. She had chatted with Mrs. Marjorie Ingersoll and spent the afternoon with her friend, Pam Ingersoll. But Kate had gleaned little of significance. What she did learn appeared to lead away rather than toward Marshall Ingersoll as the guilty party. Bytex Labs, they said, had withdrawn completely from hardware manufacture and now concentrated on its growing software line, particularly programs aimed at agribusiness and produce wholesalers.

"Actually," concluded Kate, "Marshall isn't home much. He travels a lot, Boston, Washington, D.C., Europe. If that company is working on a secret version of Katwar, the Ingersoll women haven't heard a peep."

They parted in less than an hour. Kate had a late date to go dancing with a Control Data salesman peddling a line of "miniperipherals." Doug felt a twinge of regret when she embossed their good nights with one of her little dance sculptures.

His secretary Edith Yeager called at eight the next morning while Doug was dressing. With dangling shirttail and no pants, he took notes on her relay of Susan Lindbloom's preliminary report on Otis Kramer and Tony Canzano's on the melancholy Mexican, Carlos Rey. Doug reviewed his notes at breakfast.

Kramer. High school, Harrisburg, Pa. Son of garage mechanic. Grad. Temple '50. Pro football guard, Wx. Redskins '51–'55. Commerce Dept., '56–'63. Computer sales Bunker Ramo, Hewlett-Packard. Computer consultant, D.C., since '73. A-1 credit rating. Est. income $100 K. Not well known D.C. dp circles. Believed has ties to National Security Agency. Wx. Post files have only one item: Kramer a reluctant witness before Senate committee investigating intelligence agencies, '75, on Operation Shamrock when NSA scanned all cable and Telex messages in and out of U.S. Kramer said he

worked three months on Shamrock, picking key words
from messages. More later . . . S.L.

Rey. Born '43. Reared Mex. City. College in U.S.,
Tulane. Father diplomat. Traveled widely and has Wx.
contacts, also worldwide. Computer broker on inter.
scene since '77. Reputation so-so. One source says he
made killing on big dp sale to Czechs. No press items.
Will keep trying . . . Tony.

Doug and Kate spent a week in Silicon Valley, celebrated her
twenty-fourth birthday with champagne and became fast friends,
but they made scant headway on their mission. If someone in California's computerland stole Katwar's design by cross-country electronic suction over Arpanet, the amateur Princeton Dataflo sleuths
turned up no clues to the deed. Kate became a walking guidebook
on the night life of Santa Clara County and Doug made valuable
business contacts in the Valley, but as detectives neither one
justified the Dataflo expense accounts. The sole new development
on Katwar came from the home office: Carlos Rey had phoned,
left word for Doug that Ossian, Ltd. was raising its original bid to
$9,750,000. Doug replied that while he liked the looks of the
offer, all Katwar negotiations would be postponed until he returned in two weeks.

He breakfasted with Kate the morning she would fly home.
They sat in a booth beneath one of the stained-glass globes. Dangling glass beads tinkled each time the kitchen door swung open.

"I wasn't much help," said Kate, "but I know now how we can
make a ton of money at Dataflo."

"Hurry up and sell Katwar."

"That, but I mean another bunch of money. Here's what we do,
Doug." She shoved her cup of coffee aside and leaned forward
conspiratorially, her eyes flashing. Rising steam curled about her
canted grin. "We junk all our lines and switch to video games. I
thought of one that'll outsell Folkblast."

"Tell me. I can't wait." Doug thought she looked wonderful
this morning in her gamine way. He would miss her.

"We do terrific graphics on a couple of hundred glamour babes,
see. Big boobs, gorgeous bodies. Players pick out one and try to
get her to bed by making the right approach. The machine dia-
logues with the guy after he shoves in his quarter. The quicker he
scores, the bigger his score."

"And we call it Making Out."

"No, stupid. We name it Bed Scores."

He was loath to see her go, and when she waved good-bye from the wheel of the rented Fiat, he felt the creep of loneliness for the first time in weeks.

"Watch who you undress, Doug," she called as she drove off.

He picked up a San José *Mercury News* at the newsstand and headed toward the restaurant for a second cup of coffee. At the moment, through the glass door of the main entrance, came Marshall Ingersoll. When he saw Doug, he halted and for a few seconds, they stared at each other.

Then Ingersoll put on a wide smile and advanced with his hand out. "Happy coincidence, Doug. I heard you were in the Valley, but I had no idea where."

How could that be? Doug wondered. The Ingersoll women knew where both Kate and Doug were staying, didn't they? He shook hands without enthusiasm. This meeting was unwanted. He knew little more than when he left Princeton, and a confrontation without evidence could achieve nothing.

"Sorry I can't have a coffee with you." Ingersoll was slouchy tall, fair-haired with smooth babylike skin. He had a way of tilting his head as if to avoid a blow. "I'm late for a meeting in the Game Bird room. . . . But if you're going to the Grove, I'll see you there. Paul Ellenbogan invited me."

"How's the new job going?"

"Great. But maybe I left Dataflo too soon. I hear the new cipher chip may make you a fortune."

Yet Marshall knew of Katwar's potential from the first day when they celebrated with champagne. Doug studied him. "Play any poker out here, Marshall?"

"No, I haven't found a game yet." He stared at Doug. "Say, you know . . ." He paused, squinting. "I think I still owe somebody in that Princeton game forty or fifty dollars." He pulled a wallet from his hip pocket and picked out three bills. "Doug, would you mind taking the money back? I've forgotten who I owe it to."

"Jay McNaughton." Doug declined the money. "Jay says you owe him eighty-three. But that's for the two of you to settle."

"I'll call him today." He folded the bills back into his wallet. "Funny. Until I saw you, I had completely forgotten."

Ingersoll started to move on, but Doug caught his sleeve. "Say, do you know a man in Washington, D.C., named Otis Kramer?"

Ingersoll started. "Kramer?" He tilted his head, gazed upward reflectively. "No, I don't believe so."

"He knows you. He caught me outside my house a week ago Sunday night after the poker game. He said you told him I'd be home about that time."

"You've been had, Doug. That's a crazy story. I never heard of anybody named Otis Kramer."

Doug decided he did not like this man at all.

Zap. Ingersoll had a pink, hairless body, stringy muscles, slumping shoulders. For good measure, taking a tip from Kate, Doug pictured his former employee sitting on the toilet. The image vanished almost as soon as it appeared.

"Good seeing you, Doug." Ingersoll glanced nervously at his watch. "I've got to shove on in."

The encounter raised Doug's suspicions. He felt sure his former systems programmer lied about not knowing Kramer as well as forgetting the poker debt. But why? What was his connection with that nebulous Washington character?

Later that day Doug put a professional stamp on his sleuthing by hiring a San José private investigator recommended by Jim Taliaferro. A handsome debonair epicure with a master's degree in criminology, Phil Wetherill had little in common with the hardbitten cynical fearless private eyes of the movies. Rather, he doted on the good life, believed in the evolving goodness of man and rated himself "a gold medal coward" who cringed at gunplay. Wetherill signed on at a modish retainer to explore Ingersoll's background and to keep track of his movements, contacts and finances.

That evening Doug flew to Hawaii, spent a week in a rented cottage at Poipu Beach on the island of Kauai. He lay on the sand, went night spear fishing off Anini Beach, danced at the Kauai Surf and met a slim, elegantly groomed divorcee from the mainland. She encouraged his attentions until he greeted midnight at a bar in Nawiliwili by dancing the hula with a huge Polynesian matron and matching her pelvic display thrust for thrust and swirl for swirl.

"Disgustingly cornball." His date's look couldn't have been more poisonous had he worn a T-shirt to the opera. She left without him.

In all, he enjoyed himself tremendously, even though he bruised a heel on a flying board during a brief imprudent surfing lesson. He wound up the week loose and limber, all kinks dissolved, and stayed up late the final night.

A ringing phone slugged him at 4 A.M. He could feel the trauma through the wool of sleep.

"Mr. Perry? This is Otis Kramer calling from Washington. Hope it isn't too early out there." Kramer's own watch read ten o'clock.

"Oh, no. The sun will come up any hour now." There ought to be a law against violation of time zones.

"Mr. Perry, I can get you a very healthy price for your new chip from a company in Tokyo. You interested?"

"Of course." He struggled into wakefulness. "We'll consider bids from anyone outside the Communist bloc."

"One of my clients opposes a sale to the Japanese. Claims they're threatening our whole computer industry as it is."

"Listen, we sell to whoever we want." Yanked from sleep after a mere sample of it, he felt cross and irritable. "Just what's the point of this call, Kramer?"

"To offer you a very attractive deal. If I bring you together with this Tokyo outfit, I get half of anything you net over five million."

"How about my heart, liver and kidneys too?" Doug's temper spurted. "You're talking nonsense. We've already been offered nine million."

"This Japanese deal might go much higher. And the export permit could be difficult for you. I have an in at Commerce."

"Come see me in Princeton. I'm ready to consider any offers, but the brokerage fee has got to be reasonable."

"I'd like to explain this to you now."

"No, damn it. You woke me out of a sound sleep. I don't want to talk anymore about it now."

"Another matter, Mr. Perry. I'm informed the National Security Agency takes a dim view of your refusal to give them the Katwar layouts. Your shop is the only hold-out in the cryptographers' agreement to give NSA early look-sees."

"So I've heard a number of times."

"NSA wants you to reconsider."

"Are you authorized to speak for the agency?" Doug yawned.

"I didn't say that. . . . Mr. Perry, the agency throws around a lot of bucks in the computer field. It's got clout, you know."

"Our decision was made months ago, Kramer." Since he was

awake anyway, Doug decided to make something of this web-footed hour. "I saw your friend Marshall Ingersoll in California."

"Marshall Ingersoll?" A measured unfamiliarity on a rising inflection. "I can't place the name."

"Come off it. You told me in front of my house that Sunday night that Ingersoll told you I'd be home around midnight."

"You're mistaken, Mr. Perry. How could I mention a name I'd never heard?"

"Skip it." So Marshall had called Kramer.

"I hate to be the source of any misunderstanding." Kramer sounded put upon. "I'll call you again on this next week."

"Next week I'm talking to no one. I'll be at a camp in California with no phone."

"Pity. Well then, the week after. . . . And Mr. Perry, you forgot to call me when you got that Ossian Ltd. offer."

"Don't worry. That won't be the last time I won't call."

Two hours later the sun rose in a cascade of gold and began sucking the dew from the grasses and trees of Poipu. Surf crashed against tumbled black rocks, scattering pearls of spray to the sky. In the ocean, facing the public beach, early surfers bobbed like seals, straddling their boards as they waited for the big wave. A trade breeze, soft as silk, nuzzled the palm trees.

As he flew away, leaving the island drowsing in a placid sea, he felt that twinge of sadness that often accompanies departures. Kauai had been good to him. Some day he would come back.

6

A sob. A fluted whimper. A sudden, overpowering stench of feces, perfume of despair. A rush of labored breathing, fading to moans, little more than soft convulsions of the throat. A pink bubble at the mouth. Silence.

"*Terminado.*" The major aimed the toe of his paratrooper boot at the crumpled body on the floor. "The son of a fucking whore quit on us."

The kick glanced off a beardless chin. A tooth popped from the swollen, purpled lips, bounced oddly on the stained tiles and came to rest with its bloody roots pointing toward the sound-proofed ceiling. It had joined a garden of teeth, all white as lilies thanks to the lime in a lifetime diet of tortillas. A fly lit on the molar and probed the severed roots with busy hairy legs.

"*Nada?*" Maj. Gen. Ruiz Sánchez Valdés lifted his eyes. He had been staring hypnotically at Subject 8104. "Never confessed to helping the MMB?"

"Nothing." Maj. Felipe Alcazar rolled his thick shoulders, seeking to ease the fatigue. It had been a long day and he was out of shape for this kind of work which his subordinates now customarily handled. First the appeal to reason, the solemn warning. Then, after a stoic refusal to cooperate—the usual stupidity masquerading as courage—the thing of the fingernails, followed by Code Eight which, unfortunately, brought blood prematurely to the ears. And, of course, once each hour, five times in all, switching on the current of the apparatus clamped to the *huevos*. The slow extraction with the tongs—incisors first, molars last . . . the final working over with the knuckle dusters . . . oh, he'd gone by the book all right, but this *hijo de la chingada,* this stubborn animal from a miserable thatched hut in the highlands had told him nothing.

"Not a word, General." Alcazar, a stocky bull-necked officer who headed the operations squad of the Army's elite security department, faced his superior with a hint of truculence. He had failed, true, but he was in no mood for one of Sánchez' supercilious lectures about the standards of the detachment and the pressures from *La Presidencia.* Let the General spend just one day in the cell-like rooms of Detention A, or *La Casa Dolorosa* as the people called it, listening to the monotonous litany: the screams, the hateful blubbering, strangled curses, the keening of terrified women or the contemptible weeping and gargled sobs when a subject finally broke and agreed to talk, thus gaining a half dozen hours of life before liquidation.

"Ah, Felipe, he was, after all, a *Huachel.* We don't fare well with the *Huacheles.*" General Sánchez spoke in a low voice like a bereaved relative of the *natural* as every Indian called himself.

Surprised to find the General sympathetic to his hardships, Alcazar decided to press his advantage. "Would the General indulge me by letting me check out early today? My wife and I have been invited to dinner before the ball. And that"—he nodded at the body which lay curled like a fetus—"was a tough one—without reward."

"You deserve it." Sánchez touched the major's sleeve. "I know the extra duty you've shouldered these last weeks. And tomorrow . . ." He shook his head sadly.

"Many thanks, General."

Sánchez stepped to the door of the barred, silenced room as Alcazar faced the wash stand where special laundry soap and towel waited. The General paused, stared pensively at one of the splotches blooming on the plastered walls like dark flowers, then turned around.

"I appreciate it that you handled Xichaq personally. Pepe, wasn't it?"

"Yes. Pepe Xichaq."

"Seventeen?"

"No. Fifteen, according to the preliminary interrogation officer."

"Our informer in San Juan Ojotopec says both parents are also suspect."

"Yes, I know, General."

Sánchez glanced at the body. "Any teeth left?"

"No. Full extraction. The routine."

"Felipe, let's not put him with the others for the chopper run."

"At your orders."

"Instead, I want the body stripped and driven up to Ojotopec tonight. Have the noncoms wear plain clothes and use one of the Buicks. Instruct them to deposit the carcass in the doorway of the Xichaq house."

"How about . . . ?" Alcazar put out his boot and tapped the dead boy at the crotch.

Sánchez nodded. "Yes. In this case, that's required. Absolutely." He opened the door. "Flor and I will see you at the ball tonight, Felipe."

As the door closed, Major Alcazar stepped to the wash stand and picked up the spiked iron bands that fit over the interrogator's fingers as they doubled into fists. He scrubbed blood and scraps of flesh from the instruments, then washed his hands, digging carefully under the nails. After drying, he took off the soiled canvas apron and rolled it into a bundle. At last he straightened his tie and put his tunic back on.

He walked down the corridor to the squad's ready room where

two soldiers in stiffly laundered brown uniforms sat listening to a radio soap opera. Both men had straight black hair and dark Indian features.

"I have a *huevos* job for you, Vicente," said Alcazar. "Room Seven. Notify me in my office when you're finished."

Private Vicente went to Room Seven, took down the hunting knife from the wall bracket, studied the body a moment, then cut away the pants at the belly. He recognized the trousers, a rough blue fabric with white stripes. Together with the V-necked, red-cotton shirt and an outer jacket of black wool and intricately embroidered collar of many colors, they made up the traditional men's costume of San Juan Ojotopec, a town just a few miles from his own mountain village.

Reaching to the boy's groin, Private Vicente grasped the testicles with his left hand. With his right, he sawed the genitals away from the lower belly, dropped his knife on the dirty tiles and pried open the mouth of the corpse. He stuffed the bloody organ into the toothless cavity, leaving the penis protruding from torn lips like a hibernating reptile.

Retrieving the knife, he walked quickly to the wash basin, cleaned the knife and scrubbed his hands with the brown laundry soap. He was drying his hands on the towel the major had used when the spasm hit.

He vomited. Into the basin went his lunch of black beans and tortillas. He stood weakly, grasping the white enamel as he waited for that second attack that never failed to come. Tears filled his eyes and sweat broke out on his forehead. He threw up once more, then held the basin while prolonged dry retching wracked him. He pictured the main street of Ojotopec, a muddy gash in this rainy season, flanked by scrawny pines and one-room adobe dwellings, and he wondered in front of which door the corpse would be dumped.

Room Seven's foul air, its usual slaughterhouse odor now mixing with the pungent smell of fresh urine, blood, vomit and feces, drove him into the corridor. Vicente hurried to the barracks to change his spattered shirt before reporting to Major Alcazar.

As Vicente completed his assignment, Maj. Gen. Ruiz Sánchez was being driven from the outskirts of the capital, where the operation squad's barracks, offices and Detention A were located, to the compound of the Presidential Palace in the city's center.

His armored command car argued its way through hybrid

traffic. Ancient wheezing cars from North America, dinosaurs of the auto age, fought for space with bantamweights from Japan and Europe and with motorcycles, bicycles, donkeys and hundreds of stubby Indian men and women, backs bent under loads secured by thongs and headbands, who trotted along the streets and side-walks. Everywhere the old rubbed against the new in this crowded garish seedy rancid city that the Spanish conquistadors of Central America had built on a volcano-rimmed plateau almost five cen-turies ago. Open fragrant tortilla bakeries adjoined pizza parlors or fast-food restaurants advertising jumbo hamburgers. An Indian in the bright woven *traje* of his native hamlet displayed herbal remedies on the sidewalk next to a movie theater playing a double feature, *Body Heat* and *Tess*. Under a flashing Coca-Cola sign a furtive-eyed vendor sold bananas, single cigarettes, Mickey Mouse watches, thonged sandals made from old rubber tires and little, tin-framed photographs of *Puchón,* a widely admired saint whose votaries delighted in his smoked glasses, gangster-type fedora and flaring Pancho Villa mustache.

Today General Sánchez saw none of this. He was busy reading an article written for Amnesty International by the gringo profes-sor whom he would meet in a few minutes. The General despised these busybody self-righteous intellectuals from North America and Europe who brought their prejudices and their ignorance to his own very special culture. They knew nothing of the nation's customs, traditions or spiritual values, and their ideas of democ-racy, as naïve as those of an adolescent, had no application what-ever to the stern realities faced by those encumbered with the task of governing an illiterate backward mentally stunted native popu-lation.

Sánchez flicked a page impatiently, scanned the text.

"Most Latin cities rejoice in noise," he read. "Not so this capi-tal under the volcanoes. On these gray littered streets, no one shouts. People encountering friends exchange greetings in low voices. Peddlers hawk their wares *sotto voce*. The human voice of the city is muted by day and deadened by night."

The General curled his lip in contempt, but read on, repelled but fascinated.

"An observer soon concludes that what one hears is the hush of fear. Ever since the ruling military began its systematic extermi-nation of all opposition—by assassination, torture, kidnapping and brutal repression of the most elemental of human rights—the capital city has had a tomblike atmosphere. Since the government's ears are presumed to be everywhere, the citizens hesitate to converse in public. The bars, cafes and parks, once crowded and noisy, are now half-empty and silent. This is a city paralyzed by its own national government."

General Sánchez looked up. "What shit these gringos write!"

"Excuse me, General. What did you say?" The nervous sergeant surveyed his passenger via the rearview mirror.

Sánchez held up the pamphlet. "Shit, Raúl. These gringo professors write little else about us. They distort. They insult. They lie." How right he had been to urge that purge of the National University upon *el presidente*. They had sacked a third of the faculty, all left-wing subversives infected by the so-called academic freedoms of gringoland. Most offenders had been forced into exile where they could no longer poison the minds of the nation's youth. Some, of course, had to be eliminated as examples.

"Yes, sir." The driver was relieved. The General's wrath centered on a distant target.

Sánchez hurried through the rest of the text, skimming from topic to topic, until he reached the summary on the final pages. This he read with close attention.

"The struggle in this grim unhappy land of coffee, banana and cotton plantations comes down to this: The large Indian population constitutes the greatest pool of cheap labor between Hudson Bay and Tierra Del Fuego and the ruling oligarchy, using the military as its enforcement arm, intends to keep that big pool of labor just as it is—cheap, humble, passive, unarmed, uneducated and beholden by debt.

"The oligarchy, through its army, police and secret right-wing death squads, brutally represses every effort of the Indians to improve their lot. Indian leaders are tortured and murdered, their children kidnapped and never heard of again. Agents of charitable and educational institutions working with the Indians are harried from the country. Nuns and priests have been killed, supposedly by 'bandits.' Indian co-operatives have been smashed, their leaders jailed and obscenely tortured. Indian boys are shanghaied into the army under threat of death.

"For years the guerrilla opposition made little headway. Yet, under the guise of crushing the guerrillas, government forces killed thousands of innocent citizens and wiped out entire villages because some residents were suspected of aiding guerrillas. Anyone visiting these remote native villages in the mountains and gullies knows that it is ludicrous to pin a charge of Communism on the poor proud inhabitants. Not one Indian in a hundred can define Communism or describe its pros and cons. The Indian wants to be left alone by all white men, regardless of ideology, left alone to grow and harvest his corn, raise his family, perform his half-Catholic half-animistic rituals, worship his hybrid saints and live in harmony with the land that has supported him since the days of Mayan glory so many centuries ago.

"But with the increasing severity and randomness of the repression, some young Indians have joined the guerrillas and more Indian families are beginning to befriend and succor the rebels.

"Government policy thus describes and strengthens a vicious circle. The more the regime kills and tortures the Indians and their white liberal helpers, the more the Indians gravitate toward the guerrillas—and the heavier and more indiscriminate grows the repression.

"By aiding this brutal insensitive murderous regime, the United States Government makes a grave error that will haunt it for decades. In shipping economic and military aid to this Central American oppressor, the United States Government deals the cause of human rights around the world a grievous blow. Most people will not understand why the United States condemns the denial of human rights in the Soviet Union and its satellites while abetting a government's torture and murder of its own citizens in this hemisphere."

Sánchez finished reading in a fit of fury. He rolled the booklet into a tube and beat it against his shoe like a swagger stick. When his command car arrived at the executive complex, he bolted from the vehicle and hurried up the broad marble stairway to his second-floor office. He entered by a side door, located around the corner from the door to his reception lobby.

He tossed the report on his desk and seated himself in a swivel chair. His heart beat rapidly as he thought how to counter and humble this arrogant bastard who had libeled an entire nation. Controlling his temper with an effort, he buzzed his secretary on the intercom.

"I'm back, señorita. Has the North American professor arrived?"

"Yes, General. He came promptly at three for his appointment. He has been waiting almost an hour. Shall I send him in?"

"No, no. Not yet. I'll let you know. Get me *el presidente,* please."

Now the General shot his cuffs and waited patiently. In his periods of enforced calm, Maj. Gen. Ruiz Sánchez Valdés was the very model of a military officer. Tall, with wavy black hair, firm jaw line and broad shoulders, he could trace his ancestry back many generations to Castilian and German nobility. If his skin had a slight hint of the cordovan hue so common in the Indian highlands, well, perhaps a great-great-grandfather had spent a night with a servant on the family coffee plantation. General Sánchez was, after all, a man of the people and proud of it. In the high politics in which he might soon play a more prominent role, a touch of color never hurt an officer in the plazas and *barrios* where candidates were tested.

The phone rang. *"Como le va, Ruiz?"* The President spoke in the warm solicitous tones that so charmed the diplomatic corps.

"Fine, *Señor presidente.* And yourself?" Sánchez had been a classmate of the President at military school and was thus entitled to call him by his first name, but he never presumed on their long friendship. Sánchez honored protocol at all times. "I hope your health is as good as mine, sir. I'm calling in the matter of the North American professor you asked me to see."

"Señor J. J. McNaughton, the Amnesty International man?"

"Yes, I have just read the article he wrote for that organization. General, it libels us. It is scurrilous, defamatory, packed with lies. I don't think we should dignify his accusations by sitting in the same room with the man."

"I understand how you feel, Ruiz." That personal warmth again as if *el presidente* had clasped him in an *abrazo.* "But we must go through the formalities in this case. If we refuse him interviews in the executive departments, he will contend that we feared to talk to him, thus lending credence to his baseless charges. He has a prominent sounding board in his university—Princeton, you know."

"I'll find it difficult to be civil to the son of a whore."

"But you must make the effort, Ruiz, Remember, McNaughton's organization has influence in the U.S. Congress where many ill-informed legislators already distrust our intentions on human rights. We can't risk losing U.S. military aid."

"As you wish, General. I'll do my best."

"I know you will. Remember, we have absolutely nothing to

hide. We respect the inborn rights of every man and woman, no matter how humble." *El presidente* often talked in this vein and it occurred to Sánchez that his old classmate barred the unpleasant facts of life so easily from mind because he had never visited the *Casa Dolorosa* or other chambers of interrogation. "We have a respectable human rights record and we're willing to stand on it."

"*Claro,* General. I will do my duty. . . . Oh, by the way, you know that Xichaq family in Ojotopec that founded the corn cooperative up there? A son, Pepe, has been kidnapped by unknowns and is presumed dead."

"A pity."

"Until later then. Flor and I look forward to seeing you tonight."

"Please come by our box. Gloria will scold me if you don't. *Ciao.*"

Sánchez let the gringo professor wait another fifteen minutes before notifying his secretary that he was ready.

His first look at the Princeton University professor of Latin American studies confirmed his preconception. The man wore an untrimmed reddish beard like an ostentatious mark of his calling, his features were soft and pliant and his hands looked effeminate.

Sánchez nodded curtly, as they exchanged salutations. He could not bring himself to shake hands with the bastard, but he waved him to a seat in front of his desk with as much courtesy as he could muster. The high wooden chair, ornately carved, faced the window, forcing the professor to squint in the glare of the lowering afternoon sun.

"I appreciate your taking the time to see me." His fluent Spanish, without the customary jaw-cracking *yanqui* accent, surprised the General. "I felt it necessary for my report to interview personally the chief of the Army's internal security forces."

"Detachment," Sánchez corrected tartly. "As for your report, Señor McNaughton, I thought you'd already written that before you arrived. I have just finished reading it." He gritted his teeth.

"Oh, that was after my last visit." McNaughton's russet whiskers parted in a smile. "If you'll note the date, it was 1980."

"Frankly, señor, I found that screed to be a shameless vilification of this nation, one of your country's most loyal friends." He would never understand the *yanquis*. While their government with one hand shipped weapons, medicines and dollars and gave public and private assurances of support, with the other it let its great universities piss all over a steadfast ally. "My family has lived in this country for generations, and if this report of yours had a single paragraph of truth in it, I couldn't find it." He rapped the booklet with a knuckle.

"Every fact in there came from personal observation, General, or from sources whose reliability I checked and rechecked."

"Then you're blind, Señor McNaughton. That paper is nothing but lies strung together by someone who approaches my country with malice in his heart." He could not read the professor's reaction behind that bushy beard. A coward's shield? "All generalities, no specifics. I'm surprised you have the gall to call on leaders of this government after writing such lies."

"This time, then, you should welcome me, for I come only with specific questions. . . . By the way, may I smoke?"

"No. We do not smoke in this office." And hadn't for fifteen months, two weeks and five days since he gave up the habit. Sánchez looked beyond McNaughton at the huge portrait of the Liberator storming Spanish artillery redoubts with a sword in one hand and a pistol in the other. The Liberator, who built a nation on the footings of self-discipline, had kicked not one, but two addictions, rum and cocaine.

"May I put my questions then, General?"

"Go ahead. As *el presidente* says, we have nothing to hide."

"Fine. In that case, may I have permission to visit your detachment's operations section, particularly Detention A or *La Casa Dolorosa* as the people call it?"

"There is no *Casa Dolorosa* and never has been." Sánchez bit off the words. "As for Detention A, that building is highly classified because it's filled with security equipment aside from a few rooms reserved for special prisoners. Since the building is off limits to most of our own Army, I cannot permit a visit by a civilian, especially a foreigner."

"May I take notes?"

"Of course. Next question, please. Let's not waste time. I'm under great pressure here this week."

"Can you tell me the circumstances surrounding the Army's apprehension of Juan Villanueva and his brother, Manuel, and their present whereabouts?"

"Never heard of them. Where do they live?"

"The Army seized them five weeks ago in Tecotenango."

"The Army has no Villanueva in custody and has apprehended

no one by that name within the last two months. I know. I have the short list of all persons detained."

"Why was Pablo Fuentes Montenegro taken and where is he currently?"

"I have no idea. No such name has come to this office."

"He was seized the night of May 20."

"Not by the Army."

"Could it have been the *mano blanca* or the Anti-Communist Avengers?"

"I wouldn't know, señor." Sánchez glared at his questioner. "The Army has no connection with those extremist groups."

"How about the kidnapping and subsequent disappearance of Mary O'Brien, a lay worker with the Maryknoll order? As you know, Miss O'Brien's case has aroused considerable concern in the United States."

"Mary O'Brien I do know about. Our investigation provided us with conclusive proof that she was kidnapped by guerrilla forces dressed in uniforms stripped from the bodies of an ambushed Army squad. The guerrillas murdered Miss O'Brien and scattered false clues so that the government would be blamed. You should direct your inquiries to the Marxist Mountain Brigade."

"What about Guillermo Xocop?"

"No knowledge."

"Teresa Asturias Gómez?"

"Never heard of her."

"Fausto González Ricardo."

"Not on our list."

As McNaughton turned a page of his notebook, apparently preparatory to presenting another batch of names, General Sánchez arose and walked around his desk. He placed his hands on top of a high-backed chair, blackened by age, the twin of the one on which McNaughton sat. With their heavy wood, maroon upholstery and carved legs, the pair bespoke colonial days when fashion decreed that tropical households imitate the snow-banked palaces of Europe.

"Now I'd like to ask you a question, señor." Sánchez stood with the sunlight showering his back. "Why do you make propaganda that can benefit only the Communists?"

McNaughton had to shade his eyes to see the General. "My interest is in saving lives from the machinery of governments." He had no trouble handling that tired old question. "Any government, left, right, Communist, Fascist, military, oligarchic, what have you. Amnesty International has no political ideology save the sanctity of human life."

Silence settled into the long, brocaded drapes, the gilded settee, the twin colonial chairs, the massive mahogany desk and oriental rug. In this predominantly Indian country, with its brilliant textile handicrafts, not a single native creation could be seen in the office. The General glanced at his gold-banded wristwatch, then walked briskly back to his swivel chair.

"I can give you twelve more minutes, señor. I regret that we cannot talk longer. If you had called here last week . . ."

"Can you tell me the whereabouts of Silvia Ticpan, last seen in an Army vehicle in Montes."

"We have held very few women and never one of that name." The General appeared to ponder. "Oh, a moment. Silvia. What was the family name?"

"Ticpan."

"Ah yes, a nurse in Montes. That case we did investigate fully. She was never seen in an Army vehicle. She was abducted, we learned, late at night by unknowns driving an old brown jeep that resembled one of ours. Unfortunately, we found no trace of her."

"She is still missing." McNaughton paused, eyed the General. "I knew Señorita Ticpan. I met her when she was a young girl when I first visited San Luis. Princeton friends of mine have visited her at the clinic in Montes."

"If friends or relatives have talked to you about her disappearance, I would weigh carefully what they say, Professor. The MMB has a number of apologists in the Montes vicinity."

"My informants say definitely it was an Army jeep. They noted the license number."

"They lie." The accusation came out cold, sharp. "Let's move on, señor."

"What about Jaime Quinto Schweger?"

"The name is unknown to me."

"Pepe Xichaq, a juvenile."

Sánchez glanced sharply at McNaughton. Just where was the professor getting his information? The Xichaq boy had been in custody only three weeks before his death.

"Now I do know something about the Xichaq boy. We have information that he was kidnapped by the Marxist Mountain Brigade and detained at a guerrilla camp in the north. It would not surprise me at all if the MMB disfigured the boy, brought him home in some terrible condition and then blamed us. They do it all the time."

McNaughton made notes, then said, "I take it then that you deny, as we've been informed, that two officers of your detachment broke into the Xichaq home and forcibly abducted the boy."

"Never happened. My men never break into homes unless absolutely necessary. Perhaps, again in this case, the guerrillas posed as Army officers." He appeared to reflect. "Yes, as I recall, that's just what happened."

McNaughton ran off another dozen names from his list and to each Sánchez gave similar answers. Never heard of the man. No knowledge. Never in Army custody. Name unknown.

"Just where did you get such an absurd list?" Sánchez asked at last. "Not a single person you mentioned has ever been held by my detachment." He laughed bitterly. "You're being used by enemies of your country and mine, señor."

"No, I'm not, General." McNaughton grinned. "Actually, although we always guard our sources, in this case I don't mind telling you."

"Ah." A trap?

"The list came from you, sir."

"From me?" Now what arrogant ploy . . .

"Yes, in a manner of speaking. Do you know Enrique Morales?"

"Many people have that name in this country." Sánchez proceeded with caution.

"I mean Major Enrique Morales on your staff."

"Oh. The electronics expert, deputy commander of the computer center we installed two years ago."

"That's the man. Do you know where he is now, General?"

"In Panama on annual leave."

"He *was* in Panama. Since last Thursday he's been in New York as an exile. He came with a little box. It contained a magnetic tape with the names of more than two thousand people seized by your detachment since the first of the year, people who have disappeared without a trace."

"I don't believe you." Sánchez felt his anger rise. This softmuscled insolent gringo with the fake pirate's beard dared to bait him in his own office.

"Here." McNaughton held out the photostat of some passport

pages. It showed Morales' picture and identification and a stamped visa by the U.S. embassy in Panama, dated only eight days earlier. "The tape also contains instructions from you, the Army chief of staff and the President. Some of your orders refer in explicit terms to procedures in Detention A. There is much, much more. We're planning a three-hundred-page publication this fall, verbatim quotations from the tape."

"If such a tape exists, it's a fabrication, a packet of lies like that so-called report of yours."

"Lies?" McNaughton consulted his notebook. "How about these numbers? Juan and Manuel Villanueva, Subjects 6873 and 6874 . . . Mary O'Brien, Subject 7592 . . . Guillermo Xocop, Subject 7731 . . . Silvia Ticpan, Subject 8096 . . . Pepe Xichaq, Subject 8104?"

"I know nothing of such numbers." Sánchez rose to his feet. The rage was simmering and soon, he knew, it would boil over. He clamped his jaw, seeking to corral his anger. "It is quite clear, however, that there's a conspiracy abroad to undermine this government. I request that you leave this office at once, Professor."

McNaughton closed his notebook, stood up, nodded to Sánchez and headed toward the huge oak doors. His slow ambling gait fired a new flash of hatred in the General. Damn the insolence of the man and his slovenly walk.

The moment the great doors closed, Sánchez buzzed his orderly who manned a desk in the adjoining duty room. "Go get Colonel Lemus in the communications wing. I want him here at once. No excuses."

A few minutes later Col. Rodolfo Lemus de la Cruz found himself facing his commanding general. An intense young officer with uncommon fair hair, Colonel Lemus had reached his rank years ahead of schedule thanks to his mastery of the new computer technology.

"We're in trouble, Rodolfo." General Sánchez hurried into a recital of what he had learned from McNaughton.

Lemus broke into the story. "I hate to do this, General, but I have to confirm that a reel holding apprehension and interrogation data is missing from the tape library. I discovered it this afternoon."

"Why wasn't I informed?"

"I was on the verge of reporting to you when the orderly arrived. Tapes frequently are checked out of the rack by one of our technicians, so I didn't undertake a search at once. When I did, it turned out no one had it." Colonel Lemus spoke rapidly, leaning forward in his chair. "I was puzzled. The whole area rates the highest security, as you know, and no tape ever leaves the center."

"No tape is ever *supposed* to leave the center." Sánchez liked Rodolfo and his commitment to his machine, but he could envision the traumatic scene tomorrow when the full impact of Amnesty International's coup became felt throughout the executive complex.

"Do you assume that Major Morales has indeed gone into exile in New York?" asked Colonel Lemus after Sánchez finished his capsule version of the North American professor's revelations.

"We have to expect the worst. What about McNaughton's list of names and numbers? They are authentic, no?"

"Yes, they are. As you may recall, the file lists name, interrogation number, date and place of apprehension, instructions to the interrogators, results of Detention A and final disposition."

"Did you ever have cause to question Enrique's loyalty?" The General fixed his subordinate with a cold stare.

"Never." The computer chief masked his alarm. He had had some covert talks with other young officers who shrank from the regime's excesses. And Lemus knew that on rare occasions suspected Army officers had themselves been treated to the persuasive instruments of the *Casa Dolorosa*. "In fact, in any of our discussions at the center, he was always a hundred percenter, never less."

"I never doubted his loyalty either, Rodolfo, but luckily for us, I'm on record as suggesting his transfer to a less sensitive post. I made the recommendation after his cousin, that university student, turned up with the MMB. I thought it would do no harm to shift Morales down to the Coast somewhere. However, the Palace vetoed my recommendation."

"Certainly then, General, the detachment can't be blamed in any way."

"For Morales' desertion and treachery, no. But security is another matter. *El presidente* will want to know why all this classified matter wasn't safely encoded."

"We don't have the capability for total security." Colonel Lemus hitched his chair closer to the General's desk. He was in his element now. "All our material is encrypted, as you know, but of course in this case, Enrique has the key. Besides, it's not a difficult matter to break any of our ciphers. Any halfway-smart cryptanalyst could do it in a matter of hours."

"You mean there's no way of safeguarding all that sensitive matter you deal with?" The news astonished Sánchez. "To me, while confessing I'm no expert, that seems incredible."

"At the present time, it's true, General. Computer security is mostly a farce. Of course, experts are working on the problem all over the world. There are rumors of breakthroughs too. I understand some North American engineers and cryptologists have invented a chip that encrypts in such a complex way that it would take centuries to break the computer's data into plain text."

"Is it on the market yet?"

"No, I believe not. It will be some time yet."

"What is your source?"

"A Mexican broker, Carlos Rey, was through here this week. Apparently he's involved in the sale negotiations."

"Find out when he'll be back through here. Make that a priority." Sánchez brightened. "I'd like to talk to him personally about it. Perhaps, if it works as he says, we could buy one of the early units."

But after a moment of cheerfulness Sánchez lapsed into the gloom that had been gathering since his anger subsided, and he began reckoning the extent of fallout after the traitor Morales detonated his propaganda bomb in New York.

The General and the Colonel talked longer about their predicament and agreed to meet again early the next morning to begin the onerous task of refutation and impeachment of Morales.

Alone, General Sánchez paced before his wide window overlooking half the city. Deep shadows cast by the western volcano swallowed the shabby streets. The sun had sunk behind the wooded mountain, casting a rosy aura. Smoke puffed from the crater and went rolling down the sky like cotton candy. Night would soon enfold the land as quickly as the closing of thousands of wooden shutters throughout the city.

It had not been all turmoil and bloodshed in this beautiful haunted land where the Sánchezes put down roots two centuries ago. Ruiz could remember gay carefree hours of debutante parties, picnics on the banks of sun-kissed lakes, moonlight climbs of the volcanoes, tennis at the club, diving into long green tunnels of Pacific surf or boating through river gorges where spangled parrots cried like startled children. But at heart it was a rugged somber land demanding stern measures to control and galvanize a native population that had yet to cope with ordinary machines, let alone this modern bewilderment of satellites, computers, jet planes and missiles.

Academics like the bearded McNaughton were not evil by intention, perhaps, but they did incalculable harm through their provincialism, ignorance and woeful misconceptions. Coming from nations filled with educated prosperous citizens, they just did not understand an impoverished country struggling to drag itself into the twentieth century. From their safe snug havens, they flung such loaded phrases as "savage repression," "brutality," "torture merchants," "government killers." No, they did not understand.

In the distance, just off a shoulder of the volcano, a United States-supplied helicopter beat its way to the west. Rotating blades flashed rose and violet as the craft passed through the mountain's twilight aura. As the General watched, the plane dwindled to a speck on the far horizon. Soon it would lower over the Pacific, thrash westward into darkness and drop its weighted sacks far at sea.

Very sad this nightly cargo, as regrettable as the mission of the Buick which would soon be leaving for Ojotopec. These sorry chores brought no joy to anyone. Leadership had its distressing obligations and the anguish of command took its toll of man after man. Someone like McNaughton could not possibly comprehend. General Sánchez looked at his wristwatch, sighed and turned from the window. He was late. He must change into his dress uniform, then dine out with Flor before the annual military ball.

7

Except for the slamming of a screen door and the cry of a distant bird, the timbered lodge was silent as the men grouped around the table watched the denouement of another poker hand in the specially fitted card room. A shaded drop lamp cast an even light over the green felt cover.

With all cards dealt in a hand of five-card stud, only Doug Perry and Marshall Ingersoll remained to contest the pot. Neither man had a pair showing and no flushes or straights were possible. Ingersoll, high with an ace and king over two small cards, bet the $20 limit.

Doug, showing a jack and ten high on the board, had another ten in the hole. Recalling Ingersoll's facial clues, he glanced briefly at him, noted no telltale tremor of the jaw muscle and concluded that his opponent was bluffing, only pretending to hold a pair. Perry raised $20.

Ingersoll sighed, but called the bet. "You're looking at mine," he said. "Ace high with the king."

Doug showed his pair of tens and pulled in the chips.

Ingersoll tossed his cards to the next dealer. "Just like old times." He stretched and yawned. "I can never run one on you. You're tough, Perry."

Much as he relished winning from Ingersoll, Doug felt uncomfortable playing with him. But here at Micro Mall, the luxury camp located on a Bohemian Grove hillside beneath immense redwood trees, his former employee could not be avoided if Doug wanted to join the nightly poker game, which he decidedly did.

The men crowding about the big table included a sampling of America's new computer barons: Buchanan of IBM, Stegner of Apple, Udall of Texas Instruments, Markham of Data General. Two guests from Washington, Hyer, the White House staffer, and DeGrazia, an Assistant Secretary of Defense, both had influence in the government's huge purchases of computerware. Indeed, DeGrazia had supervision over Defense's 66,000 computers, an electronic maze costing billions of dollars, much of which found its way into the treasuries of companies represented in this camp. It was said of Micro Mall that if you rolled a bowling ball past the great stone fireplace, you'd hit a dozen millionaires, several engineers and at least one man from Washington who first-named the President in private. Other camps boasted cabinet officers and governors as members, but Micro Mall made up in computer wealth what it lacked in political rank.

It was a warm silky night at the Grove, that elite encampment of the American establishment on the banks of the Russian River north of San Francisco. A summer breeze curled through the mighty redwoods. Moonlight painted an ivory path across the small lake where celebrated members and prominent guests gave noontime talks. Now someone was playing the great organ and a deep, powerful Brahms rolled down the glade to vie with the sharp cry of a whippoorwill just outside the camp. When the organ swells faded from the cathedral of redwoods, men strolling the main road in the valley burst into song. The campers were in a good mood. The Club's Low Jinks show, a comedy spoofing pretensions in the arts, had played that night in the outdoor theater to a clamorous audience.

As Hyer, the White House technology man, dealt seven-card stud with deuces wild, Ingersoll continued talking in his languid manner, cocking his head in a curious way that distanced him from the other players.

"Yeah, Doug and I used to play in the same game back when he was my boss. Sunday-night poker in Princeton. A lot of history in that game. Didn't Einstein kibbitz once in a while, Doug?"

"So they say."

"The Princeton limit is half of ours here." Ingersoll yawned again. "So smaller pots. Also less bluffing. Playing together like that, week after week, you get to know everyone's style of play. Not many surprises."

Doug shifted uneasily in his chair. It had certainly surprised him when Ingersoll welshed on his debt to Jay McNaughton. He eyed his former employee with renewed distaste. Had he mailed the money to Jay yet?

"No surprises from Doug Perry," Ingersoll continued. "Believe me, men, when Perry steps out in the betting, he's got 'em."

"Thanks for the tip." IBM's Buchanan had a country-club tan and a Mexican shirt.

"Come on," protested Markham of Data General. "Marshall's just setting us up. We've played with Perry up here. He likes to steal one now and then."

"Sucking up to the old boss, huh?" DeGrazia, the man from the Pentagon, prodded Ingersoll with his elbow.

"Maybe I should." Ingersoll's laugh was easy, confident. "There's a rumor kicking around that Princeton Dataflo has a hot new cipher chip that'll make Perry a bundle."

"Yeah, I heard that last week," said Apple's Stegner.

At once attention narrowed like water through a funnel. Several players eyed Doug expectantly. The Bohemian Grove made a point of disapproving anything that smacked of commerce. "Weaving Spiders Come Not Here," warned the Grove's motto borrowed from Shakespeare. Yet very few Bohemians traveled to the annual encampment just to attend the ritual Cremation of

Care or to saunter along shady paths for two weeks. Rubbing
elbows with fellow movers and shakers, slipping into a clubby
relationship with stewards of the American establishment proved
forever attractive to the curried breed that had been coming to this
opulent retreat for more than a century. If one could make but a
subtle distinction between weaving a web of economic self-interest
and keeping eyes and ears open as one strolled from camp to
cabinlike camp with men of power, every Bohemian and guest
knew the difference. In the case of Princeton Dataflo's new product, one didn't ask, one listened.

"The rumor's partly true." Doug felt compelled to respond although he resented Ingersoll for broaching the matter. "We're
marketing a new security chip. How profitable it'll be is anybody's
guess."

"But you're guessing on the high side, right?" Paul Ellenbogan,
always sharply tuned whenever talk drifted to computer gossip,
had the deal. With his eyes on Doug, he slowed the shuffling of the
cards.

"Nothing we have will go as high as those video murder games
of yours," Doug rejoined.

"Imagine making a fortune out of knifing, hanging and dyna-
miting people," said Jim Taliaferro. "Do you Lutherans go to
confession, Paul?"

"Is it true you're changing the company name from Logiware to
Logikill?" asked Buchanan.

"Careful," said Ellenbogan, with a grin. "This talk's getting
spidery."

"Deal!" Udall of Texas Instruments was losing.

"Let's play poker." So was Hyer.

Ellenbogan dealt a hand of Omaha, or "hold-'em," two cards
face down to each player and five cards down in the center. Finding the queen and jack of hearts in his hand, Doug raised when
the betting reached him. Two men dropped, five called the raise.
The first flop of three center cards exposed a ten and three of
hearts and a nine of spades. Doug, now holding four cards to a
flush and four to a straight with two cards yet to be turned, forced
the betting with a $10 wager. Buchanan raised him $10. Doug and
three others called. Ellenbogan's turn of the fourth card in the
center revealed a jack of diamonds. Doug, with a certain pair and
a possible straight and possible flush with one card more to turn,
bet $15 but this time got a $15 raise from Ingersoll. With a nine,

ten, jack on the board, Doug surmised that Ingersoll might have
hit a straight. A glance tended to confirm the guess. Ingersoll's jaw
muscle twitched ever so slightly. He had good cards. Doug called
after some hesitation as did Buchanan. The others dropped.

Luckily for Doug, the final flop exposed the ace of hearts, giving him a heart flush to the ace. Since no pair showed on the
board, eliminating possible full houses and fours of a kind, Doug
had a lock. Buchanan, in turn to bet, checked. Doug bet Micro
Mall's limit, $20. Ingersoll, jaw hinge pulsing, raised $20.

"One of you guys must have me beat." Buchanan threw in his
cards.

Doug raised another $20.

"Oh, oh, trouble." Ingersoll shook his head. "I just call, Doug."
He laid down an eight and queen of spades, giving him a straight,
queen high.

"I hit the flush on the last card." Doug showed his queen and
jack of hearts and gathered in more than $300 worth of chips.

"Look what I folded." Buchanan showed his hand, a pair of
threes to go with the three on the board.

"You folded three treys!" Taliaferro fingered the cards as if to
verify the claim. "You're too smart for this game."

"In this august company, I believe what I'm told." Buchanan's
wry smile belied his words. "Our guest said Perry was tough to
handle."

"Yeah, Doug's tough at the table and tough at the store," said
Ingersoll. "That makes two close ones he's beat me on tonight."

Doug savored the second win. Since he neither liked nor trusted
Marshall, losing to him would have grated. On the other hand, the
several hundred dollars he'd won from Ingersoll was but chicken
feed beside the potential profits from Katwar. Had Marshall actually stolen the design, slipping it invisibly through an electronic
network that spanned the country? Sitting here across from him,
hearing the cry of a whippoorwill challenge a prancing Offenbach
from the organ, watching Jim Taliaferro shuffle the cards, such a
long-distance theft seemed quite improbable.

"Say, Dee," said Stegner of Apple, nicknaming the man from
Defense, "I'm glad you guys at the Pentagon finally decided on a
single high-order language for your computers. You had a real
Tower of Babel going. But tell me, who came up with the idea of
calling the language ADA?"

Assistant Secretary DeGrazia peeped at his hole card, stretched and yawned. "You know, I'm not sure. All I know is that we named it ADA after Augusta Ada Byron, the daughter of Lord Byron."

"Yeah, but who put the Byrons in the computer act?"

"Search me."

"She was the Countess of Lovelace, wasn't she?" asked Doug. "And Ada Byron, the countess, worked for Charles Babbage, the mathematician who invented the first machine calculator. Is that right?"

"That's it," said Hyer.

"Bunch of Anglophiles!" Jim Taliaferro completed his deal.

"Yeah," said Ingersoll. "You'd think they could find an American to name the damn language after."

The game continued for an hour with similar random computer gossip, then broke when Taliaferro, Micro Mall's captain, took scotch and soda in hand and said that he was going to walk over to another camp, Aviary, where a songfest might continue until dawn. A dozen men, poker players and kibbitzers, clamored to accompany him. After a prolonged visit to the bar, the well-irrigated band staggered down the steep path that led to the valley floor and the roadway that passed near Aviary.

The organ music had ceased now and the whippoorwill had flown away, but the satiny night trembled with sound as the middle-aged computer executives, bent on tipsy adventure, toiled down the trail in single file. The wind sighed in high branches, a distant reveler whistled like a locomotive, somewhere two cronies argued drunkenly and floating over the lake came a crumpled chorus of the "Battle Hymn of the Republic."

Down on River Road, the main thoroughfare of the Grove, the straggling Micro Mall delegation encountered a man dressed in an English bobby's uniform who held up a hand, blew a whistle and ordered them to halt.

"You're all under arrest and held for the magistrate," he said in a fine Cockney accent. It was Sam, The Man, from Sundodgers camp. Every summer Sam, a Los Angeles corporation lawyer, brought two dozen costumes to the Grove and spent his time playing one role after another.

"I see you're from Micro Mall," said Sam. "Who's your captain?"

"I am," said Taliaferro. "What's the charge, officer?"

"Traveling St. John's highway with a known Democrat." Sam blew three blasts on his whistle.

"Who? Who?" The computer men howled their disbelief.

"Yes, officer, prove your allegation." Taliaferro, buoyed by alcohol, played an improvised part with haughty incredulity. "The Mall hasn't had a closet Democrat since the late Patrick O'Donnell. It's unfortunately true that he once voted the Democratic ticket the year Kennedy ran."

Taliaferro skirted the truth. While Bohemian Grove campers were mostly conservative, heavily Republican, 99.9 percent white and strongly old WASP, the Grove did tolerate a sprinkling of Democrats and liberals, some of whom belonged to Micro Mall. The volatile computer world, with fortunes quickly made and easily lost, attracted looser segments of society, had yet to stratify like banking, insurance, steel and automobiles.

"I'll not press the political charges at this late hour," said Sam, with imposing Cockney dignity. "However, you're all in violation for marching on a full bladder."

"What if we piss now?" By Grove tradition, members and guests, many of them elderly prostate cases, urinated in the open, aiming at mossy beds and redwood trunks, any time of day or night.

"Then you go free on probation." Sam signed the invitation with another triple blast on his whistle.

The computer crowd set drinks down on the roadway, stumbled into the woods and thrashed about with much hilarity. Assembled again after voiding, they milled on the roadway while Officer Sam took a sip from each glass, thus downing scotch, bourbon, gin, vodka, beer, wine, brandy and one surprise taste of plain water.

Doug raised a fist. "Three big Mall cheers for Officer Sam, a man who sees his duty and does it!"

Sam saluted after the ragged shouts. "Carry on, gentlemen. You're free until the Grand Jury meets." Three more blasts and Officer Sam swayed off into the night.

Not drunk enough to enjoy the mass urination and too saturated to go home, the computer lords weaved along River Road, shouting to stay-ups in such camps as Thalia, Tunerville, Parsonage, Spot, Moonshiners and the prestigious Mandalay. The unsteady travelers made slow progress. Every time they met fellow Bohemians, they stopped for beery salutations and old jokes.

Doug, lagging behind after one blowzy encounter, found himself walking beside Ingersoll.

"Has somebody put your name up for this club?" asked Doug.

"Not yet. I hear there's a ten-year or more waiting list."

"What do you think of the Grove?"

"I like it." Ingersoll stopped for another drink of his gin and tonic. "Good bunch of guys. And the entertainment's top drawer."

"This is my sixth year and I'm beginning to weary of all this hearty male-bonding stuff." A picture of Kate Warfield in one of her angular poses flashed across his mind. He missed her, a visceral feeling. "Frankly, I'd like to see some women around."

"There's always Guerneville, I hear." High-priced prostitutes, ready to entertain wealthy Bohemians in need, flocked to a bar-motel near the little town.

"No thanks. It's just that two weeks with two thousand men and no women gets mighty heavy." The chorus at Aviary had swung into "Sweet Adeline," and one bass threatened seismic convulsions in the temple of conviviality. Doug veered toward the subject that monopolized so many waking hours. "You're sure making a big splash at Bytex. Promoted to second man after only a few months."

"Lucky timing, Doug." Ingersoll slowed to a halt once more, sipped again at his drink. He stared at the glass. "You know," he said, after a long pause, "you may run into major competition on your coding chip."

Doug went into instant focus. "How's that?"

"I hear there's a European company that's going to market a security chip next year. They say it produces the most powerful and effective cipher in existence."

"Where? What country?" Doug's suspicions flared. "What's the name of the outfit?"

"Search me." Ingersoll shrugged. "I don't know the country or the name."

"Just Europe? No other identification?"

"That's all I heard." Ingersoll's drawl had a vague quality.

"Who'd you hear it from?" Was Marshall's vagueness alcohol-induced or intentional?

"A salesman friend out of Chicago."

Doug studied his former employee. Light from a nearby camp framed a picture of innocence: smooth, babylike skin, tousled hair, an expression of disinterest, almost boredom.

"Do you know anybody connected with the company?"

"Of course not." Ingersoll sloshed his drink about. "Why?"

"If you did, I'd advise him to watch his step." Doug decided to chance a shot. "We'll be on the lookout for fraud because of what happened to our beast."

"What about Susie?" Ingersoll appeared only mildly interested.

"That Trojan horse plant."

"What the hell are you talking about?" Ingersoll hiccupped, masking his reaction. On purpose?

"Oh, I thought you knew. Somebody planted instructions in the machine. Whoever did it could make Susie spill her guts any time on command."

"You mean you think somebody stole the design for your new chip?"

"Right. As you know, we designed it on the machine."

"Who do you suspect?"

"It's obviously an inside job. It could have been any of a dozen people."

"Including me, huh?"

"Yes, including you." Doug bit into the phrase.

"Jesus, Doug, you mean you've been suspecting me all this time and you didn't say a goddamn word?" Ingersoll raised his voice a notch, but remained oddly passive.

"We have no proof." The instant the words left his mouth, Doug knew he had erred. Far better to keep Ingersoll off balance.

"Even so. Living together in the same camp." Ingersoll dipped his words in indignation. "Less than decent treatment, Doug. I'd have expected you to level with me, lay everything on the table."

"We intend to act when we have all the facts." He moved to recapture the offensive from Ingersoll. "Anybody tries to market a security chip stolen from us, we'll sue hell out of them."

"Good luck," said Ingersoll drily. "Collecting on computer patent infringement suits is dicey business."

"This would be a clear-cut case. And if we've been robbed, we'll go after the thief down to his last dime." He paused. "I want you to know that, Marshall."

"Why me?" Ingersoll brandished his glass. "Christ, Perry, are you accusing me?"

"If the shoe fits . . ." Had he gone too far? After all, he had zero proof. Too many scotches.

"That's a fucking insult." Drink slurred his words, but the volume rose to a half shout. "Shit, I've a good mind to bring it up before the whole crowd at the Mall."

"That's not done here. But go ahead." Now Doug's temper spurted. "Try it." He loathed this man. *Zap. Again the naked, pink body. Childishly hairless. Scrawny. Drooping shoulders.*

The raised voices caused Jim Taliaferro and Paul Ellenbogan, strolling at the rear of the Mall pack, to turn around.

"What's up?"

"Nothing another drink won't cure." Then in a low voice, Doug said, "Bring it up if you want to, but I doubt that's a good way to get yourself into the Bohemian Club."

"Okay, we'll drop it for now. But tomorrow, Perry, I want to settle this thing. You owe me a big, fat apology."

But the next day dawned and died with no further airing of the wrangle and no apology. Ingersoll clearly avoided him. After singing at the Aviary camp until three o'clock, Doug slept late and was awakened in midmorning by one of the college-boy attendants, holding out the customary Micro Mall eye-opener, a gin fizz.

"Good morning, sir. Some of the hair of the dog." He was a tall loose-knit tennis player from Stanford.

The drink doused the fires of a gathering hangover and Doug ate a stout breakfast anchored on eggs benedict prepared by the Mall's gourmet chef, a San Francisco restaurateur. Then, since the nearby phones were for emergency medical use only, Doug walked a half mile to the civic center where public pay phones were located.

He used his credit card and dialed the number of Princeton Dataflo. Three rings, no answer. Then he remembered. Sure, this was a Sunday, the day after the Low Jinks comedy which Grove players always presented on a Saturday night. On the fifth ring, he recognized the voice of the night security guard who sometimes substituted on Sundays.

"Hello, Duddy. This is Doug Perry out on the Coast. Any of the officers around?"

"Nope, Mr. Perry. Nobody but Miss Warfield."

"Oh. Put her on."

Kate came on like bands playing. "Hey, Doug, how you doing with all those rich old farts out there?"

"All right, but I miss you."

"You had your chance, boss."

"I'm surprised at myself, Kate."

"For missing your chance?"

"Well . . . no . . . I mean that I think of you so much."

"I put the hex on you. Don't you know about my occult powers?"

"I'd believe almost anything sensational about you."

"Hey, we're making progress. . . . But I bet you called on business."

"To be honest, yes." Now he wished that he'd called for her personally. He could see her by the phone, wearing a pixie grin, warming her office with that glowing vitality. "Kate, please call either Susan or Tony and tell them to hire us some research on European computer companies. I want names, capitalization, main customers, the usual relevant data. Also what aptitude, if any, for computer cryptography."

"Got it, boss. Anything else?"

"Yes. I think you're terrific and I wish I were there to tell you about it."

"Oh." A quick intake of breath, not quite a gasp. "When are you coming home?"

"Not for a while." He applied the brakes. He had surprised himself, revealing what he'd been only subconsciously aware of. "This thing runs through Friday night. . . . Okay, baby?"

"I'm no baby, babe. Remember? Hurry back, huh?"

"I'm signed up here for the whole week. Otherwise . . ."

But he lasted only one more day. Then, claiming a business emergency, he packed his bags and had them taken to the gate and a waiting taxi. Micro Mall mates protested that the Grove play on Friday night would hit a new high for outdoor spectacles. Virtuous warriors would rout armored forces of evil while cannon boomed, battle smoke wreathed wooded hills, a massive chorus sang in triumph and the orchestra lifted a paean to starry skies. Doug murmured his regrets. He'd catch the operatic finale the next year.

"You're sure it's not a woman?" Jim Taliaferro walked as far as the camp-fire circle to bid him good-bye. Sunlight fell sparsely through the vaulted redwoods like a gentle summer shower.

"This is one hundred percent business, Jim." Doug believed it himself.

8

The president of Ossian, Ltd., dominated the office. Black-haired with bushy eyebrows and striking blue eyes, he gave an impression of physical strength and solid self-assurance. His clothes bespoke muted expensive haberdasheries in London or Rome, yet his manner was open, cordial, anecdotal. Susan Lindbloom thought Sean Hegy the most attractive man she'd met in months.

He sat in front of Doug Perry's desk beside Carlos Rey whose infrequent smile sifted through his melancholy overcast like crippled sunlight. Tony Canzano and Susan occupied the right side of the negotiating triangle.

"Of course many Gaelic scholars believe the poet Ossian never existed." Tony, eagerly taking a cue from Hegy, moved into his favorite literary specialty. "An invention, they say, of MacPherson, the Scottish writer."

"Just so." Hegy brushed a speck of lint from his pinstriped jacket sleeve. "And by analogy, does anything really exist inside our busy computers? Electrical surges, yes, but what is electricity? Bodiless energy, a phantom on the run. Yet look at the impact, Mr. Canzano. And what impact did Ossian have in the eighteenth century?"

"Tremendous. A sensation, whether or not MacPherson translated from a third-century Gaelic poet named Ossian as he claimed or merely created the epics himself."

"Precisely. You know your literary history. And so in 'Ossian' we found an apt name for our computer enterprise." The executive had a deep, resonant voice, the kind that endowed trivia with significance. "Perhaps nothing at all exists inside our machines, but what a mighty impact they're having. They're changing the face of civilization."

Doug sensed that this handsome stranger had cast a spell in the short time since he arrived at Princeton Dataflo to deal for Katwar. A bit improbable, this man. He said he was born in Paris of an Irish mother and a Hungarian father, "a lusty leprechaun snared by a Magyar con artist," as he put it. Reference works had him schooling at Cambridge, selling trucks in Africa, banking in Lebanon, then heading a computer corporation resident in the tax-easy Bahamas.

Doug had arrived home two days earlier, returned Carlos Rey's flock of calls, learned that Ossian, Ltd., thirsted for an early deal, conferred with Susan and Tony, then invited the Ossian president to fly up from Nassau.

Now, after the opening chitchat and the intricate process of feeling one another out through such odd implements as ancient Gaelic literature, Doug turned to the Katwar but not before targeting Hegy with his psychic leveler. *Zap: At once the tailored pinstripe and costly underwear vanished, revealing chest and limbs as hairy as an ape.*

"We've gone over the numbers again and estimate that we could gross around thirteen megabucks by taking our chip to market. Although a single-shot sale to you would save us on costs, we'd lose the good will of regular customers." Well fortified now, Doug took the big step. "So, considering all factors, if we sold to you, we'd need $17,500,000."

Susan shot a look of astonishment at Doug. Tony coughed to hide his confusion. Carlos Rey frowned darkly. Hegy, save for a slight elevation of his regal eyebrows, gave no hint of his reaction. "Our last offer was $9,750,000," he said.

"I know, Mr. Hegy, but we are asking seventeen-five." Doug, having reclothed the naked Irish-Hungarian, tapped his desk with a letter opener. "One comes up with a chip like Katwar only once in a lifetime."

"You've escalated far above the level we'd been considering." Hegy's shaggy eyebrows lifted, yet he did not seem unduly perturbed. "Señor Rey reported that you thought you could get ten or eleven mega from your usual customers."

"We undershot. And just yesterday a Japanese company offered us an even twelve."

"Ah, yes." Hegy nodded. "Nakamura Electronics."

Now how did the Ossian president know that name? It had been Otis Kramer, in that wacky early morning call from Washington to Hawaii, who first tipped Doug to Japanese interest. While Kramer had not mentioned Nakamura, that must have been the company. Were Hegy, Rey and Kramer all acting in concert?

"One always confronts the Japanese these days. Let me rework some numbers here." Hegy produced a palm-size calculator, that international tool of modern commerce, and began tapping the buttons. Kingdoms of numerals, empires of tallies, rose and fell within milliseconds. Hegy paused in his endeavor, squinted at the figures in the display slot, then began punching the buttons all over again. In the hush Doug's swivel chair squeaked like a cat in pain. When Hegy looked up after the second exercise, he said: "We can raise our offer to twelve-five."

Doug responded at once to this swift elevation in Katwar's value. "I like your straightforward approach, Mr. Hegy. Let me talk in another office with my colleagues." He nodded to Rey. "Our executive committee."

The trio moved to Susan's office on the floor below. Save for its off-white color scheme and a long mural-like photograph of Nassau Street in the horse-and-buggy era, the room duplicated Doug's. They stood at the window overlooking the lawns and woodlands of Forrestal Center.

"Doug, whatever got into you?" Susan searched his face for a clue. "I couldn't believe my ears when you said seventeen-five."

"Yeah," said Tony. "After we agree to hold out for twelve, all of a sudden you're asking five-five more. You trying to stretch our solid single into a triple?"

"I had a big hunch and I played it." Doug saw a streak of red outside as a cardinal swooped to a landing on the branch of an oak. "I've got a weird feeling about Hegy. I think he's ready to pay almost any amount. I doubt he'd have blanched if I'd said twenty."

"What's the hunch based on?" Tony looked skeptical.

"I can't explain. Vibrations from the guy, I guess. He's an actor, you know. That figuring he did was all stage props. Man, he wants the chip." And why so eager? "Stay with me, guys. I get these hunches at poker sometimes."

"But hell, this isn't poker." Tony, often a man to take chances, now looked apprehensive. "This company needs money, remember?"

"Yes, Doug." Susan had lost her usual smile. "I'd rather settle for a nice fat profit than shoot for the moon and get nothing."

"I've got a feeling," Doug insisted. Also the gamble had set his blood coursing, reminding him of those moments of high risk in the big money games.

"I hope you're right. On paper Hegy's got the money." Tony shook his head. "Ossian's financing is a mystery to me."

"But there's no doubt the company's solid," said Susan. "Twenty million in ready reserves at Tri-Manhattan alone."

"Anyway, if you two back me up, I think we can swing this at bigger money than we anticipated."

"You planning on fifteen?" Tony spread ten fingers, then five. "That cuts it even between Hegy and us."

"No, I intend to stick to seventeen-five until we get it."

"But what if he refuses to move up?" asked Susan. She was as baffled by Doug's new gambit as was Canzano.

"We can always back down later." Doug watched the cardinal fly away, wings flashing in the hot July sun. "Come on, hang with me. You watch. We'll get seventeen-five."

"Okay," said Tony, with a shrug. "I should argue with a ploy that might make us rich?"

"Susan?"

"All right, Doug." Reluctance slowed her response. "Let's go with your intuition."

"Okay then." Doug folded his arms. "Now we have a stickier problem. We're selling this man a three-year exclusive on a chip that may have been stolen."

"I've thought about that," said Susan. "It pains me to do it, but I think we have to tell him the truth."

"Remember the quote from George Herbert," cautioned Tony. "'Follow not truth too near the heels, lest it dash out thy teeth.'"

"You're for saying nothing then, Tony?" asked Doug.

"No. Damn it, we have to tell Hegy about the plant in the beast, but remember we don't know whether Marshall or anybody else actually stole the Katwar design. That has to be stressed."

"Okay, we're agreed. We hold out for seventeen-five and we bite the bullet on Jerry's discovery."

Back in Doug's office, they found Hegy and Rey playing tic-tac-toe on a corner of the desk. The broker led the entrepreneur five to one, but had the forlorn mien of a loser behind a curtain of smoke of heavy fragrance.

"With your consent, Mr. Hegy," said Doug, "we'd like to conduct these final negotiations with you personally. That is, if Señor Rey doesn't mind."

Rey did not. He gathered up his lighter and blue pack of Gauloises and left. However, in the interest of fair play, Hegy suggested that Tony and Susan also quit the negotiating field. Doug agreed. This manpower treaty brought Doug and Hegy face to face, and Doug motioned his guest to a nest of rattan furniture, covered in bright yellow plaids, near a foldaway bar at the far end of the office.

"My colleagues and I are agreed on Dataflo's position. First, we must have $17,500,000. That's our absolute minimum. Second, there's possible bad news we have to tell you."

Doug described Dunn's discovery of the secret instruction inside Susie, showed Hegy a copy of the printout that ended: "101:   1 W 0   7   10 1257   7 121404 - 7" and discussed the Dataflo computer's vulnerability on the ARPA network.

"We have a good idea who did it." Doug looked his visitor in the eye. "But we have no proof of any kind. Also we don't know whether there's been a theft or not. Thus far we can find no evidence that anyone has our design. However, before you proceed further, you have a right to know."

"I must say that's discouraging news." Hegy, however, did not look discouraged. Rather, he retained his stance of poised self-assurance. "On the other hand, your frank admission bolsters my faith in you and Dataflo, Mr. Perry. That kind of trust is essential if we're to proceed further." He thought for a time. "Of course, if we went into immediate production on the chip, Ossian would have a big jump on anyone who might have stolen the design."

"True enough. Our engineers and cryptology people might put you into production within six months, I'd say. Denied that kind of team help, I doubt a thief could start turning out chips in much less than a year, certainly not a day under nine months."

"By that time we should have a grip on the market." Hegy's voice had an extraordinary timbre, evoking thoughts of the theater and its resonances. "By the way, will your coaching team include that brilliant young woman?"

"Kate Warfield. By all means. Without Kate, the team's handicapped."

"Our agreement should include an indemnity clause in the event the stolen chip surfaces."

Doug leaned forward in his armchair. "Since we'd still own the patent, we'd stand legal costs if we decided to sue. But for the rest, you'd have to take your chances. Of course, Lloyd's will write you insurance against theft."

"If you decline to share the risk, Mr. Perry, the venture loses much of its attractiveness."

"Sorry, but that's the way it is." Doug gestured with open

hands. "The big mainframe manufacturers would run the risk alone. No question. Let's face it, Mr. Hegy. In this computer game, a six months' jump on a new product equals a couple of years in autos or aircraft."

"Any agreement we may reach on price must be contingent on my lawyers going over the angle of possible theft."

"Naturally. That's always understood."

"All right then, let's turn back to the money." Hegy, as if in veneration, made a chapel of his fingers. "Since we run the risk of competing with a stolen chip, we obviously can't afford to pay an arm and a leg for Katwar. I am, however, willing to raise our bid to fourteen-five."

"Mr. Hegy, our price is fixed."

"Your lack of flexibility makes negotiation extremely difficult." Hegy looked distressed as if he had abruptly discovered serious defects in a character heretofore deemed flawless. "Frankly, I had expected a more reasonable attitude."

"Ah, but you're trying to bargain while I'm selling a chip at its market value—perhaps a good deal less."

Hegy chose to ignore the distinction. "The obvious compromise between seventeen-five and fourteen-five is sixteen."

"That would be true if we were bargaining. But I assure you, we're not. I am selling a rare piece of merchandise at a fair fixed price."

"I feel I've been quite generous in raising my offer almost five million dollars." Hegy sat with his hands together as if in devotion. Quiet of voice, serene in manner, he might have been at morning prayers.

"I understand." Doug was not unsympathetic. "However, this is not a matter of motive, mood or behavior, but of the value of an urgently needed computer component."

"Do you realize I haven't even seen this super chip in action?"

"You'll get a full briefing and demonstration as soon as we agree. If you're dissatisfied with what you see, you merely withdraw your oral offer. Nothing's final until we sign."

Hegy frowned over his chapel of fingers. "As a last effort, I could go to sixteen." His words did have the ring of finality.

"That won't do it, Mr. Hegy." Doug scattered irritation like chum from a fishing boat. Actually, far from being annoyed, he felt his first doubts. Had he, after all, misjudged the man? He had been dead certain that the Ossian chief would buy at almost any price.

Hegy sat silent for a long minute, then arose and walked over to the wall. With folded arms, he inspected the Tom George abstract. He came back to the cluster of furniture, settled into an armchair and again took out his calculator. After staring at the four columns of buttons, he began playing the instrument like a child doing single-handed piano exercises.

"Whatever price I'd pay at this escalated level, we'd need a four-year franchise. Three years wouldn't justify the cost."

"No problem." Doug didn't bother to put on a show of hesitation. In the speeding computer world, anything over two years was a lifetime. Curious. Hegy must know that as well as himself. "Four years it is."

Hegy tapped noiselessly at his made-in-Japan electronic arithmetician. Doug could hear the man's regular breathing as his blue pinstripe jacket rose and fell. Outside the sun climbed higher. Inside the air-conditioning equipment clicked on again. After much tapping and peering, Hegy looked up. "Done. Much as it hurts, we'll pay the seventeen-five."

Despite his passing doubts, Doug was not surprised. At this point, after the second episode of the calculator, only a refusal to meet the asking price would have taken him aback. He did feel a spurt of elation, however. He had stood pat on his intuition and it had paid off—with an assist from his private zapping technique. But what, he wondered, had made him so sure that Hegy would almost double his first offer?

They shook hands.

"A drink to celebrate?"

"A sherry would be nice. Nothing stronger, please."

Doug pulled out the wall-hidden bar and poured a Spanish sherry. After they clinked glasses and took the initial ceremonial sips, Doug said, "Just one request. Please don't mention our computer leak to Carlos Rey. If word spread on the industry grapevine, it could hurt us both."

"You have my word." He set down his glass and clasped Doug's hand in both of his. Hegy appeared to enjoy the theatrics of negotiation as much as the substance. "I once saw a film where a British atomic secret was thought to have been filched and the security officer roared, 'Seal Britain!'" He put a hand over his heart. "I pledge that I'll seal Sean Hegy."

They called Susan, Tony and Carlos Rey back into the office and filled three more glasses. The two Dataflo officers concealed their amazement beneath proper corporate manners while the Mexican broker stared in disbelief when Hegy announced the final figure.

"Oh, why wasn't I on a percentage commission?" he lamented. "Never again, never again, will I work on a straight retainer."

"How about that bonus, señor?" asked Doug.

Rey coughed nervously, studied his drink, then looked outside. "Interesting view from here, Mr. Perry."

"Bonus?" scoffed Hegy. "Don't bleed for Carlos. His Pedregal home in Mexico City looks like a castle."

They chatted for a few minutes, exchanged plans for implementing the sale in advance of the signing. Next step: Ossian's chief cryptologist would meet with Dataflo's cryptologists to check out the Katwar, making sure the chip performed as fast and as inviolably as promised. Ossian's expert would fly in tomorrow and Hegy would stay over to inspect the Katwar with him.

"Where do you intend to produce the chip?" asked Tony as Hegy prepared to leave.

"We're not sure yet. The logical place would be our plant on Route 128 outside Boston, but we've had an interesting proposal from Latin America. . . . Well then, until the signing."

The Dataflo executives escorted the broker and computer president to the lobby door and watched them move off in a rental Cadillac Seville with Rey at the wheel.

"You're a goddamn burglar, Doug." The suppressed glee came out as Tony punched his arm.

"I'm still stunned," said Susan. "I never imagined you'd get anything like that. I'm afraid I'd have sold us out cheap."

"That's because Hegy stirred up your hormones. I saw you bat your eyes at him."

She laughed. "He is attractive."

"My God, old friends," said Tony, "we won the ball game. Doug stole home."

"We did, didn't we?" Doug watched the car disappear around the curve of College Road. "But as for Sean Hegy, I wonder . . ."

Susan linked arms with the two men. "Our money problems are over." She had a lilt to her voice. "No begging at the banks. No payless Fridays."

"Hell, we're rich," said Tony.

"It's a great feeling." Doug stretched with relief. "I hate to be strapped and I hate to borrow."

"At last we all get raises." Susan grinned.

"How much?" asked Tony.

"I'm on my way to my office and my calculator."

Now there was Katwar's creator to notify and Doug, alone in his office, felt a glow of eagerness at the thought of talking to her again. Edith found Kate within a few minutes. On the line came the voice that flew pennants.

"Doug! You crossed me up. I thought you'd call the minute you got back."

"I was beat. Slept through a night and a morning. This is the first decent chance I've had. . . . Kate, I've got good news for you."

"My news is better. Guess what I'm doing?"

"Sitting at a keyboard."

"Nope. I'm painting a kitchen."

"Where?"

"In my new apartment in New Brunswick. I'm cooking tonight. You free for dinner?"

"Sure. Best offer I've had today—and I've had a big one."

"Great." The quick catch in her voice moved him more than his multi-million-dollar triumph. "We'll do candles, wine, the works. . . . Doug, I'm excited."

"That makes two of us. What time and where do I come?"

"Any time." She gave an address near the main Rutgers campus. "What's the good news?"

"We just sold your chip. You're $875,000 richer."

"Terrific. Come earlier—and stay later."

9

The walk-up, entered from the back yard where Kate's motorcycle stood, occupied the second floor of a two-story clapboard house on Richardson Street near St. Peter's Medical Center. Narrow houses, bright with paint, shouldered one another on twenty-five-foot lots, small front porches crowded the sidewalks, green traffic signs admonished "Resident Parking Only" and window cards offered rooms for rent. An unfashionable tidy livable street.

Kate opened the door at the top of a flight of creaky stairs leading directly to an aging kitchen, newly greened, that smelled of fresh paint. Doug set a large paper sack on a counter.

Kate wore tight black corduroy pants, sling pumps and a loose silk blouse. A choker of enameled pink wooden beads contrasted with her black pouf of hair. She had never looked more appealing.

"Hi." She smiled shyly.

They hesitated a moment, then came into each other's arms as smoothly and naturally as if they had been lovers for years. This, their first true kiss, engaged them like consummation itself. They held each other, not in a fever of exploring, but with the gentle firm knowing of a couple reuniting after an estrangement. Doug had a sense of fitness, of satisfaction, as if this were exactly the way they should be together. He felt her thin angular body shaping to his, her tongue searching and her curly hair brushing his forehead. He hardened as they pressed closer. He kissed the soft nook at the base of her throat. She nuzzled. They stood together for several minutes, savoring what each had long anticipated, assuring each other wordlessly of the pleasure they found. It was an intense rich embrace, but one of quiet assurance as if every touch or small caress followed some ritual they had devised long ago.

"Uh-huh," she said lazily, when they drew apart. "I knew it."

She looked uncommonly attractive tonight, he thought, softer, fewer angles, yet her figure as trim as ever. She noticed when he glanced at her hips.

"Good fit, aren't they?" She patted the corduroy pants. "I found them in New York the other day. I thought of you when I bought them."

He knew it was not idle flattery and he was pleased. She took his hand and led him through the kitchen to the combination living-dining space, bare save for two chairs and a round, wooden table, and the bedroom where the only furniture was a large Japanese futon made up with pillows, sheets and blue coverlet, on the scarred floor.

"I've only been here three days," she said. "It'll take a while before it looks like a home. You can watch it change."

The implication of continuing visits, sketching a future, seemed in harmony with their kiss of greeting. So much seemed understood already. In fact, as they moved back to the kitchen with its fairly respectable assortment of pots, pans and utensils, he felt quite at home. He had a sense of belonging in this bare walk-up in New Brunswick, only a few miles but a whole culture away from affluent, clannish, intellectual, achieving Princeton. Everything here seemed fitting and comfortable, he pouring them drinks from the liquor and wines he had fetched, she mixing a salad dressing, the rosy hues of sunset through the small window over the sink, her sudden kiss on his forehead, the way she curved to him when he gathered her at the waist. While driving here, he had fretted again over the disparity in their ages, but now it seemed quite natural that he, at forty-seven, should be courting, as his preacher father would have put it, a woman younger by a generation.

"I'm dying to hear all about the sale of Katwar," she said, when they sat down with their drinks at the round dining table.

"Your cut will bring you almost a million." He swung into the story of Sean Hegy, the negotiations, his own refusal to drop a cent below the asking price. "And Hegy asked for you especially on the team that will coach his people."

"He'd better. . . . Hey, Doug, did you strip him?"

"Just once, at the start, for insurance." He grinned. "But I didn't have to. I had a hunch he'd pay a bundle when I first saw him."

"Am I rich?" She asked it flippantly as if she didn't care about money. Then her mind raced. "Say, I'll get a terminal, maybe a Zentec or a SAS, installed up here and my own little beast, an Apple III. Then a bed, some classy rugs and something to sit on."

"Interesting priorities, lady."

"Priorities?" She frowned. "Oh, you mean computers first, bed second? Well, the futon is okay for now. . . . You can't know how liberating it is to have my own place. One more month around Mother and we'd both go bonkers. Oh, Peggy means well, but it was past time I flew her nest and made my own. Dad agreed."

"Why here?"

"Well, I'm only a couple of miles from the Busch campus and Rutgers' Computer Science Department. And I wanted to live outside Princeton—try the real world where people talk about the Mets and stock-car racing instead of the Heisenberg Uncertainty Principle and what you've accomplished recently. It's a beautiful

town and will always be home to me, but no more Pru
McNaughtons for a while, thanks."

The name startled him. Since his return, he had thought of Prudence only momentarily, had neglected to call. Now the thought
had an edge, and he realized that with Pru he always felt vaguely
uncomfortable as if he were being tested in some way. The Educational Testing Service was not the only institution or person
around Princeton that measured people. It was a Princeton custom, that business of handing out grades in life. Strange that Kate,
the achiever's achiever, evoked images of meandering country
streams or mellow twilight while Prudence, the dilettante, summoned up teachers, blackboards and quizzes.

Kate reached out for his hand. "I'm glad you've gotten over
your block about age and 'the sticky emotional tangle with the
Warfield family' as you said in California."

"I'm not bothered about it much anymore, no, but sometime I'd
like to hear you talk about you and older men. Most women in
their twenties go with men in their own age bracket."

She struck one of her quick, fleeting poses. "So do I, lots of
them. Don't accuse me of having a father thing. I've never had a
date with a man over—what? Thirty-five, I guess. It's you, Doug
the person, that hooked me, not Doug the older man."

"I'll accept that and try to say no more about it."

"Oh, we'll talk about it again. We'll have lots of time." Again
that assumption of continuity like railroad tracks stretching across
a plain to a far horizon. "Now I want to ask about your wife. You
mentioned her only once out in California."

"What's to tell? She's been gone two years and is about to file
for divorce, or so she says. Joan, well . . . let's see. I loved her
once. We had fine times together. But then I was on the road a lot,
stayed out, found some high-stakes poker games, played around.
Hell, I couldn't seem to make it home, even after Judith came.
Joan wanted the domestic scene, nice silver and linens, security,
faithful husband, all the stuff I couldn't care less about. Then it
came to a head down there in San Luis. Judy and I loved the Indians and the thatched-hut mountain towns. Joan hated to leave
the big-city tourist hotels. Joan is a gracious, pleasing, conforming, not very hip lady. Oh, who knows about mates? It all looks so
simple, but it's damn complicated."

"Did the commitment bother you?"

"I didn't think so, but maybe subconsciously I was rebelling against marriage."

"Sounds to me like the woman bored you." The flash of her eyes seemed to say that around Kate no one would ever yawn.

"You hit it. I was bored and she felt it and left."

"To quote you, 'I'll accept that and say no more about it.'"

"That's okay. I don't mind going into it."

They refilled their glasses, scotch for Doug and vodka and tonic for Kate, and talked of the chip, Ossian, Ltd., California and themselves. Night blotted out the gray tones of dusk, the drum of traffic on nearby Easton Avenue faded to a whine and Kate said she'd better put on the lamb chops.

"Unless you're famished," said Doug, "let's skip dinner and go try the futon instead."

"Neat idea. I began to think I'd have to make the first move."

A trifling breeze nagged at the open bedroom window, but the night was heavy after the hot, humid day. They undressed in the dark. Doug lay on the mattress and waited while Kate padded to the bath, then propped the bedroom door open with a wad of newspaper. The sluggish air stirred.

He wanted her. Desire welled up like flood waters. When she came to bed, he pulled her to him with none of the earlier gentleness. Kate winced at the rough handling, but responded as if triggered. She nipped at his shoulder, held him with feral strength, crushed her lips against his. After waiting for weeks, they moved to the same swift beat. The power of her urge fired him further and he swept her small breasts with kisses. She held his head fiercely. If it were not for familiar patterns leading to coitus, the mutual aggression might have dismayed them. As it was, they let the passion carry them without restraint over the battleground of love.

Then, as suddenly as the lust had flared, they eased off and began pleasuring each other with long, slow caresses and kisses. As silently as they had accepted the fiery overture as a natural result of the weeks of tension when they wanted each other, now as silently they accepted a quieter, measured cadence as their way to love. Kate sighed, guidepost to surrender. Doug felt himself yielding, gliding out of control. It was a delicious sensation, yet tinged with fright as if to lose control was to lose himself. Then the fear slowly evaporated and the glide continued, steeper, deeper. They were dropping into the void where the mind never came.

Even as they savored this intensity of ease, this voluptuous sapping of the senses, Doug wondered if each of the world's couples found its own rhythm and cruised its own channel of love. Among the multitudes of human lovers, who fought and scratched, who screamed along the dark tunnel to orgasm, who stroked like feathers, tongued ears and throats, swatted bottoms, adored feet, thrust like demons, sucked out juices, croaked obscenities, fanned bodies with long, weeping hair, blew at orifices, suckled breasts like babies or rushed toward the little death with mangled moans and cries of rapture?

As for Kate and Doug, after a small eternity of surrendering, they bolted from their easy cadence on a surge of power. They gripped each other, locking into an embrace that seized the breath. They lusted. They fucked. She cried aloud. All thought ran from his mind like spilled water.

And then, after the mutual climax, they lay like spent animals, still clinging together, each feeling the other's rapid heart beats, the moist skin, the staggered breathing. For Doug it was all so old and yet so strikingly new. Even in this lax aftermath of lovemaking, he felt elated, a flowering of the senses and the mind. Could this be love once more?

They lay unspeaking for many minutes, their occasional caress a communion. Then Kate's yawn ended in a strangled laugh.

"Hey, Doug. A freaky thing happened. Right at the top of the wave, when I felt holy and horny all at the same time, a picture of the algorithm popped into my mind. Would you believe it?"

"No way. My mind was a total blank."

"In bright, bright red, I saw a new loop that I think will work better. Isn't that weird? Maybe I *am* some kind of freak. I'll never have to go to work, just make out with you and keep a notebook by the bed."

"Well, as I always guessed, Kate, you're a fucking genius."

They laughed and joked, fondled and kissed, traded honeyed vulgarities, revealed small secrets and slowly rekindled the fire that had burned so hotly only an hour earlier. Once more they pursued the flames until consumed and once more they lay lax and depleted.

This time Doug turned uncharacteristically moody as the dark night pressed down like a weight and the feeble breeze died. Now he did brood on the young Kate and the older Doug, on the flickering transience of being. He thought of loss, of people and things gone like smoke, of vanished hopes and plundered dreams. The pain of mortality seized him, almost made him shudder in the torpid night. It was not nostalgia. He would not, if he could, summon those shreds of yesterday—the way the dying sun showered an ochre Arizona canyon with golden fire, Judith's baby-brown eyes filling with tears when she fell and mashed her nose in her first attempt at walking, the hum of mellow Indian voices at outdoor markets in San Luis, the honk of migrating Canada geese on frosty autumn mornings. No, he did not want to relive those moments, any more than he did this explosion of love and lust with Kate, but their transience, as fleeting as moonbeams, filled him with sadness. All passed and disappeared as swiftly as the electrical cycles of his and Kate's computers. All was lost before it began. The overture offered its own dirge, the bud its wilted flower, the child's first babble its own dying words, Kate's cry of passion the dry cackle of senility. So beautiful, so magical, so short, so drenched with pain. Like Sunday-night poker, the players shuttled off and on, forever changing. Only the game went on.

"Do you think we have a real thing going, Doug?" she said at last in a drowsy voice.

"Could be." And yet so desperately short. He fought to lift the weight, to keep it light. "You mean forsaking all others?"

"I would never demand a commitment." She wanted to be serious.

"I feel so right with you, Kate. I'll be back many many nights if you'll let me."

"You're invited permanently."

"Nothing's permanent." And he sank beneath another wave of regret.

"I know. Well, you're invited as long as we both want to. Agreed?"

"Sold."

She raised up, framed his face with her hands and looked into his eyes. "So it sounds like maybe an affair. I'm happy, Doug. You're very exciting and, well, durable too."

"And already I feel like I belong with you."

She rolled on her back. "You know, I'd about decided that when I started on a real affair with a man, I'd ask him to have a vasectomy. There's no reason the woman should always have to fight the birth-control battles." She paused, breathing lightly in the dark. "But with you, no. Having kids is far from my thoughts now, but suppose we're still together a couple of years from now. How do I know how I'll feel then?"

"Smart woman. Even in romance, keep those options open." He loved her scent, a warm sweet earthy smell.

"Especially in romance. . . . So I'll struggle along with my diaphragm."

They talked and kissed and caressed and it was after midnight when Kate fetched sandwiches and milk from the kitchen and almost dawn before they grew sleepy.

Shortly after ten that morning, as Doug hung up the office phone after a flurry of business calls, he realized with a shock that a new and quite unfamiliar feeling had come over him. Looking out the window at the deep green woodland, he fumbled in his thoughts before recognition hit him. It was contentment. My God, Doug Perry contented? He grinned. Was this a permanent affliction?

As it happened, ten o'clock was the same hour when Kate answered her doorbell to find two callers, both neatly dressed, crew cut and courteous. Had the men been any younger, they might have come from Salt Lake City as a pair of Mormon missionaries. As it was, they came from Trenton as agents of the Federal Bureau of Investigation.

10

Weeks passed, a time of preparation, of tidying, of unhurried exploring through the hot summer into September. Then, just two days before Princeton Dataflo would sign away formally the rights to its Katwar security chip for four years, Doug Perry took a morning call from Jay McNaughton at the University's Woodrow Wilson School.

"Hi, Jay. That was a heads-up play Sunday." McNaughton, by clever betting, had lured several men to contest his unbeatable hand in the biggest pot of the night. "What can I do for you?" With all obstacles to the Ossian signing cleared away and with

Kate dancing on the rim of thought, Doug was in good humor. Kate had become his woman. As for Ossian, Ltd., an easy run from here to the dotted line.

"What's the chances of seeing you today, Doug?" McNaughton pressed. "There's a matter I have to take up with you."

"Ah . . ." He stalled. Prudence? While the affair with Prudence had been over for weeks, it would be messy confronting Jay now. He braced himself. "How about a drink at the Nass after work?"

"This can't wait. Can you make time at your office? This morning, if possible."

"How much time do you need?"

"Depends. An hour anyway. When I lay it all out, I think you'll want to discuss it thoroughly."

"Oh." Had something happened to Pru? "Can you give me some idea?"

"Not on the phone. Take my word. You'll want to handle this as soon as possible."

Doug pressed a key on his terminal and the day's schedule flashed on the screen in fluttering green letters. Nothing important until Stan Fowler came in at three for the final contract briefing, little more than a formality at this point.

"Okay, Jay. Come on out now. I'll clear away things for the rest of the morning."

While he waited, flitting images shaped possible scenarios. Prudence had confessed her infidelity to Jay. But why? She had appeared saddened but considerably less than devastated when he ended the affair over drinks at the Black Bass beside the misted Delaware. . . . No, she was leaving her husband. . . . Jay had found a note, letter or some other evidence. . . . Some blithe mutual enemy told Jay he'd been cuckolded by a fellow poker player. . . . Pru had forgotten her pill and had fetched up pregnant at age forty-one.

Oh hell, he hoped nothing serious had happened to her. While his yen for Prudence had blazed less than it flickered—her habit of tracking behavior with scout badges and demerits eventually wearied him—he thought of her with affection and wished her well.

As for himself, he could cope with almost anything on this lively September day with its nip in the air, the sun scattering splinters of pale gold and Kate off to her final doctoral work.

Weird, perplexing and wonderful, these weeks with Kate. They practically lived together now, half in the New Brunswick walk-up and half at his house in Princeton. People gossiped about this unlikely boss-and-prodigy pairing which violated two basic rules of affairs—never with anyone at the office and never with the wife or daughter of a good friend.

Larry Warfield had talked to him in a halting stilted way, if not like a father, at least like a reproving brother. Larry disliked the arrangement, yet he blamed Kate as much as Doug, looking upon her preference for an older man as a disagreeable phase that would pass. At the poker game, where Doug had returned the past Sunday night at the home of cherubic white-haired Hugh Talbott, the crowd who annotated other affairs with goatish humor pointedly said nothing at all about one player's pursuit of another's daughter. Instead, Talbott, a professor of primitive religions at Princeton Theological Seminary, told anecdotes about Barney Pilgrim and other gamblers of the game's early days.

As for Peggy Warfield, she was secretly titillated by her daughter's choice. She confided to close friends that she thought Larry subconsciously accepted the alliance because it implied that Kate "was still hung up on her father" like a number of girls of prominent Princeton families whom she ticked off with relish.

In the New Brunswick apartment and Princeton house, Kate herself shed all inhibitions and gave herself to lovemaking with boundless passion. She underwent a gradual change, feeling more centered, nourished and satisfied. Sex swept back into Doug's life at flood tide, transforming his world and empowering him with a subtle strength unknown since early manhood. They told each other that the more the other lover desired and cherished, the quicker each yielded to arousal and passion and the more rooted one's confidence became. Their lovemaking enriched everything they did so that even their first fight early one morning—over Doug's tipsy refusal to leave a craps table in an Atlantic City casino and go home to bed—had a strong undertow of affection. While both pronounced the three ancient words, "I love you," neither nailed them to the cross of forever.

Like a new unpredictable friend, their difference in age accompanied them everywhere. For Doug, living with Kate resembled residence in a foreign country, immersion in another culture. New people, slang, magazines, music—never before, for instance, had he listened to the Flying Lizards, the Wives, or the Talking Heads, all favorites of Kate—attitudes, clothes, aspirations, foods and films crowded his life. Now and then he stumbled on this strange terrain. He had to keep reminding himself that Kate and her friends knew no President earlier than Jimmy Carter, that the turbulent sixties belonged to moldy ancient history and that lower back pain had not yet been discovered. Sometimes he pined for familiar landmarks of his generation, but for the most part he welcomed the new scenery. As for Kate, she soon looked to Doug for counsel on how to weave and bob through what she called "the system" with a minimum of frustration and for a personal sense of those periods that he had lived through—like the Kennedy years— and that she knew only via print or old television clips.

The April-and-September romance produced one improbable side effect. Resentful of her father but tremendously curious about his new life, Doug's daughter, Judith, agreed after much haggling over the phone that she'd visit the Richardson Street apartment on a weekend. At first glance, Kate classed Judith as a plump plain sulky little girl who held her father solely responsible for the collapse of the family shelter and intended to punish him in perpetuity. Judith dumped herself in a corner like a malignant toadstool and discharged a sullen negativity that poisoned the apartment. Doug, dismayed, wanted to deport her back to Short Hills, but Kate treated the girl as though her toxic behavior were perfectly normal. She invited Judith to watch her play a video game that she had devised on her newly installed Apple III home computer. Judith pouted and demurred, but curiosity triumphed. She stood behind Kate, listened while Kate talked to her like a peer, gradually became involved and at last engrossed in the game. A half hour later it was Judith sitting in front of the keyboard and Kate standing behind and prompting. She sewed up Judy as a friend when she suggested that Judy name the new game. Judy decided on "Monsters and Maidens," and Kate appended the name to the program.

After that, Judy's sulky armor fell away as if rusted through at the joints and she stepped out as a quite normal nine-year-old girl who laughed, chattered, watched with big brown eyes and sometimes yawned or made faces. On her second visit she took to tagging after Kate and bombarding her with questions. "Do you and Daddy sleep together in the bed?" Assured that was the case, Judy considered a moment, then said they ought to buy an electric blanket for the cool weather coming. Before long she was copying

Kate's inflection and striking little Kate-like stances. Soon she insisted on staying over and began sleeping on the new couch in the big room. Judith doted on Kate.

But father and daughter drew closer too. The revelations about San Luis torture by Major Enrique Morales proved a special bond. Judy and Doug heard Morales describe the horrors of *La Casa Dolorosa* on a TV news show, and both promptly wondered whether the military terror had touched Montes, the Catholic clinic they had visited there or perhaps Silvia Ticpan herself.

When Doug phoned Jay McNaughton, the Princeton professor apologized. He had put off bringing them the bad news. The Army had indeed seized and killed Silvia Ticpan.

"Was she tortured, Jay?"

"Yeah. Horrible. Make you sick to your stomach. It's all on the tapes. I'm sorry, Doug, I hated to tell you on account of Judy."

"It'll break her heart. She wrote to Miss Ticpan at Easter and sent her two dollars for the clinic."

Doug told Judy as gently as he could, but with the bluntness of children she brushed aside his euphemisms and metaphors and insisted on direct speech. Had Silvia been raped, made to walk hot coals or thrown in a pit with poisonous snakes? That night she woke up crying and asked Doug to come hold her. He rocked her until her eyes grew heavy. "I loved her," she said, as sleep lowered. "She was my Indian friend. She was beautiful in her woven blouse."

As for Kate that summer, she prospered. Nourished by love, she gained weight and rounded off some angles. She loved having Doug nearby and the presence of Judy on weekends, "making us a mini-family," as Kate put it, filled out her life. Work at Dataflo and the Rutgers computer center remained a constant. She spent hours daily at this or that terminal.

Kate's only annoyance that long hot summer was the FBI. The two agents from Trenton followed their initial morning visit with calls and interviews directed at Kate's part in writing the leaflet urging the Institute for Defense Analyses to move to Forrestal Center. Always polite, always together and never contentious, they nevertheless pursued her like a pair of handsome, albeit peevish, admirers. Kate rather enjoyed tilting with "my Bob and Ray sleuths from Trenton," as she dubbed them. What were her motives? Why did she oppose IDA? What organizations did she belong to? Who else helped prepare the flyer? While Kate expressed her own views freely, she declined, despite persistent pressure by Bob and Ray, to name other students involved.

After the neatly cravatted and crew-cut agents learned some names from other sources, they tried to test them on Kate. At last she wearied of the game and refused to talk further. Bob and Ray tried a few more times, then gave up.

Business went smoothly for Doug through August and early September. Fowler and his legal assistants met with Ossian lawyers, haggled for weeks and finally produced a joint draft that satisfied both sides. With Hegy and Carlos Rey scheduled to be present, the formal signing of the $17,500,000 contract would take place in two days, the third Thursday in September, in Doug's office.

The original alarms over possible theft of the Katwar chip had become muted. The urbane San José private detective, Philip Wetherill, whom Doug had hired in California in July, came up with nothing incriminating in his fortnightly reports on Marshall Ingersoll. The Bytex executive traveled a good deal, including two trips to Europe that summer and regular flights to Los Angeles where he dated a "mediocre" actress. He bought a new home in Los Altos, but the purchase price was in line with his Bytex salary. Wetherill described his target's business contacts as normal and his social relationships as "conventional and country-clubby to the point of boredom." Doug began to wonder if he had done Ingersoll an injustice. Welching on a small poker debt did not, it seemed, a computer criminal make.

Nor had inquiries in Europe shed further light on Ingersoll's vague remark at the Bohemian Grove. Tony Canzano began gathering research on European computer companies the day after Doug phoned from the Grove. Upon his return, Doug hired a Princeton graduate student in computer science to spend two months in Europe searching for companies that might market an automatic ciphering chip. The young man reported in early September. He listed a number of firms engaged in computer cryptography, but said he'd heard no news of an upcoming chip similar to Katwar.

After weighing this and other reports, Doug, Susan and Tony slowly came to the belief that the Katwar was in no imminent danger of challenge by a rival security chip. As a precaution, however, Doug hired a West German computer expert to follow developments on that side of the Atlantic. All this information, relayed to Sean Hegy, satisfied the Ossian chief as well. Ossian anticipated no competition for its attack on the computer security market.

Doug had just finished composing a letter to the new German investigator when Edith notified him that Professor J. J. McNaughton had arrived.

Nagged by thoughts of Prudence, Doug greeted his poker friend with more heartiness than the occasion called for. The energy squandered on guilt, he realized, could fuel legions of space rockets. He guided McNaughton to the cluster of rattan furniture, upholstered in yellow plaids, near the fold-away bar.

"Coffee, Jay?"

"No thanks." Jay put down a weathered briefcase and stroked his auburn beard as he surveyed the room. "This is my first time in your office. Quite a layout."

They chatted about poker. No, Marshall Ingersoll hadn't sent him a nickel from the West Coast, said McNaughton. No, he couldn't understand it either, said Perry. Joint appraisal: So what could you expect when dealing with a seven-card full-time professional prick?

Poker disposed of, Jay folded his long thin hands.

"I'm not here on business." He bunched his brows. "Actually, I suppose some people would think me an innocent to come here at all. They'd say I don't understand how the world works."

Doug tightened. Here it came.

"What I want to talk about, Doug, is politics—international variety. It's about San Luis."

A band loosened as if sprung from Doug's chest. "What about San Luis?" His relief was patent. Now he was puzzled.

"Mind if I smoke?" At Doug's assent, Jay shook a cigarette from a pack. The business of lighting and inhaling served as an overture to dialogue. "The terror down there has produced an unlikely offspring. And you're directly involved."

"Because I met your friend Silvia? What do you mean, an offspring?"

"I'll get to that. But first, Doug, tell me frankly what you thought of Major Morales' disclosures."

"Awful stuff. Since we knew Silvia Ticpan, Judy and I were hit hardest by what you told us—her torture and murder."

"But in general, did what he said make an impact on you?"

"Yes and no." Doug reflected. "I paid more attention because of having been to San Luis and knowing one of the victims—thanks to you. But in general, well, what's to say? We all know some of those Latin honchos are sadistic with prisoners. After the first blast in the newspapers and TV, I guess I didn't follow the details."

"You and most Americans. I might react the same way except that keeping posted on Latin-American politics, especially San Luis, is my job. Then too, as a regional director of Amnesty International, I monitor mistreatment of political prisoners by any government." McNaughton paused, studied his cigarette as if deciding how to proceed. "So believe me when I tell you that nothing in this hemisphere can match the savagery of the San Luis junta in kidnapping, torturing and murdering its own citizens, poor people in no way allied to the Marxist guerrillas fighting down there. Some of the stories would curl your hair. Young kids mutilated and their broken bodies slung alive off bridges. . . . People blinded, all their teeth yanked out. . . . One day two Army thugs wounded a nun. The next day they burst into a hospital ward and shot her to death in her bed."

Doug shifted uneasily in his chair and McNaughton leaned toward him with an intent expression. "Hideous stuff, right, but you're wondering what this has to do with you?"

"Yes, I . . ." Did Jay solicit corporations for donations to Amnesty International?

"I'll come right to the point. I see by the papers that you've got a new cryptographic chip, chiefly invented by Larry's daughter, and that you're about to lease it for manufacture exclusively to Ossian, Ltd., of the Bahamas."

"Correct. We sign the papers day after tomorrow."

"You know I have good sources in San Luis." Jay ground out his cigarette. "I go down frequently—made my last trip there in July. Now I have reliable information that Ossian has struck a deal with the San Luis junta and plans to produce your chip—the Katwar, isn't that right?—just outside the capital. Cheap labor, no taxes, state protection, the works. In return, the San Luis military gets the chip free and first. The report's solid. It comes from three separate trustworthy sources."

"That doesn't surprise me." Doug shrugged. "I assumed Ossian would turn out the chip in its Boston plant, but come to think of it, Hegy did mention an offer from Latin America. Chip-making can move with relative ease and readily gravitates to areas offering special inducements."

"Wouldn't it bother you to have your chip turned out in San Luis?"

"Well, we know it's not the most benevolent political climate in the world, don't we?" Doug framed the remark with a small ironic smile. "But we're selling the chip to Ossian. It's their concern, not ours."

"I thought you were leasing the chip for four years and that you retained ownership and patent rights?"

"A matter of semantics, really. We think of it as selling because by the time four years are up, the chip will be obsolete."

"But you'll actually own it?"

"Yes."

"And it will be produced in cooperation with the San Luis junta?"

"If your information is correct, that's true."

"Look, Doug, you may think I have a lot of gall to come in here and grill you about your business." Jay apparently had caught the trace of irritation in Doug's voice. "I'd prefer not to, believe me, but this killer regime in San Luis tears at my guts. Silvia wasn't alone, you know. Other of my Indian friends, humble decent totally a-political people have been kidnapped, horribly maimed and disfigured and then murdered by the Army or the paramilitary gangs it sponsors." The pain showed in Jay's gentle eyes. "These military bastards are reactionary, they're cruel and they're brutal. I oppose any outside effort that lends them legitimacy or the coloration of ordinary civilized leaders eligible for American aid."

Doug reached out and touched McNaughton's knee. "I understand. We're old friends . . . but let's get to the point. You want me to do something. What is it?"

Jay, absorbed in thought, sat for a time without replying. While he waited, Doug appraised his fellow poker player from a new perspective. He'd always looked upon McNaughton as likable, but mild and pliable, colorless despite his ragged buccaneer's beard, not a man to venture forth to slay dragons. Now Doug saw the quiet fire in the gray eyes, a resolve and a durability unnoticed before. At Sunday-night poker did they all play with distorted shadows of real men?

"Yes, I am going to ask you to do something." Jay smiled. "But first I'd like to read you descriptions of what happened to four people I know. One of them is a good friend whom you know too. . . . Okay?"

"You mean Silvia Ticpan?"

Jay nodded. "I drew back from letting you read the data on her, but now I think you should. These are verbatim translations from the Spanish." McNaughton took a sheaf of papers from his worn briefcase. "They were transcribed from the magnetic tape that Major Morales brought to New York from the computer center of the San Luis Army. The tape contains the names of some two thousand people apprehended by the Army's security detachment in the first six months of this year."

Doug shifted uneasily in his armchair, braced himself mentally.

"The first file I'll read is Silvia's. You'll recall that a well-to-do uncle—there are a few affluent Indians—sent Silvia from Montes to the capital to high school." Jay put on his glasses and straightened the papers. "Then, as you know, she became a nurse, worked in a government hospital and came home to Montes to work in the Catholic clinic, Maryknoll as I remember, where you met her. Recently she held sessions in her home where the women planned to set up a co-op to sell their weavings. The junta regards all Indian meetings as pools of possible subversion. Apparently that's why Army security officers seized her in late April. Now the rest is direct from the tape."

McNaughton lit another cigarette. "I quote: 'Pursuant to orders of Maj. Gen. Ruiz Sánchez Valdés, chief of security, Subject 8096, Silvia Ticpan, was apprehended at her residence in Montes at 2317 hours, 26 April by a three-man detail headed by Captain Arenas. Escorted to Detention A in a squad car. Subject demanded to know under what constitutional provision she was seized and was forthwith silenced by Captain Arenas. Interrogated in Detention A 27–30 April by Lieutenants Casares and Valle and Major Alcazar. Targets of inquiry: How many meetings Subject 8096 held in Montes home to enlist support for MMB guerrillas, names of those attending, names of MMB contacts. 27 April: Lieutenant Casares encouraged 8096 to confess. She refused. Three fingernails extracted A.M. 8096 continued refusal. Remaining fingernails left hand extracted A.M. 28 April: Lieutenant Casares issued second-day warning. 8096 refused cooperation. Right hand fingernails extracted. Night Matron Galíndez urged cooperation. 28 April: Lieutenant Valle advised confession. 8096 contended nothing to confess. Code Eight applied four times.'"

Jay crushed out the newly lighted cigarette. "God, I hate to read this stuff." He brushed his eyes. "According to Major Morales, Code Eight involves one torturer holding a thick board on top of the victim's head while another slams the board with a mallet." His voice broke and he cleared his throat. "Back to the transcript.

"Quote: '8096 hemorrhaged before losing consciousness. Carried to sleeping cell. 29 April: Lieutenant Valle, again unable to gain Subject's cooperation, inserted electrical apparatus in 8096's vagina. Five shock periods. 8096 again lost consciousness. 30 April: Major Alcazar took charge, gave 8096 solemn warning. 8096 refused to answer. All teeth extracted A.M. Final warning. 8096 did not reply. Revived with pail of cold water. In P.M. 8096 underwent knuckle-plate operation . . .'"

Jay looked up with tears in his eyes. "Oh shit, Doug, I can't bear to read this again." Once more his voice broke. "Sweet, tender Silvia. Never in the world, as you must know, could she raise her hand against anyone. And these goddamn brutes terrorize and demolish her like this. Here . . ." He handed the papers to Doug. "You finish it."

Doug reached out again to comfort his friend, then took up the reading. "In P.M. Maj. Alcazar performed knuckle-plate operation. 8096 expired at 1632 hours." His own voice trembled. "Body taken to disposal shed by Private Vicente. Loaded on Helicopter 875 for evening flight to Pacific dumping area." Doug felt a deep chill, wondered if the room temperature had dropped. "What's a knuckle-plate operation, Jay?"

McNaughton stared at the floor. He was trying to bring himself under control. "The inquisitor puts a spiked band of metal around his hand, makes a fist and"—he coughed, cleared his throat again—"and slams the victim repeatedly in the face and torso. It rips off chunks of flesh and smashes bones. Since most people are almost gone by that time anyway, they don't last long."

Jay took out a handkerchief and wiped his eyes. Doug blinked back tears. Neither man spoke. The room's only sound, a low humming of the air-conditioning system, became a requiem for Silvia Ticpan. An image of a spiked iron fist formed in Doug's mind, but when it lashed at the face of a petite graceful Indian woman, the screen went blank. He could not tolerate the blow. Instead he saw a Madonna Silvia in nurse's uniform tending the sick.

"Doug, do you mind reading the other transcripts yourself? I can't. They're all friends."

Three other cases paralleled that of Silvia. Couched in the same curt colorless style, the transcripts told of unspeakable atrocities. Three men, two Indians and a white of European descent, survived several days of grisly ordeal—matches burned under fingernails, the head thrust repeatedly into a tub of ice water just shy of drowning, Code Eight, teeth extractions, thick metal rods rammed up the anus—only to collapse like broken toys under the spiked mauling of Major Alcazar or a subordinate.

Doug fell into a mood of sickened despair. The scenes evoked by the dry bureaucratic language weighed on him like shackles. He shied at the images of torn and bleeding Silvia crowding his mind. At the same time part of him struggled to dismiss the torture scenes as fiction. A mind seduced by Princeton's urbane peaceful life-style, seamless save for the petty irritations and bickering of an academic town, could picture electric shocks to the genitals and other barbarities only with great difficulty.

Doug gave the papers back to McNaughton. "Jesus, what incredible stuff. Imagine the sadists in that San Luis Army."

"Exactly." Jay folded the papers and put them back into his scruffy briefcase. "Usually, Doug, we don't see foreign policy issues close up like that. Instead, we deal from a high pulpit—abstractions, concepts, numbers, national interests, etc. But every issue involves human beings, and in this case I knew some of them personally. You met one of them.

"I don't know about you, Doug, but when I hear some smug official in Washington talking about supplying arms to San Luis to 'counteract the forces of destabilization,' I think of dainty hundred-pound Silvia and I want to sentence the guy to a month in *La Casa Dolorosa*. Remember, you have to multiply these four cases several thousand times to cover all the citizens of San Luis who've been murdered, defiled and dismembered by their own government in the last few years."

"You wonder why the junta would record its own crimes on tape," said Doug. "It's like the murderer leaving his fingerprints all over the room."

"We've talked about that." Jay nodded slowly. "For one thing, it reflects the incredible arrogance of the generals. They feel they're untouchable. Also there's General Sánchez's own background. He had German ancestors on his mother's side, and he's inherited a sense of discipline and order. Cataloguing his tortures and its victims is entirely in character. Then too, don't forget that many San Luis rulers of European stock regard the Indian as sub-human, so that recording their disposition is like keeping books on cattle and hogs."

Doug stood up. Outside oak and maple leaves trembled on the September breeze. He walked about with his hands in his pockets. "You have to wonder why Washington supports a government of torturers in San Luis."

"You certainly do." Jay's voice had firmed again. "There are a lot of reasons, not the least of which is the greed of a few American corporate interests down there combined with a vacuum of public opinion here at home. But now you can appreciate why I'll fight to deny support of any kind to the military thugs in San Luis who call themselves a government."

Doug walked back and stood looking down at McNaughton. "And now that you've softened me up, we come to the point, don't we? I can almost taste what you're going to ask me."

"I think we're on the same wavelength." Jay smiled. "Yes, I want you and your company to consider canceling the contract with Ossian or at least stipulate in your contract that no products can be produced or sold in San Luis."

"That's all?" Doug's short laugh had a touch of derision.

"That's all."

Doug sat down again and huddled back in the rattan arm chair. "Do you realize, Jay, that if all business judgments were to consider similar factors, international trade would grind to a halt."

"I've thought that through and I think you're wrong, but let's skip generalities. At the moment we have a specific country, a special set of sordid facts and just one business contract on the burner."

"Granted, but it's not so simple. Suppose we told Ossian to get lost and sold the chip to some big American computer manufacturer—you understand we don't produce complex hardware here. Then what? Do we tell them where and to whom they can sell Katwar? If that's your idea, forget it. Any company would tell us plain to go to hell."

"We're not talking about sales all over the world." Jay leaned toward him. "We're talking about San Luis. You mean you couldn't persuade any of the big producers to ban sales to San Luis?"

"I sure doubt it. They'd come back and say how about South Africa? How about Argentina, Paraguay, Brazil, Haiti, the Arab countries? None of them are so hot on human rights. The manufacturer would say sorry, but nobody dictates where we sell."

McNaughton nodded. "I read you, Doug, but that's all speculation. Right now we're talking only about your prospective contract with Ossian. If Ossian makes this chip in San Luis, you can't imagine what prestige that will lend the junta. A new manufacturing complex, new jobs, the introduction of high technology so lacking in the tropical countries. All this polishes the image of the military, makes the generals look like efficient administrators instead of a band of brutal cutthroats. One computer plant might even attract more high-tech industry seeking a tax break, which would further strengthen the junta's grip on the country.

"On the other hand, Doug, if you cancel Ossian or amend the contract to cut out San Luis, the word goes out loud and clear that one civilized corporation won't deal with a bloody-handed gang that mangles and kills its own people, most of them innocent of even a misdemeanor."

"Look, Jay, I think that San Luis gang is just as barbaric as you do." He hitched his chair closer. "But you're asking me to make foreign policy, moving onto turf where business doesn't belong."

"It's simpler than that. There used to be a group called the Giraffe Society whose members believed you ought to stick your neck out on issues you believed in." Jay leveled a finger. "I'm just asking you to stick your neck out."

"You're asking us to make a moral decision. Business doesn't operate that way. Business is not immoral, but its rules are built around profit, not ethics. The ethical issues are for the churches and society at large to settle."

"Every decision affecting human life has a high moral content." Jay's eyes mirrored his intensity. "It's a moral question whether your company makes poison gas for the military, manufactures guns or torpedoes or nuclear warheads or whether or not to put a plant in a country run by savage killers."

For almost an hour the two friendly poker rivals talked fitfully of right and wrong, a man's duty to his conscience, the nature of good and evil. They were self-conscious at first, more accustomed to parry ethical concerns with wit or cynicism, but gradually moved into serious deliberation. Did a person have a moral obligation, as Thoreau held, to withhold taxes from a government engaged in unlawful acts? Jay thought yes; Doug no. On the other hand, Doug argued that a government never had a right to lie to its citizens, while Jay believed a lie was justified in certain rare instances. Jay contended that a business had no right to produce unnecessary or frivolous goods if the production depleted irreplaceable natural resources. Doug said that the marketplace generally should be the arbiter with government acting as policeman in special cases. Both men agreed that torture was an absolute evil.

"So we come back to where we started," said Jay. "Here's a ruling junta in San Luis that routinely practices the torture that we both agree is an indefensible crime against human beings. All I'm asking, Doug, is that you and Dataflo refuse to help that government."

"Assuming I made that decision, just how do you envision we'd go public with it?"

"At a press conference right here in this office." McNaughton, quickly enthusiastic, swept his arm from the Arnold Roth caricature to the long window. "We'd alert the big media guns. You'd have a mob here."

"And the next day," said Doug, "our customers would call, demanding what the hell were we doing in politics. Conservative columnists would blast Dataflo for aiding the Soviet Union by snubbing a staunch anti-Communist ally of the U.S. . . . Name me one corporation that ever waded voluntarily into a hassle like that."

"I can't right off, but there must have been some. Remember, it's just sticking your neck out for your convictions."

"No, it's more than that." Doug arose, jammed his hands in his pockets and began to pace about again. "In this company I have fellow officers, more than two hundred employees, steady customers, a reputation for low-key reliability. To say nothing of profits. This is a seventeen-five million contract, Jay, making us as much money at one crack as the company has made since we started." And, he knew he might have added, preventing a possible financial crunch. Summoned back to the day's schedule by his own words, Doug glanced at his watch.

"I realize all that." Jay got to his feet. "I know it's a lot easier for me as an individual to take a stand."

"But you don't understand the business world, damn it, Jay. If Princeton Dataflo gets branded as a political ideological company, customers will leave us in droves. Believe me, man, I know these corporate types. One spurt of controversy and they take to the hills."

"I hope you'll give it more serious thought." McNaughton opened his briefcase. "Discuss it with your other officers. You keep these transcripts. Also here's a report on San Luis that I did for Amnesty International a couple of years back. It'll give you the background on the military repression."

Doug promised to read the paper. "I'm going to take up your request with my two vice-presidents and also with Kate Warfield since she has a royalty interest in her chip. I'll get back to you on the outcome, but frankly I'm not optimistic. Business is just not a political arena."

"Oh, but it is. Economics is the guts of politics." McNaughton's voice stiffened. "Why do you think those military goons beat Silvia Ticpan to a bloody corpse? The issue's cheap labor, my friend. Read the report." He buckled the leather case and tucked it under his arm. He started toward the door, halted, then turned once more to Doug. "One more thing. Don't, please, take what I'm about to say as a threat, but as an old Sunday-night buddy you're entitled to know my plans. So I want to be completely up front with you."

Doug put a hand on Jay's shoulder. "Sounds ominous." He grinned. "You gonna declare war on us?"

"No, on San Luis. I'm going to give copies of these transcripts to Kate Warfield and get her to read my Amnesty report. If Judy were a couple of years older I'd insist that you let her read the transcript on Silvia." He saw Doug's face harden. "I know, she's only nine. . . . If your Ossian contract goes through as is, I'll hold a press conference in New York and lay out the facts as I know them."

"You'd be putting a lot of heat on us, Jay."

"I repeat, nothing personal in this, but I intend to do every damn thing in my power to oust that bunch of assassins down there. That means rallying American public opinion any way we can."

"I understand." Doug edged Jay toward the door with a hand on his elbow. "But you have to understand my situation as well."

"Whatever you decide, Doug, you'll be in the thick of contro-

versy. Morales is starting on the college lecture circuit next week,
so the issue will be flaring sporadically. Also Amnesty International is putting out a special 300-page white paper on San Luis
based on the torture tape."

They shook hands at the office door. "Believe me, Jay, if I were
acting alone, you'd have had a 'yes' from me an hour ago."

McNaughton looked him in the eye. "Don't bullshit me, Doug.
Everybody in town knows you run this company."

11

The minute the door closed, Doug gave Edith Yeager instructions
to locate Sean Hegy at once, in Nassau or wherever the Ossian
chief might be. While he waited, he paced beside the great window
with its view of trim lawns and thick untouched woodlands. Jay
had shattered his calm, that sense of well-being on this gilded September day with Kate sparkling in mind and a fat contract signing
only two days off.

McNaughton's last remark stung. Had he told the truth? Would
he, Doug Perry, if sole owner of Dataflo, cancel the Ossian contract? Hmm. . . . Of course, he had only Jay's word that Ossian
had made a deal with the San Luis military. Best to nail down the
facts quickly, see what Hegy had to say. Outside a squirrel leaped
from branch to branch of a birch tree. The silvery undersides of
poplar leaves glinted in the sunlight. A couple strolled along College Road hand in hand. Then Doug saw a spiked fist whipping
toward the delicate face of an Indian woman. But his mind
balked. The fist fell away. The woman vanished.

The call from Nassau came through promptly. Sean Hegy's cultivated theatrical voice shrank the distance to room size. Good
cheer rolled from the phone. All was in order. He and his lawyers
would fly up in the corporate Learjet the next afternoon, put up at
the Scanticon and be ready for the signing the next morning. And
he hoped Doug's state of health matched his own.

"Fine," said Doug. "Mr. Hegy, there's a report up here that
you've made a deal with the government of San Luis to produce
the Katwar there. Is that true?"

"Yes, it is. I'm surprised it leaked so soon. I'd planned to announce it after the signing. They're giving us a very attractive tax break and assurances of a roof on wages. Most appealing."

"You're not worried about the disclosures of Major Morales? You'll be tied to a government painted in the press as brutal torturers and assassins."

"Oh, my junta friends and Americans I know doing business down there tell me that's mostly left-wing propaganda. Don't believe those distortions. Those tough leftist guerrillas aren't fiction, you know. Besides, the media will tire of the story long before we market the first Katwar."

"How about export permits? It's A-listed against export to the Soviet bloc, of course, but you may have trouble elsewhere too."

"No, no. My man in Washington has promises from his Commerce Department contact that permission for San Luis will be expedited as soon as we legally have a lease on the chip."

"Have you actually signed with the San Luis generals?"

"No, but we have a firm oral agreement. I fly down there the day after our signing to put it in writing. Why, is there some problem up there?"

"Well, this San Luis angle catches me by surprise." Doug paused, reflecting. "Let me sound you out on something. Would you consider manufacturing the chip somewhere else?"

"Oh, no. The San Luis arrangement is ideal for us." Hegy's voice continued to echo the resonances of the stage. Had he been an actor once?

"What if we made some adjustment on the price?"

"Such as selling at a reasonable figure?" Hegy laughed. "No, I want maximum flexibility. I don't want to be handcuffed in any way. . . . Look, Mr. Perry, if you're concerned about the San Luis generals, someone has misled you. They're trying their best to provide stable government under very trying circumstances. I anticipate excellent cooperation from them."

"I must say that's not the picture I get here."

"I think I can reassure you when we talk on Thursday. We'll be arriving in early afternoon."

"Okay then. Until Thursday."

As soon as he hung up, Doug ordered Edith Yeager to run off copies of McNaughton's report and transcripts on the duplicating machine and take one set to Susan Lindbloom and one to Tony Canzano. Both officers agreed to put aside other work, read the papers carefully and come to Doug's office for a midafternoon meeting. Then Doug postponed his legal session with Stanley Fowler for a day and spent the lunch hour at his desk with ham sandwich, malted milk and Jay McNaughton's written analysis of the savage politics of San Luis. He read slowly and when he finished, he had some understanding of a regime, steeped in a culture passed down from colonial days, that regarded Indians as an inferior species fit chiefly for hard work at wages and hours fixed by plantation owners and others of European descent who belonged to the privileged oligarchy.

Lindbloom and Canzano arrived carrying McNaughton's report and papers. As they took seats in front of Doug's desk, Tony tossed his copy on Doug's desk.

"Sadistic bunch down there," he said. "I'd hate to meet one of those guys from *La Casa Dolorosa* on a dark night. But just what in God's name has all this got to do with us?"

Doug told them of Jay McNaughton's mission, gave a condensed account of their discussion and reported that Sean Hegy, confirming the upcoming deal with the San Luis junta, declined to consider manufacture elsewhere even in return for a reduction in price. "I told Jay that I'd take the matter up with you and Kate," he concluded, "but said I doubted we'd move into an area that is basically political."

"Have you made up your mind on this, Doug?" Susan, composed as always, held McNaughton's report in her lap. She had made extensive notes on the back cover.

"No, I haven't. I'm reluctant to see Dataflo take on a foreign government." Doug tilted back in his swivel chair. "On the other hand, those transcripts . . . the Silvia Ticpan you read about . . ."

"Horrible, what they did to her," cut in Susan. "I could hardly bear to read it."

"You see, my daughter, Judy, and I met her." He told of visiting the neat one-room clinic in Montes two years earlier, of meeting Silvia's parents in their thatched-roof house with the chickens and pigs in the dusty yard, of Judy crying herself to sleep the night they heard of Silvia's murder.

"I know how you must feel, Doug," said Tony, "but you've got to realize that with a lot of those governments down there, that's the way they treat their people."

"That doesn't mean we have to go along with it," said Susan.

"Listen." Tony Canzano shot out a finger. "I don't have a single doubt about our course here. I don't want us messing in international politics in any way. McNaughton came to the wrong shop. It's not our business to chew out governments or right the wrongs of this world. Let the Pope, the presidents and prime ministers handle sin and social injustice. Our business is computers."

"Nobody's suggesting we tackle all the wrongs of the world, Tony," said Susan quietly. "Only one country's involved and the question is, do we want to help a government that mutilates and slaughters its own people?"

"We don't know a damn thing about San Luis politics." Tony rushed to battle stations. "Take it from Swift, politics 'are nothing but corruptions.' What's the objective? You trying to topple the junta? How do you know its successor wouldn't be twice as bloody?"

"Tony, reading those transcripts made me sick to my stomach." Susan's expression reflected her nausea. "I'm not at all sure I want Dataflo in effect to endorse a government guilty of such horrors."

"A contract to sell a chip doesn't endorse a government, for God's sake," Tony scoffed. "As for our image, people in the industry couldn't care less about San Luis."

"That's not the problem." Susan looked from Tony to Doug. "My problem is: Could I live with myself? Don't forget, the junta would be using our chip to hide all accounts of their tortures."

"God, this is getting far out." Tony, exasperated, was tuned to a wavelength many bands away from Susan's. "I never thought we'd consider throwing away seventeen megabucks just because we didn't like how some banana republic treated people. We've never let politics influence our decisions before."

"Come off it, Tony." Doug leaned back in his swivel chair, tapped at his foot with a pencil. "We base a lot of moves on politics. How about our lobbyist in Washington? Taxes? Price and wage controls? Inflation? Export permits?"

"Doug, are you actually thinking about breaking the agreement with Hegy?" Canzano coated the question with incredulity.

"I don't know what I think yet. I want to hear everything you two have to say. Kate too."

"Why Kate?" Tony flared. The affair between Doug and Kate, while never mentioned in Doug's presence, had supplied office gossips with heavy ammunition and put invisible strains on the

Dataflo triumvirate—for now President Perry had a new confidante on the company payroll. "She's not an officer."

"No, but she was the key to bringing in the chip." Doug, aware of the heat source behind Tony's complaint, spoke evenly. "We owe her the courtesy of hearing from her. Also Jay McNaughton warned me that he was going to give her the same papers you've read."

"Smart guy," said Tony. "He figures to pressure you through Kate." Now that it was out, everyone felt relieved. Secrets drain off more energy than humidity.

"We three will make the decisions," said Doug firmly, "but we can use Kate's thinking."

"That's right," said Susan. "I want to know what Kate thinks. After all, she brought in Katwar."

"Okay, so she's a female genius on computers, but she's still a kid emotionally." Was Tony's retort a caustic footnote to the union of boss and prodigy? "And I don't want her taking part in this decision."

"She won't." Doug said it flatly without temper. "But we owe her the courtesy. You know that, Tony."

"All right then, damn it, let's talk about money." Tony was half shouting now. "Nobody's said much about money so far. Okay, so we're goddamn near busted. We all know that. Another quarter and we may be looking to the banks to bail us out. And you two are actually sitting there, talking about giving up seventeen and a half million dollars. Jesus!"

"If we canceled, we wouldn't lose it all," said Doug. "We can still go to the mainframe manufacturers or market the chip ourselves."

"But we have no real idea how much we'd get," Tony protested. "Face it. We'd lose millions by canceling, and I find that incredible, absolutely loony, especially for a company that's damn near on its ass."

"Money isn't the whole issue here, Tony," said Susan in her quiet way.

"I can't believe my ears. Is this a business or a charitable foundation?"

And so for several hours they debated the issue that kicked up more emotion, heat and wrangling than any in their decade-long history as a successful executive trio. The longer they talked, the more adamant Tony became. He favored signing the Ossian contract, period. Jay McNaughton or any other "busybody long-distance reformer" could go to hell. "The business of business," he said, "is to maximize profits while still treating people decently." Ah, rejoined Susan, but "what is decent?" That's what the argument was all about, no? She had moved fully into the opposite corner. She felt confident Dataflo would survive whatever they decided, but if she abetted the San Luis junta by a sale of high technology, could she live with herself? Yes, but not happily. Doug raised points first on one side, then on the other, realized that he was not sure himself yet which course the company should take. His business judgment told him to sign the Ossian contract, but the small voice of conscience somewhere at the back of his skull grew larger and louder as the afternoon wore on.

"I guess we've run out of soap," he said at last. No one had injected a new idea for several minutes. "Let's go home and sleep on it and come back here at eight-thirty tomorrow prepared to decide. We ought to let Hegy know before he and his people climb aboard their jet."

"It's beginning to look like our first split." Susan shook her head sadly. "I don't like the feel of it."

"You're on the hot seat, Doug." Tony seemed to relish the thought. "But face it, it's your decision anyway. I just hope you see the light, but not become, to quote Massinger, 'blind with too much light,' . . . Aw hell, Doug, there's only one way to go on this and you know it."

Doug lingered at his desk after his associates left. No other issue had had quite these dimensions since they'd formed the company. Always before the question had been simply: What's best for Dataflo? While the answer was never quite as simple as the question, the three officers usually agreed after airing the options. Now they faced a companion question: What's the right thing to do? Here his conscience spoke at once, pointed out the path. But did following the unwritten uncodified dictates of that powerful shadowed realm, the conscience, automatically serve the best interests of Dataflo? Tony Canzano would say no. Countless executives would say no without hesitation. To turn down millions of dollars on a straight business deal that could restore the company to robust health would be lunacy, they'd say.

Yet he, Doug Perry, found no easy answer on his sleeve. Dataflo's best interests? Didn't they include a humane civilized world? A world safe for children like Judy? And could he face his daughter if he helped a regime that killed the Indian friend she loved? His mind stretched. He wondered and he pondered and several times he snatched at hazy solutions that dissolved like smoke. He suffered. He was, after all, a preacher's kid.

His private phone with the unlisted number rang. He knew it would be Kate before he lifted the instrument.

"Hi. Your place or mine?" The option danced, light as air. "We got to celebrate."

"What? You bought a new motorcycle?"

"No, stupid, telling Ossian to get lost and sticking it to those vicious generals in San Luis. . . . Jay McNaughton brought his papers over here and I cut an afternoon lab to read them. Doug, I'm with you all the way. We can sell Katwar to Cray or IBM. God Almighty, what . . ."

"Kate." He had to interrupt. "We haven't reached a decision yet. I'm meeting with Tony and Susan again in the morning."

"You mean there's actually a chance you might go through with the Ossian contract?" Her tone switched to that of a district attorney.

"We haven't decided."

"Have you decided whether to read that transcript to Judy?"

"That's a separate issue, honey."

"I happen to think it's the same one—we call it decency. Just what is it you have to decide?"

"Whether to sign with Ossian, of course."

"I can't believe it." Advance patrols of outrage. "Could we have read the same transcripts? Listen, I'll see you at your place in an hour. In case you've forgotten, Doug Perry, you wouldn't own that chip if it weren't for me. And if you think my five percent interest can't holler to the press, you got another think coming." The anger peaked. "Oh shit, Doug, you've hurt me."

He poured a scotch and soda at the infrequently opened bar and drank it slowly as he stood by the long window. The gilt-speckled afternoon had faded into muted shades of twilight. Long shadows captured the nearly empty parking lot.

He felt a weariness now after the day-long alert, the sharp exchanges, the challenges posed by McNaughton. It was all much clearer when you were twenty-four and looked at life with the shimmering certainty of youth. He recalled the day in college when he accused a sociology professor of a lack of integrity and told him, "The trouble with you, you're tainted by experience."

Now it was himself with the burden of experience. Would Kate mark a taint? For the first time since they began living together, he actually felt the difference in years as a gulf with distant shores, and it saddened him.

He finished the drink as he stood looking out the window, trying to pick out the twin dogwoods that bloomed hot pink in early May. And as he searched the mass of foliage, the scrub growth, the beeches, ashes, maples and oaks, he saw a woman's face appear in the soft twilight. It was a dark face, delicate, small-boned and suffused by a smile of compassion and fragile beauty. Then, from the shadows, an iron fist studded with needle-sharp spikes lashed out. This time Doug's mind did not block the blow, but opened wide, letting it smash into the face of Silvia Ticpan again and again. Flesh exploded. Blood spurted. A cheek bone cracked. Suddenly there was a spongy, red and gray crater where the nose had been and an eye drooped from its socket like a wilted wildflower.

And in that instant when his mind at last confronted the full image of evil, Doug Perry knew with unshakable conviction that the Ossian contract was finished. It was not one of his wild hunches, but a deep, sure, intuitive knowing. If he signed the contract, he could live with himself only in self-hatred. The ruin of a casually met Indian woman would haunt his nights.

With the decision made, he felt a sharp lift of spirit. He wanted to tell Kate at once. Had she shaped his verdict? No. She might have helped create the mood, but the flash settlement of his inner debate had been seeded long ago, perhaps in childhood in those evening hours when his God-worshipping father told him stories and talked of life and the great brooding mysteries.

Briskly now Doug folded the bar into the wall, put away papers and tidied his desk. There would be a risk, sure, but a risk bright with challenge. Who knew what changes, like widening ripples from a stone thrown in a lake, would circle from Dataflo's decision? Tomorrow, a brand new game.

12

Carlos Rey Quinto snuffed out another cigarette and peered at the German through his thick-lensed glasses. "Impossible." He looked as bleak as ashes. "It's not a question of money. Ossian won't sell to a Bloc country."

"I haven't known you to turn down a fee before, let alone one of this size." Dieter Kirchmann's pale blue eyes mirrored his skepticism. The pudgy East German's wispy blond hair and purpled beer-drinker's nose belied his acumen. "I repeat. I could get you $50,000 for this."

"You don't understand, don't understand." Rey gave off his customary toxic emanations.

"Obviously not," said Kirchmann. Never before had hard money failed to galvanize the despairing Mexican.

The two men sat at a table in the paneled Nante-Eck, one of four bars in the Swedish-built, luxury Palasthotel on the banks of the River Spree in East Berlin. They had met a number of times on Rey's business trips through Eastern Europe. Dieter Kirchmann, top purchasing official in the German Democratic Republic's Ministry of Electronic Technology, did all the computer buying for this most prosperous of the Communist nations. He also doubled as a secret agent of the SSD or *Stasi* as the people called the government's security forces. While Rey had no evidence of Kirchmann's covert role, he never doubted it for a moment. Reared under the corrupt Byzantine politics of Mexico's long-ruling party, the PRI, Rey navigated these murky waters of Communist one-party statecraft by instinct.

The bar where they drank their beer beneath an old-fashioned chandelier reproduced a prewar tavern of the old Berlin where Bertolt Brecht and his cronies gathered after the theater. Now the replica drew a crowd of Communist bureaucrats, Socialist Unity Party bigwigs and today a bantering delegation from Angola in flowered sport shirts. The relative chic of the new Palasthotel struck a popular chord among a citizenry held captive behind the

Wall in a land of dull, proletarian architecture and colorless interiors about as exciting as soap.

"Nothing is impossible." Kirchmann bent to the attack in his heavily accented English, the language in which he and Rey transacted their business. "The West's export controls leak like a sieve. You know that as well as I do, Herr Rey. We and Uncle Ivan have been able to obtain almost every electronic item we wanted, especially in computers. Now this new ciphering chip, no matter how fantastic it's supposed to be, must be obtainable for a price."

"It can't be done." Another negative from the den of gloom.

"I might persuade the ministry to go to $600,000." Kirchmann flicked suds from his lips. "That would boost your commission to $60,000."

Rey shook his head. "The laxity of export regulations has nothing to do with this case. It's Ossian, Ltd., itself. The company won't sell, not for any amount, to the Communist nations."

"Socialist nations, please." Kirchmann liked to observe the semantic niceties. "What is this? A capitalist enterprise indulging itself in principle above profit?" He sniffed in disbelief.

"What do you know about Ossian?" Rey found he gained respect by talking back to Bloc officials. "Did it ever occur to you to ask how a small company with very little track record can put up $17,500,000 in cash?"

"Our information shows that they have double or triple that sum in New York banks."

"Ah, yes. But where did it come from?" Rey, on his third beer, mopped his brow.

"What are you suggesting?" Much as he disliked these Latin ambiguities, Kirchmann had learned to suffer Rey's circumlocutions.

"I suggest only that you consider the obvious possibilities." Rey had his standards. He never gave his customers valuable information unless threatened by violence, deportation or some other ordeal such as having to brazen his way through customs with large amounts of suddenly acquired currency. A hint or two, however, seemed a fair reward for continued generous patronage.

"Are you indicating that Ossian, Ltd., may be a front for some agency of the U.S. government?"

"I indicate nothing. I merely urge you to think as if you were an officer of the *Stasi*." Rey stared morosely at his beer. "A quite improbable career for you, of course."

"Ossian is financed by the CIA. Is that what you mean?"

"Oh, I would think that unlikely."

"The National Security Agency?"

"You said it. I didn't."

Unfamiliar with the colloquialism, Kirchmann studied the Mexican broker with a frown. "May I take that as confirmation?"

"I neither confirm nor deny, Herr Kirchmann." Now Rey began to enjoy the game. His disconsolate air lifted a bit like mist rising from a bog. "I do applaud, however, your willingness to attend the logic of the situation."

Kirchmann, reflecting, said nothing. The noise in the bar increased as more officials and visitors came in for an end-of-the-day social drink. A clutter of languages vied with German. At the Angolan table a jest of some kind touched off peals of laughter.

"When do you leave here?" asked Kirchmann after a time.

"I fly to Budapest tomorrow evening."

"I wonder." The East German traced a moist circle with his beer stein. "Could you stay over another day? I'd like to go over the whole Katwar situation with my superiors tomorrow."

"Superiors?" Rey interpreted the word to mean the KGB, which had a large section in the huge Russian embassy in East Berlin.

"Yes. There are a number of alternative channels through which we might conceivably obtain the chip. Perhaps you could help us there."

"I don't see what they could be. Anyone appraising Ossian, Ltd., with full knowledge of the facts knows they'll never sell to the Bloc."

"Understood. But front or no front, Ossian will have to sell someday to the NATO countries, and that does open up some profitable channels."

"How long would I have to stay here?" Rey wanted to accommodate a good customer even though he considered this a futile exercise.

"Only until day after tomorrow. Just delay your flight to Hungary twenty-four hours."

"Frankly, if I'm to hang around here two nights, I'd rather spend them in West Berlin with the shows and the women." Rey swallowed the last of his beer. "With all due respect, Herr Kirchmann, this capital of yours is like a morgue after dark."

"And before dark?" Kirchmann beamed and his purple nose took on a sheen. "Don't answer that. . . . Go over there, by all means. So let's say we'll meet here at the Palasthotel for lunch day after tomorrow. In the *Roti d'Or*. It has a decent French cuisine. Agreed?"

In West Berlin Carlos Rey ensconced himself in a deluxe suite in the Hotel Kempinski and spent two lubricious nights gorging himself on food, liquor, music and sex. He mingled with portly German businessmen who marched with disciplined ardor to carnal pleasures in the city's smoky night spots, sex bars, transvestite shows, dance halls and kinky massage lairs.

Rey spent hours at the Purple Fox, a lavishly decorated bar offering a dozen comely hostesses who wore only high-heeled shoes, earrings and rapacious smiles. At Macao, amid the pungencies of a perfumed deodorant, he watched a naked couple copulate like jaded serpents and a Korean contortionist slowly tongue herself to a state of frenzied, if bogus, orgasm. He passed an afternoon at Kino Freude drinking margaritas and gaping at colored pornographic films while holding a succession of bosomy fräuleins on his lap.

A pounding headache awakened the Mexican broker on the second morning. Aware of his midday appointment in the other Berlin, he swallowed two aspirins and asked room service to send a double order of coffee with his orange juice and *International Herald Tribune*. By the time he had showered, shaved, pulled on his bathrobe and settled himself at the breakfast table overlooking the lively boulevard of Kurfürstendamm, he felt capable of coping once more. Rey sipped gratefully at the hot coffee, then put on his glasses and spread out the continent's main English-language daily.

A three-column feature headline on the front page struck him like a blow to his still throbbing head:

U.S. COMPUTER FIRM DENIES MIRACLE CHIP TO 'BARBARIC' SAN LUIS JUNTA

An accompanying photograph showed Douglas Perry, frowning and solemn, behind a nest of microphones with Kate Warfield standing happily to one side. The cut-line that identified Perry also labeled Kate as "the postgraduate girl genius responsible for a spectacular advance in computer security."

With the sinking sensation of a man who has just lost $100,000, Rey cleaned his spectacles on a napkin, then began reading the story.

Princeton, N.J., U.S.A.—A computer company today took the highly unusual step of canceling a profitable contract because of "moral revulsion" over alleged torture practices of a foreign government.

Princeton Dataflo, Inc., broke off a $17,500,000 deal with Ossian, Ltd., of the Bahamas because Ossian proposed to produce Dataflo's new security chip in San Luis under tax shelters and other benefits offered by the ruling military junta.

The San Luis Government stands accused by a deserting Army officer and by Amnesty International of mass torture and assassination of what Maj. Enrique Morales has called "a blood bath of its own innocent citizens."

Dataflo's action effectively denies to the San Luis Government use of the "Katwar 23," a sensational new cryptographic chip that experts say will revolutionize computer security. Information encrypted automatically by the Katwar 23 can withstand attacks for centuries without yielding itself in plain language, according to industry sources.

Apparently Kate Warfield, a 24-year-old Rutgers University Ph.D. candidate and chief inventor of the chip that bears her former computer password, influenced the Dataflo decision denying the product to the Central American military government. Miss Warfield has a royalty interest in her chip.

"I'm gratified that Dataflo canceled out," she said. "It's about time that corporations stand up and be counted on the big moral issues. The San Luis junta engages in revolting tortures that hark back to the Middle Ages.

"Princeton Dataflo is saying by this action that it refuses to help bolster the San Luis regime economically. I would hope the U.S. Government will also get the

message and deny further economic and military aid to
a military gang that murders its own people."

Douglas R. Perry, president of Princeton Dataflo,
said in a formal statement that actions of the San Luis
junta provoked "moral revulsion" at Dataflo headquarters and that corporate officers decided that they
could not aid the San Luis regime in any manner. He
said Dataflo would have gone through with the contract
with Ossian, due to have been signed last week, if Ossian had agreed not to manufacture the chip in San Luis
or sell it to the military government. Ossian refused, he
said.

Little men in iron boots tramped about Rey's aching skull. He
poured himself more coffee, lit another cigarette and turned to an
inside page where the article continued through two columns. A
State Department spokesman said U.S. military and economic aid
to San Luis would continue despite Princeton Dataflo's effort to
"make its own foreign policy." Major Morales hailed the Dataflo
decisions as did Amnesty International. Sean Hegy of Ossian said
Douglas Perry had been "misled by clever Communist propaganda," a theme also sounded by several conservative senators
and lobby organizations in Washington. The San Luis junta denied
that it ever tortured or murdered anyone and deplored "this attempt by a small Communist-duped North American company to
drive a wedge between the United States and a loyal ally." Several
anonymous computer executives expressed hope that Dataflo's action would not set a precedent for American companies embark-
ing on diplomatic ventures best left to governments.

A pessimist by nature, Carlos Rey nevertheless felt himself unduly penalized by fate this morning for a rather tame tour of West
Berlin's fleshpots. The headache and sour stomach he could take
in stride, but the loss of a $100,000 commission added flutters of
anxiety to his customary dolor. To make matters worse, a call to
Nassau brought word that Sean Hegy would be unavailable for
several days.

Rey brooded in a second hot shower, dressed slowly, downed a
third aspirin and then took a long walk along Kurfürstendamm in
the bracing air of late September. His head cleared somewhat and
by the time he checked out of the hotel and presented himself at
the metal sheds housing East German passport control in the bar-

ricaded passageway of Checkpoint Charlie, he felt back to normal, which was to say mildly despondent.

Dieter Kirchmann was already seated in the *Roti d'Or,* one of the Palasthotel's eight restaurants, and Carlos Rey could tell at once that the East German official knew the bad news. He showed Kirchmann the *Herald Tribune* headline as he took his place.

"Yes, we've heard. That wipes out Ossian as a possible source for us." Kirchmann leaned forward. "But we had already decided on another route, one where you can be of great help. We don't need Ossian at all." He smiled cheerfully as he passed the menu card to Rey. "I recommend the *escargots* here."

"Oh, not today." The very thought of rich mealy snails, no doubt afloat in a buttery garlic sauce, incited gastric rebellion. "I'll stick to something less hostile. Ah, the leek soup. Bread and soup will do it for me."

Each table had its own nook fenced off by dividers and Kirchmann had arranged Rey's chair adjacent to his rather than across the table. However, the formal restaurant was filling up with super-comrades as the people called East Germany's privileged officialdom, so Kirchmann hitched his chair closer and lowered his voice.

"Forget Ossian, Herr Rey."

"Forget it!" Rey's voice flew up in outrage. "When he canceled Ossian, that fucker Perry cost me a hundred grand."

"That's already history. If our plan works out, you'll make up what you lost."

A waiter in black tie and jacket brought Rey's soup and Kirchmann's snails, black lumps washed by a yellow sea reeking of garlic. Rey averted his eyes, but otherwise focused his attention. "Let's hear it, Herr Kirchmann."

"Do you know of rumors in the U.S.A. that someone stole or somehow illicitly duplicated the Katwar ciphering chip?" Kirchmann speared one of the snails, swabbed it in the sauce and tasted it. "Ah, delicious." His eyes, raised in judgment, snapped their opinion. "You made a mistake, Herr Rey. . . . What have you heard?"

"Nothing." Seeing no reason to break his rule against providing valuable information without financial inducement, Rey lied with becoming sincerity. Actually Sean Hegy had told him in detail about Doug Perry's fears that the Katwar designs may have been stolen, siphoned off via some Arpanet terminal. Indeed Hegy had asked Rey's advice on the matter. "No, I never heard anything like that, not like that."

"We have learned that a small computer company in the Federal Republic is about to produce an encryption chip that has almost identical capabilities as the Katwar." Kirchmann forked up another dripping snail.

Did the "we," Rey wondered, embrace the KGB? Certainly the East German had time to confer with Soviet agents yesterday. On the other hand, the *Stasi* had its own reliable sources in West Germany.

"We think this company in the Federal Republic is working on designs smuggled out of the U.S.A. If true, the fact makes the company vulnerable. But stolen or not, the chip is being readied for production." Kirchmann leaned closer, forcing Rey to retreat from the garlic fumes. "Herr Rey, we want that chip and we're willing to pay a great deal of money for it."

"You mean Uncle Ivan wants it."

"*Ach,* you are too quick to jump to conclusions." Kirchmann raised his palms, a gesture of mild dissent. With his napkin tucked at his chin, he looked like a benign paterfamilias. "Uncle Ivan obviously wants the best and latest in computerware, but in this case we act alone. Actually, we like to keep ahead of Moscow, especially in electronics. Makes Ivan come to us. Evens things up, as it were."

Kirchmann leaned quite close to Rey and spoke just above a whisper. "As you leave, notice the two men at the table to your right, the one with the orange chrysanthemums. KGB men. They had us under surveillance at lunch two days ago as well. Our lead in computerware infuriates them." He chuckled.

"Hardly news." Rey blew a lazy smoke ring. "Between your *Stasi* and the KGB, I assume I'm being watched everywhere but in the w.c., and sometimes there as well." But he suspected that Kirchmann might be telling the truth about acting independently of the Soviets in the computer area. The East Germans were proud of their technical prowess within the Communist bloc.

"At any rate, Herr Rey, if you can get the ciphering chip for us, we'll pay you $100,000 in any hard Western currency you wish."

Rey shook his head. "I'm not in the espionage business. Too dangerous. Besides, my ethical standards would not permit it."

"This is not espionage by any remote definition." Kirchmann pushed the blackened snail round and round the shallow casserole until the animal absorbed its own weight in garlic sauce. "You merely act as a broker as you've always done. A straightaway deal. Your client will be another firm over there. What that company does with the chip is none of your business. You would be totally insulated from our wicked Socialist bloc."

"I see." Rey finished his soup and lit another cigarette from a newly purchased pack. He had run out of his prized Gauloises. "What nationality would my client be?"

"British. A reputable company."

"Connected, of course, to the *Stasi* or KGB."

"Not so. You buy from West Germans on behalf of a British electronic company. Your fee is paid by the British firm. If you wish, you needn't ever see me again."

"Ah, Herr Kirchmann, who could contemplate such unbearable sacrifice." The new cigarette, an East German brand, tasted dreadful. He ground it out. "But why me as the go-between? Why doesn't your British front buy directly from the West German producer?"

"Please, it is not a front." Kirchmann looked hurt. "We merely have a friend inside the firm. . . . We want you because it makes the deal look as perfectly normal as indeed it is. You travel the world, you pick up rumors and gossip, you make deals everywhere. If the British were to approach the producer directly . . ." He shrugged. "Please, Herr Rey. You're a big boy. Don't make me explain the obvious."

After another ten minutes and yet another abortive try at the cigarettes, Carlos Rey offered to undertake the brokerage mission for $100,000. Following his two days in Budapest, Rey would fly to London, meet Brandon Nichols, representative of Sussex Integer, Ltd., at an apartment in Hammersmith and make arrangements for delivery of the chip after procurement. Then he would fly to Hamburg. The West German company handling an apparent version of the Katwar 23 was named Schnelldaten A.G., according to Kirchmann, and its headquarters was located in an old section of Hamburg near the waterfront of the port city. Nichols would pay Rey $10,000 in London and the balance when chip, designs and supporting software were delivered to the Englishman at the Langbacher Hof, a hotel on the lakefront of the inner Alster in Hamburg.

"You can go as high as $1,000,000 for the chip without checking back with Nichols," said Kirchmann. "In addition to your fee, you'll get 10 percent of any amount you save under $1,000,000."

"Who's got the money?"

"Nichols. He'll pay from his company's funds on a London bank. You'll like Nichols. He enjoys a good time."

"If you're going to produce the chip on this side," said Rey, "just the chip and software won't do it. You need an instruction team to coach your people for a month or so."

"You let us worry about that." Kirchmann removed the napkin from under his chin and folded it neatly on the table. "Don't forget, we're making progress on cryptographic chips ourselves. Your job is to swing the sale from Schnelldaten to Sussex Integer. We'll take it from there."

Rey made notes, they drank a ceremonial beer, shook hands repeatedly and parted in an alcove off the main lobby.

"This trip, you never saw me." Rey looked drawn and pale. His head still throbbed.

"Have I ever?" Kirchmann gripped his hand a final time. "We never fail you at control, Herr Rey. *Aufwiedersehen.*"

That evening at East Berlin's Schönefeld Airport, as Rey passed through emigration control en route to his *Interflug* flight to Budapest, he showed his Mexican passport and said, "By permission of Herr Dieter Kirchmann, Ministry of Electronic Technology." The emigration officer took the passport to a nearby phone, called a number, listened a few moments, then handed Rey's passport back to him without placing an exit stamp in it. Carlos Rey had visited East Germany a dozen times on computer business, but his passport carried not a single visa or exit stamp of the German Democratic Republic.

13

Growing crowds heard Enrique Morales describe the anatomy of repression in San Luis as the self-exiled Army major moved westward on the college lecture circuit. Intrigued by the controversy over Princeton Dataflo's boycott of the San Luis junta, the curious turned out to hear what the computer specialist had to say about government torture and assassination in his Central American homeland. After Morales opened his lecture tour at Harvard, audiences increased in size as he spoke, at Syracuse, Carnegie-Mellon, Ohio State, Ohio Wesleyan and Notre Dame.

By the time he reached the University of Chicago in mid-October, a thousand people, plus a press contingent, packed renovated Mandel Hall to hear him castigate the brutalities of the junta he once served as deputy commander of the Army's computer center. This night for the first time Morales openly praised Douglas Perry and Princeton Dataflo for canceling the Ossian contract and "having the courage to place moral conviction and social conscience ahead of profits." Copies of Amnesty International's condensation of the San Luis torture tape, fresh off the press, were distributed in the lobby.

Morales confronted detractors during the question period when he was asked to respond to testimony that day before the U.S. Senate's Permanent Subcommittee on Investigations. One witness, an American businessman with coffee holdings in San Luis, had denounced Morales' lecture tour as "a left-wing propaganda circus that gives aid and comfort to the guerrillas in San Luis." He also supplied the committee with confidential unspecified evidence which, he said, linked Morales to the Marxist Mountain Brigade.

Morales called the testimony "character assassination," challenged the businessman to repeat his accusation outside the privileged Senate forum and said he would reply at length the next night after his speech at the University of Minnesota. Morales refused to discuss the issue further despite a flurry of heckling.

An hour's reception followed his appearance and then the former Army officer was driven to his hotel, the Blackstone, in downtown Chicago by a member of the university faculty. Morales told his host that he needed some night air before retiring and wanted to walk around the block. The professor drove off from the hotel entrance a few minutes after midnight as Morales turned the corner into Michigan Avenue.

At 12:41 A.M. Major Enrique Morales was shot and killed in front of a tavern in the block behind the hotel. He died immediately, according to police officers who reached the scene several minutes later. The assailant shot Morales twice. One bullet entered the back, pierced the heart and lodged between two fractured front ribs.

In Princeton Doug Perry learned of the murder on the morning news of a local radio station, WHWH, as he drove his BMW through Forrestal Center and into the Dataflo parking lot. The broadcast contained a few excerpts from Morales' last speech, including his praise of Perry and Princeton Dataflo for denying its security chip to the San Luis junta.

At once a picture of the Latin Army major took shape in Doug's mind. He saw Morales as he had two weeks ago when Jay McNaughton brought the former San Luis officer to Dataflo headquarters for a visit. Short, stout with shining black hair, Enrique Morales had that special woody complexion that denotes some Indian ancestry. He showed no emotion during their half-hour meeting, sitting unsmiling and impassive for the most part. Morales offered formal thanks for Doug's act of opposition to the junta and expressed belief that the regime would ultimately fall if U.S. public opinion could be marshalled against it. Aside from an impression of strength and durability, Doug gained no insight into the man's character and had to take Jay's word that Morales had acted out of deep respect for individual rights and not from a spirit of revenge for some personal reverse in the labyrinth of military politics.

Doug felt little shock over the news of Morales' sudden death. Did one ever experience the "shock" so freely ascribed to people by the media when a prominent person met a violent end? Yes, he knew the feeling that day a rifle bullet tore into the head of President Kennedy in Dallas or when Martin Luther King, Jr., and Robert Kennedy fell before assassins' fire in the bitter spring of 1968. A small piece of himself had died with each man and his world view altered perceptibly. Ever since those killings he had felt less secure, more uncertain and vulnerable. At the same time the black shadow of the unknown, falling at seeming random, set the rest of life's landscape in vivid contrast. Now living had a poignancy, an immediacy and beauty unfelt before.

But Morales had been an enigma, and Doug's first reaction was a guess as to the assassin. He assumed Morales had been killed by an agent of the paramilitary hit squads that the San Luis junta secretly financed. Jay had told him that Morales fully expected that attempts would be made on his life and that the major knowingly incurred that risk the day he walked out of the computer center with the magnetic tape hidden in his briefcase.

Doug's thoughts veered at once to the impact of the murder on himself and his company. Certainly the killing spelled more trouble. For one thing, the press and television would be plaguing him again for comment. He and Dataflo would be pitched back to page one and the evening news shows where they had spent altogether too much time recently. What he had feared most had happened. Princeton Dataflo was getting an image as a political crusading controversial company with a slightly leftist hue. Customers were becoming restive. Salesmen reported spots of resistance here and there even among purchasers who swore by Dataflo products.

Any way one viewed the matter, Princeton Dataflo's image had suffered in the data-processing industry in the month since its cancellation of the Ossian contract. Plenty of people applauded Dataflo's stand, but they tended to be professionals and academics, not industrial buyers of computer components. Now the murder of Morales, Doug sensed, would only compound the company's predicament.

Tony Canzano was waiting at Edith's desk when Doug walked into the reception room leading to his office. He could tell at once that his old friend and business associate had not come on a happy mission.

"You look like you missed some sleep last night, Tony." In his office Doug pulled up a chair for the vice-president. "You heard about Morales?"

"Yeah." Tony settled into the chair. "He brought my problem to a head." He hesitated, avoiding Doug's gaze. "This is the toughest scene I've faced since we started Dataflo." Again he hesitated, then blurted, "Doug, I've come to resign."

"Jesus!" Now Doug did feel shock. And yet, somewhere in his subconscious he had sensed that this might happen. "Mind telling me why, old friend?"

"Sure. I've felt out of place here ever since we canceled the Ossian deal. I thought then that you and Susan were 180 degrees wrong, and I still do." The words rushed out. This was a chore on which Canzano did not want to linger. "I've had long-standing offers from Sperry and Cullinane, as you know. A couple of days ago Cullinane upped its bid, offering me a package with a lot of goodies in it. I went back and forth, but then this morning when I heard about Morales, I decided. Doug, I'm going to move to Cullinane."

"I don't get the connection with Morales," said Doug quietly. He was finding the defection hard to absorb.

"His murder will put us right back in the middle of this messy fight. Everybody and his brother will be calling from the media.

But hell, Morales is just the symbol. This company dumped itself into politics, Doug, and business and politics don't mix. I want to do my business straight. Remember how Lewis Carroll's Duchess said things would improve 'if everybody minded their own business.' "

As if adding an exclamation point, Edith's buzzer sounded. Answering, Doug listened, then said, "No, no. Not now. Have them call later." He turned to Tony with a shake of his head. "That was NBC and the Washington *Post*."

"We've become the media's favorite company. And all the far-outs love us. They call us the overseas Ralph Nader." Tony grimaced. "If you want to help the downtrodden San Luis Indians, call Princeton Dataflo."

Doug winced. How could Canzano scoff so readily when he too had read of that iron fist smashing into the soft flesh of Silvia Ticpan in the *Casa Dolorosa*? And how could he airily dismiss San Luis Indians as "downtrodden" when whole villages had been burned out by government troops, men emasculated, mangled bodies thrown on door stoops as "lessons" to the families? But it was too late now for such reminders. Hours of talk had not changed Tony's perception. He had his own mind set.

"Anything else?"

"Well, you know I never agreed with your decision against turning the Katwar designs over to the National Security Agency. I couldn't see how that would hurt us competitively. I thought it was our patriotic duty. That still rankles, Doug."

"Is that the whole story for leaving, then?" Doug rode a wave of regret. They had been through so much together.

"Frankly, no. There's the whole business of Kate Warfield. You're relying on her judgment now which means the original threesome no longer runs this company."

"That's not true, Tony." Yet he knew the time for debate had passed.

"I think it is. She sat in on our session about turning the Katwar over to the NSA. And if it hadn't been for your, well, connection with Kate, we'd never have ditched the Ossian deal."

"Kate's views didn't sway me. What convinced me was the viciousness of the San Luis military." Doug spoke with no intent to persuade. He knew it was too late.

"That's not what she told the press. She made it very clear that she'd influenced the company that owned her chip. . . . But we're rehashing now. I've made up my mind, Doug. This is all very painful. I'd like to get it over with. You know how much I think of you and Susan personally."

So they switched to talk of finances. Tony and Susan each owned 33 percent of the stock. Doug owned 34 percent. After much discussion, Doug proposed a five-year period during which Tony would receive dividends—if any—while Doug and Susan gradually bought him out. Tony tentatively agreed, subject to checking with his lawyer. Perhaps, said Doug, Princeton Dataflo should go public if the Katwar proved successful.

"One thing you don't have to worry about," said Tony, as he rose to leave after an hour that left them both drained. "I'm not another Ingersoll. Nothing I've heard, seen or done at Dataflo goes with me. I value our friendship too much. Also a lot of my life is in this company. I want it to start rolling again."

When Tony put out his hand, Doug clasped him in a bear hug. As they parted, Tony brushed at his eyes, then hurried from the room.

Dejected, Doug sat quietly at his desk for some time, finally called Susan with the news. She said she'd try to persuade Tony to change his mind, but they both sensed the futility of the attempt.

Doug sorted through the priorities, trying to decide what move to make next. As he pondered, Edith put through a call from Larry Warfield who came on the line from the Second National Bank with a bass version of his daughter's contralto sparkle.

"Hey, Doug, did you hear the news?"

"The Chicago murder?"

"No, a local blast. About Gary Jameson?"

"What about Gary?" *He saw his old poker nemesis stripped: scrawny limbs, lumpy belly, a scattering of pale hairs on a sunken chest.*

"You haven't heard?"

"No." Doug knew the banker loved to spin his stories on a web of suspense. "Come on, Larry. Let's have it."

"You ready for the biggest surprise of the fall social season?"

"Fire away."

"Gary has come out of the closet."

"What?"

"You've got it. Our long-time poker pal announces himself as a homosexual, moves out on Brenda and the kid—the two older ones are married—and sets up housekeeping with his thirty-year-old gentleman lover on Bank Street."

"For Christ's sake. And I thought that Beverly Hills hair-do that Gary adopted last spring was for a new woman."

"He spread false rumors. Now he's come clean. It wasn't a woman, but a male car-wash commando from Trenton."

"Where'd you hear all this?"

"You can bet the limit he didn't announce it in the *Packet* or *Town Topics*. Peggy got it straight from Brenda Jameson at lunch yesterday. Brenda's furious. Gary moved out last weekend after a dramatic family-type confession."

"What about his job?"

"I don't know. He's still a cryppy at IDA. With all their hush-hush work on codes and ciphers, a secret homosexual might be a problem for them. But now he's in the open, he's not subject to blackmail. It'll be interesting to see what IDA does."

"And the Sunday-night game? I'm not sure how I'd feel about playing with him now. He's the least likable of the guys in my book anyway. I wonder how the others feel."

"I'll check around. . . . Some game!" Larry laughed derisively. "One deadbeat, Ingersoll. One international incident, McNaughton. One guy who's older than his father-in-common-law. That's you, Perry. And now a gay cryptographer."

"If he stays, how'll you tell those fag jokes of yours?"

"No problem." Larry Warfield let silence briefly capture the line. "At his age, you know, they'll be calling Gary a Gay Panther."

As he hung up, Doug realized that all the poker regulars, and perhaps some of the occasional players, would hear the Gay Panther crack from Larry before the day ended. For the banker, life's mission was finding an audience for his shaky jokes. Doug could picture Ira Bickstein receiving the word at his office above the sweeping lawn and pond of the Institute for Advanced Study. The mathematician would hook his dark brows in a scowl and make some mordant remark.

Edith buzzed after Warfield left the line. "This is about that poor Indian friend of yours who was so horribly tortured." Like other Dataflo employees, Edith had read the San Luis documents at Doug's behest. "A man who says he's her brother is calling from Miami."

"I didn't know she had a brother. Put him on."

Doug heard a high-pitched voice speaking badly fractured English. "Meester Perry, I am Pedro Ticpan, the brother of Silvia. Thank you for helping my country."

"It was a matter of principle. The least I could do for your sister. What brings you to the United States?"

"I come for help." The voice quavered. "I myself will take revenge on Major Felipe Alcazar, the killer of my sister. His hands run red from the blood of *naturales*."

"His acts are beyond words."

"You will help us obtain what we need?"

"I'm not sure I'm the right person."

"I was told you would help. If I get a ride to New Jersey, can I come talk to you?"

"Yes, but . . ." What would this involve? "If it's supplies you need, I'm not your man."

"You heard about Major Morales? Those sons of whores want to kill us all. But they can't. We are too many. As Fidel says, we shall win. Again a thousand thanks. *Hasta la vista, señor*."

Doug felt uneasy about the conversation. What kind of help did Pedro Ticpan want? Was he talking about guns? When he came here, it might be wise to have a third person, perhaps Stan Fowler, present. Three telephone calls, coming in rapid succession, intensified the edgy feeling. Newsmen from the Washington *Post, NBC* and *National Public Radio* wanted Doug's reaction to the Morales murder. While he deplored the killing in words that struck him as banal and faintly insincere, he declined to speculate on the identity of the assassin or to discuss other aspects of the San Luis conflict. The *NPR* woman, for instance, probed for his answer to a charge by a spokesman for the San Luis junta that "Princeton Dataflo, while boycotting a firm friend of the U.S., sells its products to people who serve the Communist cause." Doug termed the accusation "a ridiculous lie," but refused to expand the comment. He wanted no more media attention and he began to envy the executives of large companies who could hide, faceless and silent, behind public relations departments that specialized in protecting the corporate image.

He had scheduled an afternoon meeting with Tony and Susan at which they were to decide to whom to sell the Katwar 23. Control Data, IBM, Digital Equipment and Amdahl had all expressed interest in acquiring the chip, but at a much lower figure than the $17,500,000 Sean Hegy once offered. Now with Tony off the team, Doug would confer with Susan alone. Again that stab of regret over Tony.

He wanted to get Susan's thinking on an idea that had come to him last night. Kate had stayed in her own apartment studying, and Doug had spent the evening at his home reading. A magazine article about troubles in Silicon Valley turned his mind to Jim Taliaferro with whom he'd chatted on the phone only once since their summer encampment at the Bohemian Grove. He pondered. Could Jim produce the Katwar? Sure, why not? Eniplex had the facilities, could tool up swiftly and God knows he trusted Taliaferro. Suppose they went into partnership with a fifty-fifty split? The idea threw off sparks, and by the time he went to bed Doug was afire with plans.

Now, as he prepared for the meeting with Susan, he gathered his thoughts once more. Just what were the financial and production numbers at Eniplex? He was about to phone his research "department"—one very bright woman and her secretary—when Edith announced a call from California.

"It's your friend Mr. Taliaferro from Eniplex."

Doug had a bounce in his voice when he answered. "This is weird, Jim. I've been thinking about you since last night. I came up with a hot idea. Matter of fact, I was going to call you later in the day and try it out on you."

"Great minds." Taliaferro was under full power. "That's why I'm calling you. I had a brainstorm too. I tried out my idea on a couple of our v.p.s and they liked it."

"My idea involves the Katwar chip," said Doug.

"You want us to produce it."

"Bull's eye!" Doug was excited now. "How the hell did you know that?"

"I didn't. I guessed. Because that's why I'm calling you. We want to produce your chip and we think it would be a good deal for both parties. You haven't sold it yet, have you?"

"No. Things slowed down after we withdrew from the Ossian deal." He told of the inquiries and interest by the four large manufacturers. As Doug talked, he could visualize his friend sitting in the sun-flooded office that commanded the resortlike spread of Eniplex, Inc. "We'd figured on closing with one of them before long, but I'd rather do business with you."

"You realize you'd never get the price now that Ossian offered?" Taliaferro slid into his bargaining voice.

"Of course. But that chip will still bring good money. It's one hell of a product, Jim."

"But we both know somebody could show up with a bootleg copy."

"Could be." Doug was wary, but firm. "However, when it comes to timing, quality, reliability, servicing—all those goodies—we can beat any stolen chip with our hands tied."

"So what price did you have in mind for us?"

"No price. We have the chip. You produce it and sell it. We split profits fifty-fifty."

"Now *you* hit the bull's eye." Taliaferro's laugh was exuberant. "Fifty-fifty was exactly the deal I was going to propose. You've got the chip. We've got the production plant and the big sales force. Whatever the net, we split it down the middle. No loading of expenses by us. You're welcome to send an auditor out here to check our costs as we go along."

"Right on." Doug took wing. "Let's write us a simple one-page contract. None of those long goddamn things that lawyers cook up for people who don't trust each other. You with me?"

"All the way. This'll get us both off the hook." Taliaferro punched it out. "You're running in the red like you told me out here. And we're sagging on the memory boards, as you know, and we've been casting around for a new product. The Katwar will fit us beautifully. From your standpoint, Doug, you'll avoid a long negotiating hassle with one of the big outfits. In the end, you'd probably have to settle for a poor price. . . . Also you still face the chance that somebody may have stolen the Katwar 23, a tough thing to handle in a contract. But with us, we already know about that and we're willing to share the risk with you. . . . And just what is the current status on the Trojan horse problem?"

"As of today, we have no evidence that anyone is producing a stolen Katwar." Doug told of sending a graduate student to Europe after Marshall Ingersoll's remark at the Bohemian Grove that a European firm might produce a security chip. "He drew a blank. Now we have a German consultant who lives in Frankfurt keeping a steady watch over there. Of course, Europe's a lot of ground, but he's found nothing suspicious up to now.

"As for Ingersoll, I told you about hiring Phil Wetherill, the San José detective. He's come up with zilch so far."

"Good news," said Taliaferro. "You know, plenty of companies are having security troubles these days. Out here in the

Valley people are into a different kind of scam." He paused. "We've had heists where employees carried off newly produced chips by the sackload. Intel lost 10,000 memory chips to one inside gang. At Apple, some employees carted off entire Apple III computers. So we've become very theft conscious here at Eniplex. You can bet that if we produce the Katwar, we'll have triple-A security for it. . . . Doug, I think this deal makes real good sense for both of us."

"Our image doesn't bother you, Jim? A lot of people in the industry are shying away from Dataflo. They think we're too political since we boycotted San Luis."

"We discussed that here. Doesn't scare us. For one thing, once we get the Katwars coming off the line, they'll be our chips in the customers' minds, not yours. For another, this is California, man, and that kind of shit doesn't frighten business." Taliaferro laughed again. "Out here people swing from left to right and back again like weather vanes in a storm. Anyhow, Doug, I'm with you on San Luis. I told my Latin American salesman last week. 'No sales of any kind to those thugs running San Luis.' "

"Okay. Any other questions from your end?"

"Nope. How about you?"

"Yeah, a couple. One thing, if we agree on this, I think you ought to take over Wetherill and his investigation of Marshall Ingersoll. Maybe I haven't been insistent enough with Wetherill. Either he should step up his surveillance and financial checking or maybe you should put a new detective on the job."

"You still suspect Ingersoll then?"

"I do. I don't feel right about the guy. I'm confident he planted that instruction in our beast. He may have stolen the chip design and sold it before Wetherill got on his case. I'd feel better if we knew the man's movements day by day."

"Okay, I'll handle it. What else?"

"How soon can you hit the market with Katwar?"

"If we sign right away and you give us a good coaching team," said Taliaferro, "we can have it out the door by Memorial Day."

"Fine. I think we have a deal, Jim. I have to clear it with my associates, but I predict they'll love it. I'll call you back tomorrow."

They spoke briefly of the Morales murder and traded several gossipy items about fellow Micro Mall campers.

Soon after they hung up, Doug had an enthusiastic yes from

Susan, and that night at the house on Hun Road, Kate quickly agreed that her chip might thrive under a partnership with Eniplex. "The main thing," she said, "we'll be doing business with a guy you trust."

A few days later, during the third week in October, Doug and his poker-playing lawyer, the ponderous but painstaking Stan Fowler, met Jim Taliaferro and his attorney in Chicago. It took but several hours to draft an agreement satisfactory to both sides. Doug would send a four-man team to Sunnyvale to help Taliaferro's company gear up for production. Kate would fly out if and when needed. The security chip, enabling computer users to protect their electronic files via history's most powerful ciphers, would be called the Eniplex Katwar.

Taliaferro flew back to the West Coast that night, but Doug joined a table-stakes game in the Congress Hotel organized by some acquaintances in the computer business. He bought $1,000 in chips as his stake in the poker game. By midnight he was $3,000 ahead, but when play ended at 4 A.M., he had lost $600 and a night's sleep.

14

The cold rain drove into the Alster lakes like darts, creating a boundless domain of tiny fountains. Traffic bleated in the slick streets and water raced along the gutters. In the harbor of the Elbe, one of the world's busiest ports, the downpour flogged the bawling gulls and lowered visibility, forcing the great ships to sound their fog horns as they slipped along like phantoms.

A doorman held a large umbrella to shelter Doug and Kate from the mid-November rain as they left the limousine which had brought them from Hamburg's Fuhlsbüttel Airport. Their hotel was the Vier Jahreszeiten, a deluxe establishment on the shore of Binnenalster, the smaller of the two lakes that grace the center of West Germany's largest city.

As they were about to enter the hotel, Doug saw a man down the block hailing a cab. Despite the rain, mist and distance, something about him, his carriage perhaps, struck Doug as familiar.

Messages raced from eyes to brain to voice box at speeds and with magic patterns that no computer could match.

"Carlos! Hey Carlos!"

But the man, hunching his shoulders and gripping the collar of his trench coat, entered a cab which moved off through the rain. Doug stood watching the taxi until traffic swallowed it.

They mounted steps to the entrance hall that looked toward a tapestry of a royal hunting scene. Doug's shoes were soaked. He stamped his feet on the marble floor.

"Do you think that was Rey?" she asked.

"I thought so, but I'm not sure."

They walked to the reception desk through a pillared lobby with gilded chandelier and stiff formal furniture. After they registered, the women desk clerks, trim in white shirtwaists, made a name search but could find no Rey or Quinto booked as a guest. They had no more success when they looked through the past week's guest list.

A basket of fruit and candy awaited them in their spacious room which opened on a balcony overlooking the rain-swept inner Alster. The room was handsomely appointed, but neither Doug nor Kate took much notice as they fell into bed with grateful sighs. Both were exhausted. They had taken the night Lufthansa flight from New York via Düsseldorf and by the time they reached the hotel, it was after ten in the morning.

Unsettling news had forced the couple to jettison their schedules at office and campus and fly to the West German port city. Doug, undone by word from a number of independent sources, made the decision abruptly just two weeks after signing the contract with Jim Taliaferro for production of the Katwar.

First of the troubling reports came from Otis Kramer, the shadowy Washington operator. Doug hadn't heard from Kramer in months, had almost forgotten the pot-bellied computer consultant who accosted him outside his home late on that sultry June night. Now, out of the blue, he called from Paris.

"Mr. Perry, are you aware that somebody stole the recipe for your Katwar chip? And did you know it's being produced in a foreign country?"

"Where did you hear that?" Doug went on the alert. "In Paris?"

"From a source of bed-rock reliability." Kramer ignored the

last question. "Surely you're aware that the chip's design has been stolen?"

"No." He could picture Kramer, flabby, vapid expression, and he could feel the moist palm of his handshake. "Eniplex is producing the Katwar under contract."

"I know." Over the phone Kramer's heavy breathing sounded vaguely obscene. "But so is another company."

"There in Europe?"

Again Kramer slid by the question. "They'll make millions. Would you like to know the company's name, address, officers, the whole bit?"

"Sure." The news, whether fact or rumor, chilled him.

"It's yours for $15,000, Mr. Perry. For that you get the entire rundown on the illegal producer."

"I don't buy information."

"Not even if I give you the name of an employee who'll talk for a price?"

"How would I find this employee?" He didn't trust Kramer.

"I'll tell you that when we meet and talk."

"Where?"

"You name it. Just bring the fifteen grand."

"What guarantee that you'll provide the needed information?"

"My word, Mr. Perry."

That sealed it. "No thanks."

"I don't understand you Dataflo people. You refuse to act in your own self-interest." That raspy breathing again. "You'll be sorry, Mr. Perry. That illegal production is going to cost you a fortune."

"I'll take my chances."

Kramer tried a bit longer, then at last ended the trans-Atlantic conversation on a note of bemused regret. "It's a pity. With my help, you could catch the thieves."

A day later, while he still wondered whether Kramer was hawking fact or fiction, Doug took a call from Westwood, Massachusetts. It was Tony Canzano phoning from Cullinane Database Systems where he'd been on the job but a few days. The exchange of pleasantries proved a strain and Canzano quickly came to the point.

"I have a tip for you, Doug. Strictly Dataflo business. I take it there're no new developments on possible theft of the Katwar?"

"It stands just where it was when you left." With Canzano off the team, Doug hesitated to tell him of Otis Kramer's disconcerting offer.

"Here's the scoop. Last night I met a computer salesman who's big in Europe, his territory. He says an encryption chip that sounds suspiciously like the Katwar is being offered on the gray market over there."

"Who's the producer?" Alarms rang. "Do you have a name or a place?"

"No, damn it. He says the chip's being made somewhere in West Germany, but by whom or in what city, he doesn't know."

Doug plied him for details, but Canzano knew little more. "I wish I did," said Tony. "I got a lot of money tied up with you, Doug, and I don't want to see old Dataflo take a beating. Remember what Tennyson said: 'The jingling of the guinea helps the hurt that honor feels.' Good luck."

Doug tried to reach Hans Engen, his German consultant in Frankfurt, but Frau Engen told the operator that her husband was in Japan on business. She had no number for him. Doug stewed for a time, conferred with Susan Lindbloom, then decided he must call Jim Taliaferro. The circuits to California were busy and when he reached Taliaferro an hour later, the Eniplex president said he had been trying to phone Doug as well.

"We ought to get up a telepathy act," said Doug. "We both seem to reach for the phone at the same time."

"I hope you have better news than I do." Taliaferro was not in good humor. "We're in trouble, Doug. It looks like a copy of the Katwar is being made in West Germany. Have you heard anything from that German consultant you hired?"

"Not a thing. I tried to reach him in Frankfurt this afternoon. That's why I was calling you." He told Taliaferro of the talks with Kramer and Canzano. "But Tony had no particulars you could sink your teeth into. How about you?"

"Oh, I've got particulars all right. How accurate is another matter. According to my information, this enciphering chip is being produced by an outfit called Schnelldaten A.G. in Hamburg. I'll spell that."

Doug made notes. "You got an address?"

"Yeah, Rambachstrasse 13. I understand that's just a couple of blocks from the docks in Hamburg."

"Where did you get this dope?"

"From Paul Ellenbogan. One of Logiware's video games salesmen in Europe picked it up. Paul and I look out for each other."

"What about Ingersoll? Did Phil Wetherill dig up anything interesting?"

"You're a jump ahead of me. The Wetherill agency has come up with a real eye-opener. Remember that Wetherill reported to you about Ingersoll making regular flights to L.A. to lay an actress?"

"Yeah. Wetherill called her 'mediocre.' Whether upright or horizontal, he didn't say."

"Turns out the woman is either a side-line or a blind. What Ingersoll really goes to L.A. for is big-stakes poker. He makes a no-limit game in Culver City at least once a month. Did you know he played that kind of poker?"

"Hell, no." Doug thought a moment. "Very strange too because Marshall knows I like a high-stakes game now and then. You'd think he'd have said something."

"Right. Just what went through my mind."

"Do the Wetherill people know how long he's been playing in L.A.?"

"Since last spring. And he's had some hefty losses, they report."

"He told me in late June in San José that he hadn't found a game out there yet."

"He lied," said Taliaferro. "Another big item. Wetherill's people found out that Ingersoll quit his job with you and moved to Bytex Labs just a month after he dropped a bundle at a game in New York. It's a game reportedly bankrolled by the Mafia."

"Jesus! Things begin to add up. . . . How about Ingersoll's travels?"

"Wetherill got all Ingersoll's trips from an informant in Bytex's travel department."

"Any trip to Hamburg?"

"Come on, Doug. If so, I'd have told you first thing. Let's see here what the list shows." Taliaferro paused. "Okay. Three flights to Europe this year. One to Paris in June. Another to Munich in August, and late last month he flew to Zurich."

"Of course, he could have gone on to Hamburg from any of those points without telling anyone."

"True. All in all, Doug, we've got a problem. It looks like somebody is after our ass."

They talked for another ten minutes. Weighing the matching reports from Kramer and Canzano as they assessed this new peril to the success of Katwar, the two executives agreed that the German firm had to be investigated promptly and somehow blocked if indeed it was marketing a stolen version of the Katwar encryption chip.

"Tell you what, Jim." Doug made a swift decision. "I'll fly over to Hamburg and look into this personally. At your end, I think you ought to put Ingersoll under twenty-four-hour surveillance."

"Will do. Also I'll put my legal people to work on the West German law. We ought to know just what our rights are over there."

Before they rang off, Doug committed himself to fly to Hamburg as soon as possible while Jim promised to call that evening with the names of several electronic executives in the Hamburg area with whom Eniplex had dealings.

That night Kate quickly joined the battle to protect her chip. She insisted on accompanying Doug. She would make up her Rutgers' work later. Doug put Susan Lindbloom in temporary command of the company, promised to bring his daughter, Judith, a surprise present from Germany and had his bank transfer $20,000 to Deutsche Bank's Hamburg branch. With Dataflo's deficit, his own funds had begun to shrink as well, but he held this to be a reasonable gamble. Hamburg harbored some heavy poker games, he knew, and if Ingersoll had indeed gone to the city, he may have found a high-stakes game and perhaps left some traces of his stay there. A long shot, but what the hell, he craved a night's play anyway in the big German port city. On a hunch he obtained a small photograph of Ingersoll from Dataflo's personnel files and tucked it in his wallet.

Making his apologies to Hugh Talbott, who again was holding the Sunday-night game, Doug learned that Mrs. Talbott, who had fled Hitler's Germany as a girl, had a nephew in Hamburg who worked for a private investigation firm. The relative, Klaus Bloch, had spent several years at Miami University in Ohio. "Sounds like just the kind of guy I'll need over there," said Doug. Talbott offered to call the young man.

Both Kate and Doug hoped that their mission met with more success than their abortive trip to California. "Still," said Kate with a laugh, "if we hadn't gone to California together, I wouldn't have made that first pass."

Twenty-four hours later they were flying over the Atlantic.

They slept soundly for several hours and when they awoke in early afternoon, the rain had stopped. A feeble sun struggled to break through the overcast that covered Hamburg like a soiled bandage. Kate peeped over the fat *Federbett* that served as both sheet and down-filled quilt and let her eyes roam around the room. It was done in opulent eighteenth-century style, green marble fireplace, crystal chandelier, a long antique mirror and thick pale green carpeting overlaid with an oriental rug. Matching drapes framed the glass doors and balcony that looked down on the inner Alster lake.

"I thought the company was hard up," she said, as Doug took her in his arms. "We fly economy class, but we go to bed deluxe." She snuggled against his chest.

"I'm picking up this tab myself. I figured you'd earned a little luxury. This Four Seasons is a famous hotel, family-owned for three generations." Doug yawned. He felt nerveless and lazy. "Well, time to go to work. Let's start by calling Mrs. Talbott's nephew and the leads Jim gave us."

Doug put in a call to Frankfurt for the German computer consultant he had retained. No, said Frau Engen, her husband was still in Japan, would not return for a day or so. However, Doug did reach Klaus Bloch, Mrs. Talbott's nephew, who agreed to meet them the next morning at breakfast. He had heard from his aunt, he said, and would put himself at Mr. Perry's disposal for as long as needed.

"We start work in the morning." Doug turned to Kate.

She was sitting before the dresser's ornate mirror, brushing her black halo of hair. He thought she looked stunning and he kissed the nape of her neck. Kate sighed. She felt deliciously female, ripe with love.

"Did you ever see one of those harvests in the wine country where people crush the grapes with their bare feet?" she asked.

"No. Why?"

"Reminds me of the way I feel these days."

"The grapes or the feet?"

"I'm all of it, kind of a big luscious harvest." She turned to him. They kissed. "Lover." She resumed brushing her hair, but after a time she laid down the brush.

"Oh, Doug." She stared at him, an odd longing in her eyes. "Will you grieve for me when I'm gone?"

"What a wacky thing to ask." He was about to make a flippant retort when he noticed tears at her eyes. "Jesus, honey, I'm a quarter of a century older than you. Whatever gave you the idea that you'll die before I do?"

"You're so indestructible, you know, so solid." She said it admiringly, laced with love. "I think you'll always be around."

"I sure don't feel that way." And now he saw plainly in Kate what he had only glimpsed before. For all her brilliance, she was sapped by feelings of insecurity. Big Doug was her rock, and that must be much of his attraction for her. A rock? Good God, sometimes he felt as rattled and empty as a tin-roofed barn in a hail storm.

Kate went back to her brushing. Her sad mood had passed. "Maybe Carlos Rey's here under an assumed name," she said. "But why?"

"My feeling about Carlos is that he'll make a buck wherever and however he can. If he's here in Hamburg, you can bet it's more than coincidence."

"If Schnelldaten is selling a copy of our chip, he'd be after it as a broker, wouldn't he?"

"Damned right he would."

Later at the nearby Schümanns Austernkeller, where waiters in white tie and tails looked as somber as the ancient oak paneling, they ate a hearty German meal, including a Hamburg specialty dish, pears, beans and bacon. Then they hired a car for a night tour of the city. They drove around the two lakes, passing consulates, mansions and parks on the large Alster where the denuded weeping willows graced the banks in summertime like leafy chapels. They toured the financial and commercial districts, solemn at night and a bit forbidding under a new cold drizzle, then drove along the waterfront where cargo ships that had come sixty miles down the River Elbe from the North Sea were being unloaded beneath flood lights. They crossed the St. Pauli district, teeming with strip joints, honky-tonks, girlie spectacles, bars and dance halls. Men, many of them merchant seamen, tramped the sidewalks past gravel-voiced barkers. Women in low-cut gowns or hip-hugging pants, peddlers of sex by the hour or minute, popped in and out of doorways.

Cruising dark streets near the waterfront, Doug ordered the driver to stop at Rambachstrasse 13. An old three-story stone building, apparently one of the few that came through the Allied blanket bombing of World War II, it looked seedy and unremarkable. A busy bar splashed with the ubiquitous Astra beer signs faced a wine shop and apartment complex across the street. An adjacent doorway gave access to the upper floors. Doug inspected the name plates beside a set of doorbells. One read "Schnelldaten A.G." The computer company had located in a dowdy section of the city where small shops, taverns and rooming houses for sailors crammed together off the well-traveled Ditmar-Koel Strasse. Whatever its mission, Schnelldaten apparently intended to do it on the cheap. As the rain had grown heavy again, Doug and Kate soon returned to the hotel.

They met Klaus Bloch at breakfast in Restaurant Haerlin, a room of muted opulence named for the hotel's owners. Glazed ceramic cherubs smiled down at fresh-cut flowers, stiff linens and upholstered armchairs occupied for the most part by German businessmen. Waiters and waitresses in formal uniform served the expensive spread of breads, buns, jellies, jams, honeys, eggs, cold meats and coffee with ceremonious briskness.

Bloch was a lean dark-haired intense man in his thirties who spoke ready English with a Midwestern accent and had a way of fixing his total attention on a person. He wanted them to call him Buddy, the nickname he had picked up at Miami University in Ohio where he had studied liberal arts and played on the tennis team. He was now a partner in a private-detective agency with two other men his age. Buddy agreed that his firm would spend the next few days investigating Schnelldaten A.G. and attempting to locate Carlos Rey in the city either under his own or an assumed name. Doug and Kate would spend the time contacting the electronic specialists recommended by Jim Taliaferro and exploring this bustling vibrant sometimes tough city of nearly two million people, a floating metropolis where buildings rested on piles to thwart a water table almost as high as that of Venice.

On his rounds that day Doug, in addition to meeting several computer executives, had a printer run off a set of calling cards with false name and address. On the second day he withdrew $10,000 from his Deutsche Bank balance and placed it in a hotel deposit box. Always a good idea in an open-end operation like this to have ready cash at hand, he told Kate.

"Are you going to play poker here?" she asked.

"Maybe. If Ingersoll has been here, he probably played. Good way to track him."

"Terrific excuse too." She dismissed his motive with a roll of her eyes.

That night Doug reached Hans Engen in Frankfurt. The consultant had just returned from Japan and he agreed to come to Hamburg promptly after a good night's sleep. The news that Schnelldaten reportedly was selling a security chip surprised him.

The Bloch agency's inquiry revealed the name of Schnelldaten's chief officer, Ludwig Frischauer, but little else about the concern. About all that people in the computer business knew was that Schnelldaten was new, small, undistinguished and not affiliated with any trade association.

But Doug was not prepared for what he found when he arrived on the third morning at Rambachstrasse 13 with Buddy Bloch accompanying him as interpreter. The doorway beside the tavern opened on a flight of worn steps leading to a second-floor wooden landing where an abbreviated corridor offered several doors, one of which announced Schnelldaten A.G. in small black letters.

Doug rapped and entered a room hardly larger than an ordinary elevator. A woman, straw-colored hair skinned back in a bun, sat tapping with crimson fingernails at a typewriter considerably older than she was. Startled, she regarded the two men as she might a pair of intruders. A wooden railing enclosed her work space, leaving a narrow strip with a single unpainted chair for visitors. Doug noted a door at the rear of the enclosure.

Bloch, neatly dressed and mannered, said that he and an American businessman from New York wished to speak to Herr Frischauer. Doug handed over one of his new cards:

Steelman Bishop
Monarch Computerware, Inc.
New York City

Did Herr Bishop have an appointment? *Nein,* but he sorely needed one of Schnelldaten's products and was not disposed to haggle over price. Urgent that he see Herr Frischauer at once. The typist, obviously skeptical, frowned, glanced at the card a second time. Then she began squaring her papers tidily beside the typewriter, centered a pencil precisely on the papers and moved a small bottle of nail polish from the suburbs of her desk to a central location just above the pencil. *"Einen Moment, bitte."* She slipped into the inner office, shutting the door behind her.

Reappearing after several minutes, the secretary unloaded a cargo of negatives on Bloch. No, Herr Frischauer could see no one today nor at any time this week. Impossible. A schedule packed as tightly as a World Cup soccer stadium. Perhaps next week if Herr Bishop would be so kind as to leave a note of his hotel and room number.

Klaus Bloch looked to Doug for instructions after the translation. The Fräulein with the crimson nails took her seat again with a prim smile and began disassembling the elaborate mosaic she had crafted beside her typewriter.

"Oooh!" Doug cried out in pain and slumped to the floor, clutching at the wooden railing as he fell. He writhed about, moaning and kicking spastically. He let out an agonized shriek, whimpered and panted, then howled once more.

The interpreter looked down at Doug in dismay. The secretary ran around the railing. Out of the inner doorway burst a bald-headed man in vest and shirt-sleeves who carried his suit jacket as if intending to finish dressing on the way to lunch. All three people bent over Doug. The woman stroked his temples while the bald-headed man peered into his eyes and put a hand over Doug's heart.

While they inquired anxiously in salvos of German, Doug loosened his collar, rolled on his back and motioned them to move aside. The Schnelldaten man stood up and put on his jacket, tugging at the cuffs for a proper fit. Doug lay quietly, opening and closing his eyes, breathing deeply and at last smiling wanly at the three Germans. Then, with the Schnelldaten man assisting him, Doug got slowly to his feet and began to brush himself off.

"A seizure," he said to Bloch. "Please extend my apologies to these kind people."

"Unnecessary," said the Schnelldaten man. "Fräulein Kranz and I both speak English." His was a fine British brand encased in a Teutonic accent. Solicitous, he bustled about Perry, dusting off sleeves and straightening his jacket. "And how can we be of help, sir?"

"If I could just sit down and rest for a while. The attack won't return if I remain calm." Doug grimaced. He had banged his elbow falling, and it felt as if a needle had pierced the nerve.

"I'm Ludwig Frischauer, Herr Bishop." The German bowed and offered his hand. "I'm at your service. Please come sit in my office until you feel better."

Doug let himself be helped into the inner room while Buddy Bloch with a bemused expression settled down on the lone chair outside the railing.

Frischauer guided Doug to a straight-backed metal chair and seated himself behind his desk. The top was heaped with pamphlets, order sheets, letters, newspapers and computer digests, all neatly stacked but apparently unseparated by category as if the owner prized a kind of orderly chaos. Frischauer himself fit the same pattern. He had the requisite number of eyes, ears, lips and other appurtenances, but they lacked ordinary cohesion so that he managed to look harried, distracted, weary and shrewd all at the same time.

"So. We shall sit here and have ourselves a quiet chat. Time heals." Folded hands would have been appropriate to the soothing words, but actually they hovered like wrens at the nests of printed material. Frischauer pulled out one envelope, as quickly shoved it back again. Then he scratched at his hairless head. Doug had the impression of an owl with all the head feathers plucked out.

Frischauer made profuse apologies for having failed to receive Perry earlier. Mountains of overdue work, customers complaining, a nasty headache, etc., etc. Doug believed not a word of it.

Striving to recover his equilibrium, Doug spoke slowly of Hamburg, New York and Monarch Computerware. He learned that Frischauer, a former instructor of electronics in a Stuttgart technical school, had opened Schnelldaten's Hamburg office less than a year ago.

The office, not much larger than the cell-like reception room, had one window, an art calendar with an industrial river scene by Max Beckmann, a dusty rubber plant, a photograph of a four-man rowing crew and a flashy poster of a French computer exhibit dated April 1978. A nondescript beige paint covered the walls.

"Where is your production plant located, Herr Frischauer?" The time for recovery had arrived.

"But we have no manufacturing plant." Frischauer seemed genuinely surprised. "Since we make nothing, we have no need for one."

"Then I'm under a misapprehension. I was given to understand that you made computer components."

"Not at all." Frischauer's delicate little hands fussed at one of the stacks of papers. "We buy and sell anything to do with computers from five-hundred-mark items of software to mainframes that cost a fortune."

"My informant had you all wrong then, but no matter. Actually what I came here to buy can just as easily be purchased from a broker."

Frischauer waggled a finger. "No, we're not brokers. We're in a special compartment of our own. Perhaps wholesaler would be closest in concept for an American."

"You have a warehouse in Hamburg?"

"We don't have warehouses. You see, Herr Bishop, we have no possessions except those in transit from the producers to those who buy from us." He looked not only wise, but pleased with himself as though he had explained it all with great clarity. "Just what was it you wanted to buy?"

"I'm in the market for a ciphering chip. I was told you had a fabulous new chip that encrypts more powerfully than anything going."

Frischauer, after an instant of thinly veiled surprise, frowned and pursed his lips. "Sounds quite elegant." Now he looked like a puzzled, featherless owl. "We don't have anything like that for sale. . . . Wait a minute." He fished around in one of his heaps and pulled out a page torn from *Computerworld*. "Here. Your American weekly describes something of the kind invented by a young woman in New Jersey."

The issue was three months old. Both Kate and Doug were quoted in the article which, fortunately, did not carry his picture.

"We don't deal across the ocean," continued Frischauer, "so I can't help you. I'd suggest you contact the New Jersey company when you return to the U.S.A."

Doug felt thwarted. This man and this office had a spurious quality. Just what was it? He resorted to his old tactic. *Zap: A hairless pulpy chest, fat belly, mouse-colored pubic hair, veined and flaccid legs. Remembering Kate's device, for good measure he seated the man in a New England outhouse in January.*

The image boosted Doug's morale. "You have no ciphering chip of any kind for sale?"

"None." Frischauer appeared quite pleased at the limits of his stock.

Doug tried another tack. "Do you know a Mexican computer broker named Carlos Rey Quinto?"

"No. It seems to me I've heard the name, but I've never met him."

Doug sketched a thumbnail word portrait of Rey. "Anybody like that call on you here?"

"Never." Frischauer's reply now had an edge of wariness.

"How about an Otis Kramer of Washington, D.C.?" He described him briefly.

"Again no." Frischauer's tone became crisp. His ailing caller was recovering too swiftly. "You're the first American ever to come into this office. . . . You act like a detective."

"I'm not one." Doug chanced a random shot. "Of course Marshall Ingersoll of California has been here." He fished Ingersoll's photo from his wallet and held it in front of Frischauer.

The German no more than glanced at the picture. "I repeat. No American except you has been in this office." He was openly hostile now.

"It's just that you might have forgotten."

"I do not forget." The amiable bustling gentleman who had helpd Doug off the floor turned belligerent. "You're abusing our hospitality here, Herr Bishop. Now that you've recovered, I must ask you to leave. I am extremely busy."

They sparred for a few moments, but Frischauer, pressing firmly on Doug's sore elbow, propelled him from the room, shutting the door with a smart click.

Bloch was chatting with the stenographer-receptionist. She held a cigarette between two crimson-tipped fingers and Doug became aware of an unmistakeable thick pungent odor.

"Oh," he said, "you smoke Gauloises."

"Not usually." She inspected the burning cigarette as if for flaws. "A salesman left these here yesterday and I decided to try them." She held up a blue pack with the traditional winged helmet. "Would you like one?"

"No thanks. . . . Was the salesman a Mexican named Carlos Rey?"

"No." But in the split second before her negative, Doug noted a most revealing look. "No, a German from Bremen."

Perry reflected on that look as he and Bloch went down the creaky stairs. Once, passing a table in a New York restaurant, he had seen a woman glance at her dinner partner. He caught only that one momentary glance, but sensed that in some strange fashion he had been privileged to witness the emotions of a lifetime.

Hurt, vulnerability, hunger, longing, the sweet raging sadness of existence, all laid bare in that single moment. Now Fräulein Kranz's fleeting expression had some of that same quality: surprise, defensiveness, curiosity, alarm, a deep vulnerability. He felt he knew her intimately. Fräulein Kranz was a barricaded, lonely woman.

"Those seizures," asked Bloch, when he and Doug reached the sidewalk, "do they happen often?"

"Yes, Buddy." Doug placed a hand on the investigator's shoulder. "I get one every forty-seven years."

Bloch smiled, chuckled hesitantly, at last broke into laughter. Doug joined him. He felt quite proud of his acting ability, but rued the injured elbow.

"Our first job is to find Carlos Rey," said Doug. "There's no doubt now the man's in the city or was yesterday."

"We'll give it top priority. Now tell me what Herr Frischauer said."

As Doug related the conversation, Bloch stopped him repeatedly. He wanted to know in precise detail who said what to whom. They agreed as they cabbed back to the Jungfernstieg area, where both the hotel and Bloch's office were located, that in addition to the effort to find Rey, the agency would probe the backgrounds of Frischauer and Fräulein Kranz whose first name, Bloch had discovered, was Ute.

"I'm convinced the guy's a liar," said Doug. "As for her, she's defensive and lonely, so maybe she could be reached. One way or another, we ought to get a break here. . . . By the way, Buddy, where's the best poker game in Hamburg?"

"There are some in St. Pauli. I don't play myself, but I've heard gamblers talk about one at Cafe Monaco off the Reeperbahn. It's safe and honest and runs all night."

"Thanks. The bell captain at the hotel mentioned the Cafe Monaco too. Apparently it has a good reputation."

"Oh, I think so. They never have trouble there."

They left the cab on Jungfernstieg, the promenade of the smaller Alster. Bloch returned to his office on Bleichenstrasse and Doug steered for the hotel, moving briskly on the broad walkway beside the lake. The rain had stopped during the night. Now a northern breeze harried the clouds, scoured the sky and left large plazas of blue overhead. The sun, warm for November, glinted on a dozen steeples that lanced the sky above water-bound Hamburg and its canals, ponds, lakes and river. By contrast, the facts about Schnelldaten remained cloudy. Doug had a strong suspicion now that Frischauer and his odd little company were dealing on the worldwide gray market, probably in violation of German law and perhaps with a handle on an imitation Katwar. As for Carlos Rey, he most certainly was here to buy from Frischauer.

Kate was waiting for him as he entered the hotel lobby. "Buddy's people just called. They have a break for us." She handed him a slip of paper. "They're sure Rey is using the name Edmundo Fernández and that he's staying at the Langbacher Hof on the other side of the lake. Let's go."

"Hold it, Kate." Doug raised a hand. "Hans Engen is due here at noon from Frankfurt. I want you to meet him. Also somebody ought to be here in case Buddy phones with new leads." He gave her highlights of his visit to the Rambachstrasse office.

She whooped when he told her of his sham seizure. "Up to your old stunts."

He rubbed his elbow. "I didn't mean to lose an arm at it."

"You be careful, lover. We need all your parts."

"So you hold the fort here. I'll be back as soon as I find out what gives with Carlos."

It was a five-minute walk around the small lake to the Langbacher Hof. An Indian summer sun lured people to the Jungfernstieg or Virgin's Walk where mothers pushing baby carriages belied the lakeside avenue's name. Flags flew in the plaza and refreshment carts rolled past the moored sightseeing boats. Swans glided on rippling waters. It was a fine coppery day that assured handsome Hamburg and its well-dressed citizenry that autumn had not yet yielded to winter. At another time Doug would have strolled and basked in the sun. As it was, he quickened his pace.

The desk clerk at the Langbacher Hof was most helpful when Doug asked for the room number of Edmundo Fernández. "You just missed him." He waved toward the lobby door. "He checked out not more than ten minutes ago."

"Do you know where he went?"

The desk clerk frowned, surveyed Doug from head to shoes. The Langbacher Hof protected the privacy of its guests.

"It's imperative I see him." Doug slid a fifty-mark note across the counter.

"He cabbed to the airport." The voice was low, refined. The currency disappeared in a pants pocket.

"Is he flying back to Mexico?"

"No, to Berlin, I believe."

To the taxi driver at the entrance, Doug offered a twenty-mark bonus for speed and the Mercedes rolled the seven miles to the airport at a perilous clip. On the curves the tires squealed in protest. Doug paid in advance and bolted from the cab the moment it stopped.

Under the complex antiquated pact governing Berlin since the end of World War II, no German airlines flew into the western half of the divided city and only Pan American flew from Hamburg to West Berlin. The departure board listed Pan Am's next Berlin flight at 1:30 P.M., just twenty-three minutes away.

Doug raced to the departure area where buses ferried passengers from the terminal to departing airliners. He pushed into a security booth where a guard frisked him for lethal hardware. No tools of the hijacker's trade being detected on his person, he was passed and permitted to hurry to the waiting room for the Berlin flight.

A long queue moved slowly toward the door leading to one of the ferry buses. Doug's eyes, sweeping the row of faces, halted midway. There was Carlos Rey, that vat of gloom, looking as doleful as ever. He carried a flight bag and took a last few nervous puffs on a cigarette before crushing the butt underfoot.

Doug got a whiff of the familiar odor as he approached. "Forever Gauloises, eh, Carlos?" He grasped Rey's arm.

The Mexican broker might have been a schoolboy apprehended by his father in the town cathouse. He swung around with a startled look, recognized Perry, snatched his arm away and rushed off, pawing other passengers aside, toward the boarding gate for the bus.

15

Startled by Carlos Rey's quick move, Doug Perry lost a moment before he set out after his man. Then Doug too shoved surprised passengers aside, lunged forward and managed to grab the Mexican broker just before he reached the doorway leading to the airliner bus.

Doug clutched the rear folds of Rey's trench coat, pulled hard, then linked his arm and swung Rey around.

Other passengers, looking on with apprehension in the manner of travelers who shun involvement with any untoward event, moved toward the bus with quickened step. Rey tried to shake loose, but Doug held fast. The boarding agent started toward the two grappling men.

"Knock it off or I'll tell him you stole money from me." Doug spoke swiftly in a low voice. "Then I'll appeal to the police."

"I have to make this plane." But Rey stopped struggling.

"There's another one in an hour or so. All I want from you, Carlos, is some information."

"No. I have to leave." He looked as melancholy as ever.

Doug tightened his grip. "Then I'll put the police on the trail of Edmundo Fernández."

Rey gaped, started to speak, then sighed and peered at Doug through his thick-lensed spectacles. "Necessity breeds deception as well as invention, Mr. Perry."

The uniformed Pan American agent stood beside them. "Just what is the difficulty here?"

"We're business partners," Doug explained. "I just caught him before he left. There's an urgent matter we have to handle."

"Is that right?" The agent turned to Rey after eyeing Doug with unveiled suspicion.

"Well, you see . . ." Rey hesitated. Perry dug his nails into Rey's arm. "Yes, that's right, that's right. You see, I didn't realize at first who it was." His somber mien, however normal it might be, lent weight to his disclaimer.

"We'll just sit down here for a while, if we may," said Doug.

"As you wish." The agent, who wore a lavishly coiffed toupee, did not appear entirely convinced. He nevertheless moved off to shepherd the last of his customers to the ferry bus while glancing over his shoulder at the two men.

Doug motioned Rey to a seat and sat down beside him. Jet engines whined outside and the building quivered as an airliner thundered down the runway and vaulted into the sky.

"A true surprise." Rey tried to recover his poise. "Yes, very surprising meeting you here."

"I doubt that." Doug shook the proffered hand. "I called to you three days ago. You were hailing a cab alongside the Binnenalster. I thought you heard me."

"Oh, no." Rey's customary look of bereavement had darkened. "I'd have been very pleased to see you."

"Then why did you try to run away from me just now?"

"It was a shock . . . I don't know . . . you frightened me." He appealed with his large dark eyes. He wanted off the hook.

Doug did not insist. "What brought you to Hamburg?"

"I have a German-Brazilian deal cooking." He looked as drained as bottom flats at ebb tide.

"No doubt." Why did the man suffer so? Against his will, Doug felt a tug of compassion. "And it involves a cipher chip just like the Katwar."

"Oh, no. Not at all." Rey failed to bring it off. He could be read, if not like a book, at least with some study like the fine print on a contract. "Is somebody producing a security chip around here?"

"Come on, Carlos, let's not play games." Doug stared into the Mexican's eyes, black pools that evoked those days of Indian empires before the Spaniards came with their horses and their tubes of fire. "I know all about your call at Schnelldaten. Fräulein Kranz even offered me one of your Gauloises."

"I don't know what you're talking about." At mention of his favorite smoke, Rey pulled out a blue pack and lipped a cigarette.

"No? Listen, Rey, if you don't come clean about yourself and Schnelldaten, I'll see to it that you never make another goddamn deal in the United States. I've got connections, you know, and I can get you blackballed in the data-processing industry like you wouldn't believe."

Rey said nothing. Instead he lit the cigarette and blew out a shaft of smoke. Again that thick, roasted smell that Doug would always associate with the sorrowing Mexican.

"And I'll put a private detective on the tail of Carlos Rey, alias Edmundo Fernández, who'll follow you all over the world until I damn well find out who stole our Katwar chip and just what you had to do with it. I warn you, Carlos. You're traveling on thin ice, and the law is not far behind."

"I didn't steal your chip, Mr. Perry." Breaking his considerable silence, Rey looked down at the floor. "I had nothing to do with anything like that."

Now Doug surmised that Rey might talk. "Was it stolen?"

"I don't know." Rey shook his head. "I heard that it might have been, but I honestly don't know whether it was or not."

"But Schnelldaten is selling a security chip just like the Katwar. Isn't that right?"

Rey, continuing to stare at the floor, flicked ash from his cigarette, inhaled again. He was hunched over with elbows on his thighs. He said nothing.

"Isn't that right?" Doug shook Rey's arm.

"Maybe." Rey glanced up at Doug. "I'm willing to tell you what I know. You want to hear the story?"

"Of course, damn it. Why do you think I grabbed you out of that boarding line?"

"Okay, then." Rey cleared his throat. "About six weeks ago a client approached me about getting hold of a new security chip. It was just after I read about you canceling the Ossian contract—a bad mistake, by the way, Mr. Perry, in my opinion. Anyway, I was out the $100,000 that would have been due me from Sean Hegy and I was feeling low."

How did Rey measure his own mood levels? If his constant malaise rated as normal, then "low" must have verged on desperation.

"What's the client's name?"

"That's confidential."

"Bullshit. I want that name." *Zap: Sagging brown flesh, a surgical scar, creased belly, fatty chest.*

The tactic failed. "You won't get it." Rey lifted his brooding eyes and for once looked straight at Doug. "If you want this story, you'll have it my way. Otherwise I don't talk." His voice, schooled in the graceful evasions of Spanish, became suddenly harsh.

Doug realized that Rey too could get his back up. He reminded himself to soften his approach. "Okay, Carlos, tell it the way you want to."

Rey took a long drag on his cigarette. "All right then." He squinted, protecting his eyes from the smoke. "The client gave me the name of an intermediary I was to meet in London. I did meet the party there and got a down payment on my commission. However, the party wanted me to hold off for a month—just why, I don't know. When I finally got the green light, I came here to Hamburg this week, apparently arriving about the time you did." Smoke swam about them. Doug coughed. "It's true I did hear you call my name, but I didn't want any diversions right then. I was concentrating on getting that chip. I went to the upstairs office of Schnelldaten on Rambachstrasse and met the boss. I guess you saw Frischauer too?"

Doug nodded. "Yeah. He did a good job of lying to me."

"I told Frischauer I was in the market for an encryption chip and that I understood he had one. He said he did have a model for sale, but that he'd already sold it to another customer. I told him that was okay, that I'd buy a copy of the circuit diagrams and chip layouts from him and was prepared to pay a lot of money for a good copy. He asked how much, and I told him 'high up in the six figures.'"

The airline agent, on his way back from the boarding bus, arranged a few chairs as he scrutinized the two men. Pan Am's Flight 102 to Berlin rolled toward a runway with a keening of demons. Rey ground out his cigarette.

"Frischauer said he'd sold the chip outright," he continued, "but he'd see what he could do. I was to return yesterday, which I did—that's when I mislaid the cigarettes that Miss Kranz found. This time Frischauer said the people who bought the chip refused to make a copy of the designs, not for a million or for any other price. I hung around another day, but Frischauer told me on the phone this morning that they'd again refused and there was no hope."

"Frischauer told me that he had no security chip for sale." Doug recalled the German's act. "Come to think of it, though, he didn't say he never had one. . . . He denied knowing you despite my description of you."

"Of course, the man is not to be trusted." The Mexican implied that he, Rey, by contrast was the quintessence of trustworthiness. "He deals on the gray market outside the regulations of the West German Government."

"Do you think Frischauer sold a stolen copy of the Katwar?" Doug locked his eyes on Rey's.

"If I had to make a guess, I'd say yes, but believe me, Mr. Perry, I have no evidence of any kind to support that."

"Any idea who did buy the chip from Frischauer if that's what happened?"

"I don't know, but I have my theory."

"Which is?"

"The Soviets. I think the KGB got to Frischauer before I did.

As a matter of fact, maybe that party . . ." His voice trailed off. He appeared to be exploring a new line of speculation.

"Maybe which party?"

"I wondered if the party I saw in London may have dealt secretly with the Soviets. That month's delay lost the chip for my people."

"If you were in my shoes, where would you start in order to discover whether Frischauer sold to the Russians?" Doug's mind raced ahead.

"I just wouldn't know, wouldn't know." Rey brooded. "I know very little about Schnelldaten. In fact, I've picked up only one interesting fact about the company. A small thing, I guess, but they do have space in a building at Wirtsweg 62. That's also near the wharfs, I think. I heard Fräulein Kranz direct someone to that address over the phone."

"Frischauer told me Schnelldaten didn't have a warehouse."

"I don't know. The Wirtsweg place sounded like another office or maybe a meeting place. Who knows? I'm sorry I can't help more."

"What's your guess as to who sold the chip to Frischauer?"

"I wish I knew." Rey's mouth had a stubborn set and it was apparent that whatever he knew he would not disclose it.

Doug fired his next question without warning. "Do you know Marshall Ingersoll?"

"I've heard of him, yes. He used to work for you, didn't he? But I've never met him or had any contact with him."

"Has he been here in Hamburg?"

"I have no idea." Rey gave no sign of dissembling.

"What about Otis Kramer?" Doug recalled that when he and the Mexican first met, Rey denied knowing Kramer.

"Ah, Kramer." Rey tilted his head. A smile, as wan as winter's sun, slipped on and off. "Be careful of that one, señor. You know he once worked for the CIA, covert operations, eh? Then later for the National Security Agency. Now he's like the old freebooters. He'll pick up a dollar or a peso anywhere he can. He rattles around everywhere. Once I picked up his trail in Jakarta. He pretends he still has ties to the intelligence agencies. Maybe, but I doubt it. Not to be trusted. Decidedly not."

"He called me in Princeton, told me the Katwar had been stolen and offered me the name and address of the illegal producer for $15,000. I refused."

"That's Kramer." Rey nodded in recognition. "He picks up all kinds of rumors and gossip, but who knows the truth of what he peddles?"

"You told me when we first met that you didn't know him."

"I didn't and I don't. I've never met the man, yet I feel I know him like I know my own skin."

"You going to Berlin on business?"

"Yes. I have several computer clients there." He busied himself extracting another cigarette from the blue pack.

"West or East?"

"Señor!" Rey looked as sadly reproving as a basset hound. "I told you I got burned once on a Bloc deal. There's no profit for me doing business with the Communists."

Doug continued to grill the broker for another quarter of an hour, but learned little except that Rey had suffered a bad cold in London and that in Berlin he would be stopping at the Hotel Kempinski. "Under my own name," said Rey, with the resolute look of a criminal vowing to go straight.

Doug accompanied him to the Pan American counter and stood by while he negotiated a reticketing. Then, at Doug's prodding, Rey wrote out his itinerary for the next two weeks: West Berlin, London, New York, Mexico City.

"Carlos," said Doug, in parting, "I hope you've told me the truth. If you haven't, I warn you, I'll ruin you on the U.S. market."

"Everything I've told you is the absolute truth, Mr. Perry. In the years ahead I expect to call on you many times, many times." He tapped his flight bag as if to lend body to the promise.

No sooner had he left the despairing broker than Doug was enveloped in a cloud of regret. He did like the man despite Rey's evasions and obvious duplicity. His dolor was so pervasive that it took on a tragicomic cast. How extraordinary that a person should remain despondent for so long without doing away with himself. Doug wished that he'd thrown an arm around the Mexican's shoulders and tried to cheer him up. Hell, Carlos, he could have said, it's an insane world and we're all nutty inmates, so why not relax and enjoy it until they cart you out of the asylum in a pine box? On the other hand, he wanted to smash the broker in the face. Rey had no compunction about dealing for a chip stolen from Doug and Kate. He was a man of powdery loyalties.

Returning to the Vier Jahreszeiten room, Doug found Kate

happily presiding over an investigative enterprise involving both Buddy Bloch and Hans Engen. The Frankfurt computer consultant turned out to be an elderly pink-cheeked gentleman who wore a fresh rose in his lapel and carried himself with old-world courtliness. Engen paid strict attention to everything said, and his shrewd questioning gave Doug a feeling of confidence. Bloch also had impressed him.

Doug briefed them on the scene with Carlos Rey, including the Mexican's suspicions that Frischauer might have sold the security chip to the Russians. He also noted that Schnelldaten apparently had additional space at Wirtsweg 62.

They divided the assignment, Bloch to investigate Frischauer and Fräulein Kranz personally and Engen to learn everything possible about Schnelldaten. They would report the next day at breakfast; would contact Doug or Kate in the meantime if developments so justified.

"We're making headway, lover," said Kate after the two Germans left. She struck a little pose that suggested—what exactly? Happiness? No. Too bland. Ferment, perhaps. Yes, that was nearer. Kate at her liveliest and most vital.

She was standing by the picture window overlooking the inner Alster and he joined her in the warm afternoon sunlight. They gazed on a rare summery scene for mid-November. Flags flapped in the breeze on the nearby plaza, swans coasted about the lakes like a proud marine nobility and a few sailboats, not yet stored for the winter, cut shining wakes through the dark waters. Whether the hint of progress on their mission was illusory or actual, today's seeming advance elated both Kate and Doug and when they looked at each other, they laughed at what they read in the other's mind.

"You too?" he asked. "At the top of the afternoon?"

"So what's wrong with broad daylight, lover?" She casually opened the top button of her shirtwaist.

The languid movement fired him. She always called him lover now, and that too often aroused him. He swept her into his arms. Their kiss was eager, demanding. He undid the two remaining buttons of her blouse and slid his hand from one breast to another as if fearful they might vanish. Then they fell to undressing each other like feverish children.

They tore the fat *Federbett* from the recently made bed and seized each other as if in combat. Charged by the touch of their bare bodies, they reacted in a kind of spiritual frenzy, spiritual because they loved each other and frenzied because they lusted for the outer manifestation of what they loved. Yet even amid their cries and thrusts, Doug wondered anew at this phenomenal act of love, this rude, harsh grappling to possess the unpossessable, to vent the unventable, to discover the undiscoverable. It was truly mysterious, this carnal beatitude that dwarfed everything else in life. It was a magnificence apart, a cathedral of lust, a vale of tenderness, a great raw chunk of divinity that brought human beings together with the power of hurricanes. What indeed was a trifling security chip beside this passion that seared the flesh and transfigured the soul?

At last, the frenzy gone, they lapsed into their familiar rhythm, an undulating roadway of kisses, strokes and sighs. Lounging on this plateau of desire, they slowly worked themselves once more into a state of passion that spiraled ever higher and stronger until it consumed them. Neither spoke for many minutes.

"Weird," said Doug, at last. "I've been wondering why your undoing a button on your blouse would shoot me into sexual orbit. They say search your childhood for the trigger, and I remember now my first time." He talked in a low, lazy voice. "Want to hear about it?"

"Of course, lover. I want to know everything about you."

"Well, I was fifteen and I was cutting the grass for a neighbor in Des Moines where my father was a pastor for a couple of years. The neighbor was a big-hearted bosomy woman whose husband was always off traveling somewhere. It was July, and she invited me into the kitchen for a soft drink. After a time she asked if I had a girl friend and began talking 'suggestively' as my mother would say. Then she unbuttoned the top of her dress and this tremendous wave of frightened excitement came over me. The rest is kind of vague except that the bed upstairs was a four-poster with a lace canopy over it. I felt like I was camping out with Zsa Zsa Gabor, the big siren of the day."

Kate snuggled to him and kissed his throat. "Whenever I see you yawning in the daytime, I'll just undo a button. How exquisitely simple."

"And you? What image from your childhood sets you off?"

"A trim ass. Ever since I was a kid, I've been turned on by a slim pair of hips on a man. Just like yours, Doug."

They talked and laughed and traded romantic bewitcheries,

then made love again and fell asleep. When they awoke after their nap, twilight misted the lakes, sails and swans could be seen no more and long shadows paved the way to nightfall. They were dressing when the phone rang. Doug answered.

"Doug, this is Jay McNaughton. I got your number from Susan Lindbloom." The professor of Latin-American politics eased through the preliminaries. "I'll make this short. Between us, it looks like a coup by younger, more liberal officers is in the making down in San Luis. One of them, a very young colonel named Lemus, heads the Army's computer center. He was Major Morales' superior officer. Lemus is in Miami now, and he wants to talk to you. Would you be willing to talk to him in strict confidence?"

"I guess so," Doug said. "Now that I'm in this deep, I may as well help get rid of those thugs who run the country."

"I told him I thought you would. . . . Okay, he'll phone you shortly."

The call from Miami came through a few minutes later. "I am Colonel Rodolfo Lemus de la Cruz." The strong Latin accent, stressing all the wrong syllables, complicated preliminaries, but Lemus bulled ahead. "Mr. Jay McNaughton said we could talk in total private. Many young officers are ashamed of the Army's brutalities and of our government's sorry record on human rights. We want San Luis to return to the family of civilized nations. We intend that government forces stop killing innocent civilians, confining military action to the fight against the guerrillas." He told of further aspirations while Perry strained to sort out the meaning from the colonel's erratically accented English. "I'm here in the United States to seek support for our position."

"And how do I fit in?"

"Should our group come to power," said Lemus, "we want to be able to announce that you'll reconsider your cancellation and produce the security chip in San Luis."

"The chip is now being made in California," said Doug, "by another company under a partnership agreement. However, I'd certainly be willing to talk to the other company and see what could be done. Perhaps an auxiliary plant could be located in San Luis. . . . But only on one condition."

"What is that, Mr. Perry?"

"That six months elapse during which there are no government murders, kidnappings or torture of noncombatants in your country."

"It would be difficult to change the Army completely around in such a short time. Brutality has become a way of life."

"Nevertheless that's my condition. If the new junta, or whatever, maintains a clean human-rights record for six months, I'll sell you the Katwar chip and do everything I can to locate some computer production down there. I'll let Professor McNaughton be the judge of the record."

"May I relay that promise to my fellow officers?"

"By all means. And hell, Colonel, if you can bring it off, I'll come down there with Jay McNaughton and help you celebrate a six months' anniversary."

The news lit a fuse for Kate and she took off like a rocket into blue-sky rejoicing. "See what happens, lover, when you make a stand for your convictions? You *can* make changes. You can. You can." She struck a pose of triumph, arms flung upward.

"Hold it, baby . . ."

"I'm no baby, babe."

"Hold it anyway. This is just one colonel talking. There's no coup down there yet, no halt to the killings, no nothing. For all we know, Lemus and his friends may never get the plot off the ground. Maybe they'll be knocked off themselves. Maybe, maybe."

But Kate wanted no part of caution, no prudent assessing of risks, chances, probabilities. "The good colonels will bring it off, you watch." For Kate the world had its good colonels, cousins of the good fairies that made wishes come true, and if one stood up for the right, well then, right would prevail.

"Kate, Kate, why get your hopes up . . ." But he never finished the sentence. She had turned from a mirror and she looked spectacular in her new dress, nubbly brown and purple wool, that hugged her hips—as slim as those she admired in men—and hinted of cleavage at the bosom. She was radiant, bursting with life. He loved her deeply, a love that intuitively embraced all the disillusions, the shocks and traumas down the long corridor of years that stretched before her. Kate had known only the good colonels of life as she soared from one success to another. For all her genius, she was, dear God, but twenty-four. He wanted to cry.

But he did not. Instead he kissed her, told her she looked splendid in her new outfit and offered her a variety of choices for dinner. She selected Fischereihafen, a restaurant with a view of the river, where they dined on oysters and lobster and watched the workings of the great port at night.

"This is lovely," she said, reaching for his hand. "But I had a strange feeling coming in here. That man in the brown suit who followed us in. I think he got out of the car that was behind us."

"You think we're being followed?"

"I'm not sure. Yes, I guess so. Anyway, it's a possibility. Vibes, you know?"

"I doubt we're being followed, but it's possible. Let's keep an eye out."

But they soon forgot and gave themselves to the spangled view. The port slept under a carnival of lights. The lights festooned the angular container ships moored at the piers, poked into the shadows of sheds and warehouses and glistened on the dark waters. Downriver metal cranes traced geometric patterns above one freighter that was being loaded under floodlights. An occasional small boat bustled through black waters on its nighttime missions. Gulls swooped under a misted moon and here and there a star shone through drifting clouds. After dinner, over coffee, Kate and Doug held hands as they surveyed the harbor with quiet contentment.

The cabby on the ride back to the hotel proved to be fluent in English and unusually talkative and friendly, a mutant in the German breed of silent businesslike drivers who raced to their destinations as if every narrow street were a speedway and every cobbled lane a Grand Prix course. This one chattered about bars, soccer, Bonn politics, homosexual shows, shipping and the eccentricities of Japanese tourists.

"Where would a stranger go to play big-stakes poker in this city?" asked Doug.

"In St. Pauli. There are a number of big games on streets just off the Reeperbahn." The driver turned to face them, narrowly missing an oncoming fender in the process. "I can take you there in no time."

"I don't doubt it. Which game draws the big gamblers?"

"Not tonight, lover." Kate had a lilt to her voice. She had drunk only one glass of wine. She was high on life.

"The Cafe Monaco," said the driver. "I saw a Venezuelan bet 9,000 marks on a pair of threes one night. A Dane won the pot, calling with a pair of sevens."

"Where do Americans go to play?" Although Doug thought of Ingersoll, he himself felt the urge. He hadn't played poker for a month, not since that night in Chicago after he and Taliaferro signed the production contract.

"That depends." The driver eyed Doug in the rearview mirror. "Those that like the big bets go to Cafe Monaco."

"You're the third man to mention the Monaco. Is it safe there?"

"Safe as home. If you win a lot, they'll even give you an escort back to the hotel."

"Doug!" Kate cocked her eyebrows. "You're not considering playing tonight, are you?"

"Think of it as work." He grinned. "If Marshall came here to sell your stolen chip, he probably played poker in St. Pauli."

"That's just an excuse." She was hurt. "If you play, I want to go along."

"No." The driver, ignoring speeding traffic, turned his head again. "That's no place for respectable women."

"Who says I'm respectable?" She growled it.

"You can't go. You know that, Kate."

"If you'd agree not to play tonight, I could make you a big winner some day."

"What's that supposed to mean?"

"I've worked out a program . . . No, I refuse to bribe you."

"I've decided to play tonight, Kate."

"Men!"

The taxi pulled up in front of the hotel. Doug told the driver to wait. On the sidewalk, he took Kate's arm.

"Look, honey. Jim Taliaferro's investigator tells us that Ingersoll likes the big games. It would be foolish not to follow up on that. If I hang around the poker crowd, I may get a line on him."

"You just want to play." Now Kate grew angry. "And you're coming up with a very flimsy justification."

"Untrue. I do like to play, sure. But it makes sense to look for Marshall in places he'd be apt to go."

"So much for making love in the afternoon." She cracked the words like a whip. "I can't believe it. At least in Atlantic City, I was with you. . . . You'd leave me alone in a foreign country for the whole night?"

Doug glanced at his watch. "It's eleven already." They were

moving through the lobby. "I'll play a few hours and be back by three. . . . I'll tuck you into bed before I go."

"Oh, no." She wrenched away and ran to catch an open elevator. As she entered, she turned. "You better hire yourself another room, Perry. Where I sleep, I'm putting on the night chain." The elevator door closed.

Doug stood for a moment musing. He had half a mind to go up to the room, but now he was irked. Why was Kate so snappish? He turned and went to the registration counter where he withdrew 10,000 marks and $5,000 in travelers' checks from his deposit box. He wanted ample ammunition for the hours ahead.

"Women!" scoffed the cabby as they drove off. "I remember the time I decided to go to Amsterdam and my wife . . ."

16

They surged along the sidewalk, quick-eyed, fretful, lonely, a human river of discontent that emptied into the Reeperbahn, main artery of Hamburg's St. Pauli district which catered to every craving save that for sleep. Here garish signs flashed through the night, barkers lured restless men with visions of aphrodisia, strippers toiled till dawn and the vendors of vice took cash or credit cards.

In a block off the Reeperbahn the river of men poured past an arcade of video games and the den of a bare-bosomed palmist. An Oriental massage parlor advertised twenty-four-hour service in blinking lights. Nearby a noisy beer hall featured a Bavarian band in *lederhosen,* Turkish belly dancers and a troupe of shrill transvestites. A bus stopped in front of the hall, disgorging a load of Japanese tourists whose tickets entitled them to one cocktail or two beers.

Doug Perry pushed his way through the Japanese to reach the swinging doors of Cafe Monaco, the adjacent establishment. The Monaco made a pretense of posh. The bouncers wore black tie, and waiters draped white towels over their arms. A long bar of polished cherry wood stretched along one wall. Sleek women in clinging evening dress lounged on the bar stools and smiled invitingly. In the shadows hostesses and their partners danced to soft music. Doug made his way to the rear via the cabby's instructions.

A huge man with biceps the size of grapefruits beneath his dinner jacket guarded a curtained doorway. Doug showed his wallet, stuffed with currency and travelers' checks. The strong man nodded and held the velvet curtain aside.

The rear room was unlighted save for a drop lamp over the poker game. Doug counted nine men seated around the large round table, which was covered with green felt and fitted with recessed compartments to hold money and drinks. A smoky haze as thick as morning fog on the Elbe wreathed the room. Two old-fashioned spittoons rested on the tiled floor, and half-burned cigarettes littered the gambling area.

A man who wore an open-necked sport shirt beneath his jacket stood watching the play with folded arms.

"You speak English?"

"Nah." He had a narrow head and a streetwise look. "Only Brooklynese." He spoke in a stage whisper from the side of his mouth and his eyes never left the field of play.

"My first time here. What's the drill?"

"The fat guy with the blond hair is the house man." He shifted his mouth toward Doug. "He deals for everybody, cuts the pot for the ante—ten marks. Dealer's choice, but only five and seven-card stud, draw and hold-'em allowed. Pot limit." He leaned closer. "A seat's about to open up. The guy in the hat says he's leaving."

Between Brooklyn and his own observation, Doug soon learned the format. Each player became dealer in turn, although the cards actually were shuffled and dealt by the Monaco's laconic heavyweight. Only German marks, then more than two to the dollar, were used in the game. The player designated as dealer put ten marks in the center and at the end of each hand, Fritz, the house man, took ten marks from the winner's earnings and stuffed the money into a slotted box as the Monaco's cut.

Players communicated in monosyllabic German, but Doug guessed that he could identify an Italian, an Englishman, two Germans and a Turk. A burly man in a crew-neck sweater and a blue cap occasionally growled an expletive in an unknown language. He drank whiskey, laughed a good deal and appeared to be winning.

"A Yugoslav off the freighter *Gospic*," said Brooklyn in his side-mouthed whisper. "He comes here every voyage, or so he says."

Thanks to years of poker, Doug soon took in the pattern of play. These men were big-money gamblers who seldom bet less than the size of the pot which swelled rapidly as each hand progressed. One winner raked in 4,000 marks or about $1,800, the next 2,500 marks and the third more than 5,000. When a man wanted his drink replenished, Fritz pressed a button, summoning a waiter from the cafe. But the players drank sparingly except for the hearty Yugoslav sailor who took his whiskey neat.

Studying individual styles, Doug concluded that the Yugoslav was a conservative player behind his camouflage of tipsy conviviality. He folded an open pair of queens when the Turk, flamboyant in a white linen suit and pink shirt, bet 1,000 marks on the last round of five-card stud on an ace-king high. The Turk stayed almost every hand. He bet heavily, often bluffing and cursing in French when he lost. One of the two Germans, a stout unsmiling business type, never played unless he had good cards and Doug dismissed him as a threat. The other German, thin, young and stony-faced, fingered his cards like a professional. He played patiently with sudden bursts of aggressive betting, and Doug decided he merited close scrutiny.

The man who wore an expensive felt hat left the game an apparent loser and his place was taken by Mr. Brooklyn. The American unaccountably dusted off the chair with a handkerchief, blew alternately on the fingernails of his right and left hands and sketched the Sign of the Cross at his chest. Doug made a mental note to monitor the superstitious New Yorker for possible telltale gestures. The American played less than he watched and Doug surmised that he was a man with limited funds who was content to wait for excellent cards before risking his money. The player Doug pegged as an Englishman turned out to be Irish and keenly observant of every move made at the table. When the Italian left the game, cramming a sheaf of bills into his wallet, Doug waited for a nod from the house man and then took the vacated chair between the blue-capped Yugoslav and the man from Dublin, who it turned out, hummed constantly, specializing in themes from Beethoven and Tchaikovsky.

Doug had decided to play a waiting game for a half hour or so until he had sorted out personal styles and habits more thoroughly, but on the second deal, a game of draw without opening requirements, he drew a pair of aces along with three minor miscellaneous cards. The lean young German opened for ten marks and attracted three calls. Doug raised the limit of the pot, 60 marks. Three men behind him dropped. The German and the three original callers met the raise.

All took three cards on the draw save the Turk who took but one. Doug, as was his custom, opened his hand card by card. First was the two of clubs. Second he saw the deuce of spades, then the two aces, giving him two pairs. When he squeezed the fifth and final card into view, he felt a jolt that raced through his system and stepped up the heart beat. It was as if he had swallowed a double shot of bourbon or inhaled deeply of nitrous oxide. While he remained outwardly impassive, his body set up a clamor and to quiet the interior turmoil, he palmed his neck, tilting his head slightly to the right. To an observer, Douglas Perry appeared to be in a quizzical, reflective mood, a man perhaps weighing the value of less-than-impressive cards. Actually elation gripped him.

The fifth card was the ace of hearts, giving him a full house, three aces and a pair of twos. Now all thoughts of a slow, unobtrusive entry into the game vanished like smoke. Instead he geared for combat, as totally and as fiercely absorbed as the deep-sea fisherman who feels a powerful tug on the line and knows he has hooked a marlin.

The young German, frowning over his cards, bet 350 marks, just a shade less than the size of the pot, thus signaling that he had improved his hand. Brooklyn called. The Turk, who had drawn but one card, called the 350 and raised 1,000 marks. The Irishman beside Doug folded his hand while humming the popular bar from Beethoven's Fifth. Doug studied the pot and players, called the required 1,350 marks and raised another 2,000. The pot now held nearly 6,000 marks.

The young German, coolly professional, tossed in his cards. Brooklyn, after prolonged hesitation, also folded. That left only the Turk. He restudied his cards, shrugged and pursed his lips, provoking an elaborate shift of facial scenery that would have done credit to an actor in the old nickelodeon movies.

"*Und noch Viertausend.*" The Turk called the 2,000 and raised 4,000.

Zap! Undressing the Turk, Doug saw mottled dark skin, flabby breasts, lint caught in a gummy belly button and a scattering of gray hairs in the pubic thatch.

At the same time he boosted his estimate of the Turk's hand from a straight to a flush. Mr. White Suit, drawing one card, had filled a flush, he guessed. He might, of course, have made a full house. However, Doug's aces full would top any hand short of a rare four-of-a-kind or an even more improbable straight flush. In games without wild cards, Doug never rated an opponent's hand higher than a full house. The few times he had lost to four-of-a-kind and the lone occasion when he bowed to a straight flush, he took the large losses without grumbling. Such extraordinary hands fell outside the bounds of normal play, and no gambler conceded their existence until he had been raised several times.

The pot held almost 12,000 marks. Doug counted the currency in his wallet. He had 6,500 marks left in cash and the $5,000 in American Express checks. He waved the checks at fat Fritz and turned to the Irishman.

"Ask him if I can use these travelers' checks to raise?"

The brief exchange in German slid down a negative chute. "He says it's up to White Suit. Players are not obliged to accept anything but German marks, but since only White Suit is involved, he may take the travelers' checks if he wishes."

"*Nein.*" The Turk waved the checks aside, thus ending the matter.

"Okay, so I'll raise what I can." Doug matched the Turk's last 4,000 marks and raised a final 2,500.

The Turk quickly tossed in two 1,000-mark notes and one for 500. They rose like sailplanes on a small current of air, hovered fitfully and slowly fluttered down to crown the heap of currency. The center of the table held more than 20,000 marks or about $9,000.

The room fell silent. The Irishman stopped humming. Dark splotches slowly spread at the armpits of the Turk's white-linen jacket. Through the curtained doorway came the muffled beat of dance music. Doug's own pulse quickened once again. This was that moment, that razor-thin slice of time, that instant before revelation, for which gamblers lived.

"Aces full." Doug spread his cards on the table, the two black deuces huddled beside three splendidly naked and regal aces.

"*Merde!*" The Turk fanned out his cards face up. He too had a full house, three jacks and two fives. He had run only a neck behind, but in poker the sole reward for players who finish second is chicken soup if they happen to have Jewish mothers.

Fat Fritz inspected the cards of both players, pointed his finger at Perry and took ten marks for the house. Doug needed both hands to scoop the money into his trough. One 100-mark note dropped to the floor and the Yugoslav retrieved it for Doug.

"You walk in from street and win big pot," he said in labored English, tipping his light blue cap. With his bushy blond hair and easy grin, he looked like an advertisement for Dutch Boy paint.

"Beginner's luck." Doug tossed off the gambler's bromide, but behind the casual facade victory messages raced to the body's outposts like electrical impulses shooting through a computer. Every nerve had gone on alert. He knew the signs. He had zoomed into his poker high, a psychic aerie reached only during the big money games. It wasn't the winning alone. His sensations would have been comparable, if less heady, had he lost to the sweating Turk. It was rather the risk, the suspense, the constant combat by which a man tested himself in hand after hand, alone without the usual advisors, subordinates, bosses or friends. It was the lure of the unknown, the instant exhilaration produced by good play. Let others seek the deceptive rush of cocaine. For Doug high-stakes poker did the job so thoroughly that three or four sessions a year sufficed to slake his desire for that other state of consciousness.

Snatched up to the poker heights by this swift action so early in the play, Doug sensed that, win or lose, he would be here until the game ended. He also knew that Kate had been more right than wrong. He came to the Cafe Monaco primarily because the gambling fever had struck and only secondarily to track the spoor of the elusive Marshall Ingersoll. He did not particularly like this lust to gamble in himself, but at least he admitted it. He hoped Kate would understand. He loved her as he had loved no other woman, and he would pay her tender attention tomorrow and the next day and the next and the next. But not tonight. This night he pursued his old temptress, the courtesan Lady of Chance.

Doug drew small, uninteresting cards on the next few hands, but then in a game of seven-card stud, he found himself with two kings in the hole augmented on the fourth card by a third king. He bet strongly through several rounds, encountered what turned out to be a spade flush held by the florid German businessman and wound up winning with another full house, kings over fours. As he drew in the 9,000-mark pot, he knew this would be one of those hot nights. The fever mounted.

Aside from the humming Irishman, whose repertoire ranged the masters, and the Yugoslav, who kept laughing and drinking, the players were a silent bunch. All but the Turk sat impassive, even grim, while Fat Fritz, the beefy dealer, wore a look of marbled indifference. His hands, however, were in perpetual efficient motion, gathering cards, shuffling, dealing, fingering the winner. The Turk tried to use his rubbery face as a medium of false advertising, but he lacked subtlety. He looked lugubrious with good cards and jubilant with bad ones and consequently fooled no one.

As his subconscious absorbed the nuances of play, Doug became aware of tensions beneath the surface. The Germans did not like the Turk who symbolized, despite his bankroll, the wave of "guest workers" who came to do West Germany's menial labor and stayed on with their pointed shoes, oily hair and alien chatter in the cafes. The dealer did not like the Irishman humming. Too private. The Irishman did not like the Yugoslav's laughter. Too loud. The American from Brooklyn did not like Doug. Too lucky.

After an hour's play, pastel-tinted German currency threatened to overflow the small bin in front of Doug. He guessed he was about $15,000 ahead. With studied unconcern, he placed his wallet on top of the cash, excused himself for a few minutes and left the room. He had two motives. He missed Kate and wanted to phone his apologies for leaving so hastily. He would tell her of his good fortune and say he'd be back for breakfast. Also he considered the move good psychological gamesmanship. A man who would leave a clutter of cash untended before eight strangers was bound to inspire awe and uncertainty. If he cared so little for money, would he not squander it in outrageous attempts to bluff? More subtlely, the move was calculated to suggest a naïve trust on his part, encouraging other players to take advantage of this innocent ready-for-the-shearing American.

Kate did not answer although the hotel operator rang the room repeatedly. Disappointed, Doug surmised she either refused to pick up the phone or she had gone out for a drink or a midnight stroll.

Returning to the game, he found his Yugoslav neighbor in a happy unbuttoned mood. He had just won a fat pot from Brooklyn who was busy blowing on his manicured nails to propitiate the gods of chance. Doug let several hands go by without participating, then bet 1,500 marks on a broken flush in a draw game. Two players dropped, but the German businessman called his bluff and won the pot with two small pairs. Doug hoped the sacrifice would lend him a reputation as a loose player.

For three hours his fortunes went up and down like a yo-yo. He drew consistently good cards and won thousands of marks on threes-of-a-kind, two straights and a flush, but he lost other thousands when rivals nosed him out on the last card of stud hands. The heavy action, matching anything he had experienced in major league poker, fueled his gambler's high. He was completely involved, his mind centered on the tactics and nuances of the game and the personalities of the players. Never did his thoughts stray from the green-felt field of combat and its cone of light shining through the haze of tobacco smoke. Not once did he think of computers, his company or the Katwar and only fleetingly of Kate herself. As the night wore on, he lost less than he won, and the currency in his trough gradually underwent a subtle change of color, fewer of the pale gray 100-mark notes and more of the beige 1,000-mark variety. At 3 A.M., when several men stood patiently outside the circle of light waiting to play, Doug guessed that he was more than $20,000 to the good.

The Turk, who had become the game's big loser, called for five-card stud at his turn as nondealing dealer. Fat Fritz dealt Doug a king in the hole and a ten up. The opening round drew only modest bets, no one raising the young German's 10 marks wagered on an ace. As his second up card, Doug drew a king and when the betting reached him, he raised 400 marks on his pair of kings. The young German, the Turk and the Yugoslav called, the others dropping out. With no apparent change on the next card, the German checked his ace and Doug bet 1,000 marks on his half-hidden pair of kings. The German called as did the Turk with a queen high and the Yugoslav with a nine high.

On the last card no one improved his hand except the Yugoslav, sitting to Doug's left, who paired an open four. His hand showed the pair of fours, an eight and a nine. Now high on the board, he looked at the other players, grinned, then tapped the table near his cards, indicating that he checked. The German and the Turk also checked.

When it came Doug's turn to act, alarms sounded. His intuition told him that the Yugoslav, a careful player, may have hit a second pair or perhaps three fours. He doubted the seaman would have stayed through the strong betting without a pair. Though his intuition told him to check, a sudden impulse seized him and he bet 1,500 marks. Perhaps the Yugoslav had stayed with an ace in the hole.

The seaman shoved back his blue cap, took a shot of whiskey and stared at the pot. It contained about 8,000 marks. He grinned at Doug once more, called the 1,500 marks and raised 5,000. The German and the Turk dropped.

Doug felt the trap snap shut. The Yugoslav had at least two pairs, maybe three fours. Doug had gone against the instinct and thrown in 1,500 marks on a hunch. Should he now call the 5,000? If he had one rule in this master game where psychology and chance danced their ceaseless ballet, it was that he never, but never, acted against intuition twice in a row.

With a shake of his head, Doug turned over his cards. Fat Fritz, the silent house man, pointed at the Yugoslav. Glowing in triumph, the sailor pulled in the money.

Had he run a bluff? While Doug would never know, he felt certain that the Yugoslav had checked a locked winning hand, then sandbagged him after Doug stepped out with his 1,500-mark bet. Had the man had a pair of fours from the start? Was a four the Yugoslav's first up card? Doug could not remember and the recognition of the memory lapse hit his fatigue button.

Suddenly he felt very tired. A glance at his wrist watch showed 3:15 A.M. All at once the poker high, so cherished for hours, collapsed like a pricked balloon. When he could no longer remember the sequence of cards, it was time to quit, no matter that he'd planned to play until the end. His decision made, his mind promptly veered elsewhere, to Kate, to the Katwar, to his mission here.

He looked at the convivial Yugoslav beside him. If he played here every time his freighter came to port, wouldn't he remember other players? Doug chanced a shot. "I'm quitting. You're way ahead. How about buying you a drink?"

The husky seaman, his shoulders like hawsers, sat back, stretched and yawned. "Yah, I'm tired. We go to bar for drink." He was a powerful man and while dormant violence slumbered beneath his sunny disposition, Doug judged him to be a friendly sort if not provoked.

Doug gathered up winnings that crammed his wallet to the bursting point, persuading him to transfer some of the bills to his pants pocket. He and the mariner departed under a mix of neutral and hostile stares. Only the Irishman, still humming his fragments from the classics, smiled a good-bye.

Doug and the seaman took seats on stools at the long bar where several inebriated spenders fed drinks to buxom hostesses. A number of couples swayed in pelvic togetherness on the darkened dance floor. Doug saw one of the dinner-jacketed bouncers signal a group of B-girls who were lounging in a booth. Two practitioners of the carnal arts, one with flaming red hair, promptly bore down on the winning poker players. Doug waved them off, but they persisted until the Yugoslav gave them each a twenty-mark bill, patted their rumps and told them to go away.

"I keep steady woman in Hamburg." He seemed to think his act of dismissal needed an explanation.

Doug ordered drinks, straight scotch for the seaman and vodka and tonic for himself, as they traded names and fragments of personal history. The Yugoslav said he was second mate on the *Gospic,* a cargo vessel plying between Dubrovnik and the ports of western Europe, chiefly Hamburg. He had sailed up the Elbe to Hamburg so many times a year that he considered the city a second home. His name, he said, was Kosto Gavrilovich. When he learned that Doug sold computerware in the United States, Kosto said that the *Gospic* was equipped with an American-made computer for navigation, engine room computations and sundry housekeeping chores.

But poker, not computers, forged their bond. Kosto, loquacious and afloat in alcohol, said he hit the Cafe Monaco at least once every voyage, kept "thousands of marks" ahead and never had cause to quarrel with the house. The Monaco ran the cleanest poker game in St. Pauli.

Kosto downed half his scotch at a gulp. "Doug, why you don't call my fours?" There was a sly tinge to his smile of triumph.

"Because, Kosto, you had three of them. Or maybe two pair."

"I had ace in hole." He beamed in pride, his blue cap tilted rakishly.

"No, you had me beat and you sandbagged. I watched you, Kosto. You play 'em close despite all that booze."

Kosto laughed, a single explosion that startled the bartender. "You figure me out, huh? Well, I figure you too."

"And what did you find?"

"Oh, no. Why tell? You come back one day. You easy to read sometimes. Not always." He spread his arms, a gesture of magnanimity. "But sometimes."

They gossiped about the game, ordered another round of drinks. Doug had metaphors for some of their gambling rivals. The Turk was a faulty space rocket. He made a great fuss just off the launching pad, then sputtered and dropped into the ocean.

Brooklyn was a groundhog, forever frightening himself with his own shadow and scurrying back into his hole. Kosto named the young German as the game's best player although he'd had poor cards all night. Doug agreed.

"I like you." Kosto slapped him on the back, a bearlike swipe that nearly knocked Doug off the stool. "Americans okay."

"You're all right yourself, Kosto." Doug saw his opening. "Have you played with many Americans here?"

"Oh yeah. Usually at least one in the game."

"I'm wondering whether a friend of mine from California ever played at the Monaco." He described Marshall Ingersoll as best he could, mentioning the slouch, the babylike skin and the peculiar languid manners.

"No, I don't remember man like him. When he play?"

"Oh, anytime this year."

"He drink much?" Kosto himself took another belt. The man could absorb an enormous amount of alcohol without losing control.

"No. But he has one habit at poker. Whenever he pulls a good hand, he clenches his jaw muscle. Like this." Doug demonstrated.

"Oh yeah!" Kosto's eyes widened in recognition. "Do I remember that guy. Yankee Jaw! I saved lots of money on account of him."

"When?" Doug went on the alert again.

"My last time here." Kosto thought. "October—about a month ago."

"Do you remember the date?"

Kosto reflected while taking another swallow of scotch. "A Tuesday night. Maybe twenty-four, twenty-five October."

Doug consulted a small plastic calendar from his wallet. "Tuesday, October 26?"

"Yeah, I think. He was here in August one night too. When he had good hand, his jaw went like that." Kosto imitated the muscle clenching.

Kosto explained that he first noticed the bulging hinge muscle when Yankee Jaw bet 1,000 marks on a lock pair of queens in five-card stud. Kosto called the bet to his regret, but learned his lesson. Thereafter he called Yankee Jaw or bet into him only when the telltale muscle failed to quiver. Other players who had failed to mark the singularity lost money to the American.

Doug took his personnel department's photograph of Ingersoll from his wallet and showed it to the freighter officer.

"What are you? Police?" Kosto frowned. For the first time, the big man's mouth had a hard set.

"No, I'm in computers like I said. But listen, Kosto, this guy pulled a job on me." He gave the Yugoslav a condensed version of the possible theft of the Katwar. "I'm trying to find out whether he brought a stolen chip here to Hamburg." He looked Kosto in the eyes. "Believe me, I have nothing to do with the police or any law-enforcement agency."

Kosto studied Doug, fingered the picture, then visibly relaxed. "Yah, that's the guy. He never quit doing it." He tensed his mandible muscle once more in exaggerated fashion, slapped Doug on the back and broke out laughing. "I save plenty money when Yankee Jaw bet."

So, Marshall Ingersoll had come to Hamburg late last month after flying from the United States to Zurich. And earlier in August, when Wetherill, the San José investigator, found that Ingersoll had flown to Munich. Of course, poker-playing in St. Pauli did not mean that Ingersoll called at the Schnelldaten office, but Doug felt sure now that he had. He became convinced for the first time that Ingersoll indeed had stolen the Katwar designs, sucking them electronically and invisibly over 2,500 miles from Princeton, New Jersey, to Sunnyvale, California. And Ingersoll had brought the chip's designs here to Hamburg and sold them to that shady gray-market operator, Ludwig Frischauer, he of the bald head and fluttery hands. While Doug had no proof of the sale, he had no doubt now that it had occurred.

"Aside from his jaw troubles," asked Doug, "was Ingersoll a good player?"

"*Comme ci, comme ça.*" The *Gospic* officer wobbled his right hand. "Not like you, Doug." Once again he thumped Perry on the back.

They downed another drink, talked of computers, ships, women and nations, shooed away another assault by satin-gowned hookers, exchanged home addresses, bought one final round, pledged lasting amity and staggered out to the sidewalk. Apparently it had rained heavily while they played, for the pavement was wet and the gutters still ran with water. Kosto vowed to protect Doug from robbers by sharing a taxi with him. At the entrance to the Vier Jahreszeiten they once more plighted friendship, this time of the eternal variety, a palship to be fortified by exchange of visits between Princeton and Dubrovnik, that Dalmatian princess city of walls, villas, gardens and limestone mountain. Then Kosto, bellowing good-byes in five languages, rode off to the harbor and his officer's berth aboard the *Gospic*.

In the elevator to the fourth floor room, Doug remembered Kate's threat to bar his entry with a chain lock. Would he have to plead through a doorway crack? He walked down the hallway to the room, fumbled for his key and unlocked the door. It swung open easily. So Kate had relented. He took off his jacket in the dark, not wanting to startle her with a sudden light, emptied his wallet onto a little table in the reception hall and scooped up the currency in both hands.

He would kiss her awake and baptize their love by showering her with some $20,000 in marks. Then he'd turn on the light so that she could rejoice with him in the fruits of victory.

He approached the bed, his way illumined by the first pink rays of sunrise coming through the window. He stopped. The puffy *Federbett,* spotless and unwrinkled, lay on top of a carefully made bed that had not been slept in. Kate was not in the room.

17

Kate Warfield sailed down the fourth-floor corridor like a sloop on a stormy reach. She was furious at Doug. He had dumped her in the hotel lobby in the middle of the night and taken off for some stupid poker game on the sleazy Reeperbahn. She wasn't his first love at all, but the "other woman" who ran a poor second to gambling. Or maybe she placed a mere third or fourth. Who knew what other addictions or indulgences had captured his desire? And the nerve of the man in deserting her so soon after that crushingly tender lovemaking high above the sunlit Alster lakes with their sailboats and regal swans. Callous, really. At least he could have seen her to their room and caressed her until she fell asleep. It's true he did offer to tuck her into bed, but of course she refused. So why didn't he persist and do it anyway? Truly shabby treatment. She recalled that summer night when she practically had to drag him away from the casino in Atlantic City. Would that become the pattern? For a man older than her father—and she became abruptly and unpleasantly aware of the age gap—Doug certainly acted immaturely at times. Also he was stubborn, insensitive and selfish.

She bore down on their room, then halted before the door without reaching for her key. Once inside, what then? She knew she couldn't sleep. She paced about, undecided, the smoldering fury flaring once more. What she needed was a good stiff nightcap. She retraced her steps, waited for an elevator, went down to the lobby and made her way to the Simbari bar.

Kate settled into a red leather armchair at one of the tables, oblivious of the admiring glances from men at the bar. She was well into a brandy and a bout of self-pity when she saw Klaus Bloch heading toward her table. The young investigator had an air of urgency.

"May I?" He placed his hand on the back of the chair opposite her.

"Of course, Buddy. Please sit down." She returned his formal little bow with a smile that taxed her. Although relieved to meet any acquaintance at this juncture, she was not in a hospitable mood.

"I've found something of possibly great importance." His intensity gave him an added dimension. Kate decided he actually was handsome in his trim controlled well-barbered way.

"Care for a drink, Buddy?"

"No thanks." He leaned forward and lowered his voice. "Hans and I discovered the Schnelldaten's additional space at Wirtsweg 62 is actually very large, the whole second floor. Tonight I've been following Ludwig Frischauer. He went home about six to the apartment he's renting near the lake in the Uhlenhorst district. He came out at eight carrying a piece of luggage and took a taxi back downtown. But instead of going to the office he went to Wirtsweg 62. . . . By the way, where is Mr. Perry?"

"Who knows?" She looked upward, beseeching the heavens. "To be honest, Buddy, he's playing poker. I believe he went to some place called the Cafe Monaco."

"That's too bad. This may be a critical night and I wanted instructions from Mr. Perry."

"Never mind about Doug. I'm in charge when he's off somewhere." She couldn't resist giving the "somewhere" a flavor of irresponsibility, of feckless cruising about. "So what's happening on Wirtsweg?"

"A lot of night work. Six men, including Frischauer, are up there right now. They appear to be in a hurry."

"How do you know. Were you there?"

"Not quite." Bloch's smile had a touch of self-deprecation. Kate boosted her appraisal from handsome to very attractive. "I have a point for surveillance across the street. Rental space, so to speak. I slipped the night watchman a hundred marks." As he told it, Bloch had set up a portable telescope, enabling him to see inside Schnelldaten's work space through a narrow aperture in pulled blinds. He could pick up parts of people and objects, enough to form a reasonable conjecture as to the whole. "They're obviously working fast. A deadline maybe?"

"Just what can you see there, Buddy?" He had Kate's total interest now.

"Sheets of heavy paper spread on tables. Also long computer printouts. Graphic designs of some kind."

"If they have my chip . . ." The mere thought acted like a transformer, converting her fury at Doug into anger at unknown men gathered in a warehouse at midnight. In both cases—one actual, the other potential—a violation of self was involved. "Come on, let's go." She craved action. "I have to see this myself." She tossed off the remainder of the brandy and slipped a ten-mark note under the glass.

"Miss Warfield." A note of restraint. He failed to rise along with Kate. "I'd rather not go back there without Mr. Perry."

"Come on, Buddy." She prompted his elbow. "I can take care of myself. We'd waste a lot of time trying to find Doug."

Bloch obliged reluctantly. Whatever his political beliefs, he obviously remained a conservative on those battlefields of feminism where the sexes deployed their tanks and lobbed their shells. They walked to a nearby parking garage, climbed into his black Volkswagen and rode toward the riverfront. Above the city's modestly elevated profile, steeples and towers pierced tumbling night clouds and fingered a few pale stars. Bloch drove about a mile to the district where Wirtsweg was located. A dimly lit area of warehouses, small factories and show windows featuring marine supplies, machinery and electrical equipment, it included high wooden fences, well splashed with theatrical posters, that bordered construction sites. Crowded with wholesalers and jobbers by day, the district was all but deserted at night.

As they crossed Wirtsweg, Bloch pointed to a man pacing the sidewalk halfway down the block. "They've posted a lookout." He turned sharp right into an alley and drove to the middle of the block, parking behind the building where he had stationed himself for observation.

It was an aged narrow brick warehouse seven stories high and topped by a steeply slanted tile roof. The night watchman, a bony old man with bad teeth, occupied a cubicle off the stairs leading from the alley. Buddy Bloch introduced Kate as his assistant and handed the custodian another twenty-mark bill.

"Güten Abend." The old man had a look of genial greed. He waved them into his dark dominion.

Picking her way behind Buddy, Kate circled great coils of marine rope smelling of tar, hemp and brine. It was a pleasant rich odor, evocative of thriving ocean commerce and therefore comforting to Kate on this dubious midnight mission to an unpeopled district of a foreign city.

"Seven floors crammed with this stuff," offered Buddy. "Must be a couple of acres of rope and rigging." Also hawsers, cordage, tackle, bowlines, cord, painters, wire rope.

A concrete ramp led to the second floor and more cylinders of cordage. Now the smell was heavier, mustier, more pervasive. Bloch led the way to one of three front windows of the narrow old building. Had the place shrunk in its latter years like the frail residents of nursing homes? Bloch had wiped a corner of the dust-coated glass of the tall, uncurtained window to permit use of his telescope. The instrument stood on shiny metal legs, black snout peering outward like a creature from space.

The building across the street was dark save for bright lights on the second floor. Venetian blinds had been dropped and closed at all four windows so that no one could see in despite the blaze of illumination thrusting through cracks in the blinds and streaming out the sides. The one exception was the window directly opposite the one where Bloch had mounted his telescope. There the blind failed to reach the windowsill by several inches, permitting observation of a thin band of objects and activity within.

Buddy Bloch squinted through the eyepiece of his scope, made several adjustments and turned the instrument over to Kate. "Orthoscopic," he said. "The four lenses give good definition. . . . Of course, you only see a slice of whatever's going on. The fluttery hands belong to Frischauer."

Frustration saddled Kate the moment she placed her right eye to the instrument. She could see hands, parts of shirt-sleeved arms, a slice of a chair, papers strewn over a table top, the flash of a hand ring, a sampling of the dingy rear wall and the spigot of a water cooler, but she could make little sense of what she saw nor could she imagine the whole from this layer of random parts. It was somewhat like having a fine orchestra seat for a play oddly being performed behind a wall fitted with a gun slit. Or for Kate, a puzzle fan, she was being shown a few scattered pieces of a jigsaw layout and challenged to identify the complete picture—Office Party, Political Campaign Headquarters, Midnight Inventory or White-collar Crime?

But Kate, never a quitter, kept her eye pressed to the scope. As she became accustomed to the light, distance and fragmented images, she noted a detail here, another there and began to make informed guesses as to the missing segments. She saw a pair of hands at what looked like a keyboard and filled in, to her satisfaction, a computer terminal with display screen. She saw a dark, rounded object which under concentrated mental focus became a spool of magnetic tape. Thick sheets of paper held some kind of writing, but when she shut out other visual stimuli she saw that it wasn't writing, but sketches. A longer look confirmed her conjecture.

"Chip layouts," she said, without taking her eye away.

"What's that?" Klaus Bloch stood in the dark beside her. His own eyes scanned the sky. He wanted to be ready to yank Kate back from the window in the event the foaming clouds should roll away, letting moonlight illumine deeply shadowed Wirtsweg and its buildings. He never lost awareness of the bulky lookout who paced up and down the sidewalk across the way.

"Chip layouts, a bunch of them." She wished she could magnify each detail by a factor of ten. "Kind of like blueprints. They're drawings you'd use to manufacture a chip, for instance."

"Would you use them during a coaching session?" Bloch asked while maintaining his vigil.

"Sure, Buddy. Just what's going through my mind. If Frischauer sold our chip, he may have people instructing the buyers."

"And if they're working this late," added Bloch, "they may be under time pressure. Time to leave maybe."

"Yeah. . . . Wait a second . . . Holy Jesus!" She had halfway anticipated what she thought she saw, but the realization came as a shock. "That one layout describes a hunk of the Katwar. I can't be sure because it was only held up for a few seconds and it's some distance off. Still, I'd swear that's the piece where the input latch stores data in the RAM. . . . The thieving bastards."

Kate took her eye from the scope and straightened up, ready for action. She peered at the lighted floor across the street, took in the guard below at a glance and swung to face Bloch.

"That's my chip those people are messing with." She felt invaded, defiled, as though someone had broken into her apartment and ransacked it.

Bloch reflected, frowning. "I wonder . . ."

"Let's go over there and break it up." Outrage gripped her.

"No, Miss Warfield. That could be dangerous. This is the gray market, remember. They may be armed. If they're Soviet agents, as Carlos Rey suspected, they're almost sure to carry guns."

"Doesn't scare me." She could not imagine anyone actually shooting her. That was the stuff of movies and paperback thrillers, in no way connected to real life and Kate and computers and ordinary people like Buddy Bloch.

"Well, it worries me." Bloch drew her away from the window. "I don't carry a gun. Our laws are very strict."

"So what do you propose?" Her challenge was defiant.

Buddy Bloch proposed to escort her back to the hotel, then return and maintain the surveillance until the men left. He would follow them in his car and report back to Kate and Doug at the hotel when the targets settled down somewhere. Behind the words lay his thinly veiled conviction that it would be foolhardy, indeed disloyal, to act now without Perry's approval and direction. This was man's, not woman's, work.

"I'm not going back to the hotel." Although her fleeting pose parodied intransigence, she was nonetheless determined on her course. "Don't you understand, Buddy? That's *my* chip they're pirating."

"Still, I think the sensible thing . . . Now what's that?" He pointed to the street and drew Kate close to the dusty pane. A taxicab rolled down Wirtsweg and halted in front of the building opposite them. The guard ducked into the entrance. At once three men wearing topcoats, one carrying a suitcase, hurried out and entered the cab. The car's overhead light flashed on as the rear door opened, making the passengers clearly visible. One, nervous and young, smoked a cigarette. Another was hatless and bald. The third, a heavy, rather shapeless sort, adjusted a snap-brim hat.

"The bald-headed one is Frischauer," said Bloch.

"I'll bet the young one is the chief technical coach. Hey, the sloppy guy seems familiar." Kate concentrated, putting her memory to work in that odd shuffling of images, fragments of thought and tenuous associations that often succeeds brilliantly and inexplicably within seconds and sometimes meanders fitfully for months without resolution. Hadn't she seen a picture of him? Who had it? Oh yes, Tony Canzano. Tony had shown her a picture of the Washington computer consultant. "I think . . . my guess is it's Otis Kramer. Remember? Doug told you about him."

"How certain are you?" The light had stayed on but a few seconds.

"So-so. I've never seen him, only a picture."

The taxi moved off with a smooth meshing of gears. In a moment the red taillights vanished around the first corner.

"Damn." Kate brooded at the window. "I'd have given a year's pay to follow them. I'll bet it was Kramer." Once more her anger at Doug flashed. Had he been here, he could have made the identification with ease. Of all the nights to go gambling!

"At least we can follow the others." Klaus Bloch took her arm. "My guess is they're about to leave too."

The building across the street put an exclamation point to his guess. Most of the lights went out, leaving the second floor veiled in a single ghostly light.

Bloch led Kate at a fast walk through the great cylinders of marine rope down the cement ramp to more hairy coils and the metal cubicle of the night watchman.

Bloch, only half pausing, spilled a few liters of German and pressed more currency into the hand of the old man who responded with a grin of happy venality.

"I told him to dismantle my telescope and keep it for me." Bloch and Kate scrambled into his black Volkswagen. He started the engine and drove back up the alley to the first side street, extinguished the headlights, then turned left and moved slowly to Wirtsweg where he halted just shy of the intersection so they could keep No. 62 in view. One light still burned on the second floor and the guard had renewed his beat in front of the building.

"They're still there, but I'm sure they'll move out soon," said Bloch.

"Kramer!" She boiled at the thought. "Who do you suppose the other guys are?"

"Rey told Mr. Perry that he guessed it was the Soviets who bought the chip. Probably. At least it's a reasonable guess. If we can tail them when they leave, we'll have a chance of finding out for certain."

Kate peered down the dark street. She wanted to attack the strolling guard, rush into the building, lash out with her fists and rip up the tapes and papers. "Doug's visit this morning must have tipped off Frischauer that he was being watched."

"Right. You can bet Frischauer wasn't fooled for long by that fake seizure." Bloch kept the motor running, the gears in neutral. "So if he and Kramer were running an instruction school for the buyers at No. 62, they would want to wind it up as soon as they could. That would explain this late night session. Maybe we're seeing a split, Kramer and Frischauer and their technician going their way and the buyers going theirs." The motor puttered along like a gabby neighbor, a friendly sound on the empty shadowed street.

"Which means the guys we'll try to follow are the ones with the designs for my chip." A rational deduction, as logical as the computer's central processing unit or her own Katwar, but tonight she was in no mood for the strict causality of her profession. She wanted action, any kind of action. She'd rather cruise haphazardly around the city looking for Otis Kramer than sit here patiently and quietly. And where was Doug at this hour? Playing cards with strangers. Damn him.

"Here we go." Bloch pointed to his right. A blue sedan rolled toward them along Wirtsweg. Bloch promptly put the Volkswagen in reverse and backed into deeper shadows a dozen yards to the rear. The sedan crossed the intersection at considerable speed. Kate noted the driver in overcoat and hat, but saw no passengers. Bloch moved their car back to the corner as soon as the sedan passed. "BMW," he said, triggering Kate's image of Doug's BMW at home and another round of hostile thoughts of her lover. Lover? The word grated.

The sedan stopped beside the guarded building. At once the last lights went out on the second floor. The guard opened a car door. Two figures emerged from the building, each carrying light luggage, apparently dispatch cases. They ducked into the sedan. The guard slammed the door and got in beside the driver. The BMW took off.

"You didn't tell me one was a woman." The swirl of a skirt had caught her eye.

Bloch wheeled the Volkswagen into Wirtsweg, following the red lights of the sedan. "I didn't know." He was accelerating swiftly without headlights.

"You just assumed they were all men." She was about to accuse the German investigator of sexism when she realized that she had made the same mistake. Now she recalled that when the glitter of a ring was seen through the telescope, the ring-bearing hand was quite feminine. With a hint of gloss at the nails? Kate, in her testy fractured mood would have brooded over this example of brainwashing by the dominant male culture were it not for the blind rush of the Volkswagen. They were traveling at an alarming speed for a car without headlights.

18

Klaus Bloch gave the dark street ahead his full attention, driving in top gear with his hands at ten and two o'clock of the wheel, his neck craned forward and his mouth set in a hard lipless line. Warehouses, plants and office buildings flew by, great fluid hulks slipping through the night under a moonless sky. The few stars had fled. A storm menaced. Black clouds swirled, sculpting gargoyles, raging rivers, ebony brontosaurs with reptilian tails. The small car rattled and bounced. Kate was thrown back against her seat when Bloch suddenly accelerated, narrowly beating a truck that surprised him at an intersection. The truck driver vented his outrage in a blast of horn that echoed down the lonely street.

The BMW turned into Ost-West Strasse, a well-lighted thoroughfare with a goodly amount of traffic for 2 A.M. on a weekday night. Bloch switched on his headlights and maneuvered his car to the rear of a commercial van. "Keep your eye on the BMW," he ordered Kate. They were perhaps a hundred yards behind it. Soon the blue sedan turned into Holstenwall, one of the arteries ringing the downtown section, increased its speed as it curved around toward the Alster lakes. Just shy of the twin bridges between the lakes, the speeding car swung to the left, wheeled through a plaza and wound up on Rothenbaumchaussee, a wide avenue leading north and connecting with highways that ran through the soft lowlands of Schleswig-Holstein as far as the Danish border.

Bloch dropped back while navigating the connections to Rothenbaumchaussee, then spotted the BMW again and maneuvered his Volkswagen two vehicles to the rear of the target car.

He cursed in German. "I wish I dared get closer. We've got to get the number on that license plate."

They rolled northward through the blackening night, passing two universities on the left and the large Rotherbaum sports complex with soccer field and tennis courts on the right. Once more the BMW increased its speed. Neither Kate nor Bloch spoke. The German drove with full concentration while Kate focused on the BMW, making sure she kept it always in view.

At the head of the larger Alster lake, the blue car switched onto a main highway, the Alsterkrugchaussee. Now the BMW accelerated yet again, running north at about seventy miles an hour.

"Not much doubt now," said Bloch. "They're heading for the airport. It's just a few kilometers further."

Suddenly the sedan braked sharply and turned left into a side street. Bloch switched off his lights just before following into the turn and as a result missed a parked car by inches.

The blue BMW, slackening speed only enough to avoid crashing, roared down the narrow street of modest stone houses, turned again with a screech of tires and vanished from view. Bloch flicked on his headlights for a moment, negotiated the turn on the verge of disaster but managed to keep the Volkswagen upright. Taillights of the car ahead appeared once more as it raced along a curving road lined with airline cargo offices, some of which had night lights that silhouetted desks, chairs and hat racks like sentries of a sleeping army. Taillights of the sedan again disappeared as it turned another corner.

When the Volkswagen swerved in pursuit, still without lights, Bloch no sooner straightened the wheels than he was forced to jam on the brakes, bringing the car to a jolting halt.

"Verdammt!"

The blue BMW had stopped at the end of a short truncated

street perhaps a mile distant from the lighted terminal building and directly in front of an open chain-link gate, part of the metal mesh fence topped by three strands of barbed wire, that apparently circled the airport. Thirty or forty yards from the gate, on the circular apron at the beginning of a runway, sat a two-engine propeller-driven airliner, wing lights winking, passenger windows darkened, props revolving, headlights aimed down the runway. Apparently poised for take-off, it nevertheless had its stairway lowered.

A man in a windbreaker jacket held the chain-link gate open and three people, one of them a woman, raced through heading for the airplane. Two carried dispatch cases and their arms flapped wildly like broken-winged birds.

Bloch was about to leap out when the BMW, which had backed up and turned around, vaulted forward with a cat's howl of rubber and shot past the Volkswagen. If Bloch had not slammed his door shut again, the sedan would have smashed the door and mangled his arm. As it was, the BMW all but took the paint off the Volkswagen's fenders. Bloch swiveled around, tried to read the license plate of the fleeting car, but the numbers blurred like ink in the dark.

Kate meanwhile bolted from the other side of the Volkswagen and ran toward the gate, about fifty yards distant. But the man at the gate now threw it shut with a clanging of metal and ran to the airliner. Reaching the entrance, Kate grabbed the metal handle and twisted. It failed to open. She rattled the gate, put her fingers through the opening in the mesh and fumbled at the closing mechanism. Nothing happened. When slammed shut, the gate had locked automatically. Bloch, arriving a few steps behind Kate, also tried to force an entry but with no more success.

Their chase brought to a rude halt in an isolated wing of the airport, they could only stand and peer through the high mesh fence like children barred from a party. They saw four people run to the airliner, rush up the steps and disappear inside. Immediately the stairway ramp folded into the plane, the two propellers went into high spin and the plane began to roll down the runway. Headlights lanced the way. Soon the craft fled into the sky, wing tip and belly lights winking like fireflies, and was swallowed by the night. Black clouds heaved eastward in the plane's wake. Lightning flashed on the far horizon.

"I caught the letters on the fuselage—CCCP," said Kate. "Russian, right?"

"Right. How about the number? I thought I saw 87321."

"Yeah, 873—I didn't get the last two."

"Let's get to a phone." Bloch tugged at her arm. "I've got a night-duty friend in the tower." They ran to the car.

He swung the small vehicle around and headed back toward the main thoroughfare. "Obviously, it was all arranged and timed to avoid going through exit procedures at the terminal."

"Do the Soviets fly into Hamburg?"

"No regular run, but now and then they come nonsked. Trade delegations, sports teams, conventions, stuff like that." He looked to both sides as he drove, searching for a phone booth. "The timing of that getaway had to be right on the button. The plane couldn't wait too long or the tower would begin bugging the pilot."

"And someone had to handle the gate from inside."

"Right. Plenty of advance work for that operation."

Returning on the Rothenbaumchaussee, speeding toward the heart of the city, Bloch spotted a phone booth near an entrance to the Rotherbaum sports complex. He parked at the curb.

"You've got a decision." He turned to Kate. "This is now a case for the police, and my friend at the airport tower will report it unless I cook up another story. Do you want the Hamburg police in on this?"

"That's for Doug to decide." Thinking of him for the first time since they left the warehouse with its tarry smell of ship's rigging, she again felt anger. Gambling in some seedy joint on a night like this. The gall, the irresponsibility.

"He's not available. I need to know right now." Bloch fingered the door handle.

"Then no." Pure intuition. "No police." She didn't even bother pretending to herself that sequential thought played a part.

"Okay." Buddy trotted across the avenue to a public phone. She watched as he dropped in two coins and dialed.

The long-threatening storm hung over the city like a depression. Kate herself felt dispirited even though the chase had set her adrenalin flowing. Not much doubt now that designs for her Katwar were flying east on tumbling clouds, a saddening thought yet one rimmed with maroon, her color for pride. Sure, pride. Hey, how about that? The once pudgy awkward and embarrassed thirteen-year-old, that numbers and computer freak, had grown up within a few years and produced a chip that the whole world wanted. People stole, lied and cheated for it. Now Big Ivan, that vast superpower, had contrived a whole intricate operation to filch it. Of course, that meant all manner of complications: police, FBI, perhaps West German and Interpol agents. Who knew where it all might end? A far cry from the fun and games that day they cele-brated her breakthrough at Princeton Dataflo with champagne and grass. Kate brooded as the first drops of the advancing storm splatted on the pavement and nearby trees began swaying like drunken dancers.

Bloch remained at the telephone for many minutes, apparently making several calls. When he returned through the rain on the run, he started the car and drove off at once.

"That was an Antonov 32, CCCP No. 87321, two turbo-prop engines, short-to-medium range." He paused to regain his breath. "Its flight plan to Moscow calls for a refueling stop in Warsaw. It's carrying the Russian national gymnastic team that took part in the European championships here the last two days. I should have remembered. I'd read about it in the papers."

"What about the wait at the end of the runway."

"My friend Stefan, one of the controllers, says the Antonov pilot suspected electric troubles and spent a quarter of an hour at the end of that runway checking it out." Rain rattled on the car roof. Buddy Bloch drove as swiftly as the slick roadway permitted. "I woke up one of my partners. He's going to check the airport, the *Hauptbahnhof* and the bus terminal for any signs of Frisch-auer and Kramer, either together or alone. Not much chance, but we have to try." He pressed the accelerator. "If only we'd got-ten that plate number."

"And where to now?" Kate rubbed her hands in the warm draft from the heater. With the sudden downpour, the temperature had plummeted.

"First to Frischauer's apartment. Then I want to pay a visit to Ute Kranz."

He wheeled the small car across the Kennedy bridge at the foot of the large Alster lake and into the Uhlenhorst residential district as water streamed over the windshield and the wipers beat a swift tattoo. He pulled up before a venerable stone mansion that had been converted to apartments. They ran through the rain to the portico and Bloch pressed the button of No. 4. He rang repeatedly without response, then thumbed the button of the superintendent's flat. This did bring an answer after a number of rings. A head protruded from a basement window and aimed a grouchy protest their way. Bloch's twenty-mark note appeased the super, a grizzled oldster with a bad cough, who moderated his complaint into a kind of peevish conversational badminton, the super tapping back Buddy's questions in short tart sentences.

"As I expected," said Buddy, when they regained the shelter of the car. "Frischauer didn't come back after he left at eight with the suitcase. It's a furnished apartment, two months' rent in advance, that Frischauer leased two months ago. He'll never return now."

Bloch drove through the Hohenfelde and St. Georg districts into a working-class section near the main railroad station. As they stopped for a traffic light, Kate said she thought the car behind, a brown Opel sedan, may have been following them. No, said Buddy, that car had just turned into the street. Don't worry, he added, he was monitoring the rearview mirror. But Kate did worry. Somehow that brown Opel did not fit a normal pattern. As they drove through the city, the storm passed to the south, turning the sky from black to mottled gray. The rain stopped, but the chill remained, enclosing them once again in an ordinary damp cold November night, far from the summerlike fluke of the previous day.

Ute Kranz lived in a modern four-story brick apartment complex at 26 Danziger Strasse across from two Portuguese restaurants. The area behind the huge railroad terminal was rough and brash, filled with noisy bars, pornographic shops and small cheap hotels where brassy hookers, lounging in doorways, bargained with their johns. By contrast, Fräulein Kranz's building opened onto a rustic courtyard that held dozens of small gardens cultivated by tenants in the growing season. Her apartment occupied the first floor off one of several entrance hallways.

She opened her door after a half dozen rings and appeared only mildly surprised to see them. Though quickly armed and apprehensive, Fräulein Kranz gave a simultaneous impression of shyness and vulnerability as if her defenses were made of eggshell and would shatter at the first unkind word. A scarf, binding her straw-colored hair, was tied beneath her chin, giving her an aspect of innocence. She wore a stylish housecoat.

The entry into her parlor was less by invitation than by Ute

Kranz's retreat, for Bloch had planted one foot firmly inside the door. A lighted floor lamp revealed a tastefully decorated room with hand-tooled ottoman, a deep leather armchair and a mauve-velvet love seat. Kate and Bloch sat side by side on the love seat facing Fräulein Kranz in the armchair.

"I suppose this is about Schnelldaten." Ute Kranz spoke English. She folded her hands, the brightly polished nails lying like scattered cherries in her lap.

"Yes," said Bloch. "Since I came to your office with Mr. Steelman Bishop . . ."

"No need for that," she interrupted, with a sad smile. "I know his real name is Douglas Perry. And I suppose this is Miss Kate Warfield, the genius who invented the ciphering chip?"

Bloch sat dumbfounded. Kate preened. "Invent might be too strong," she said, "but I did have a lot to do with it, Miss Kranz."

"I know you did." Again that shy private look. "I know a lot about you and Mr. Perry and Princeton Dataflo, and I'm sure I know why you're here. I expected you sooner or later."

No need to smash the eggshell defenses, Kate realized. This woman would crack them from within. Strangely, although Kate had known her but a few moments, she trusted Ute Kranz.

"I think I can tell you most of what you want to know." Fräulein Kranz got to her feet. "But first, let's have some cakes and coffee. It's almost four in the morning."

Buddy Bloch, accustomed to battering his way through sullen opposition, was so disarmed that he merely gaped at her. Kate offered polite thanks. Recovering and fearing a stratagem of some kind, Bloch followed the woman down a short hallway to the kitchen where indeed she put on a pot of coffee. He lingered at the door, chatting about Hamburg and the weather.

Not until she had wheeled a dark wooden cart into the parlor and served coffee, cream, sugar and date-and-almond cakes did Ute Kranz begin to talk.

"You see, Herr Bloch, I knew who you were yesterday within a few minutes after you left." She sipped at her coffee. "Herr Frischauer said at once that he thought the American was Douglas Perry of Princeton Dataflo. We'd seen pictures in the trade papers. He had me check the hotels. I started with the best, of course, and found Herr Perry registered at the Vier Jahreszeiten. On a hunch, Ludwig asked me to try a Kate Warfield at the same hotel and so I found that you too were registered." She smiled at Kate. "I have no hesitancy in telling you all I know. For one thing, I don't like chicanery. For another, Herr Frischauer dismissed me with a month's pay at five o'clock this—yesterday—afternoon, so my only loyalty is to myself."

"Schnelldaten is finished?" asked Bloch.

"*Kaputt*. I saw it coming. The Rambachstrasse office lease ends next Monday, and when I mentioned renewal several times Frischauer put me off."

"How about Wirtsweg 62?" Bloch had taken out a pen and notebook.

"Oh, you know about the large space? Yes, that lease also expires soon—on 1 December. No move was made to renew that either."

"Frischauer left his apartment with a suitcase last night," said Bloch. "Do you know where he went?"

"No." Fräulein Kranz passed the date-and-almond cakes. "But I imagine he is leaving or has left Germany. Switzerland perhaps. Or maybe . . . he knows the Azores Islands. My best guess would be Brazil. He has a brother in São Paulo."

"You talk like he's a fugitive," said Kate. "From what?"

"I think Ludwig is either running from you or he's running from the law. I think he has been dealing in stolen computer parts. I can't prove that. I have no evidence, but in my heart I believe it." Ute Kranz finished her coffee and tapped a cigarette from a pack. "Let me tell you what I know and then you can ask questions." She lit the cigarette and savored the smoke while exhaling. "Frischauer opened the Schnelldaten office in Hamburg early this year. He says he's from Stuttgart, but had no confirming papers that I saw. I joined him in May in answer to an ad for secretarial help. Right from the start he was secretive about everything. He placed most of his own calls and didn't want me listening when he picked up from me after an incoming call."

Ute Kranz spoke calmly and quietly, yet with a sense of relief as if she were happy to unburden herself. She smoked steadily, one hand supporting the elbow of her smoking arm. "The curious thing was that I had no books to keep, nothing to keep track of. There wasn't any inventory. All I did was pay the rent, answer the phone and type formal business letters that he'd dictate. Queer letters. They never named a specific product. It was always 'the part you referred to' or 'the component you are looking for.'" She described this gossamer operation at some length.

"In August a Mr. Harvey Ryerson of New York showed up at the office. As soon as he came on the scene, everything speeded up. The space on Wirtsweg was rented, we worked longer hours, and people, some from the United States, came and went. Since I had to know what was going on to be of any use, Frischauer told me that he had obtained rights to a new miracle enciphering chip that would make Schnelldaten a lot of money when he sold it. Then came that day in September when the papers and television carried the news, Miss Warfield, about you and Mr. Perry refusing to sell your security chip to the rulers of San Luis in Central America."

Ute Kranz addressed Kate exclusively now, almost as if Bloch had been whisked from the room. The day the San Luis story broke, she said, Frischauer sat down with her for a long talk, explaining that in the history of science and technology "important advances often strike two great minds at the same time." Such was the case with the fantastic security chip that Harvey Ryerson had brought to Schnelldaten from a mysterious "inventor recluse," never named, who lived somewhere in the United States.

Frischauer, she related, sent out news over the "European computer *Flüsterpropaganda*" of the availability of the super-cryptographic chip. Soon this word on the grapevine was picked up by a Finnish company named Vaasa, A.G., which bid high for the part—in the neighborhood of $4,000,000, she heard—and in early October a company of Finns arrived to tape instructions and receive coaching on building the chip from Ryerson and other American computer experts. It was her understanding that the Finns completed their lengthy instruction course this week and would fly home to Helsinki today or tomorrow.

"I was suspicious of Frischauer and Schnelldaten for some time," she concluded, "but not until Mr. Perry and Mr. Bloch appeared at the office did I come to believe definitely that Frischauer was dealing with a stolen invention although just how one steals such a thing is beyond me."

"Believe me, the way it's done is very tricky," said Kate.

"How do you know the buyers were Finns?" asked Bloch.

"I was told so and I saw the three Finnish passports one morning when Frischauer had me log in the date—names, addresses—for the office file."

"Did you ever meet them?"

"No. They never came to the Rambachstrasse office. They worked out of the Wirtsweg loft."

"Did you ever see any correspondence from Finland about them or letters to them?"

"No . . . why? Do you doubt they were Finns?"

Bloch shrugged without replying. Instead he steered the conversation to Ryerson. Had he been here steadily since August? How did she know he brought over the security chip designs? How did she know that was his real name? Where was he right now?

"Right now he's at the Europäischer Hof on Kirchenallee." Ute Kranz obviously disliked Bloch's prosecutor's manner, but she appeared to answer without hesitation. "He's been in and out of here since August, steadily here for the last few weeks. As for the chip designs, and who brought them, I only know what Frischauer told me. About his name, let me tell you what happened."

Her story came with a blush or two, some laughter and the smoking of several cigarettes. She said that Ryerson, soon after arriving, asked her out for dinner and dancing, but since she had a steady man then, she proposed that a friend, Carla, accompany him. Carla and Ryerson hit it off and wound up sleeping together several nights a week. One night after considerable drinking, Ryerson slept soundly, but Carla found herself wakeful and fidgety. She got out of bed to make herself some tea. She saw a tan wallet lying on the floor and became curious since the wallet she'd seen Ryerson handle many times was black. Looking idly through the tan pocketbook, she found papers and cards in the name of Otis Kramer. One laminated card even bore Ryerson's photograph along with birth date, residence and other identification for "Otis Kramer." Another card, frayed and old, appeared to class Kramer as an official of some U.S. Government agency. Carla placed the tan wallet beside the black one in the inner pocket of the jacket hanging in her closet. She told Ute of her discovery, but never mentioned it to Ryerson-Kramer, and the next week ceased dating him. "She became frightened. Carla's a cautious one."

"Did you tell Frischauer about the dual identity?" asked Bloch.

"No, never." She was fussing at the tea cart, stacking plates and saucers, brushing crumbs into a neat mound. "I was very suspicious, of course, and I thought of going to the police."

"Why didn't you?" asked Kate.

"What would I say?" Fräulein Kranz appealed with her soft

eyes. "Then too, my job paid very well and I didn't want to lose it. You understand?"

"What was Carlos Rey's connection with all this?" Bloch asked it with an air of testiness. He sensed an unspoken empathy between the two women.

"Nothing at all that I know of. He tried to buy the chip for a client of his, but he was too late. Frischauer already had sold it to the Finns and they weren't interested in selling or leasing to anyone."

"Did you ever hear the name Marshall Ingersoll?" Kate locked eyes with Fräulein Kranz.

"Marshall Ingersoll." The secretary repeated the name slowly as if the sound might tap her memory. "No, I don't believe so."

Kate described the Bytex executive, tall, blond, smooth, babylike skin, languid manners. "An American from California."

"No. I don't recognize the name or the description." She appeared to be quite straightforward. Indeed, Kate had the feeling that Fräulein Kranz's fragile defenses might self-destruct under any attempt at deceit. "Of course," she added, "several Americans were brought over by Ryerson-Kramer, but they worked over on Wirtsweg and I never saw them or heard their names."

Bloch questioned for another half hour, plowing old ground without turning up any new information of significance. At the conclusion, he offered Fräulein Kranz 500 marks for inconveniencing herself at this odd hour. She declined politely but firmly. She was, she said, only too glad to help a woman whose prize invention had been stolen. She escorted them to the door, bidding them good-bye with the same shy vulnerable look Kate had noted upon entering. "Call me again if I can help," she said as she closed the door.

Full daylight greeted them as they walked to the parked Volkswagen. It was after six o'clock and already the streets of this workers' district were coming alive and some of the neighborhood storekeepers were opening their doors. A stiff chill wind blew from the north, flicking at the damp pavements and promising a raw day under dull gray skies.

Buddy Bloch dropped Kate at the entrance of the Vier Jahreszeiten. He would check in at his office and return for the eight o'clock breakfast with Perry, Kate and Hans Engen.

Kate rehearsed her opening line as she took the elevator to the fourth floor and walked down the corridor to the room she shared with Doug. She felt torn. On the one hand, she was bursting with news and wanted to deliver it in a fine shower of sparks. On the other, the indignity of Doug's desertion still galled her. After a quick tussle, she decided on her line: "You bastard!"

She unlocked the door and stood in the small reception hall. The main room was darkened, the drapes drawn. Looking in, she saw Doug asleep, huddled on one side of the wide bed. A note on hotel stationery had been affixed to the doorway with Scotch tape: "Sweet Kate, Open your luggage, the plaid carry-on. Present for you. Love, Doug."

When she pulled the bag from the shelf of the closet and opened it, she found herself gazing at a pastel sea of money, marks of all denominations. Another note crested the swell of currency: "Sweetheart, I won about $20,000. This half's yours. Spend it in sybaritic living. I love you deeply. INGERSOLL WAS HERE! Doug. P.S. Wake me when you come in."

When she pulled the *Federbett* off him and punched him awake, she changed her rehearsed line. What she said was: "Doug, you bastard, I love you."

19

The breakfast meeting of the two Germans and the two Americans in the hotel's Haerlin restaurant stretched through half the morning under the ministrations of a primly efficient waitress. They drank countless cups of coffee to drown Doug's pounding headache, the gray legacy of his drinking bout with Kosto Gavrilovich, the bottomless Yugoslav, and to revive Klaus Bloch and Kate after a sleepless night. Only Hans Engen escaped the look of battered luggage. He looked as fresh as the new rose in his buttonhole.

They devoted an hour to swapping information gained from Cafe Monaco, the surveillance on Wirtsweg, the scene at the airport and the talk with Ute Kranz. Also Bloch reported that a check at the Europäischer Hof showed that one Harvey Ryerson had checked out early last night. Hans Engen contributed a full rundown on Schnelldaten. The company had no track record, was unknown to the computer societies, was rumored by several Hamburg electronic specialists to be trading on the gray market and had only a small bank balance with no established line of credit. However, large amounts of foreign currencies had passed through the Schnelldaten account and been withdrawn.

The exchange of information went smoothly, but the minute the four people got around to the subject of what to do next, they fell to arguing. The Germans wanted to inform their authorities at once. Klaus Bloch felt his career would suffer if he failed to take the story of the airport escape in the Antonov 32 to the state police of Hamburg that day. He had friends among the officers who would never forgive his failure to cooperate with them. Hans Engen was equally insistent that they must go to the *Bundeskriminalamt,* or BKA, West Germany's criminal investigation agency, with the entire case. Perry, on the other hand, wanted no authorities alerted until he had conferred with his associates, particularly Jim Taliaferro, and lawyers in the United States and determined the next move. The future of the company, he said, depended on proper handling of the Katwar robbery. The argument grew heated. At one point Herr Engen, contending his reputation was at stake, threatened to quit, forego his fee and call the BKA in Wiesbaden.

Doug at last proposed a compromise. "Look, gentlemen, I understand your position. Now you must appreciate mine. The way I see it, time is not terribly important here except in tracking down Frischauer and Kramer. The chip is gone. We lost it to the Soviets. The circuit diagrams and chip layouts probably are already being worked on in Moscow. Nothing we can do today or tomorrow will bring them back. Face it, we've been had."

He appealed with open hands. "So give me three days. Here it is Friday morning. At noon on Monday, you'll be free to tell what you know to the authorities. At the same time I'll go to the FBI in the States. I must have time to get legal advice, see what my company's rights are in this case, a bizarre one, you'll have to admit. How about it? Only three days and most of that a weekend when nothing much could be done anyway."

And so it was agreed: A lid on the case until Monday noon. In the meantime Engen and Bloch would devote full energies to finding Frischauer and Kramer. The breakfast meeting ended in midmorning after Doug wrote checks for the substantial fees of the two Germans.

Kate and Doug quickly wound up their Hamburg mission, making a midday plane to Frankfurt for connections with a late-afternoon flight to New York. A shaft of light, knifing through the patchwork overcast, gave them a final look at Hamburg from the climbing airplane. Sunlight glinted on steeples and spires, painted the lakes, waterways and river with streaks of silver and cupped the old Hanseatic League city in a great bowl of autumnal colors. Then clouds closed in again, blotting the ground from view.

"I guess we blew it again," said Kate. "As detectives, we'd make a fine pair of bookends."

"I don't agree. We nailed down the main fact of the Katwar being stolen and . . ." Doug grinned. "We made expenses."

In the huge Frankfurt airport, where they spent two hours between flights, Kate settled into one of the hundreds of plastic sling chairs with a copy of *Barron's*. "Maybe I can get some tips on where to invest those ten G's, gift of your guilty conscience."

Doug's first phone call, to Jim Taliaferro, caught the Eniplex president before breakfast nine time zones distant in his Los Gatos, California, home. Doug briefed his Katwar partner on the bad news from Hamburg and in turn learned one startling fact that he relayed to Kate.

"Ingersoll has disappeared," he said. "He drove to L.A. in a rented car and left it at the airport, so it's assumed he took a plane somewhere. Neither his family nor Bytex officials know where he went."

But it was his daily call to his own office that jolted Doug.

"Mr. Perry, you got a distressing letter yesterday in the afternoon mail." Edith spoke in her best medical diagnostician's voice, smooth, low, in no way calculated to alarm. In her soothing vocabulary "distressing" meant catastrophic. "I tried to reach you last night at your hotel, but you were out. So I took the liberty of telling Susan Lindbloom, and she had me read the letter to Stanley Fowler."

"If it needs a lawyer, it must be awful. Go ahead, Edith, read it."

"Yes, Mr. Perry. It's on the stationery of the United States Attorney, Newark, New Jersey."

Re: Federal Grand Jury Investigation
District of New Jersey

Dear Mr. Perry:

Your conduct is being investigated for possible violation of federal criminal law involving the sale abroad of computer parts of strategic value without valid export permits.

I am informing you of this fact in order to afford you an opportunity to testify before the Grand Jury or to inform it of the identity and the substance of the testimony of other witnesses or of other evidentiary material that you wish to present to the Grand Jury.

In the event that you wish to testify yourself before the Grand Jury, you will be granted that opportunity at 10 A.M., Monday, November 22, at Room 481, Federal Courts and Post Office Building, Federal Square, Newark, New Jersey.

If this date is not convenient, an adjustment can be made. However, the Grand Jury is nearing the end of its hearing in this matter and it could not receive testimony from you later than the 24th, the day before Thanksgiving. Feel free to call me if you wish to appear and have any questions pertaining to your appearance.

In event that I do not hear from you or an attorney acting on your behalf by the above-specified date, I shall conclude that you do not wish to testify before the Grand Jury or present any other evidence to the Grand Jury.

Very Truly Yours,
Banning T. Osgood
Assistant United States Attorney

"Of all the damn . . ." His exclamation went winging through space to an orbiting satellite before returning to earth and the maze of telephone lines leading to the Princeton Dataflo office. "What the hell is this all about, Edith? What does Stan Fowler say?"

"Mr. Fowler called Mr. Osgood for further information and to tell him where you were." Edith hesitated. "I hate to say this, Mr. Perry, it's so . . ."

"Come on, Edith. Let's have it."

"You're being accused, Mr. Perry, of secretly passing the Katwar security chip to the Russians."

"Oh, for God's sake." It was preposterous. "What's that two-way WASP name again? Osgood Banning?"

"Banning Osgood, sir."

"Yeah, well, tell Stan to meet our plane at Kennedy this evening." He was steaming now. "We're due in at seven-ten."

Kate, putting aside her financial magazine, at first took the news as a joke, then recalled her misgivings about being followed in Hamburg. "It happened again early this morning," she told Doug. "I had a feeling that Buddy and I were being followed on the way to Ute Kranz's. You suppose Bob and Ray and their cousins have been tailing us all over? What a scene!"

Doug glanced around at people slumped in the sling chairs awaiting the flight to New York. The thought that one of this restive, vaguely apprehensive crowd might be a federal agent watching Doug's every move struck him as outrageous. Doug Perry, slipping strategic computerware to the Soviets! How idiotic could they get in Washington? His worst crimes were speeding or running an occasional red light on an empty street late at night. He'd never even cheated on his income taxes by padding deductions like so many of his friends.

But then when his anger subsided, he began to examine his position anew. A weird crime, this one, when seen from the outside. A chip had been stolen in an unwitnessed transcontinental heist that left no fingerprints, no marks, no evidence of any kind. He was convinced now through the ever-mounting circumstantial evidence that Marshall Ingersoll had been the thief, but who in authority would suspect Marshall or even think that a robbery had been committed? Such a crime: As evanescent as moonlight, as ephemeral as mist, as undocumented as a sneeze. Legions of electrical impulses had fled unseen from New Jersey to California, bloomed fitfully on an unknown video screen and been gathered as swiftly as cut flowers on printouts that Ingersoll guarded as life itself. Now the papers and tapes rested in the laboratory of some computer technicians in Moscow, leaving no more measurable residue in the West than a pilfered dream. Doug's initial outrage trailed off to a fit of brooding.

The eight-hour flight to New York seemed more like eighty. The bright dream of Kate's Katwar, a happy mix of genius, romance, wealth and professional triumph, had turned very somber indeed. Now he was being accused of smuggling this cryptographic marvel to agents of the Soviet Union. He hoped that Stan Fowler

could shed light on this preposterous charge. Jesus, what a mess—
and just when he was ready to tell the whole story to the FBI.
Now he would have to tell it to a Grand Jury.

20

A sharp November wind picked at bony trees in Newark's Federal
Square, rattled panes in the Peter Rodino Federal Building, that
"house of a thousand eyes," and whistled past the store front of
Simpson & Miller offering twenty-four-hour bail bond service:
"Get-en in jail is your business, get-en you out is MY business."
The wind pasted scraps of paper like blemishes on the steepled
tower of Grace Episcopal, an old brownstone church wrapped in
withered ivy that provided the area's sole relief from the ponderous monotony of government architecture.

Doug Perry lowered his coat collar as he entered the Federal
Courts and Post Office Building and walked the length of the old-
fashioned postal lobby with its marble floors, high balcony and
hooded lamps on chest-high writing desks. He rode the elevator to
the fourth floor. A security guard eyed him balefully as he passed
through a boxlike electronic contraption that frisked him for lethal
weapons. Silently cleared, he followed a corridor as directed to
Room 483.

The waiting room for the adjacent Federal Grand Jury was not
calculated to inspire confidence. Dirty beige walls enclosed three
chairs, a worn bench, a metal hat rack and several desks seemingly strewn about at random. A window overlooked a huge parking lot on Walnut Street and beyond it the devastation of the
Newark skyline. The distant view framed vandalized and gutted
buildings, treeless vacant lots, piles of rubbish, sooty apartments
and unkempt sidewalks. The city might have been mutilated in
some forgotten war and never restored or perhaps left to crumble
by an army still laying siege to its outskirts. Compared to the once
war-leveled city he'd left only three days ago, industrious Hamburg, with its vitality, tidiness, elegance and brawn, Newark was a
city of sorrow.

But the ironies of history mingled only briefly with thoughts of his own predicament, for just a few minutes after his arrival, Doug was summoned before the Grand Jury. A worried juror with a pronounced Adam's apple popped his head into the anteroom, asked if he were Douglas R. Perry and ordered him to follow.

Doug found himself at the rear of a low-ceilinged room, paneled and furnished in somber browns. Members of the Grand Jury, seated in swivel chairs bolted to the floor, turned to watch his progress to the front of the room where the foreman, portly and florid with a shock of white hair, sat on a raised platform like a judge. Doug was directed to the witness box, equipped with chair and microphone and located at a level slightly lower than that of the foreman. He seated himself between the foreman and the court reporter, a haggard man who grimaced as he rubbed his lower back. Doug looked out over several rows of faces. A swift count revealed twenty people—or less than the full Grand Jury membership of twenty-three which Stan Fowler had mentioned in his briefing. About half of them were women and a half dozen were black.

At the foreman's request, Doug raised his right hand and swore to cleave to that triad of truths that no witness, however virtuous, had ever managed to honor in totality since the dawn of jurisprudence. Long before Einstein the relativity of truth had been enshrined everywhere save in courts of law.

A tall lean young man who wore a vestless blue suit, smoothly tailored, had been lounging against a side wall. Now he approached Doug with a slouchy confident stride and a wisp of a smile that spelled breeding. Crew, tennis or lacrosse at his Ivy League college? Doug guessed his age at twenty-nine or thirty.

"I'm Banning Osgood, Assistant United States Attorney," he said. Doug had not doubted it for a moment.

Osgood carried Doug through a litany of identification and asked whether he had received a letter inviting him to testify, if he wished, "before this Grand Jury which is investigating your conduct for possible criminal violation of the Export Administration Act covering shipment or transfer of strategic materials to certain prohibited countries?" Doug said that he had.

"That act provides penalties of a fine of $50,000 or five times the value of the material, whichever is greater, or five years' imprisonment, or both. Were you aware of that?"

"Yes. I've been briefed by counsel."

"And do you know your constitutional rights? That you can refuse to answer to avoid self-incrimination? That you can leave this room and consult an attorney waiting outside?"

"Yes." Doug nodded. "I was briefed on my rights by my lawyer."

"And your attorney accompanied you to this hearing?" said Osgood. "He is waiting outside, is that right?"

"No, sir. I came here alone. My lawyer's back in Princeton. He wanted to come with me, but I said no. I have absolutely nothing to hide, will answer any questions and don't need any legal advice whatsoever in this preposterous hearing . . ."

"Just answer the question, please, Mr. Perry," admonished the young prosecutor. He was low-key, not unkind. "You'll be given ample time at the conclusion of my questioning to make any statement you want."

"We could dispose of this in no time if you'd just let me tell my story." Doug felt the onset of anger. He must guard against outbursts, Stan Fowler had cautioned. Any good prosecutor could make a fool of a hot-tempered witness.

"Mr. Perry." The man sitting on the raised platform tapped his gavel. "I'm Matthew Shedlin and I'm the foreman of this Grand Jury. We have our regular procedures here which protect the rights of the defendant in every respect. We of the Grand Jury are trying to determine whether or not there's enough evidence to warrant sending you to trial. Kindly observe the procedures and help us in this very serious task. Right now the Assistant United States Attorney is questioning you. Later members of the jury may have questions. Then you may make your own statement, taking as long as you wish. All right now, let's get along, Mr. Osgood."

"Mr. Perry, is it a fact that your company this year designed and built a new computer chip that advances the art of electronic cryptography by many years?" Osgood strolled about with his thumbs hooked in his belt.

"Yes."

"Would you please describe briefly for the Grand Jury the origin, size, power and capability of this chip."

Sparing no superlatives, Doug took several minutes to turn out a commercial for his prize ware.

"And this Miss Kate Warfield that you mention as the chief inventor, you have a special relationship with her, do you not?"

"Yes, I live with her."

"Now, Mr. Perry, am I correct in believing that this chip in the hands of an unfriendly or adversary nation would be very disadvantageous to the United States?" Osgood leaned against the witness box. "That is, it would take us centuries to break an enemy's ciphers and codes if the enemy were using your Katwar chip?"

"That's right. Of course, somebody eventually might successfully attack Katwar-produced ciphers, but as of now they're invincible—unless you've got a couple of lifetimes to spend on it."

Osgood ambled toward the windows with their outlook on Newark's battered profile. "Did you happen to see any of the television news this morning?"

"No. I was busy getting dressed and driving here."

"For your information, Moscow announced early today that a Soviet scientist has invented a computer chip that automatically enciphers texts in so many billions of ways that Soviet secret communications will become unbreakable. Does that surprise you?"

"No. I was expecting it." He recalled betting Kate as they flew home that the Russians would claim invention of a security chip before the end of the year.

"And why did you expect it, Mr. Perry?"

"Because I have evidence they stole the Katwar from us."

"You say they stole it. You will not contest then that the Russians now possess the Katwar security chip?"

"Hell, no. As I said, they stole it from us. It happened just last week in Hamburg when . . ."

Foreman Shedlin rapped his gavel. "Please, Mr. Perry, just answer the questions. You'll have your turn later. Nobody is trying to deprive you of your rights, believe me, sir."

"Mr. Perry." Osgood, leaning against a windowsill, addressed him in a conversational tone. "Is it a fact that a committee of cryptologists, private, university and government, agreed in 1981 to submit their papers on new developments in codes and ciphers to our National Security Agency?"

"That's what the press reported, yes."

"The NSA is the U.S. Government body that concerns itself with making and breaking codes, is it not?"

"So I understand."

"And isn't it a fact that U.S. code and cipher researchers thus far have complied unanimously and voluntarily with that guideline?"

"That I don't know."

"Well, if I told you that Mr. Cyrus Wolansky, chief of the public cooperation section of the National Security Agency, made that statement, you wouldn't dispute it, would you?"

"No."

"As it happens, Mr. Wolansky made one exception to that unanimity. He told this Grand Jury that your company, Princeton Dataflo, declined to submit its Katwar designs to the NSA despite a request. Did you so refuse?"

"No formal request was ever made, but we never turned over the Katwar specs to the NSA, no."

"Well, didn't a Mr. Gary Jameson call on you one day and remind you of the voluntary agreement to which all cryptologists were adhering?"

"Yes, but it wasn't a request and Jameson's not with the NSA. He's a code man at the Institute for Defense Analyses in Princeton."

"The Institute has a close affiliation with NSA, doesn't it?"

"Yes."

Osgood loosened his collar. The room was growing warm. "And didn't you tell Mr. Jameson that a vice-president of your firm wanted to turn over your Katwar materials to the NSA, but that you as president overruled him?"

"I did tell him that, yes." Doug squared his jaw. But off-the-record, damn it. So Gary too had been interviewed by the government. And he'd talked freely. How deep had this investigation gone? Doug felt decidedly less at ease than when he took the oath.

"So, Mr. Perry"—Osgood advanced toward the witness box with folded arms—"all the cryptologic research in this country has been turned over to the government out of a sense of patriotism with one sole exception. Princeton Dataflo declined at your insistence. Isn't that true?"

"Yes, but I can explain, if I may."

"Go ahead." Osgood stood a few feet away with cocked head and arms still folded.

"Development of the Katwar," said Doug, "cost my company many months and tens of thousands of dollars. We're in business to make a profit. There's no law compelling me to give an invention to the government. I took the position that we'd sell the chip on the open market where the National Security Agency could buy it just like anybody else. Nothing will be withheld from the government. I'm just as patriotic as the next man."

"But you deprived the NSA of the advantage of early use of your chip, didn't you?"

"That's one way of putting it."

"And as we stand at this very moment, the Russians have this chip, but your own government still does not have it. Isn't that true?"

"Yes, but not through my intention. The Soviets stole our chip."

Osgood strolled about the room, head down, thumbs tucked in his belt. "Now Mr. Perry," he said after a time, "is it a fact that Miss Warfield, with whom you have this special relationship, was questioned by agents of the Federal Bureau of Investigation?"

"That's right."

"Let me read you a leaflet." Osgood swerved about, pulled a printed orange sheet from his pocket. With deliberation and studied emphasis, he read the blast at the Institute for Defense Analyses that Kate had helped write the previous June.

"Do you agree with the criticism of IDA and the U.S. Government as expressed in this flyer?" Osgood gazed at Doug with clear blue untroubled eyes.

"Some of it, yes, but it's greatly exaggerated, rather juvenile in tone."

"Well, let's see now. . . . Do you believe that U.S. foreign policy has been obsessed with fear of Communism?"

"Not consistently, but sometimes it has. Under President Reagan, yes, and when John Foster Dulles was Secretary of State in the fifties, yes."

"Do you agree that the Institute for Defense Analyses, which works on classified defense projects, is 'a mercenary of the Pentagon' to quote the flyer?"

" 'Mercenary' is a loaded word. IDA does have government contracts."

"Quoting the leaflet once more, do you agree that U.S. military policy is in the image of Dr. Strangelove?"

"I think the flyer says that the world at large holds that image. No, I don't agree. I don't like my country having such a huge military establishment with tremendous nuclear overkill, but the men who run the Pentagon are decent men for the most part, not crazy Dr. Strangeloves."

Osgood folded the sheet and tucked it back in his pocket. "Miss Warfield helped write that pamphlet, didn't she?"

"So she said."

"And agents of the FBI questioned her about her role in the preparation of it?"

"Yes."

"Now Mr. Perry, there came a time, did there not, when you reached a verbal agreement to sell your Katwar chip to Ossian, Ltd., a data processing company headquartered in the Bahamas, for $17,500,000?"

"Correct."

"That was an enormous amount of money, wasn't it?" Osgood, on the prowl once more, neared the windows. The sunless November skies settled like lead over the maimed city.

"Enormous, no. A good agreement for us, yes."

"Well now, let's have a look." Osgood consulted a note fished from his coat pocket. "Wasn't that about six times more than Princeton Dataflo's profit in its best year ever?"

"Yes."

"Wasn't seventeen and a half million dollars considerably more than Dataflo's total profits in more than ten years of operation?"

"That's right."

"And isn't it a fact, Mr. Perry, that your company has been running in the red for the last five quarters."

"That's true."

"And that you needed something like this Katwar chip to turn the company around into profitability?"

"Yes, we're counting on the Katwar."

"Actually, Mr. Perry, isn't it true that Princeton Dataflo wasn't far from broke this year?" Osgood settled down on the window ledge.

"We are fairly near the point of going to the bank, yes. We need the Katwar to pull us out. No doubt about that."

Osgood inspected lint on his sleeve, finally picked it off. "Now Mr. Perry, wasn't the price Ossian was willing to pay far above the price you might have gotten from companies like Control Data, Wang or IBM?"

"Yes."

"No other product of Dataflo had ever brought anything like that amount, had it?"

"No."

"And then there came a time in September, didn't there, when you suddenly canceled the agreement with Ossian, just a day or so before the formal signing."

"That's right."

"Will you please explain, as briefly as possible, the circumstances of that cancellation to the jury?"

Doug told of the visit by Jay McNaughton, of reading the accounts of torture and murder in San Luis and of Ossian's proposal to fabricate the chip in San Luis under special benefits offered by the military dictatorship there. He sketched the discussion over company policy with Susan and Tony and told of his own tormented deliberation and eventual decision.

"So, you broke off a deal that could have enriched your company, which was almost broke, and that also would have helped the economy of a friendly nation, one that our own country supplies with military and economic aid, isn't that right?" Osgood spoke in a soft coaxing voice as he sat on a windowsill, his arms folded.

"I broke it off because the San Luis junta engages in revolting torture of human beings. I refused to help that kind of barbaric regime in any way. . . . Our loss of the big money hurt. No question."

"Isn't it true that our government provided San Luis with $55,000,000 in military aid and $30,000,000 in economic aid last year?"

"I don't know the figures. That sounds right. . . . What is this, an interrogation of my political views?"

Osgood ignored the complaint. "And isn't it true that our government has very friendly relationships with the government of San Luis?"

"Yes, but a lot of Americans, including me, vigorously dissent from that official U.S. policy. We don't believe we ought to be friendly with a gang of cutthroats and torturers."

"And isn't our military aid sent down there to combat a Communist-led insurrection?"

"That's the excuse. However, the San Luis Army kidnaps and murders thousands of innocent citizens, mostly Indians, who have nothing to do with the guerrillas. As to Communist-led, I never heard that."

"Aren't some guerrilla leaders open Marxists and one faction even takes the name Marxist Mountain Brigade?"

"That's true as I understand it, but I don't think there's any evidence of outside help from the Soviet Union."

"From Cuba?"

"If so, I haven't heard it."

"Your company's decision to cancel the Ossian contract was not unanimous among the three executives heading Princeton Dataflo, was it?"

"No, Anthony Canzano, a vice-president, dissented."

"Is that the same man who opposed your decision withholding the Katwar chip from the National Security Agency?"

"Yes."

"He took the position in this case, did he not, that it was not the business of your company to enter international politics by rebuking a foreign government?"

"That was one of his reasons. He had a number."

"Yes, and wasn't another of his reasons that he thought turning down that enormous amount of money was stupid business?"

"He thought it wasn't good business. Stupid, I don't know."

"Wasn't the NSA incident still another reason he left?"

"Yes."

"As a matter of fact, Mr. Canzano felt so deeply in this case that you'd taken Dataflo into an area where it didn't belong that he resigned from the company. Isn't that true?"

"Essentially, yes. He did receive an attractive offer from Cullinane, however."

"Mr. Perry, did you ever hear of the Logan Act?"

"No."

"It forbids private U.S. citizens from dealing with foreign governments in an effort to influence those governments on matters involving official U.S. policy or measures."

Foreman Shedlin tapped his gavel. "Just a minute, Mr. Osgood. Isn't that traveling far afield from the charges under consideration here?"

Osgood waved an arm dismissively. "No matter. . . . Now Mr. Perry, sometime after the cancellation of the deal with Ossian . . ." Osgood paused. His roaming had taken him to the back of the room where he carefully inspected the imitation oak paneling, scratching at the veneer with a fingernail. "Sometime later you received a visit, did you not, from a Major Enrique Morales, a deserter from the San Luis Army who came to this country to rally Americans against the San Luis Government?"

"Yes. He also brought a magnetic tape holding proof of a couple of thousand abductions, torture and murders of San Luis citizens by their own army and government hit squads."

"And why did you confer with Major Morales?"

"I didn't 'confer.'" Doug felt another flash of irritation and reminded himself to keep his cool. "Jay McNaughton brought Morales by for a visit. Morales thanked me for canceling the Ossian deal, and we talked some about his lecture trip. He was killed a few weeks later in Chicago."

"Do you know a guerrilla in San Luis named Pedro Ticpan?"

"I know of him, yes." Now where was the prosecutor headed?

"Didn't you, in fact, have a phone conversation with him?"

The question stunned him. For a few moments Doug did not reply. "Yes, I did." My God, had the FBI tapped his phone? That meant a court order. He began to feel caged, hounded, targeted for some opaque reason he could not comprehend.

"What was the nature of that conversation?"

"Ticpan is a brother of Silvia Ticpan, an Indian nurse in a Catholic clinic down there. I met Silvia and her parents when my family and I visited San Luis two years ago. Silvia was horribly tortured to death by the San Luis Army. I didn't know she had a brother, but Pedro called me from Miami one day, thanked me for trying to help his country and asked if he could come to Princeton to talk to me."

"And did he, in fact, come to see you?"

"No. I never heard from him after that."

"Did he not ask you if you'd help him obtain supplies for the guerrillas?"

"I don't know about guerrillas. He said he wanted to take revenge on the major who tortured and killed his sister and asked me if I would 'help obtain what we need'—I think those were his words."

"And you agreed?"

"I did not." If Osgood had heard a tape, why did he twist implications of the exchange? "I told him I wasn't sure I was the right man for him."

"But you agreed to talk in person with him?"

"Sure. I'll talk to anybody."

Osgood sauntered toward the front of the room in the relaxed almost indolent manner that somehow annoyed Doug more than a bombastic attack would have. The prosecutor stopped in front of the witness box and stared at him. "Now Mr. Perry, you knew, did you not, that Pedro Ticpan was the commander of one of the crack units of the Marxist Mountain Brigade, the main guerrilla faction fighting the government of San Luis?"

"No, I didn't. I knew nothing about him."

"You didn't know his long record as an active Communist subversive in San Luis?" Osgood continued his cool staring.

"No. I had no idea then or now what he did or believed."

"You knew, did you not, that Pedro Ticpan wanted you to help finance the purchase of munitions to overthrow the legal government of San Luis?"

"No, I didn't."

"Mr. Perry, didn't Ticpan end your conversation with a salute to Fidel Castro, the Communist-bloc Cuban dictator?"

"He quoted him, yes." As Doug saw more fully the nature of the web being spun about him, his temper rose. "Say, Mr. Osgood, was the government tapping my phone, and if so by whose orders?"

Foreman Shedlin again rapped his gavel. "Please, Mr. Perry." He looked as though the reprimand pained him.

"There is more than one end to a telephone line." Osgood's small smile played with the ambiguity. He was a man who patently enjoyed his job. Now he broke off the eye-lock with Doug, strolled back to his perch on the windowsill and gazed outside. Scraps of refuse, choreographed by the wind, danced fitful patterns against a sullen sky. The prosecutor toyed with a shoelace as he reflected.

The room's brief silence ended in a tremendous belch by the court reporter who promptly grabbed for his lower back. Several jurors tittered. The foreman tapped his gavel in feigned reproof. As Doug surveyed the men and women who would judge him—to indict him and send him to trial or not to indict him—he could gain no clues. One matronly woman knitted patiently at a child's sweater, the needles clicking as rhythmically as rails under a rolling train. In the rear row a well-groomed patrician, pink as an investment banker, folded his arms and frowned. Doug had noticed him glancing frequently at his wristwatch, no doubt aware of the millions of stocks, bonds and money instruments that were fluctuating by mighty fractions while he sat here idle. On the other hand, thought Doug, maybe he was a dentist pining for his drill. Two black men carried on a whispered dialogue over some private joke. Two seats away a young black woman in a tailored suit read *The Wall Street Journal*. A doughy white woman, whose blue polyester suit overflowed a front-row seat, yawned and closed her eyes.

"Mr. Perry." Osgood came to life. The hunt was on again. "Do you know a Marshall Ingersoll?"

"Yes." But no question could have surprised him more. Now what?

"Do you know where he is today?"

"I have no idea. I heard he left home in California without saying where he was going."

"Who told you that?"

"James Taliaferro of Eniplex, our partner in producing the Katwar chip."

"Has Ingersoll communicated with you in any way since his disappearance?" Osgood lounged against the sill, his arms folded and feet crossed.

"God no." Doug was astonished at the line of questioning. "I'd be the last . . ."

"Is it a fact that Marshall Ingersoll has lost large amounts of money playing poker recently?"

"So I heard."

"From whom?"

"From Jim Taliaferro. You see, we hired a private detective to check up on Ingersoll, and the investigator reported the poker losses to Jim who told me."

"You hired a private detective to investigate Ingersoll?"

"Yes, sir."

"What's the detective's name and address?"

"Philip Wetherill, San José, California. I don't have the street address with me, but he's in the phone book."

Osgood made a note on a pad, then resumed stalking about the room. After a bridge of silence, he asked: "You play big-time poker too, don't you, Mr. Perry?"

"Yes."

"And you've lost a great deal of money. Isn't that right?"

"Not as much as I've won." Now why was the young prosecutor trying to link him to Ingersoll and poker losses? Doug had thought he'd divined the thrust of the earlier questioning. Now this Ingersoll-poker curve threw him off balance.

"Are you trying to tell this Grand Jury that you're a consistent winner?" Osgood loaded the line with skepticism.

"No, but over a lifetime, I'd guess I'm a fair amount ahead." The fond claim of every gambler, he realized as soon as the words left his mouth. Did he really know? . . . Ah, poor invalid truth, ailing whole truth and that sickly sibling, nothing-but-the-truth.

"But recently you've lost, haven't you?"

"Not at all. I've played twice recently. Last month I dropped $600 in a game in Chicago, but last week I won about $20,000 in Hamburg, Germany."

"Twenty thousand!" Several nodding jurors snapped to attention. "You won $20,000 gambling at one sitting in Hamburg, Germany?" Osgood spaced and stressed the words as though the revelation had cosmic significance.

"Yes, sir."

"Now, Mr. Perry, isn't it true, as a matter of fact, that you play poker nearly every Sunday night in Princeton, your home town?"

"Yes, but that's a different story." Doug shrugged it off with a smile, his first of the morning. "That's just for fun, a friendly game. We have a $10 limit."

"You can bet $10 on a single card?" Osgood swept the jury with a look of shared poverty at the feet of riches. "Doesn't that produce big pots for the winner, two or three hundred dollars?"

"Once in a while. Most pots are around a hundred or under. A man is lucky to win $300 in a night in our game."

"I see, just a small friendly game." Osgood said it drily, his first venture into sarcasm. He let the thought sink in, then asked, "Marshall Ingersoll used to work for you, didn't he?"

"Yes, he was our chief systems programmer at Dataflo for five years."

"And he played in your Sunday-night game?"

"Yes." Wherever this was leading, Osgood had been supplied with solid investigative research.

"So you were quite friendly with him, were you not, in your essentially friendly game."

"No, sir. I wasn't. I was never friendly with Ingersoll. He was an employee and an acquaintance."

"He left your employ early this year to accept an executive post with Bytex Laboratories in Sunnyvale, California, is that correct?"

"It is."

"And you parted in friendly fashion, didn't you?"

"No. Ingersoll left a lot of hard feelings around Princeton. He borrowed $83 at the Sunday-night game and never repaid it. Hasn't to this day, as far as I know."

"Did he owe the money to you?"

"No. To another player. But I never could be friendly with a man who welshes on a gambling debt. Not to be trusted." He struggled with words. "Frankly, it's sleazy, piss-ant behavior."

Banning Osgood yawned. "I take it that welshing on a gambling debt is at the apex of your code of values." The government's attorney was leaning against the rear wall now. In his roaming he had circled the room several times.

Taking the remark as mere observation, Doug did not reply. In the silence, the click of knitting needles sounded like drum beats.

"Speaking of values, Mr. Perry, did you ever pay federal income taxes on your gambling winnings?" Osgood said it casually as if an after-thought had slipped out by mistake.

"That line is not appropriate, Mr. Osgood." Foreman Shedlin stroked his crest of white hair. "The defendant is here because of allegations that he transferred strategic materials to prohibited areas in violation of federal law. That's the charge on which we'll either indict him or vote a no-bill. He's not accused here of violating the tax laws."

"I stand corrected," said Osgood promptly, "and withdraw the question."

"I don't mind answering," said Doug. "I did pay federal income taxes on gambling winnings two separate years during the seventies. Also I plan to pay this year because of my big win in Hamburg. . . . Ask me anything you want, Mr. Osgood. Aside from a few computer secrets of my company, I have nothing to hide. Nothing."

A man of perpetual motion, Osgood set off again on his rounds, thumbs hooked in his belt. The man's brain was both well-stocked and orderly, Doug conceded. Only once had the attorney referred to notes.

"Mr. Perry, you and Miss Warfield flew out to California early this summer to confer with Marshall Ingersoll, did you not?" Osgood spoke while sauntering and without raising his head.

"We didn't go to confer. We flew out there to investigate our suspicion that Ingersoll may have stolen our chip."

"Well now, you did speak to Mr. Ingersoll, didn't you?" For once the question had a sharp edge.

"Only in passing. He came to a meeting in the motel where I was staying." Doug described the brief encounter.

"That was all?"

"That was it, period."

"But you did see him again in California, did you not, at a men's camp where you both slept under the same roof for a number of days?"

"That's right."

"Will you please describe the all-male Bohemian Grove for the benefit of the Grand Jury?" Osgood had reached the window again and settled down on the sill.

Doug sketched a picture of the encampment under the redwoods. "So inside the Grove," he concluded, "I also belong to the Micro Mall camp, largely composed of computer people. Ingersoll was a guest of another Micro Mall camper. Not until I reached California did I learn he'd been invited."

"Actually, Mr. Perry, the Bohemian Grove encampment, almost exclusively white, brings together some of the most powerful businessmen, politicians and opinionmakers in the nation, doesn't it?"

Doug nodded. "Not everyone fits that description, but there are quite a few well-known and influential men, yes."

"And you and Ingersoll, this man you say you suspected of stealing your highly valuable chip, were together in the same lodge for nine or ten days, were you not?" The tone was steadily sharp now.

"Yes, but not by my choice, I assure you."

"As a matter of fact, you played poker together in very friendly fashion, did you not?" Osgood advanced toward the witness box.

"We played poker." Doug felt anger flicking at him like a temptor. "There were seven or eight men in the game."

"And weren't you at all times on a friendly basis with this man you contend welshes on gambling debts, indulges in 'sleazy, pissant behavior' and was under suspicion of stealing from you?" The prosecutor stood only a few feet away, his eyes boring into Doug's.

"It was a gentleman's game." Just who was the informant for all this? One of those two guests from Washington, Hyer of the White House or DeGrazia, the Assistant Secretary of Defense who supervised the military's vast computer networks? "I could hardly denounce Ingersoll or refuse to play because of him."

"Now, Mr. Perry, to be open and forthcoming with these jurors here, isn't it true that late one night after a poker game, you and Ingersoll had a long private talk on one of the pathways under the redwoods?" Osgood rested an elbow on the scrollwork top of the witness stand and gazed at Doug.

"It was more of an argument than a talk." Doug felt Osgood's proximity as a physical threat, had to restrain himself from pushing the prosecutor away. "He told me that a rival security chip was being produced in Europe. I took that as a sly warning, got mad and told him he was under suspicion for the theft. He blew his top. We started shouting at each other."

"But you continued to live under the same roof and eat at the same table and play poker together, didn't you?"

"No, sir. I left two days later without waiting for the usual Grove windup."

"You left because of your aversion to Ingersoll?" The attorney lowered his brows in disbelief, bit off the words. "Just couldn't stand the sight of the man?"

"That was partly the reason. Also I was anxious to get back running the company." To say nothing of his hunger for Kate and his surfeit with milling throngs of men without women. Ah, the whole truth. Should the law, by some miscalculation, ever blunder into the whole truth, it would smother to death in a trash heap of verbiage and tangled motives.

Osgood turned from the witness and walked slowly back to the window where he resumed his favorite post, leaning against the sill like a college professor bored with his phlegmatic class and yearning for his sabbatical. He gazed at Perry as he might at a sluggish student.

"Now Mr. Perry, you and Marshall Ingersoll both went to Hamburg, West Germany, did you not?"

"Yes, but not together. When I heard that our chip, which we thought had been stolen, was being produced maybe in Hamburg . . ."

Blap. Matthew Shedlin's gavel again smacked wood. "You know better than that, Mr. Perry." He gazed down sadly at Doug like a father disobeyed. "Just yes or no, please."

"You have just returned from Hamburg, is that right?" asked Osgood.

"Yes."

"And while in that city did you not call at the office of Schnell-daten, A.G., dealers in computerware?"

"Yes." So Kate was right. They had been followed.

"Did you go to Schnelldaten in company with Ingersoll?"

"No. I never saw Ingersoll in Hamburg." Now he glimpsed where the young prosecutor was heading. Somewhere, somehow, in the vast warrens of the federal government, someone apparently hatched the ludicrous idea that Ingersoll and Perry had teamed up to smuggle the Katwar to the Soviets. Incredible. Yet why else these insistent questions about Ingersoll? What, if not a criminal conspiracy theory, could this attorney with the reversible WASP name be spinning? Doug began to regard Banning Osgood as the enemy. How should he handle this astonishing perversion of the facts? He desperately needed the advice of a lawyer, and he understood now why Stan Fowler had deplored his decision to come here alone. And who was the informant who started federal agents on his trail? Otis Kramer? That shady character who played his serpentine games?

"How long did you stay at the offices of Schnelldaten?"

"About an hour."

"Did you talk with a Ludwig Frischauer, head of the firm?"

"Yes."

"And you made final arrangements, did you not, to sell, give or otherwise convey your Katwar chip to Schnelldaten for transfer to another party?"

"Absolutely not." Doug's temper broke its bonds. "That's a damn false insinuation and anybody who told you that lies."

"No more of that, Mr. Perry." This time Foreman Shedlin brought his gavel down with a bang.

Denied a vent for his rage, Doug resorted to his old gambit. *Zap: Banning Osgood's expensive clothes fell away, exposing the naked man. Unfortunately, Doug gained no advantage. Try as he would he could not reshape the trim firm-muscled young body, still showing a vestige of summer tan from Martha's Vineyard or perhaps Nantucket.*

"What then did you talk to Ludwig Frischauer about?" Osgood appeared quite content with Doug Perry's outburst.

"I tried to find out whether certain people I suspected in the theft of our chip, Ingersoll among them, had been there. Frischauer denied knowing any of them."

"Did you use your own name when you called at Schnell-daten?"

"No." The question startled Doug. Whoever the federal agents were, they had been very thorough.

"What name did you use?"

"Steelman Bishop."

"Isn't it true that Ludwig Frischauer and his Schnelldaten has a shady reputation and that he largely deals on the illegal gray market?"

"I learned that after I arrived in Hamburg, yes."

"Yet, using an assumed name, you called on Frischauer and conferred with him anyway?"

"Sure. I wanted to find out whether he was brokering our stolen chip."

"Mr. Perry, if you didn't go to Hamburg with Marshall Inger-soll, how did you know he was there?"

"I found out in a poker game."

"You found out in a poker game?" Osgood, still lounging near the window that offered its cityscape of leaden skies and drab streets, dropped each word separately like a burden. "Was that the same game where you won $20,000?"

"Yes."

Osgood guided Doug through a description of the game and its location, by no means overlooking the Reeperbahn's reputation, its splash of fleshly entertainment and its congregation of voluptu-ous vulpine hookers from all parts of the globe. "And how," the prosecutor asked with unveiled skepticism, "did you learn at this big-stakes poker game in the rear of a luxurious bordello that your former employee, Marshall Ingersoll, had also visited Hamburg?"

"I learned it from a Yugoslav merchant marine officer named Kosto Gavrilovich. He sat next to me in the game."

"And you just leaned over and asked him if a Mr. Ingersoll had been to town and this Yugoslav sailor obliged by saying oh yes, of course. Was that it?"

"No, Mr. Osgood. Despite your sarcasm, I did learn about In-gersoll from Kosto. Do you want me to tell how that came about?"

Osgood waved. "Please."

Doug described the encounter in great detail, including Gavrilo-vich's imitation of Ingersoll's jaw clenching and their laughter over the mutual profit gained from the discovery of Ingersoll's facial philanthropy. He noted that the grand jurors, especially the men, followed him as closely as they might an adventure movie.

"You are quite at home, are you not, Mr. Perry, with the deception that is such an integral part of the game of poker?"

"Mr. Osgood," cautioned Foreman Shedlin, "that kind of implication is not necessary or proper here."

"At any rate, you say you learned about Ingersoll at a big poker game in the St. Pauli district. Now, did you also learn that a Russian gymnastics team competed in Hamburg at the same time you were there?"

"Yes."

"And that this delegation was accompanied by a large number of KGB secret security agents?"

"I don't know. I would assume so."

"And also cryptographers and computer experts?"

"Again, I have no knowledge, but I'd guess so."

"And isn't it a fact that the airliner taking this group back to Moscow waited in the pitch dark at the end of a runway to take aboard unauthorized passengers who had spent many hours at Schnelldaten?"

"My guess is yes. Miss Warfield was at . . ."

The prosecutor, advancing, again interrupted. "And you knew, did you not, that these Soviet experts were taking the designs of your Katwar chip back to Moscow?"

"Well, I sure thought so. The chip had been stolen . . ."

"So knowing all this, Mr. Perry, you naturally rushed to the proper authorities to report the facts, did you not?" Osgood stood beside the witness box, his eyes fixed on Doug's.

"No, I didn't. We had . . ."

"You did not report anything to the authorities?" Osgood raised the pitch of his voice and stretched the sentence like an accordion.

"No. If you'd just . . ."

"You did not report to the Hamburg police?" He draped the inquiry in incredulity.

"No . . . Mr. . . . ." Doug knew he could not contain his anger much longer.

"You did not report the facts to the BKA, West Germany's criminal investigative agency?"

"No." Doug clenched his fists.

"You did not call the American consul in Hamburg?"

"No."

"You did not call our ambassador in Bonn?" The questions came in rapid cadence and high decibels.

"No, sir." He was furious now.

"You did not attempt to contact the CIA?"

"No."

"Nor the FBI?"

"No."

"In fact, Mr. Perry, you had no intention whatsoever of going to the FBI, had you?" He asked it belligerently.

"That's not true." Doug struck back at a half shout. "I planned to go to the FBI this noon."

"You planned to go to the FBI this noon." Osgood tucked his thumbs in his belt, shook his head slowly and sadly and plodded with drooping shoulders back to the window and its view of urban ruin. He had turned his back, his posture said, on this affluent defendant with his shoddy fabrications, preferring instead the honest decay of a city moldering in poverty.

The young prosecutor let silence hang for seconds that seemed like minutes, then asked in a weary tone, "Mr. Perry, over the long months when your company was almost broke and when you contend your chip had been stolen, did you ever once contact any law enforcement agency?" His was the manner of a young man disillusioned by the extent of the world's malefactions.

"No." God, how would he fight his way out of this trap? "If you'd just let me explain, Mr. Osgood, I'd . . ."

"You never contacted your Princeton police?"

"No."

"Never picked up the phone and called the district attorney of Mercer County?"

"No, I . . ."

"Never once got in touch with the FBI?"

"No."

"As a matter of fact, Mr. Perry, from the moment you say the chip was stolen, through the after-midnight hour when Soviet agents spirited it away to Moscow from a city where you were staying, right up to this very second, you have never asked the help of local, state, federal or foreign law enforcement officers. Now isn't that the simple truth of the matter?"

"I have not done so, but if I just might have the chance . . ."

"That's all, Mr. Foreman," Osgood cut in loudly. "I have no more questions."

Foreman Shedlin leaned down toward Doug. "Mr. Perry, we'll recess now for lunch. When we take up again, Mr. Osgood will put to you whatever questions members of the jury want asked. After that, you may make your statement, taking as long as you wish." He thumped his gavel. "The witness may step down. Please be back by 1 P.M."

21

Hands jammed in his pockets, Doug paced about the small anteroom that seemingly served as a repository for odds and ends of unwanted furniture. Soiled gray skies hid the noon sun as if the ailing November day already had passed into the gloom of dusk. Lights shone in the Colonial Coffee Shop across Walnut Street as the restaurant handled its lunch trade of lawyers, bureaucrats and those enmeshed in the complexities of federal law.

Doug had returned here promptly after buying a hot dog at a sidewalk cart outside the courthouse. "Cheer up, man," said the black vendor, noting Doug's troubled look. "If you was black, the judge'd double your time."

Alone now after two hours on the stand, Doug confronted the dimensions of his predicament. One thing was certain. He could have used sound legal advice this morning. But had he been foolhardy to come here without Stan Fowler? His poker buddy had implored Doug not to go unaccompanied by counsel. "What you'll gain by grandstanding in front of a jury as a persecuted man," Stan had said, "you'll more than lose in a hundred little traps the prosecutor sets for the unwary witness." While Doug acknowledged that Fowler spoke from experience, he nevertheless honored his intuitive feeling that jury members would award him points for coming alone. And just in case one of them might quiz him this afternoon about talking to his lawyer, Doug had quelled his impulse to telephone Fowler during this lunch break. He would face this thing alone—this wildly absurd fiction that the young government prosecutor had pieced together for the Grand Jury.

How in God's name had government lawmen hit upon the astounding theory that he and Marshall Ingersoll had conspired to sneak Kate's elegant chip to the Soviets? What an unjustified nutty perverse premise. He, Doug Perry, who loved his freedoms, reveled in the scramble of competition and prided himself on his ability to go it alone! Who could think that he connived to share his own woman's prize achievement with a ponderous system that scorned personal liberties, suppressed competition and glorified that abstraction in monotony called the state? Totally impossible.

Yet, putting himself in the place of one of the jurors who had stared at him for two hours with neither hostility nor sympathy, he could see that the tapestry woven by Banning Osgood might make sense. First the disclosure that the Soviets now had Dataflo's miracle security chip. . . . Then the fact that he'd refused to turn over the Katwar designs to the National Security Agency, perhaps, in hindsight, a mistake. . . . The implication that Kate, his woman, was a left-winger who despised her own government and that Doug shared her views. . . . The broad suggestion that he backed Marxist guerrillas against a San Luis regime that Washington supported with money and weapons and that he let ideology override good business judgment in canceling the Ossian contract that would have rescued a hard-pressed Princeton Dataflo. . . . The Assistant U.S. Attorney's questions left the clear impression that Doug was a close friend of Ingersoll and conferred with him in Sunnyvale, the Bohemian Grove and Hamburg. And that heavy emphasis on poker—designed to show a man of dubious character, perhaps often a heavy loser, who might be susceptible to Soviet lures? His conduct in Hamburg, as traced by Osgood's questions, pictured him dealing with a shady gray-market broker who fronted for the Soviets. Also what juror would credit Doug's implausible story that he learned about Ingersoll's visits to Hamburg from a Yugoslav in a poker game where thousands of dollars changed hands? Finally, after pinning Doug by implication as a Communist sympathizer, the young prosecutor showed that not once in six months had Doug contacted a law enforcement agency. Doesn't an honest man who suspects both theft of his property and its capture by Soviet agents go at once to the police?

While Doug reasoned that a court trial would surely vindicate him, the prospect of devoting a year of his life and a big chunk of his savings to a legal battle dismayed him. And an indictment, though it carried no legal presumption of guilt, did tarnish a person's reputation. If he were indicted, Princeton Dataflo would suffer. So would Kate, his daughter, Judith, Dataflo employees, even Jim Taliaferro and Eniplex.

To escape the taint of indictment he must convince the jurors of his innocence and that meant an appeal to the gut as well as to the head, mixing emotion with fact, yet keeping his recital simple, comprehensible and coherent. He was not skilled at public speaking, but now he must excel in relating the story of Katwar. He set to work outlining his defense and marking in memory the main points to stress.

He barely heard the knock an hour later. It was the juror with the active Adam's apple who again summoned him to the witness stand where Foreman Matthew Shedlin greeted Doug with a pleasant, if noncommittal, smile. The jurors looked well fed and content. Banning Osgood, at his favorite post, leaned near the window with its view of a ravaged skyline.

"You're still under oath, Mr. Perry," said the foreman, "so we'll take up where we left off. Mr. Osgood will put several questions to you that members of the Grand Jury want answered."

"Mr. Perry." Osgood nodded. He wore a fresh blue shirt in contrast to the morning's white. "The jury would like to know whether you consulted with an attorney during the recess?"

"No. The only person I spoke to was the hot dog man down on the sidewalk."

"The jury wants to know whether you ever belonged to the Communist Party?"

"No. Last thing in the world I'd ever join."

"Again from the jury. Do you approve of the Russian system?"

"Flatly no." He called up his noontime thought. "The Soviet system denies personal liberties, bans competition and glorifies the heavy gray state, all of which are anathema to me."

"Did you ever discuss with anyone going to the police with your suspicions?"

"Yes, but I'd rather cover that in my statement so it will be in context."

"Was Marshall Ingersoll ever a guest in your home or did you ever visit in his?"

"Never."

"Mr. Perry, as a final question, the jury wants to know how your chip was stolen if indeed it was?" His chore finished, Osgood strolled from the windows and took a seat near the jury facing Doug.

"I'll cover that at length in what I have to say."

"All right, Mr. Perry," said Foreman Shedlin. "The floor's yours. Take as long as you want, but try not to ramble, please."

"Okay. First let me say something about Mr. Osgood's line of questioning. I realize it was very broad, since he wasn't trying to build a case, but just highlight enough evidence to warrant a trial." Doug hitched forward in his chair and made use of the microphone. "But how the government prosecutors ever got this weird idea that I gave or sold the Katwar chip to the Soviets is beyond me. All I can say is that it stuns me and also frightens me. The only thing I've done with the new security chip is order and encourage its development and production. But I can see how a juror, listening this morning, might conclude that I may have betrayed my country, something I've never done or contemplated.

"So let me tell you the whole story of Katwar from its beginning until last week in Hamburg when, I have strong evidence to believe, the Russians took a duplicate of it to Moscow. First, how was it developed and who did it?" Expanding on his answer of the morning, he described the long days and nights of exploration in the basement of the Dataflo building, Kate's dramatic breakthrough and the office celebration that followed.

"Now, folks, to understand computer crime, you have to realize that a clever systems man can steal you blind without ever leaving a trace." He told of the hectic scene that bright day in June when Jerry Dunn discovered the secret instruction that enabled someone to command Susie, the computer, to release any or all of its stored information to a terminal thousands of miles away. He pictured the Arpanet and its hundreds of computers scattered about the country and abroad. He explained in detail how a crafty technician might plan a Trojan horse operation.

"So all of us, Miss Warfield included, saw that we could have been robbed of the Katwar designs," he continued. "But the question was: Had we been robbed? On that, we had absolutely no evidence. It reminds me of a story I heard about the atomic-bomb-making facilities down at Oak Ridge, Tennessee, during World War II. One worker quit after a year, charging it was all a big boondoggle because nothing ever came out of the tall smokestack that he could hear, see, smell, taste or feel. We had a similar situation. There was no evidence that we could hear, see, smell, taste or feel that our Katwar designs had been sucked electronically out of the computer where the chip was developed. Still, we thought it might have been.

"We all believed Marshall Ingersoll was our No. 1 suspect, but we had no evidence to take to the police or district attorney. For one thing, we didn't want to accuse a man without at least some circumstantial evidence. For another, most law-enforcement officers still know very little about computer technology and it would be very difficult to explain the Trojan horse operation so that we'd be taken seriously." Doug leaned forward, pushed the microphone aside and spoke in a loud firm voice. "I ask each of you jurors. What would you have done in my shoes? Would you go to the police, accusing someone of a crime, a someone who might be innocent, when you had not a shred of evidence to offer? Or would you first try, as we did, to find some evidence on your own? That's why Kate Warfield and I went to California, that's why we hired a private detective on the Coast to investigate to see if any of our suspicions were warranted. I think any of you would have done the same thing. That's the decent and fair way to go rather than to rush to the police with a lot of wild accusations that you can't substantiate. Also, don't forget, if we made public charges, the market price of our Katwar would fall because a producer would fear competition from a stolen chip on the gray market."

After describing his California trip and his encounters with Ingersoll, Doug switched to cancellation of the Ossian deal. "Mr. Osgood has made much of the fact that my company is hard up and that I turned down a great deal of money from Ossian. That's true and don't think my mouth didn't water over the prospect of bailing out Dataflo with all those millions. But the military government of San Luis had offered Sean Hegy tax and other benefits to produce our Katwar chip down there. In essence, our chip would have been bolstering and adding prestige to a savage killer regime that I abhorred. I refused to help a gang of cutthroats masquerading as a government. That's the simple fact of the matter.

"Remember that I'd read that sickening transcript on the torture and killing of Silvia Ticpan, the beautiful little Indian woman my daughter and I met in San Luis once. I wish all of you would read those accounts. They bring generalities of torture down to the reality of smashed faces, yanked teeth, battered heads and electric shocks to the genitals. . . . Look, I was no hero. Any of you would have canceled that Ossian contract after reading that frightful stuff—no matter how much money it cost you."

Doug let his eyes play about over the rows of jurors so that he made brief eye contact with each one. "Now the thrust of the prosecutor's questions was that because Communists oppose the San Luis junta that our country supports I must be a Communist sympathizer because I also oppose the junta and its barbarities. Of course, Mr. Osgood never said that outright, but when you think about it, wasn't that the clear implication of his questions? Now that's about as unfair and as irrational as calling one of you a Communist sympathizer because you wanted to go ahead with the Olympic Games in Moscow back in 1980 while your government was boycotting the Games."

Doug mentioned Kate's help in writing the IDA flyer, his conversations with Major Enrique Morales and Pedro Ticpan. "Here again, the only purpose Mr. Osgood could have in bringing up those trifling incidents is to leave the impression that I'm some kind of leftist subversive who would be eager to smuggle a chip to agents of the Soviet Union. Actually, ladies and gentlemen, if you follow Mr. Osgood's reasoning to its conclusion, he's saying that if you don't agree one hundred percent with your government's foreign and military policies, why then you must be a Communist subversive. Now, we all know that's nonsense. This is a democracy where each one of us thinks for himself or herself, thank God—or ought to."

Doug continued the story of Katwar, including the production contract with Jim Taliaferro's Eniplex and wound up with a lengthy, step-by-step narration of what he and Kate did in Hamburg. "So at that final breakfast with Klaus Bloch and Hans Engen, we were convinced of these points: One, Soviet agents had flown stolen Katwar designs to Moscow on a plane bearing the Russian gymnastic team. Two, Ludwig Frischauer's fly-by-night firm provided the Soviets with the stolen Katwar designs at a big price. Three, Otis Kramer of Washington, D.C., was definitely involved in getting the chip to Frischauer and perhaps to Soviet agents as well. Four, Marshall Ingersoll had been to Hamburg several times during the period when Frischauer acquired the designs."

Doug leaned over the edge of the witness box, speaking directly to the jurors. "But remember, while we were all convinced of those four points, we had no proof. As I told you, the two Germans wanted to inform their authorities at once, but I wanted time back home to check with my legal counsel, Susan Lindbloom, Jim Taliaferro and others. So that's why we agreed on the deadline of today noon. Since West Germany is six hours ahead of us, no doubt Bloch and Engen have long since told the German authorities just what I've told you.

"I would earnestly urge this Grand Jury to call witnesses who will buttress and amplify my story at all points along the line. Among these people are Kate Warfield, Susan Lindbloom, Anthony Canzano, Jerry Dunn, Jim Taliaferro, Paul Ellenbogan and other members of the Micro Mall camp, Philip Wetherill, Professor J. J. McNaughton and the two Germans, Hans Engen and Klaus Bloch." Doug looked at his wristwatch. He had been talking almost an hour and a half.

"Would you spell Canzano and Wetherill for me, please?" asked the court reporter who had seldom taken his eyes from Doug's lips during the long monologue.

"I guess that's about it," said Doug in conclusion. "I'm not guilty of violating any federal law in this operation and I'm astonished that anyone suspects me of doing so. I'm sure that Mr. Osgood and those who pursued this investigation of me did so in good faith, but they're on a totally wrong track. Their targets should be Ingersoll and Kramer, not me, and I'm confident that if you call the witnesses I've suggested, you'll come to the conclusion that I've done nothing wrong. Thank you."

The jury room, frozen like a still life in the last few minutes of Doug's presentation, dissolved into small noises and movements. Jurors coughed, yawned, whispered. Several stood up and stretched. The court reporter rubbed his lower back.

"Any further questions?" asked Foreman Shedlin.

"Just one," said Osgood after a silence in which no juror raised his hand. He had strolled back to the window ledge.

"All right, Mr. Osgood."

"Mr. Perry, in reference to your decision to go to the FBI this noon, did you call any FBI office to make an appointment?"

"No, sir, I did not. The minute I heard the contents of your letter last Friday, I knew my first priority was to prepare for this appearance."

"So, to this moment you have not contacted the FBI or any other law enforcement agency on this matter?"

"No. Of course, Mr. Osgood, I'd have looked pretty silly going to the FBI *after* receiving your letter."

"That's all, Mr. Foreman." Osgood lounged against the sill with folded arms, his blue shirt still crisp.

"Mr. Perry, we'll continue to hold you under subpoena until we complete our inquiry into this matter." Foreman Shedlin tapped his gavel lightly. "Please do not leave the state without notifying the U.S. Attorney's office. All right, you're excused now. You may step down."

As Doug walked past the jury, again fixed in their bolted swivel chairs, no one glanced at him and he searched the impassive faces in vain for a clue. The only sound was the rhythmic click of knitting needles.

22

They played the last game of the year at Larry Warfield's lakeside home the Sunday night before Christmas. Snow powdered the air, coated bushy evergreens and skeletal hardwoods and vanished soundlessly in dark waters of Lake Carnegie. The poker table stood on the Warfields' heated, glassed-in porch, snug yet part of the ivory night. Light from the drop lamp bathed the whitened lawn that sloped to the lake. The hush that accompanies a windless snowfall settled on Princeton like a prayer.

Nine players crowded around the blanket-covered table. Hugh Talbott, the game's historian, had pronounced this the "fortieth anniversary of our founding" and urged everyone to come. The celebration would include presentation of a special prize to the first winner of both ends of a high-low hand. A festive air prevailed as Larry broke open two new decks. Cheers and groans greeted Ira Bickstein's latest Jewish mother routine. More groans, mingled with boos, saluted Larry's new camel joke.

Doug's own mood was wary, febrile, tense, yet excited, not unlike those extraordinary highs that seized him during the big-money games at moments when the flick of a card would decide whether he won or lost several thousand dollars.

A telephone message from an anonymous caller just an hour earlier had provoked a drastic change of mood.

For Doug had grown steadily more disheartened in the month since his testimony before the Federal Grand Jury in Newark. He had expected an early resolution, a quick vote to erase the charges against him. Instead, the case dragged on day after day, muffled in the secrecy that surrounds Grand Jury proceedings. He knew that a few of the witnesses he'd recommended had been called—Kate, Jim Taliaferro, Susan—but they reported a consistently strong adversarial, if not hostile, line of questioning by Banning Osgood and another assistant U.S. attorney.

Hans Engen and Klaus Bloch mailed Doug copies of the statements they had given to the German BKA and Hamburg police. Doug personally delivered these to the U.S. Attorney's offices in the Rodino Federal Building, but aside from a receipt and a smile from the sleek black receptionist, he might as well have scattered the documents along the New Jersey Turnpike for all the response they elicited from the prosecutors. Hans Engen cabled one day saying he understood that the BKA had evidence that Otis Kramer had recently opened a large Swiss bank account. Doug sent the cable registered mail to Banning Osgood, but heard nothing. Indeed, the prosecutors and Grand Jury lost themselves in the silence of caverns.

Carlos Rey phoned from Washington to say he'd picked up a rumor that Otis Kramer had tipped the Justice Department that Douglas Perry may have slipped the Katwar to the Russians. "Be careful of that one, Mr. Perry," he said. "As I told you, he's slippery. Plays all sides."

On the West Coast Marshall Ingersoll casually turned up at home and at the Bytex executive offices as if nothing had happened. Ingersoll told friends, according to Phil Wetherill's report, that he had burned out on the job and had spent a month recuperating at a seaside Mexican village near Puerto Vallarta. Wetherill checked, found that Ingersoll never had been in the hamlet. Although possessing several promising leads, the detective still had no solid evidence linking Ingersoll to the Katwar theft.

Some news from the West Coast was positive, however. Jim Taliaferro accelerated preparations to mass produce the Katwar and now forecast that they would hit the market soon after Easter, pricing the security chip at $1,250 a copy. Advance orders augured heavy demand around the world.

Doug and Kate ate a light Sunday supper at the planked table in the kitchen of his Princeton house where shimmering copperware, relic of another life, hung beside the stove.

"Cheer up, lover. If they don't indict you, we'll fly down to Jamaica and have a ball." Kate struck one of her poses. "If they do send you to trial, you'll learn a lot of law while you make your triumphant march to acquittal."

He forced a smile. "I'd like to relax, God knows, but it's hard. This Grand Jury thing has me uptight."

"I know a secret that might help." Teasing, she was in one of her mercurial moods.

"What is it?"

"Promise to love me forever?"

"Eternity plus."

"Tony Canzano's unhappy in his job. He wants to come back."

"You're kidding." But his spirits lifted at the prospect.

"No. Jerry Dunn got it from a friend at Cullinane. Tony heard a rumor you were in trouble, and he wants to return and help support the company."

"I'll call him first thing tomorrow and open the door. Five-to-one he'll throw me a quote from Wordsworth or Pope."

"And tell you that now he won't have to steal home."

Doug did not reply. The conversation fell away. He lived in spells of silence these days.

"If it were a big game tonight," he said at last, "I wouldn't play. I never play real poker when I feel low. Bad psychology. I did it once years ago and lost my shirt."

"So why go tonight?" She reached out and took his hand.

"Oh, a friendly game's different. No pressure. Besides, I haven't gone in a month, you know. I promised your father I'd show tonight. Hugh Talbott's making a big deal about this being the supposed fortieth anniversary."

"Okay. I'll keep my promise too. I told Judy I'd work on a program for a new video game. We think there ought to be fewer war games and more female-type electronic fun, so girls would play in those mall arcades too."

"Kate, you've been wonderful with Judy." He tightened the handclasp. "She's a different kid since you came into her life—and mine."

"Oh, we're pals." She made light of it. "Or rather I'm big sister, I guess."

The phone rang. Doug took the instrument from its nearby wall bracket.

"Mr. Perry?"

"Yes."

"I'm not supposed to do this." A male voice, mellow and easy. Possibly a black accent. "But just in case they don't give you the vote, it was nineteen to two."

"Oh, you mean . . ." But the phone clicked dead.

He felt the jolt like a thump on the back and when he told Kate, they fell to swapping excited speculations and questions. The Grand Jury, of course, but did it meet on Sundays? Nineteen to two to indict him—or not to indict? Would a juror call like this if Doug had not been cleared? Yes, he might. There were cruel people in the world, even on juries.

"It's just got to be our way," insisted Kate. She believed as ever in good colonels and good jurors. "That man took a risk in calling you. You won, Doug. I know it."

He was already at the phone calling Stanley Fowler. He caught the lawyer just as he was pulling on his overcoat to go to the poker game. Fowler, ever cautious, made Doug repeat the anonymous message several times.

"Okay, I'll get right on it," he said. "If they did clear you with a no-bill, the prosecutors ordinarily don't inform the defendant or his lawyer, not unless asked. I never heard of a Grand Jury meeting on Sunday. Maybe they voted Friday. I'll try to reach Osgood or someone else in that office. . . . Look, you go on to the game. I'll get there when I can. Just hold a seat for me and forget this for a while."

"Forget it! Stan, as a psychologist you'd make a good plumber."

Jay McNaughton dealt the first hand, five-card stud, deuces wild, $5 tax on a wild-card showing. Because of the large number of players, seven-card stud and draw poker had been banned for the night.

"What do these numbers have in common?" asked Larry Warfield. "1776, 1812, 1492, 1980?"

"We give up," said Hugh Talbott promptly. "Tell us."

"In Bulgaria, they're adjacent rooms in the Sofia Hilton."

The volume of laughter reflected the players' generous mood. "When I first heard that," said Doug, "it was the Warsaw Hilton."

"I never knock the Poles since Solidarity," said Larry.

"Come on," said Buck, "play poker."

"Deal!" said Al.

No wild cards showed on the first round. Larry bet $2 on his ace showing. Five players called, among them Doug with a jack up and a queen in the hole.

"You won't believe this, but I finally got a check from Marshall Ingersoll." McNaughton withheld dealing the third card, savoring the suspense.

"Frame it, tiger." Ira Bickstein lowered his dark eyebrows in a scowl. "If you cash it, it'll bounce."

"Already banked it." Jay grinned, tugged at his rusty beard. "What there was of it."

"What do you mean?"

"He owed me $83, right? . . . Well, the check read $33."

The game exploded. Guffaws. Boos. Yelps. Derisive laughter. "A born prick is a prick forever," said Buck. "Maybe he can't take it with him, but Marshall can sure try," said Larry Warfield. "He's keeping the rest for his favorite charity," said Doug. "The guy will O.D. on thrift some day," said Ira.

"Give him a break," said Hugh Talbott. "Marshall's an honest man. He's paying on the installment plan, $33 down and five bucks a year."

"Deal!" shouted Al.

On the third card, Larry Warfield drew a wild card to his ace, paid the $5 tax and bet the limit, $10. Everyone else dropped and Larry pulled in the small pot. The game proceeded uneventfully for several hands.

When it came Doug's turn to deal, he chatted as he flicked out the cards for straight stud. "I ran across Ingersoll's trail in Hamburg last month when I played in a pot-limit game."

"I hear you won big over there." Hugh Talbott's crown of white hair matched the winterscape outside. It was snowing steadily now.

"Not bad." Precise figures on wins and losses seldom surfaced at the Sunday-night game. Doug told how a Yugoslav seaman identified the American whose jaw muscle twitched every time he held good cards. Doug strung out the tale, hoping to allay his anxiety while waiting for Stan Fowler.

"Had to be Marshall," said Milt, when the laughter subsided.

"Yeah, for sure." Doug made no mention of showing Ingersoll's picture to Kosto Gavrilovich. Among the Sunday-night players, only Stan Fowler knew of Doug's pursuit of Ingersoll and his subsequent Grand Jury appearance.

"I hope Ingersoll dropped a bundle in Hamburg," said Larry Warfield.

The banker bet $5 on his king high in the second round, was raised by Milt who showed a queen, four. Four players called.

"Say, Doug, I never congratulated you and Jay for your stand on San Luis," said Hugh Talbott. The professor of primitive religions occasionally swam against the game's current of bantering. "That took real courage."

"Thanks for both of us," said Jay.

"Hey tiger, quit trying to raise the moral tone around here," admonished Ira Bickstein. "This is poker, not Sunday-night vespers."

"Play poker," said Buck.

"Yeah," said Al. "For Christ's sake, deal."

Doug's deal produced the first large pot of the night. Larry Warfield's pair of kings beat out Milt's queens and Jay McNaughton's nines after a spurt of betting. The banker raked in some $150 in gold, red, white and blue chips.

Doug was on edge as he passed the cards to be shuffled again. He glanced at his wristwatch—8:45. He wondered if Fowler had been able to reach any of the prosecutors. Outside the snowfall thickened. A white haze obscured the lake and branches of the tall blue spruce beside the house sagged under snowy burdens.

"I'm dreaming of a white Christmas," Hugh Talbott sang, off key as usual.

"I regard that sentiment as blatantly racist and anti-Semitic," said Ira Bickstein. The Institute for Advanced Study mathematician was winning and consequently in a good mood.

In a hand of Omaha, two cards down to each player and five common cards down in the center, Doug found he'd been dealt a pair of aces. He raised $5 when the betting reached him. The first flop of three center cards exposed an ace, eight and five, giving Doug three aces. He raised again, this time $10. Three players stayed. The next card turned was a jack. Doug bet another $10. The flop of the final card produced a ten and Doug bet $10 despite the straight possibility offered by the center cards. Larry

Warfield raised $10. Doug called. Kate's father showed his hand, the king and queen of diamonds. Together with the ace, jack and ten on the board, he had a winning straight. The banker's stack of chips was growing.

"One of those nights," said Doug, as he tossed in his cards. He hadn't won a hand.

"Larry's been winning all summer and fall," complained Buck, in a voice that accused the gods of injustice.

"We don't miss Gary Jameson a bit," said Milt. The Institute for Defense Analyses cryptographer, Doug's nemesis, had been a consistent winner. "And by the way, what's with Gary?"

"I invited him to the game at my house a couple of weeks ago," said Jay McNaughton. "Gary said no thanks. He felt some of the guys might object to playing with him since he came out of the closet."

"That's putting it mildly," said Larry Warfield. "Who wants to play with crossed legs all night so the Gay Panther can't cop a feel?"

"Tell the truth, tiger," said Ira. "The real reason you don't want Jameson back is that you couldn't tell those fag jokes of yours."

"I hear the Trenton car-wash queen left him," said Milt, "and Gary's living with a guy from the economics department."

"Impossible," said Jay McNaughton. "There's no such thing as a gay economist. In that dismal science, they're all dreary."

"Play poker," growled Al.

"Okay," said Larry, the dealer. "Five-card stud, deuces wild, high-low. Deuces up cost you $5. If you win both ends, you get Hugh's anniversary prize."

Doug looked at his watch—10:05. Where was Stan Fowler? Tension tightened once more. Had he been indicted after all and Stan was reluctant to tell him? Well, at least he had an ace up for this high-low game. When he looked at his hole card, his anxiety level dropped several notches. The hole card was a wild deuce.

Doug bet $4, the limit in high-low games, and got a raise from Ira Bickstein who had a three showing. Doug raised back. Five players called. On the third card Doug drew a six and Ira a four. Doug bet out once more, was raised by Ira. Four players called. On the fourth card Doug drew a deuce and paid the $5 tax. He now had three aces and four cards to a perfect low. Ira drew a seven. This time Doug and Ira went the limit of three raises. Only one other player, Jay McNaughton, called. On the final card Doug drew a three, giving him three aces for high and a six-four unbeatable low. Ira, on the other hand, drew a six, giving him seven, six, four, three on the board. A wild card or a five in the hole would give him a straight. A wild card or an ace in the hole would give him a seven-six low. Jay McNaughton had two nines and two small cards showing.

Doug checked. Ira Bickstein bet $4. Jay called. Doug, although he had a lock low, just called. Now the players had to announce their intentions in turn, the man who bet out going first.

"Low," said Ira. So he did not have a straight. His best possible low hand was seven-six, assuming he had an ace in the hole.

"High." McNaughton's best hand was three nines.

"High and low." Doug turned over his hole card, the wild deuce, and took in the pot, almost $200. It was his first winning hand of the night.

"Once Ira goes low, Doug has a lock for both ways," commented Larry Warfield, not without envy.

"Nice betting, tiger," Ira conceded.

"So to Douglas R. Perry," said Hugh Talbott in the booming voice of a sports announcer, "goes the surprise fortieth anniversary award, a prize that evokes thoughts of our distinguished forefathers in this game . . ."

"Foreplay fathers," cut in Larry Warfield.

"Illustrious fathers of foreplay," corrected Ira Bickstein.

"Quiet!" shouted Talbott.

At that moment the porch door flew open and there stood Stan Fowler, his overcoat, gloves and fur hat coated with snow and his pink face creased in a triumphant grin.

He pulled off his gloves, looked at Doug and jerked his thumbs upward. "You won!" He motioned with his hand. "Come on out in the kitchen and I'll tell you about it."

"No secrets," objected Milt.

"Business," replied Fowler. "Confidential stuff between lawyer and client."

Standing in the kitchen beside the sausages, cheese, bread, apples and cookies that Larry Warfield had laid out for hungry players, Stan took off his snow-flecked outerwear and hung them on a peg near the back door. Then he clapped Doug on the arms, the closest the conservative lawyer ever came to an embrace.

"The Grand Jury voted a no-bill on you late Friday." He spoke in a low voice. "I had a helluva time tracking down Osgood, finally got him at the house of some woman friend." He glanced toward the door, making sure he was not overheard.

"How did you put it to him?"

"Oh, I didn't say anything about our tip." The lawyer took a bottle of beer from a nearby tub and unscrewed the cap. "I just said a month had gone by and asked if there had been any resolution of your case yet. He said yes, as a matter of fact, the jury voted Friday afternoon against indicting you. He claimed he was going to call me tomorrow morning with the news. Maybe he was and maybe he wasn't. U.S. attorneys are under no legal obligation to let a defendant know about no-bills."

"Does that clear me for good, Stan?"

"Yeah, that's it." Fowler took a long swallow of beer. "Short of them finding some new evidence, which we know doesn't exist, you're home free. . . . He kind of hinted, though, that the investigation will continue on Marshall Ingersoll with Otis Kramer becoming a target instead of you. He said there had been 'talks with West German authorities.' Sounds to me like Osgood contacted the BKA in Wiesbaden."

"Stan, that's terrific." Doug felt light as a balloon. "I just wish I'd had the sense to have you outside that jury room in Newark. We might have ended it that same day."

Fowler shook his head. "No, Osgood said the fact that you faced the jury alone, with no lawyer waiting outside, made a favorable impression on them. It appears you did right."

"Come on, you guys," shouted Larry Warfield from the poker table.

Hugh Talbott also called. "Your prize is waiting, Doug."

"Bring me a beer," said Milt.

"You go in, Stan," said Doug. "I've got to call Kate."

She answered on the first ring. "I'm in bed with the phone beside me. I knew you'd call. It's good news, isn't it, lover?"

"The best." He relayed what Fowler had said.

"Wow!" She yelled it. "Listen, let's go some place and celebrate. My treat. We'll use that money you gave me. Jamaica? Hawaii? Tahiti? You name it and I'll go."

"It's a deal. I love you, Kate."

"Not good enough. You got to be crazy for me like I am for you. Wake me up when you get home and we'll start the celebration tonight."

The world outside wore a gown of shimmering white. The snowfall had stopped and a fragment of moon rode the edge of ragged clouds. Frail moonlight silvered the wavelets on Lake Carnegie, etched a pathway on the sloping white lawn and danced fitfully on sagging boughs of the blue spruce.

The players made room for Stan Fowler, the tenth man at the crowded table, but Hugh Talbott commanded Doug to remain standing. The white-haired Princeton Theological Seminary professor reached under his chair and brought out a package wrapped in red tissue paper and tied with Christmas ribbons.

"On this fortieth anniversary of the founding of the world's only endowed poker game," he intoned, "it gives me deep pleasure . . ."

"Deep-throat pleasure," heckled Ira Bickstein.

". . . great pleasure to award the championship high-low prize to Douglas Roper Perry, fine poker player, responsible citizen, good friend and . . ."

"Skilled cradle robber," concluded Milt.

"Strike that remark." Talbott held the package high. "It is fittingly symbolic that our winner is a computer specialist because this award comes to us from one of the early players who himself made an immense contribution to the dawning age of computers. . . . Doug, take it. It's yours."

Doug unwrapped the prize while players taunted and heckled. It was a book. He held it up for all to see: "Theory of Games and Economic Behavior" by John von Neumann and Oskar Morgenstern. The flyleaf revealed an autograph of Von Neumann dated 1946, Princeton, N.J.

"Seminal work." Ira Bickstein, who as a young graduate student in mathematics had worked with Von Neumann, said it with respect.

"All work, no semen," amended Larry Warfield.

"What makes you think Doug reads books?" asked Stan Fowler, downing his second beer.

"Who said he could read?" added Milt.

"Say Larry, I heard a new camel joke in Pittsburgh last week." Fowler drew a cigar from his vest pocket and bit off the end.

"Come on, play poker," said Buck.

"Deal!" said Al.

Doug lost $50 in the next pot, his pair of tens bested by Larry Warfield's pair of queens. As the game wore on, Doug continued to lose, but the lower his stack of chips, the higher his spirits. With the threat of indictment no longer hanging over him, he felt unbound, liberated, galvanized. Thoughts of Kate filled him with euphoria. They would take off on a long vacation, go anywhere she wanted to go. He not only loved her, he was proud of her. Kate's Katwar chip would advance the art of computer cryptography by years. Too bad the Soviets had a copy, but they were bound to get it sooner or later anyway. Here at home, with advance orders flowing into Jim Taliaferro's Eniplex, the Katwar was bound to earn millions for both companies. And tomorrow he'd invite Tony Canzano back into the fold. Whatever their political differences, he loved the guy like a brother. With Susan, Tony and Doug together again, there would be no stopping Dataflo. Soon they'd go public with their stock.

"Hey Doug, you're high." Jay McNaughton, the dealer in a new hand, broke in on his thoughts.

"Understatement of the year," rejoined Doug.

"Do your meditating at home," groused Buck.

Doug bet $2 on his king high, but his mind continued to wander. At the end of the hand of five-card stud, he found himself with a king, queen, ten, nine showing. He had a five in the hole. Larry Warfield had a pair of sixes showing and Hugh Talbott had a pair of fours up. Larry and Hugh both checked. Doug, faking a straight, bet the $10 limit. Larry called. Hugh dropped.

"All yours, Larry." Doug threw in his cards. "I can't even run one tonight."

"You may take Larry's daughter," said Ira, "but you can't take his money."

Cleaned out of chips, Doug had to buy another $50 worth from Larry who had won so many, he no longer bothered to stack them. As Doug gazed at the banker's disorderly heap of gold, blue, red and white tokens, his mind flipped back to his own big winning night in Hamburg and then, through association, to the cab ride with Kate just before he went off to play.

What was it she had said? "If you'd agree not to play tonight, I could make you a big winner some day. . . . I've worked out a program. . . . No, I refuse to bribe you." And what did Judith say one day? Something about Kate knowing more about poker odds than he did? Could Kate have . . .

"Larry, who handed you the winning poker recipe?" Doug

chanced the shot while the other players were busy laughing at Ira
Bickstein's newest Jewish dialect story.

"It's just clean living, Doug." But the banker, uneasy, averted
his eyes.

"I heard a young woman made a computer study for you on
how to win at the game?"

"Well, it never hurts to have smart relatives."

It was true! Kate must have worked out poker combinations on
her computer and given her father a formula for playing a winning
game. So, it was Daddy first, lover second. Wait until he got home
tonight. Of all the sly, underhanded, double-crossing . . . and
then he pictured Kate striking one of her poses, no doubt mimick-
ing blameless innocence, and he broke out laughing.

The door opened a crack and Peggy Warfield peered into the
masculine enclave. "Jay . . . Doug!" she called. "I hate to interrupt, but you two would want to know. They've had a coup in San
Luis. It's on the eleven o'clock news."

Both men hurried into the living room followed by Stan Fowler
and Ira Bickstein. The rest of the men continued the game.

Peggy Warfield, a flowered housecoat garnishing her formidable
bosom, stood by the television console. A young man in a trim
military officer's uniform dominated the screen. "He's the leader,"
said Peggy. "I heard George Ball predict this just last week at the
Brendan Byrnes'."

The officer was speaking into a nest of microphones in a high-
ceilinged room marked by heavy colonial furniture. Through an
arched window in the rear, one could see helmeted soldiers patrol-
ling a plaza massed with people. A legend at the bottom of the
screen read: "Col. Rodolfo Lemus de la Cruz, leader of the
junta."

". . . this opportunity to talk on American television," Colonel
Lemus was saying in heavily accented English. "At 1800 hours tonight we installed a new government dedicated to equal justice for
all citizens of San Luis. From now on, we will respect individual
rights. The state will not torture, kidnap or murder anyone, regardless of his political beliefs. The fight against terrorist guerrillas
will continue, but no one outside the guerrilla forces will be
harmed by this government. Any soldiers, policeman or member
of a private squad violating human rights will be promptly
arrested and imprisoned."

The colonel looked quite boyish despite his severe uniform and cap. "The old regime's torture chamber, so hated by the people who called it *La Casa Dolorosa,* is being burned to the ground tonight. From this moment, San Luis reenters the family of civilized nations. . . . We will forego asking military aid of the United States for the time being, but we will solicit economic help until our commerce, torn apart by violence, is restored to its former health."

Lemus looked straight at the camera. "Now a brief personal word. I'm a computer specialist in the army. As you may know, an American company, Princeton Dataflo, refused to let its computer components be built in San Luis because of the viciousness of the government we deposed today. But the head of that company, a Mr. Douglas Perry, has given me his word that if we maintain a clean human-rights record for six months, he will see that manufacture of computer parts begins here. We of the new junta appreciate that promise, and we make one of our own. Within six months San Luis will be ready not only for Mr. Perry's company, but for any other business that wants to locate in a country of great scenic beauty where the people and their government live in friendship and harmony and where every individual is treated with dignity and justice. Thank you."

The network's segment on San Luis wound up with details of the coup—bloodless save for the death of three occupants of a tank that exploded from unknown causes—names and biographies of the new five-man junta and comment, mostly favorable, from a number of capitals around the world.

"My God," said Ira Bickstein, "this is your night, tiger. You win the Von Neumann prize and now you're all over the tube as the hero of the latest Latin revolution."

"And that's not all his good news tonight," said Fowler obliquely.

Jay McNaughton gathered Doug in an embrace. "It worked, Doug! By God, I think for once we did the old world a good turn."

"You're the key man, Jay." Doug hugged his friend. "Without you, I'd never have known the truth down there."

Back around the poker table, Ira relayed highlights of the TV news show to the six men who had elected to continue playing. They listened with only mild interest. No background was needed, for the roles of Perry and McNaughton had been well known since the day three months earlier when Doug made headlines by can-

celing the Ossian contract. Talbott led a brief, ragged cheer for the
two men while Doug's mind swung back to Kate. The good colonels had triumphed after all. Perhaps Kate was one of those star-
kissed people whose wishes all came true. Then his thoughts
veered sharply to that old scene that often haunted his dreams—a
steel-spiked fist lashing into a face of dark tender beauty. He
winced. Would that image never fade?

The players hurried into the next deal with only minimal regard
for San Luis. Sunday night was not for politics, good works or the
canonizing of saints, but for the thrust and feint of poker.

Two hands later, Peggy Warfield put her head in the door.
"Kate says the phone's ringing off the hook at your place, Doug."
She was timid about breaching the male sanctuary. "She won't say
where you are."

"Good," said Doug. "I'll handle the calls tomorrow."

They played without interruption for half an hour. Then, as
they began the last round of the night, Jay McNaughton held off
his deal. He laid the deck to one side.

"Look, we haven't done right by Doug." He tugged at his pirate's beard. "He did the right thing, but we haven't come clean
with him."

"You sure haven't," said Doug. "I've only won one hand all
night."

"Here's a guy who loves this game," resumed Jay, "but we've
been taking advantage of him."

"Damn good thing too," said Ira.

"What are you talking about?" Hugh Talbott was puzzled.

"You all know," said Jay.

"Not me."

"What the hell . . ."

"You mean?"

"Right." Jay rubbed the back of his neck. "The old Doug Perry
giveaway."

A ripple of laughter soon became a wave that toppled over and
engulfed them. All except Doug. He watched bewildered as Larry
pounded the table, Buck dug his elbow into Milt's ribs and Hugh
Talbott leaned back laughing so hard that tears misted his eyes.

"You do the honors, Stan," said Jay. "You're his lawyer."

"Delighted." Fowler ground out his second cigar butt of the
night. "As your counsel, Mr. Perry, it's my duty to inform you

that you've given away hundreds of dollars over the . . . How many years have you played in this game?"

"Twelve." What was coming? He'd picked up no clues.

"Given away hundreds of dollars in the twelve years you've played in the Sunday-night game," continued Stan. "We call it the Doug Perry giveaway. Ready for the revelation of our big secret?"

"Can't wait."

"All right. Doug, every time you have a very good hand, say a full house or better, you do like this." The lawyer palmed the back of his neck, rubbing gently and tilting his head slightly to the right.

The pack howled.

"I don't," protested Doug, but he sensed the truth at once. In the soundless certainty of kinesthesia, he could feel his hand going to his neck even as he pictured three aces and two deuces, a flabby white-suited Turk and a garden of pastel German currency in Hamburg.

"Oh, but you do," said Fowler.

Nine men palmed the backs of their necks in imitation and once more the players broke up over the disclosure. Doug watched as Hugh Talbott whipped out his handkerchief to dry his eyes. Ira Bickstein shook his head in mock reproof of such innocent insensibility. Even Jay McNaughton's kindly smile had a touch of condescension.

How the mighty had fallen. Here he was in an hour of triumph, surrounded by some of his best friends, and they sat taunting him for failing to recognize a physical quirk that any high-school boy would have sensed. In the moment of lauding him, they hauled him back to earth.

Doug sighed. "I guess I ought to say thanks." He remembered Kosto Gavrilovich's comment about "reading" him sometimes. My God, how many thousands had this neck mannerism cost him in the big games?

"We'll take you anyway, tiger," said Ira.

The half moon broke free of clouds, drenching the ivoried land in a brilliance of scattered jewels. A pathway like splintered copper thrust across the lake. A single night hawk winged through the dust of moon beams and the great blue spruce, heavy with snow, ruled over a kingdom of trackless white.

"Play poker," said Buck.

"Deal!" said Al.

EPILOGUE

The Federal Grand Jury in Newark spent several more weeks hearing testimony involving alleged criminal violation of the Export Administration Act by Otis Kramer and Marshall Ingersoll. Then, after a hurried conference with high Justice Department officials in Washington, the U.S. Attorney suddenly withdrew the case from the Grand Jury without explanation.

Douglas Perry, divorced by Joan, married Kate Warfield on the second anniversary of her Katwar breakthrough. They named their first-born, a daughter, Silvia Ticpan Perry.

Princeton Dataflo and Eniplex, Inc., located a phase of the Katwar manufacturing process in San Luis after the new junta halted the random army killings in that Central American country. Both companies grew and prospered. The Katwar chip ruled the world of computer security for several years. Then a cryppy at Stanford University, using a brace of Cray computers, discovered how to break any Katwar cipher within an hour and the Katwar went the way of the Gatling gun, the Victrola and the Packard convertible.

Ossian, Ltd., was dissolved a few months after a congressman from California charged in a House speech that the company, headed by Sean Hegy, "a former European character actor," was actually a subsidized front of the National Security Agency. Some time later reporters discovered Hegy on the payroll of NSA's COMSEC division.

Under the heading, "Moscow Drops $4,000,000 in Coding Scam," a German criminology journal printed an article that the U.S. press never managed to confirm or negate. The story stated that America's National Security Agency, using a Washington computer consultant and a California data processing executive as decoys, had lured Russian KGB agents into buying a copy of a U.S.-invented coding chip from a Hamburg intermediary for $4,000,000. NSA technicians had planted a "trap door" in the duplicate chip that would have enabled the American agency to decode all of the Soviet Union's military and diplomatic messages. Unfortunately for U.S. intelligence agents, said the journal, the KGB discovered the ruse and banned all use of the chip in Communist bloc countries.

ACKNOWLEDGEMENTS

Many people willingly gave of their time and energy, helping me to understand the world of computers. Indeed, I found no one in this swiftly advancing technology who refused to share his or her knowledge. Computer scientists and technicians are a zealous lot, eager to explain the mysteries of their microchips. Of the many who helped me, these should be thanked by name:

Robert W. Lucky, executive director research communications sciences, Bell Laboratories; Saul Amarel, chairman computer sciences, Rutgers University; Paul S. Henry, chief optical systems research, Bell Labs; Howard J. Strauss, associate director Princeton University's computer center; Charles Hedrick, Rutgers University computer scientist; Ellwood Kauffman, K-Squared Systems; Jan A. Rajchman, vice-president information sciences, retired, RCA Laboratories.

On other phases of research for the novel, I'd like to thank Nicholas K. Findler, State University at Buffalo computer scientist; Sam Glucksberg, Princeton University professor of psychology; John O'Brien Cullen, Pebble Beach, Cal., and Stephen Crandall, Assistant U.S. Attorney, Newark, N.J.